Praise for *The*

"Maggie Anton utilizes the characters' authentic voices to address social justice while still entertaining the reader with an engaging romance."

—Jackie Ben-Efraim, Special Collections Librarian,
American Jewish University

"In *The Choice*, Maggie Anton presents a tale of characters inspired by Chaim Potok's novels, imagining their future struggles and triumphs. Using her unique blend of historical fiction, Jewish history, and Talmudic text, Anton provides a glimpse at American Jewish life in the 1950s and allows us to share in the lives of powerful yet familiar characters. Thank you, Maggie, for letting us know what happened next!"

—Rabbi Marla J. Feldman, Executive Director,
Women of Reform Judaism

"Maggie Anton gives evocative voice to the generation of our mothers, whose questions and bold solutions, especially about the most intimate of subjects, laid the foundation for the contemporary transformation of women's status in Jewish learning and law."

—Rabbi Susan Grossman, Senior Rabbi, Beth Shalom Congregation,
Columbia, Maryland, and co-editor of *Daughters of the King*

"*The Choice* is a marvelous piece of Midrash (early rabbinic interpretation of a classical text) or, as it's called today, fan fiction. Anton aptly illuminates the Talmudic dictum 'Better to dwell in tandem than to sit abandoned.'"

—Rabbi Burt Visotzky, Professor of Midrash and
Interreligious Studies, Jewish Theological Seminary, and author of
A Delightful Compendium of Consolation and *Sage Tales*

D0931966

"Maggie Anton's new book. *The Choice*, takes us into the Jewish world of love and learning and the love of learning. One can only be grateful for such an intriguing and engaging work. Maggie Anton's combination of history, imagination, and feminist reading of classical Jewish texts is impressive."

—Rabbi Laura Geller, Rabbi Emerita, Temple Emanuel of Beverly Hills, and coauthor (with Richard Siegel) of *Getting Good at Getting Older*

"*The Choice* is an engaging love story of a young couple determined to honor religious traditions in the face of changing social mores and radical intellectual advances of the post–World War II era. Anton's novel is simultaneously heartwarming and provocative, providing a fresh and stimulating perspective on American Jewish society during the 1950s."

—Jody Myers, PhD, Emeritus Professor of Religious Studies, California State University, Northridge

"Maggie Anton creates a rich tapestry of characters, situations, and conundrums that imaginatively envisions how, if women had been welcomed into Talmud study and decision-making, conversations might have unfolded and decisions been made, underscoring the importance of including the entire community in discussions of evolving moral values, belief, and ritual practice. The integration of serious Talmudic discourse between a woman and a man negotiating their own relationship vis-à-vis Jewish practice is a delight to read."

—Rabbi Amy Scheinerman, author of *The Talmud of Relationships*

"What a love of learning infuses Maggie Anton's *The Choice*! And how wonderfully she engages Jewish learning, women's lives, and feminist issues in her new novel."

—Rabbi Dr. Miriyam Glazer, Emerita Professor of Literature, American Jewish University, and author of *Psalms of the Jewish Liturgy*

"Reading Maggie Anton's new book made me realize how much progress has been made in regard to women studying Talmud. *The Choice* is not only a novel but also a guide to learning about the role of women in Judaism and should be required reading in classes on the topic of women and mitzvot and women and Talmud study. Buy a copy for yourself and get a copy for your *chevruta*, study partner."

—Rabbi Ellen S. Wolintz-Fields, Executive Director,
Women's League for Conservative Judaism

Praise for the Rav Hisda's Daughter Series

"Anton, the author of the acclaimed Rashi's Daughters trilogy, has penned her best book to date. Complex discussions of Jewish law and tradition as well as detailed description of the culture and customs of the times enhance truly wonderful storytelling. This absorbing novel should be on everyone's historical fiction reading list."

—*Library Journal* (starred review)—also chosen by *Library
Journal* as "Best Historical Fiction of 2012"

"Another excellent historical novel from Maggie Anton, *Rav Hisda's Daughter* explores the life of a young Jewish woman on the cusp of adulthood in third-century Babylonia. . . . As always, Anton's book is a good introduction to traditional Jewish learning, and perhaps, like Anton, readers will be motivated to discover the sources for themselves. . . . Those readers who enjoyed the Rashi's Daughters series will find this first book of Anton's next series pleasurable and educational—be sure to check out the extra resources available online."

—Rachel Sara Rosenthal, *Jewish Book Council*—also selected
as a Fiction Finalist, 2012 National Jewish Book Awards

Praise for the Rashi's Daughters Series

"With only scraps of information about Rashi's daughters, Anton has brought these three women to life. A stunning achievement. You will not be able to put this book down, and you may even find yourself rushing off to study Talmud. So curl up in your favorite chair and savor every moment."

—Judith Hauptman, Professor of Talmud and
Rabbinic Culture, Jewish Theological Seminary,
and author of *Rereading the Rabbis*

"Thanks to Anton, we have a wealth of images now, focusing on the world of 11th Century France as seen through the eyes of Joheved, Miriam and Rachel, Rashi's daughters . . . letting us see how life was lived, how religion was practiced, how religious law and superstition were inextricably entwined in the lives of people, how politics affected people's lives. Her books are as laden with knowledge as any scholarly tome, but the richly woven fictional plots, based on what Anton could find out or deduce, make reading the stories like eating an ice cream sundae—rich, delicious, and with enough substance to satisfy."

—*Atlanta Jewish Times*

"Anton has [created] a fictional narrative in three volumes, based on the lives of Rashi's three daughters. Building on the allegation that, because he had no sons, Rashi studied with his daughters, Anton imagines a community of learned and loving women. They each married intellectually gifted men and, in concert with their husbands, enriched and perpetuated their father's work. Anton's writing is fluid and her research and knowledge of text, history and ritual impressive. Each sister emerges as a unique, vividly portrayed individual."

—Gloria Goldreich, *Hadassah Magazine*

"This carefully researched work of fiction by Maggie Anton provides a rare glimpse into the little-known medieval Jewish world in which Rashi lived and worked."

—Naomi Ragen, author of *An Unorthodox Match*
and *The Ghost of Hannah Mendes*

"Regardless of what is based on solid evidence and what she created, Anton is a genius in all three of her Rashi's Daughters novels. As Anton says, the legacy of Rashi's daughters is that they recognized the value of Torah study in the Jewish world, wanted an education for themselves as well as their husbands and sons and performed the rituals reserved for men. These novels would make a fantastic collection for any woman's study group, book reading group or discussion group."

—*Kansas City Jewish Chronicle*

"Brings fascinating practices to light, from those connected to developing wool fabric with existing or emerging technologies to marriage customs and laws amongst the Ashkenazi and Sephardic Jews. Jewish practices are tied into the teachings of the Talmud, allowing readers to enter this religious world more fully. I am sorry that Rashi did not have additional daughters for Maggie Anton to write about."

—*Historical Novels Review*

"With a compelling combination of drama, suspense and romance, Anton takes her readers on a journey to Troyes, France during the eleventh century. . . . Anton creates characters who engage us with their ideas and their struggles. In the tradition of Diamant's *The Red Tent*, this is historical fiction that brings our heritage as Jewish women closer to home. Rashi himself leaps off the margins of the Talmud page to take shape as son, husband, father and grandfather."

—*Lilith Magazine*

THE
CHOICE

Also by Maggie Anton

Rashi's Daughters, Book I: Joheved (2005)
2006 IBPA Benjamin Franklin Gold Award Winner
in the First Fiction category

Rashi's Daughters, Book II: Miriam (2007)

Rashi's Daughter, Secret Scholar (2008)
for YA readers

Rashi's Daughters, Book III: Rachel (2009)

Rav Hisda's Daughter, Book I: Apprentice (2012)
2012 National Jewish Book Award Fiction Finalist

Enchantress: A Novel of Rav Hisda's Daughter (2014)

*Fifty Shades of Talmud: What the First Rabbis Had to Say
about You-Know-What* (2016)
2017 IBPA Benjamin Franklin Gold Award Winner
in the Religion category

THE
CHOICE

A Novel of Love, Faith, and Talmud

MAGGIE ANTON

Banot Press
www.banotpress.com

ORDERING INFORMATION
Quantity sales: Special discounts are available on quantity purchases by corporations, associations, and others. For details, please contact the "Special Sales Department" at the above address.
Orders by US trade bookstores and wholesalers. Please contact BCH: (800) 431-1579 or visit www.bookch.com for details.

Publisher's Cataloging-in-Publication data

Names: Anton, Maggie, author.
Title: The choice : a novel of love , faith , and the Talmud / Maggie Anton.
Description: Los Angeles, CA: Banot Press, 2022.
Identifiers: ISBN: 978-0-9763050-3-3
Subjects: LCSH Journalists--Fiction. | Rabbis--Fiction. | Jews--Social life
    and customs--Fiction. | Talmud--Study and teaching--Fiction. | Brooklyn
    (New York, N.Y.)--History--20th century--Fiction. | Jewish fiction. | Love
    stories. | BISAC FICTION / General | FICTION / Jewish | FICTION /
    Romance / General
Classification: LCC PS3601.N57 C46 2022 | DDC 813.6--dc23

Cover designer: Lorna Nakell

Printed in the United States of America
26 25 24 23 22   10 9 8 7 6 5 4 3 2 1

For all those nameless and forgotten women:
our mothers, grandmothers, and daughters.
Zee-khro-not lee-vrah-khah
(May their memories be for a blessing)

PREFACE

FIFTY-FIVE YEARS AGO, I was one of many readers who fell in love with Chaim Potok's brilliant and powerful duet of novels, *The Chosen* and *The Promise*. Which is why, when I read the author's later work, *Davita's Harp*, I couldn't help but notice that *The Chosen*'s protagonist appears in the final chapter as Davita's handsome classmate. Could this have been a Chekov's Gun? (*If, in the first act, there is a rifle hanging on the wall, in a following act it must be fired.*) It seemed to me that Potok had intended the two would eventually get together.

Fast-forward to 2013. I was finishing my sixth historical novel, *Enchantress*. Potok (of blessed memory) had been gone for ten years, but his characters still rattled around in my head and were refusing to leave. So, with the idea of continuing their story, I reread the first two books. As a feminist, I was astounded at what short shrift the female characters received. The hero's mother, who dies before he can remember her, is nameless. Nor does he seem to know anything about her or want to. His Hasidic friend's mother is also nameless, and despite the prominence of Hasidic women running their households in real life, she has a minimal presence.

So I decided to write yet another novel I wanted to read that had not been written, again focusing on overlooked Jewish women. My novel, set in mid-1950s Brooklyn, would be wholly transformative, giving names and backstories to girls and women who are inspired by but do not appear in Potok's work and, in the process, commenting on and criticizing Jewish women's unequal and inferior legal status.

There would be love, history, a little baseball, and of course, Talmud. Because for me, an additional frustration with Potok's first two novels, in which Talmud study is so entwined with the plot, is that no actual Talmud appears—not one line of Gemara. It was this frustration that drove me to include genuine Talmud in my Rashi's Daughters trilogy, so that when Rashi teaches his daughters, the reader learns along with them. Thus I created a plot for my novel in which the hero and heroine's relationship blossoms as they study Talmud together.

I have not written a sequel to Potok's works; rather, and not unlike the Talmud, I have written a commentary—my Gemara to his Mishnah. I was being respectful to his writing and true to life in New York's Jewish world in the early and mid-1900s. I found researching the latter personally motivating because this was exactly the Jewish world my father's family inhabited. Research was both easier and more challenging than it had been for my earlier novels. A great many twentieth-century sources are available online—so many, in fact, that it was overwhelming.

Like my other historical novels, the basic plot is a romance where the protagonists experience many trials and triumphs during which their relationships with one another and with Judaism are tested. Ultimately, they, along with the readers, are rewarded with a happy ending.

"That's right. I spoke until the bell rang." *He still remembers that.* It was flattering but also unsettling.

"You were so articulate. You made history real," he said. "I'm not surprised you became a journalist. You always did write the best essays." He took off his glasses and looked at her intensely.

As their eyes met, Hannah felt a jolt of exhilaration.

"It's good to see you again." Nathan glanced at her left hand as he polished his glasses. "But your last name didn't used to be Covey."

A frisson of fear tightened her stomach. "No, I'm not married. Nor have I been." She kept her voice calm; this was not the time to dwell on how many men considered single women fair game. "My father was the war correspondent Michael Covey, killed during British-Arab crossfire in Jerusalem when I was nine. He's the reason I became a journalist, to honor his legacy."

Then her chin began to quiver. Her father had showered her with unconditional love, and she missed him still. She needed to compose herself.

"You have my sympathy," Nathan murmured. "My mother died when I was two, and my father never remarried. So we're both orphans."

"I'm very sorry about your mother, but now I'm not actually an orphan. My mother remarried, and Samuel Eisin adopted me. But I use Covey as my byline." She sighed in resignation. "Even with a master's in journalism from Columbia, I doubt the *Freiheit* would have hired me if I weren't Michael Covey's daughter." *And if editor in chief Moe Novick hadn't belonged to the same Communist circle as Mama before the war.*

He nodded. "I like your scarf. It's a good color for you."

"Thank you." She suddenly felt self-conscious. She'd carefully chosen her outfit, a tailored navy suit and light blue button-down shirt, to reinforce her professionalism. At the last moment, she'd added a blue patterned scarf that brought out the color of her eyes.

She turned toward the door. "To keep anyone from seeing a woman in your office, can we go someplace outside Spektor?"

"Of course." He jumped up, grabbed his coat, and followed her out. "A café a few blocks from here is usually empty around now."

Hannah, who lived less than a mile away, knew it well. Haredi Jews didn't think it was kosher enough, so nobody there was likely to object to Rav Mandel and a woman having coffee together. And she could order lunch when they were finished.

Nathan sat quietly while she opened her notebook and took up a pencil, then said, "I've never been interviewed before. I assume you ask me questions and I answer them?"

"Why don't you tell me how you came to be Spektor's first, and youngest, professor of rabbinics?" Hannah liked her subjects to stray into other interesting topics, so she gave them a long leash. "Of course I've done some research on you, and if there's more I want to know, I can prompt you. So why not just start at the beginning?"

He gave her a cheeky grin that revealed his nervousness and amused her. "Well, I was born at Brooklyn Memorial in 1929."

She smiled back. "Somehow I doubt you could tell me much about your birth. How about starting with your decision to attend Spektor and how that led to your current position?"

"It wasn't an actual decision to attend Spektor as much as just knowing that's where I'd go." His voice was clear and resonant. "As far as I can remember, my father would praise their Talmud professors, especially Rav Rabinovich. And with a reputation for secular excellence as well, Spektor was at the top of my list."

"You sound like their promotional brochure," she gently scolded. "I know how smart you are. I went to school with you. You could have had your pick of Ivy League universities."

"But I wanted to be a rabbi."

"Like a pulpit rabbi, in a congregation?" She'd assumed that with his father's scholarly background, Nathan would also want to teach.

"I'd always intended to get *smicha* from Spektor, but as the horrific news of what happened in Europe filtered out, I realized how important it was for us not to lose American Jews as well."

Hannah didn't want to be sidetracked. "I'd like to hear about how your career path changed, what made you decide to teach at Spektor."

Nathan hesitated. "My first year was awful, particularly with Rav Klein. I'd rather you not write about it."

"Just tell me and then we can decide together how much should go into my article," she urged him. "I won't write anything unless you approve it."

He closed his eyes, and Hannah prepared herself for the tricky part—keeping him talking until it all came out.

"I was in my last year at Spektor and in the most advanced Talmud class, always taught by Rav Rabinovich. But this was just after the war, and in a coup, Spektor brought over one of the greatest surviving European scholars, Rav Avram Klein."

"That was around when your father's book was published," she said. "It was, and still is, a marvelous work. I reread it to prepare for this interview."

Nathan beamed. "Thanks. Others weren't so complimentary." Then he sobered. "That book caused me no end of tsuris with Rav Klein. Like other

Orthodox Talmudists, he believes the Vilna Shas Talmud is the definitive depository of the Oral Law. Never mind that it was compiled and printed less than a hundred years ago. For him the very idea that its text is inaccurate, that there are different versions of Talmudic works, altered either intentionally or through scribal errors, is sacrilege." Nathan's expression darkened. "Rav Klein declared that anyone who taught this way was a heretic."

"That's putting it diplomatically. I know Yiddish well enough to read his newspaper articles." Hannah put distaste into her voice. "It must have been difficult for you to study with a man who attacked your father so publicly."

"You can't imagine." Nathan spat out the words. "The only reason Rav Klein could write those vicious articles is that he used me to explain my father's methods." His voice changed to mimic a whining old man. "Please, Mandel. I don't understand what your father means here. Please. Could you explain it to me?"

She felt a rush of sympathy for him. "But you had to help him—you needed his approval to be ordained."

"I never dreamed Rav Klein would sucker me into betraying my own father." His next words were like stone. "I almost hated him."

Hannah noticed his past tense. "And now?"

"I accept that Rav Klein was desperate to save remnants of the yeshiva world he saw being destroyed around him. My father understood this and forgave his cruel words." Nathan then sighed. "Rav Klein eventually apologized for how he'd wronged me, and now I tolerate him. After all, he did give me smicha, even though on the oral exam, I used my father's methods."

"What?" Hannah couldn't contain her excitement. "You rebelled and used text criticism on your rabbinic ordination exams? That was brave of you."

"My first and only rebellion." He gave her a wan smile. "By the way, until this moment, the only people who know are the dean at Spektor, Rav Klein, Rav Rabinovich, Benny Stockser, and my father."

"Benjamin Stockser? The son of Reb Stockser who stopped being a Hasid and refused to succeed his father as rebbe?" Nathan's story had just gotten even more interesting.

His expression became guarded. "Yes, except that he's still a Hasid. We've been best friends since we were fifteen."

She waved her hand in dismissal. "You haven't finished telling me how you ended up teaching at Spektor."

"My father's book didn't just make trouble for me. It got so bad where he taught, the yeshiva he founded, no less, that he accepted a professorship at the Conservative Seminary." He shrugged. "Actually, he was offered one in Spektor's rabbinics department, but Rav Klein made them withdraw the offer."

"Let me guess," she said. "That's the position you now hold."

He nodded. "Rav Klein could hardly protest Spektor hiring me when he himself had just given me smicha."

"But he knew what you'd be teaching."

"He said he could keep an eye on me at Spektor."

"So you gave up becoming a pulpit rabbi?"

"It was a prestigious offer, and I realized that what I really wanted to do was teach Talmud and continue to study it." He leaned forward, and his eyes lit with enthusiasm. "Yes, we Jews revere the Torah, despite its focus on priests, purity, and Temple sacrifices. But it is Talmud that informs and rebuilds Judaism after the Temple's destruction. The most important—critical even—aspects of modern Jewish life come out of Talmud. The existence of synagogues, our liturgy, and the blessings we say, how we keep Shabbos and other holidays, how we observe *kashrus*—all of these are based in Talmud, not the Torah." His voice rose with fervor. "Without Talmud, Judaism would be a very different religion, if it even still existed at all."

She felt herself fill with awe. "You love Talmud."

He blushed. "I do."

"So you must enjoy teaching a subject you love."

"I enjoy teaching students who want to learn . . ." He no longer sounded so enthusiastic.

"But . . . ?" Hannah hesitated to encourage him to continue.

"Many of my students despise my methods. They agree with Rav Klein that text criticism is a threat to the Talmud's sanctity. They come to class to attack me rather than learn from me."

She nodded. "At the beginning it must have been hard that you were pretty much the same age as your students."

"Yes. Some had been my classmates the year before."

"You could have used a miracle like young ben Azariah whose hair suddenly turned gray when he became head of the ancient academy in Israel," she said. "Everyone respected him then."

"The rare students who get excited about my methods make it all worthwhile . . ." Nathan's eyes widened in surprise. "You know Talmud." It was an accusation, not a question.

"I know a little Talmud," she admitted. *Of course he's shocked. Women aren't supposed to study Talmud.* Still, she persevered. "Speaking of Talmud,

I'd appreciate you teaching me something about what exactly you do so I can explain it to our readers. Something less detailed than your father's book, and maybe a few examples of how you used textual criticism in your smicha exam."

Nathan cleared his throat. "Talmud isn't something I can teach anyone in an hour."

Well, he hadn't said no, and he loved teaching Talmud. Hannah made a sudden bold decision. "I know that," she replied in Hebrew. "I've wanted to study Talmud ever since I discovered it was so important. I read the Mishnah and learned Aramaic, but I still needed help—except nobody would teach me, not even my stepbrother. He said even a father is forbidden to teach his daughter Talmud, which only made me more determined." She stopped abruptly, petrified that she'd come on too strong.

Nathan was speechless for almost a minute. Then he switched to Hebrew to ask her, "How did you learn to speak Hebrew so well?"

They continued in Hebrew as Hannah replied, "To make a long story short, I spent four summers in Israel between 1949 and 1952 with my aunt Elizabeth, my real father's sister. She's a nurse, and I helped her care for the refugees. I still frequent the cafés and clubs that Israelis patronize."

Not that she dated anyone she met there. To her chagrin, the Israeli men were no different from college boys. They only wanted to get into her pants. And insisted a married woman shouldn't work outside the home. Almost as bad, they all smoked like chimneys.

Nathan interrupted her reverie by gushing, "So that's where your wonderful Israel stories in the *Freiheit* come from."

"I still have more they haven't published yet."

"How did your aunt end up in Israel? Where did you live? What was it like there?" He couldn't seem to contain his excitement. "Tell me everything."

"Nathan, I'm here to interview you, not vice versa."

When his face fell, she chose to be open with him. She'd wanted to study Talmud ever since grade school, when the boys went off to Talmud classes while the girls remained behind to learn Psalms and the Prophets. She'd asked her teacher about Talmud, but he'd brusquely replied that it was a complicated legal work that girls couldn't study. Which only left her more eager to discover what was in this forbidden text that men didn't want women to know.

This could be her opportunity. "If you teach me Talmud, I'll tell you all about my time in Israel."

Nathan just stared at her, apparently taken aback by her audacity. As Hannah waited anxiously, church bells began to chime.

"I'm sorry, but I have to teach at three." He stood and put on his coat. "We can continue later. How about same place, same time on Thursday?"

She barely managed a nod before he raced out. The waitress asked if she wanted anything more, but her appetite was gone.

Appalled at how she'd scared him off, Hannah berated herself as she waited for the check. What if he canceled their next meeting? What if he asked Moe for a different interviewer? After working so hard to overcome society's disapproval of working women, she'd be back where she started, copyediting the male reporters' stories and writing about Hadassah and Sisterhood luncheons.

Her heart grew heavy with sadness. Now she'd never get to study Talmud. And she'd never see Nathan again, either.

That evening Nathan's mind was a whirl. He'd been astonished at Hannah Eisin appearing out of the blue in his office, but he wasn't surprised she wanted to study Talmud. After all, it was a more prestigious subject than Torah. While he tried to think of a diplomatic way to refuse, the memory of her reciting Kaddish for her father, despite their teacher telling the class that girls didn't say it, came to him unbidden. It still rankled him that Hannah hadn't received the Rashi Award at graduation, though she'd earned it.

It made sense that so many rejections and prohibitions had whetted her appetite to learn the secret text men spent years studying. But what could he do? It was against Jewish Law to teach a woman Talmud.

The next night self-doubt assailed him as he recalled the first time he saw her. He'd tried not to stare like the other students, but he'd never seen a blond Jewish girl before. They were only in fourth grade, but he was struck by how pretty she was. And now she was a remarkably beautiful woman.

So, why not teach her Talmud? Wouldn't it be refreshing to have an eager beginning student for a change? Exciting even, after teaching the same texts for years at Spektor? Those ancient rabbis who said women were too light-headed to study Torah didn't know any modern-educated women like Hannah. Suddenly animated, he jumped out of bed and strode around his room. And look how prepared she was; she knew Hebrew and Aramaic, had already studied Mishnah. Hadn't there always been exceptional women who were scholars, some in Talmudic times and others later, like Rashi's daughters?

Then his shoulders sagged as his enthusiasm dissolved. He couldn't get around the tenet that women were forbidden to study Talmud.

Though he kept reminding himself of this, by the third night Nathan knew he could no more refuse to teach such a serious student than he could stop breathing. And he had to admit that it would be a pleasure to spend several hours a week with such a good-looking woman. No, he wouldn't disappoint Hannah—or himself. After all, Pesach was coming soon. He could teach her from Tractate Pesachim, where the Talmudic sages discuss the Seder's many rituals. Surely today's rabbis would permit a woman to study the part of Talmud she needed to know to fulfill the mitzvos of Pesach properly.

Then why not teach her some Talmud? It's not like I'll be opening a Talmud school for women. Besides, it will only be for a little while. He chortled to himself. *After all, I've already rebelled against Orthodoxy's increasing strictness once. And it went very well.*

Three days later, heart in her throat, Hannah walked into the café half an hour early. She didn't realize she'd been holding her breath until, seeing Nathan sitting at the back table, she let it out in relief.

As soon as she slid into the booth, he dispensed with preliminaries. "If I were to teach you Talmud, it would have to be somewhere private," he said in Hebrew. "And we couldn't tell anybody, not even our families or best friends. If anyone at Spektor found out, I could lose my job." He smiled weakly. "Then I'd have to take a pulpit."

To make sure she understood clearly, Hannah quietly restated what he'd said in English. When he nodded, she remained outwardly calm, but inside she exulted.

He gave her several days to memorize a Mishnah in Tractate Pesachim that focused on the Seder. "This particular section isn't difficult," he said with assurance. "You'll be familiar with its subject. We have a month until the festival begins, so it will be preparation for both of us."

Then, launching into the interview, he supplied her with a few simple ways he'd emended the text in his smicha exam. Once she understood them, she questioned him about his life outside Spektor. He enjoyed baseball (shared Dodger season tickets with a friend), the theater (especially Broadway musicals), and dancing (patronized dance halls at least twice a month). She didn't ask why he wasn't married. He still lived with his father at the same address in Williamsburg, which he gave her. Before parting, they settled on Tuesday and Thursday study sessions, when his father taught evenings at the Jewish Community Center. Finally, they exchanged phone numbers.

The night before their first class, Hannah tossed and turned but couldn't sleep. Her heart beat wildly as her emotions swung between excitement and apprehension. She couldn't believe she was finally going to fulfill her longtime desire to study Talmud, the text that saved Judaism after Rome destroyed the Second Temple—and with a top scholar. But lurking in her mind's attic was the fear that made her break into a cold sweat, the dread that had kept her from dating since college—that of being trapped in a room with a man intent on taking advantage of her. Again.

Nathan was also filled with trepidation. He wasn't concerned about being discovered teaching Talmud to a woman as much as he was afraid she wouldn't be the excellent student he'd anticipated. Then it would be a million times worse than ending a dating relationship. An ex could date other men, but Hannah wouldn't find another teacher. He hated to be just another man slamming the door in her face, not when she wanted to do this so badly.

Plus, there was the conundrum of his father wanting to meet H. M. Covey. As soon as Nathan mentioned the interview, Abba (Hebrew for "father") begged him to arrange a time when the reporter could tell both of them about Israel. Nathan couldn't bear depriving Abba, devoted to the new Jewish state, of the pleasure. Yet he didn't want Hannah to feel pressured that this was a quid pro quo for his teaching her.

Tuesday evening, Hannah stood in front of Nathan's building, battling the terror of being alone with him. Her stomach was in a knot, but she forced her legs to climb up the stoop. At the threshold, she shrank back, paralyzed by the potential unspeakable consequences of being sequestered with a stranger. Nathan seemed to be a mensch, but that frat boy—she hated his name—had as well. Until he lured her up to his room, locked the door, and she couldn't bear the memory of what he'd done to her.

Before she could bring herself to push the buzzer, Nathan opened the door.

Once inside the apartment, Hannah recognized immediately that two long-term bachelors lived there. Not that it was dirty or untidy, but except for the occasional bright-colored book spine, everything was a faded gray, navy, or brown. There were no decorative throw pillows on the French-style couch and chairs, which Hannah assumed had been picked out by Nathan's long-deceased mother. The only art in addition to a map of Israel were pictures of Franklin Roosevelt and various Zionist heroes. Bookshelves filled every available space, but they held no photos or other personal memorabilia. No vases, silver serving pieces, or any of the typical tchotchkes overflowing in most homes. Not even the Mandels' Judaica was on display, and surely they owned at least a set of Shabbos candlesticks and Kiddush cups.

Thankfully, she didn't see any ashtrays.

The sadness of that bleak living room took the edge off her fear, and the aroma of coffee further allayed her anxiety. She was also reassured by the yarmulke on Nathan's head. She took a deep breath and followed him into the dining room to start their session. "Ooh, fresh coffee," she said, observing the pot and cups on the table. "How thoughtful of you." Still, she sat in the chair closest to the front door.

Taught that it was immodest for a woman to take her gloves off in front of a man she didn't know well, Hannah pulled hers off under the table while Nathan poured out two cups of coffee. He then added the same amount of milk and sugar to hers that he'd seen her use at the café.

"Just the way I like it," she said, pleased yet disconcerted that he had noticed and remembered such a detail. When he took his seat catty-corner to her, she realized she'd still have to move fast to beat him to the door should he try to detain her. Unable to rid her mind of that scenario, she fumbled to find the Mishnah that began the tenth chapter of Tractate Pesachim.

Nathan wasn't surprised she was nervous. He was too. But he was prepared. "Rashi says that a teacher should always begin with a joke, that students learn better when they're laughing."

She swallowed hard. "Okay. Let's hear it."

"The Long Island Rail Road train was moving even slower than usual when it suddenly stopped. When it didn't start up in a minute, an impatient passenger asked the conductor what happened. 'There's a large tortoise on the tracks,' came the reply. 'But we stopped for a tortoise ten minutes ago,' the passenger protested. 'I know, but we caught up with it again.'" Nathan flashed Hannah a grin.

She burst out laughing and felt a weight lift from her shoulders.

Hannah positioned her finger on the spot in her book that he was pointing at in his. First she read in Hebrew, then translated it into English. "On the eve of Pesach, from before the Evening Sacrifice, a person does not eat until nightfall. Even the poorest in Israel does not eat unless he reclines. And they give him no less than four cups of wine, even if from charity."

Nathan clarified this, although he doubted she needed any explanation. "So we are discussing the first night of Pesach, when a celebratory banquet, not yet called a Seder, is held." He pointed to where the discussion began. "We'll start with the Gemara's debate about reclining and the four cups of wine."

Hannah had expected to arrive with questions about the Mishnah. "There are many things we eat that night." It was an effort to avoid saying *Seder.* "Does the Mishnah mean we recline with the first food we eat or with a particular ritual item?"

He smiled, both pleased and relieved. She had anticipated what the Sages would discuss. He helped her translate the Gemara that followed, which was trickier than Mishnah because it was in Aramaic and written in a shorthand style that left out many words and all the punctuation.

Satisfaction competed with mounting tension as Hannah sensed Nathan's physical proximity. She focused on the former feeling and strove to decipher the first two sentences. "The Rabbis stated: one reclines while eating matzah. Not while eating *maror*" (the bitter herb).

"Correct. Now let's see how the Tosafos, commentary written by Rashi's disciples, explain this." Nathan pointed her to Rashi's grandson Rashbam's interpretation.

Hannah felt proud when she came up with a short explanation he approved. "Rashbam says that when eating matzah, you recline in the manner of free men because the matzah celebrates our freedom," she said. "But you don't recline with the bitter herbs because they recall our slavery." *That makes sense.*

Heartened, she continued with the Gemara's next sentence, which was merely a one-word question. "Wine?" She squinted questioningly at Nathan.

"Now we're on the Mishnah's third sentence, where the Sages ask about reclining while drinking the four cups," he replied. "I warn you, this debate gets tricky."

Hannah read one line and saw that it was indeed tricky. In the Gemara Rav Nachman first says that wine requires reclining, then immediately after, Rav Nachman says that wine does not require reclining. "Whoever edited the Talmud certainly didn't care about consistency."

"It is those inconsistencies, and how the Gemara attempts to resolve them, that make Talmud study so interesting," Nathan replied. "Look how it anticipated your confusion."

Sure enough, the Gemara recognized that the conflicting statements also puzzled others. It declared that there was no dispute; Rav Nachman's two statements did not disagree. One referred to the first two cups and the other to the last two cups. But when Hannah read the next sentence, she saw the contradiction was not so easily resolved.

The problem, she learned, was that it is still unclear which two cups Rav Nachman thought required reclining. She had to chuckle at how there were again two divergent opinions. One explained that the first two cups require reclining because it is then that freedom begins. In other words, since reclining is a sign of freedom, one should recline when discussing the Exodus from Egypt. By contrast, the last two cups do not require reclining because by that time the discussion is finished.

She looked up at Nathan, who was grinning. "What's so funny?"

"We've come to our first variant text. Rashbam's says 'It is then that we are discussing our freedom's beginning' instead of 'It is then that freedom begins.'"

Hannah considered the variant text and felt the thrill of comprehension. "The time between the first two cups and the last two cups is when the Haggadah tells the Exodus story of the Hebrew slaves leaving Egypt," she said. "So when we've finished it, the people have already become free."

"Excellent." Nathan, admiring how understanding made her face light up, didn't want to dampen her enthusiasm. He was excited as well, but it was late. "However, we'll have to stop here. I must warn you, though, that the matter isn't resolved yet."

Elated that she'd actually studied and understood some Talmud, thankful that Nathan had behaved like a gentleman, and now frustrated that their session had ended so soon, she couldn't wait for two days to pass.

The following morning Hannah went to the *Freiheit*'s office to turn in her previous day's work and pick up new assignments. She tried to arrive before the linotype machine began operating, when the newsroom would be only moderately noisy rather than deafening. But there was no way to avoid the cigarette smoke air that, even early in the day with the wall-mounted fans whirling, clouded the room. Her eyes stung as she wove her way through the tables and desks to her in-box, deftly dodging the copyboys racing around the room.

"Copy," yelled a reporter as he dropped his finished story in the out-box. Immediately a copyboy rushed over to take it to any of the editors who were also shouting "Copy" to indicate they needed more work.

Hannah was lucky that she could do most of her work at home, thus avoiding the cacophony and acrid air. Every day Moe left her at least one article circled from the morning paper that he wanted translated from Yiddish into English for the weekend edition. There were also articles that others had translated earlier waiting for her to edit. In addition, Moe had an arrangement with El Al crews to bring over the latest Israeli newspapers. It was her enjoyable task to find interesting stories to translate.

But her most important and pleasurable assignment was finalizing her lengthy interviews with people she'd met in Israel, primarily refugees from

Arab countries and Europe. These were published every other week, in both their Yiddish and English versions. She was sorting through her in-box when Moe interrupted her with the latest Israeli newspaper.

"How'd your interview with Rabbi Mandel go?" He peered at her through his wire-rimmed glasses. "Learn anything interesting?"

"He actually used text criticism in his smicha exam, which I'll explain in the article." She grinned as she added, "And he goes out dancing several times a month."

An hour later she stuck her head in Moe's open door. "There's an exciting article in *Haaretz*, but I'm not sure we should print it."

He waved her in. "Let's see it."

She pointed to a photograph of a line of youngsters, all on crutches. "It's about a new children's rehabilitation center for polio patients. But toward the end, it says that the center will have to start serving children with other disabilities once the new polio vaccine is available in Israel." She was so excited she couldn't stand still. "It reports that Salk's field trials, on nearly two million subjects, have proved it's safe and effective."

Moe's eyes opened wide. "But . . . but," he stammered. "There hasn't been any announcement about a successful polio vaccine."

"Not yet." After a moment to think, she asked. "Dr. Salk is Jewish. Couldn't he be in contact with Israeli colleagues?"

"It makes sense." Moe nodded slowly. "Even so, I don't think we should print anything until it's official. But I'll nose around and see what I can find out. I have my contacts too."

By Thursday evening, Hannah had finished two drafts of her interview with Nathan, one in English and the other in Yiddish. When she knocked on Nathan's door, she was less afraid of being alone with him than before but still sat closest to the door.

As they reviewed their previous learning, she told him, "I prefer Rashbam's text, which implies that since we recline because that is how free men eat, we should recline as we hear how we became free," she began. "But why not continue reclining after the story is told?"

"Wonderful. You anticipated the Gemara again."

Elated, she read, "'Others explain it this way: the last two cups require reclining, for it is then that there is freedom. The first two cups do not require reclining because it is then that we are reciting: "We were slaves."'" Confused, she squinted at Nathan. "That makes sense too, but we don't follow either opinion today. We recline the entire time."

"Just one more sentence," he urged her.

"'Now that it was stated this, but it also was stated that, both these and those require reclining,'" she concluded. "I see. In other words we have two valid opinions, one saying we recline with the first two cups and the other that we recline with the last two cups. So we follow both and recline for all four cups." She looked up at Nathan, hopeful that he'd approve.

"Precisely." He sighed with pleasure, and relief, at how well their learning was going. The Rabbis who called women light-headed as an excuse not to teach them obviously hadn't encountered any like Hannah. "Though the Sages usually rule leniently when *derabanan* is uncertain, here, where it deals with wine at Pesach, a lenient ruling would eliminate reclining for any of the four cups, effectively nullifying the mitzvah."

"What do you mean 'derabanan'?" She'd never heard the word.

Nathan hesitated as he considered how to best reply to a question whose answer yeshiva students learned when they started Mishnah. After just a week of teaching, it was evident that Hannah was a fine pupil, with a quicker mind than some of his current students. She also had a different mind because she asked questions he'd never heard before, questions no yeshiva student would even think to ask. He gazed at her beautiful face, which no longer looked triumphant, but ashamed and disheartened.

"It's brave of you to ask when you don't know something," he praised her. "Too many students are afraid to show ignorance, but how else can we learn? I don't want you to ever be afraid to ask me questions. Okay?"

She nodded and grinned. "So what does derabanan mean?"

He chuckled. "It's complicated." The smile she gave him in return made her look so lovely it almost took his breath away. This was going to be challenging in ways he hadn't anticipated. "I think explaining it will be how we'll resume next week. But in addition, we'll be looking at the Gemara's discussion of whether a woman reclines in the presence of her husband. You should find it interesting."

Interesting? That was a word Hannah's parents used to describe something they disliked but didn't want to disparage openly.

TWO

NATHAN'S MEMORY was drowsily reprising the showstopping "Hernando's Hideaway" as the taxi turned onto his street late Saturday night. The musical *The Pajama Game* was a lengthy show, and afterward he'd taken Barbara out for coffee. It was already Sunday morning. But as the cab approached his building, his pleasant lethargy evaporated. His living room window was brightly lit.

Something must be wrong, terribly wrong. A vision of his father crumpled on the floor hit Nathan like a sledgehammer in the chest. He threw some bills at the cabbie, raced up the stoop, and fumbled to find his keys. It was only a modest relief when Abba, his thin face creased with anxiety, opened the door.

"Thank Heaven you're back." Solomon Mandel spoke hurriedly. "Benny called right after Havdalah—you just missed him. Sharon went into labor Friday afternoon and the baby hasn't come yet, so he needs you to wait with him at the hospital."

"*Gevalt.*" Nathan did a quick calculation. "It's been thirty hours."

"Benny said the baby was breech, so they expected a long labor" was all Nathan heard before he was out the door.

Nathan entered the maternity waiting room, his gut a tight ball of fear.

Benny gazed up at him with bleary eyes. "I was afraid you wouldn't come," he whispered. "I thought I'd go crazy here alone."

Nathan had seen firsthand how Benny's father, leader of the Vinitzer Hasidic sect, had raised his son in silence, never speaking to him except when they studied Talmud. The experience had left Benny unnerved when he needed to talk and had no one to talk with.

Nathan took the chair next to Benny. "What's happening?"

"Sharon started feeling contractions yesterday," Benny began. "They weren't very strong, but we heard that second babies come faster. We didn't want to violate Shabbos, so we came over before sundown. That's when we learned the baby was breech. Since she'd already delivered one child safely, the doctors decided to let this one come naturally. They warned me it would take time, but it seems like I've been here forever."

"I'll stay with you as long as it takes." Nathan noticed Benny used contractions, which he did only when he was distraught, so Nathan tried to lighten the conversation. "One advantage of beards is that you can go a few days without shaving and nobody notices."

"It makes my Haredi patients more comfortable too," he replied.

Nathan couldn't help but smile. "It doesn't hurt, either, that you look like Freud."

Benny closed his eyes, and Nathan noted that the walls were still the same pale green as when Abba had been hospitalized here nine years ago, after Abba's first heart attack. By that time, Benny, whom he'd befriended in the Brooklyn Library stacks two years earlier, had become such a good friend that Nathan lived with Benny's family for a month until Abba recovered and came home. The hospital walls had been the same green when Abba had a second coronary and Nathan was no longer welcome in the Stockser home. He shuddered at the memory of those agonizing years when Reb Stockser, outraged that the State of Israel had been established without the Messiah's arrival and that Nathan's father was a vehement Zionist, forbade Benny to have any contact with Nathan.

Abba hadn't been in the hospital since. But Nathan was here in 1951 to sit with Benny while Sharon labored to give birth to their son, Eliezer. And again, two years later, he'd cried here with both of them on that terrible day when Eliezer died of polio.

Benny interrupted his reverie. "Why the sigh?"

Nathan wasn't going to remind Benny of the deceased child. "I was thinking about the second time Abba was in this hospital." It wasn't the entire truth, but it wasn't a lie.

Benny sighed deeply. "That year was tough on me too." After a lengthy silence his expression brightened. "Your father said you were on a date tonight. Was it with the same Barbara you've been seeing since October?"

"It was." To forestall the inevitable questions, Nathan added, "I like Barbara a lot, but I'm not ready to propose to her."

Benny rolled his eyes. "Sharon said she wanted to marry me after just a couple of months, and then it only took me a little longer to fall for her too."

A cloud of gloom settled over Nathan. "How I envied you for that. I still envy you for it."

Benny's eyes narrowed with suspicion. "Sharon said you two were only friends."

"We are. I envy you finding your bride so quickly." Nathan shook his head in frustration. "You married the first girl you dated, while I've been dating since college without success."

"So, *nu*? What are you waiting for?"

Nathan didn't know how to describe falling in love, only that he knew he hadn't experienced it. "I'm waiting for someone who makes me feel the way you and Sharon obviously did when you got engaged."

Benny blushed, then his brow furrowed. "My good friend Dr. Freud would say it has something to do with you growing up without a mother."

Suddenly the door swung open, and a nurse beckoned to them. Benny raced toward her, while Nathan, heart pounding, stayed seated to give them privacy.

The conversation didn't last long.

Benny slumped down on the couch and closed his eyes again. "It's going to be several more hours at least, but labor is progressing."

Nathan waited for more, but Benny's measured breathing slowed into soft snores. He leaned back and wondered what was wrong with him that the more girls he dated, the less any of them stood out. Without finding an answer, he dozed off as well.

The sun was up when another nurse woke them. "Rabbi Stockser," she called out, demonstrating that here, "rabbi" was a more honored title than "doctor" or "professor."

Benny jerked awake, and the nurse smiled. "Mazel tov, you have a baby girl." She beckoned him to follow her. "You can see Mrs. Stockser now."

Nathan, flooded with relief, gave Benny a fierce hug. "If it's all right with you, I'll go home to get some more sleep."

"I'll phone you later," Benny called out as the door closed behind him.

Envy gnawed at Nathan as he walked down the lonely hall. He and Benny were the same age, but his friend had married and fathered two children already. *What am I waiting for?*

The following Tuesday Hannah searched frantically for the scarf Nathan had complimented. "Mama," she finally called out. "Have you seen my blue paisley scarf?"

"It's in the laundry. It was stained."

"When will it be ready?"

"I don't know, maybe Friday," came Deborah's annoyed answer. "What's so important about that scarf? Wear one of your other blue ones."

Hannah sighed with disappointment and resignation. She'd do the laundry tomorrow and make sure it was clean for Thursday.

This time Hannah fought to ignore the demons that had stymied her the week before. She marched right up the stairs and immediately rang the doorbell.

Nathan had the coffee ready. He was so eager to answer her question that he started before they sat down at the table. "The Gemara differentiates between laws derived from the Torah and those mandated by the Rabbis. Torah law is called d'oraita and Rabbinic law derabanan."

Again taking the seat near the door, she slipped her gloves off into her lap and picked up the comforting hot drink. Unlike their previous sessions, when Nathan had worn the same gray flannel suit as when she interviewed him, tonight he had on a herringbone sports coat.

"For example," he continued, "the Sages derived the laws of not eating meat and dairy together from the commandment 'You shall not boil a kid in its mother's milk.' Thus they are considered d'oraita."

"What about not eating chicken with milk?" she confidently challenged him. "Birds aren't mammals."

Pleased that she'd found the obvious objection and was brave enough to confront him with it, he smiled. "You're right. Extending this prohibition to poultry is considered derabanan because the Rabbis enacted it as a fence around the Torah," he said. When she didn't comment, he directed her to the new page. "Let's continue where we left off, starting with 'woman.'"

Hannah's annoyance rose as she read, "'A woman with her husband is not required to recline.'" She scowled at Nathan. "So a husband is his wife's master?"

"Not necessarily." He told himself it was good that she had a strong reaction to the text. "Some versions don't say anything about the husband, merely 'a woman is not required to recline.'"

"'A prominent woman is required to recline,'" she continued. Of course, few women back then were free. Most were ruled by fathers or husbands. "But it doesn't say what makes a woman prominent."

Nathan pointed to the commentary. "It doesn't need to. The Tosafos declares that all women are prominent and thus required to recline." He halted for emphasis. "Which is what we do today, for women in our time are surely no less prominent."

Somewhat mollified, Hannah read about whether waiters serving the Pesach meal recline (yes), sons in the presence of their fathers (no), and students in the presence of their teachers (it depends). Her finger followed the text until she got to a sentence that grabbed her attention. "'Rabbi Yehoshua ben Levi said: Women are obligated in the four cups, for they too were involved in that miracle.'" Then she stopped, her finger keeping her place.

Fascinated by the anomaly of a pink-enameled fingernail moving across a page of Talmud, Nathan didn't catch her entire question. "Excuse me, could you repeat that?"

"I read in a Mishnah that women are exempt from commandments that have to be fulfilled at a particular time, like hearing the shofar at Rosh Hashana or waving the lulav at Sukkos. So how are we obligated to drink the four cups of wine on Erev Pesach?"

"Very good," he congratulated her, hoping to make up for being distracted. "I wasn't sure you'd recognize the problem. Yehoshua ben Levi obviously knows about this exemption, which is why he gives a reason to override the Mishnah. He also obligates women to hear the Megillah read on Purim and to kindle lights on Hanukah for the same reason."

Hannah warmed at his praise. "Miriam and Joheved were involved in Pesach and Esther in Purim, but what did women do in Hanukah?" She wasn't afraid to ask questions now. And she was curious to hear his answer.

"Rashi says that the widow Yehudit got the Greek general drunk and killed him, but the Tosafos explains that in these three historical instances, Hebrew women faced the same dangers as men."

"Yehoshua ben Levi has good reasons to obligate women to drink the four cups, and I assume this applies to other Pesach mitzvos like eating matzah and maror—" She waited for Nathan to agree. "But how did he get the authority to overrule the Mishnah like that?"

Nathan had never heard that question before. He had to think awhile before admitting, with some embarrassment, "The Gemara doesn't explain. It only records those three instances where he does it."

Now Hannah had even more questions about men's and women's different ritual obligations. Especially since the Torah didn't mention any such distinction. But as long as "exempt" didn't mean "forbidden," she was glad to be exempt. She'd have a choice about what to do.

Mondays at the *Freiheit* were slow for Hannah since her only responsibilities were to pick up those Yiddish and Hebrew articles that needed translating into English. Editing didn't start until Tuesday. She took a deep breath of the fresh air, her last before she left, then went inside and emptied her in-box. Only senior editors merited individual desks. Everyone else did their work crowded around three large tables. Hannah chose a spot as far as possible from the foul-smelling cigar smokers.

The Israeli Sunday newspapers had already arrived, so she began to peruse them. The front page was full of politics; nothing new there. But an interior story piqued her interest. She began to skim it but soon went back to the beginning to read it slowly.

When she was finished, she rushed to Moe's office. "Moe, come look at this."

He met her at the door. "What's so exciting?"

"Remember those jars of ancient scrolls they found in a cave near the Dead Sea?"

"Vaguely. It was just before the State of Israel was founded. Right?"

By this time Hannah's enthusiasm had attracted onlookers. "Yes, in 1947. The Hebrew University bought three scrolls and the Syrian Orthodox archbishop of Jerusalem, the other four. Then, when war broke out in 1948, he hid them." She stopped briefly for effect. "But nobody knew where, and many people thought they were lost or destroyed."

Moe's eyebrows rose as his face lit with interest. "But they weren't?"

"No. The archbishop smuggled them to New York, where Syrian Christians hid them until last year. Can you believe they placed an ad in the *Wall Street Journal* to sell biblical manuscripts dating back to 200 BCE?" She was amazed at the wonder of it all. "And in an incredible coincidence, the Israeli archaeologist whose father originally obtained the other three scrolls saw the ad and purchased the additional four for Israel."

"Anything good in them?" Miriam called out.

"Much better than good," Hannah replied. "One of the scrolls is a nearly complete copy of the Book of Isaiah. And the text is almost exactly the same as we have today, even though it's two thousand years old."

Nobody said anything until Moe turned to Hannah. "Drop everything and translate this article. I want it in tomorrow's paper. Take your time on the English version, but make sure it's ready by Friday."

Hannah had promised her mother she'd come home early to help prepare for Pesach, but now she was stuck in the newsroom until her translation was finished. The linotype was up and running when she finally dropped the Yiddish version in the out-box and yelled, "Copy." Between the din and smoke, her head was throbbing, but the great story was worth it. And Mama wouldn't be too upset at Hannah coming home late once she explained what she'd been working on.

The weekend before her next Talmud session with Nathan, their last before the Pesach holiday week, Hannah looked through the Mishnah for other mentions of women's exemptions from what the Rabbis called "time-bound positive mitzvos." She wanted to understand how and why the Rabbis instituted this policy. But she ended up more irritated than enlightened. Women were not included in Grace after Meals, did not go to Jerusalem for the festivals, and were exempt from the laws of sukkah. Yet women were obligated to say Hallel, psalms of praise recited on holidays.

It didn't make sense, and at their next Talmud session she began her onslaught before even starting her coffee. "I couldn't find any explanation in the Mishnah for women's exemptions from mitzvos done at a particular time," she complained. "Nor why they're applied so inconsistently. Or where the idea that mitzvos can be differentiated this way came from."

"While I want you to have questions, that doesn't mean I'll always have answers," Nathan confessed, taken aback by her reproach. "The Sages ask the same questions. In fact, they have one of the longest debates in the entire Talmud on this subject, in Tractate Kiddushin."

"So . . . ?"

"There is no decision." For a moment he wished they could study that sugya together when she had more experience. "The Gemara never explains the exemption, but modern scholars speculate it's because of women's many household and childcare obligations."

Her eyes narrowed, and Nathan realized he'd made a mistake. "Hannah, I need to apologize. I never should have brought up this topic, one of the most difficult in the entire Talmud," he said. "I wanted to intrigue you, not frustrate you."

"I am intrigued—"

"And frustrated," he interrupted her. "But it's my fault. I've been a poor teacher, trying to teach algebra to a first grader."

Hannah could hear the shame in his voice. "No, you're a good teacher. I'm really looking forward to my family's Seders this year because of all you've taught me."

"Let me try to explain these exemptions again."

"Okay." Hopefully, she wouldn't be so confused.

"According to Jewish tradition, God gave Moses the Written Torah on Mount Sinai," he began. "But it's Orthodox dogma that Moses received the Oral Torah there as well." When she nodded, he continued. "In the Written Torah there are two kinds of commandments: positive ones like 'honor your parents' and negative ones like 'don't murder.'"

"Which apply to both men and women," she said.

"According to the Written Law, yes. But the Oral Law, in the Mishnah, divides the positive mitzvos into those that can be done anytime, like putting a mezuzah on your doorpost, and those done at a specific time, like eating matzah during Pesach."

"And it exempts women from the latter."

"Although the Gemara does take issue with this." He hesitated to decide how to summarize these conflicts simply and concisely. "You've already seen Yehoshua ben Levi's solutions, but another problem is that Judaism can't function if women are exempt from Shabbos. Also, there's the difficulty of defining *exempt*. Does it mean a woman is permitted to do these mitzvos if she wants, that she should do them, or that she shouldn't do them? The debates in the Talmud are so convoluted most men can't follow them."

Her curiosity aroused, she asked, "How do they obligate women to observe Shabbos?" Surely Nathan knew the answer to that.

He did. "The Rabbis decided that for holidays with both positive and negative commandments—Shabbos and Yom Kippur, for example— women and men have the same obligations."

Hannah kvelled at how quickly she'd understood his explanation. "Pesach has positive and negative commandments too. Besides reclining, drinking wine, eating matzah and maror, we don't eat hametz and don't work."

Nathan's heart leaped when her eyes had lit with sudden insight. "Yes," he encouraged her. "That would obligate women to observe Pesach."

"So Yehoshua ben Levi used the miracle aspect to further obligate women to Purim and Hanukah, but he couldn't find a miracle for women to observe Sukkos."

"Brilliant. You're thinking like a Talmudist."

She beamed. "Nathan, I can't thank you enough for studying Talmud with me. You've been a good teacher."

Nathan couldn't recall a student ever complimenting him. "Not as good a teacher as I'd like." Then, to his surprise, he continued with, "To make up for my deficiencies, we can study together for another month or so after Pesach and finish the sugya."

Hannah was overcome with astonished delight. "I'd love to, but are you sure? You're a busy man with so many demands on your time."

"I'm absolutely sure." It felt wonderful to be so appreciated. "I want to leave you with a better impression of me." Yet Nathan still hadn't found a way to broach the awkward subject of Abba wanting to hear about Hannah's Israel experiences.

She'd returned her notes to her briefcase when she gave him the opening he'd hoped for. Handing him the final draft of her article about him so he could approve it, she looked at him earnestly. She still felt guilty for pressuring him into teaching her. "Now that I see how much work teaching Talmud is, I realize why my request caught you by surprise." She spoke quickly before she lost her courage. "I shouldn't have been so brash, practically forcing you to accept me or risk hurting my feelings."

"I'm flattered you think I agreed to do this because I'm too nice to reject you, but I can't think of a better use of my time than giving a beginner a taste for Talmud."

"Well, anytime you want to talk about Israel with me, you only have to ask."

So he did. "I know H. M. Covey needs confidentiality, but would you consider letting my father join us? He's a fervent Zionist, and it would mean so much to him."

To Nathan's great relief, Hannah shrugged.

"I'm sure your father would be discreet," she replied. "And it's not as though my family and the *Freiheit* staff don't know my double identity."

"We could meet on a Sunday," he said. "I don't teach that day."

"I have an idea," she replied. "If we do it during Chol HaMoed [the intermediate days of Pesach], my aunt Elizabeth can come with me. Now that she's back home in Boston, she spends Pesach with us. I think she'd love to share her impressions of Israel."

"Perfect. Both Spektor and the Seminary are off that week."

The first day of Pesach, Hannah happily hummed a holiday melody as she helped her mother, aunt, and fourteen-year-old half sister restore the dining room to its pre-Seder condition. The dining table leaves and folding chairs were back in storage, along with the laundered large tablecloths and matching napkins. Aromas of beef brisket and fried matzah lingered in the air as she swept the floors. Tomorrow her family would attend the second-night Seder at Tante Essie Helfman's house.

For Hannah, the previous night had been one of the best Seders in years. As always, the large company included Mama and Dad, plus younger half siblings Rae and Jake. There were other relatives, like older stepbrother Dovid, his wife and their three young children, Samuel's cousins the Helfmans, whose daughter Naomi was Dovid's wife as well as Hannah's childhood friend, and Aunt Elizabeth. After moving to their large home on President Street, her parents began welcoming immigrant families who had nowhere else to go on Pesach. Last year, when the Eisin immigration law firm successfully prevented the Department of Justice from revoking Moe Novick's citizenship and deporting him, Moe and his wife joined their Seder as well.

Hannah was proud that, though Dad's legal work and real estate investments provided more than enough income for their family, Mama remained a dedicated employee at the immigrant aid society where she'd worked since before they married. After the war Mama's resettlement work had been critical during the refugee crisis. Now, ten years later, there were still immigrants coming to America whose difficulties required her expertise. So Samuel Eisin always reminded everyone that thousands of years after the biblical Exodus, Jews were still fleeing countries where they'd been mistreated and persecuted.

Hannah's studies with Nathan had opened her eyes to how the Talmud informed the Haggadah's narrative, making it more exciting than ever. Yet it was excruciatingly frustrating having to restrain herself from exposing her newly acquired knowledge during the men's lively discussions, during which the women were silent. But Moe made her forget her resentment.

When she left the table to bring out dessert, he caught up with her in the hall, a conspiratorial look on his face. "I need you to come in early on Monday," he whispered. "A little bird told me that there's going to be an announcement about the polio vaccine, and I want you to write the story."

Though her heartbeat quickened at the thought of such an inside scoop, she asked, "Why me? Why not someone with better Yiddish?"

"I need a writer who can capture the world-changing importance of the event." He gave her a quick smile. "And to reward you for finding that initial Israeli article and bringing it to my attention."

Then, as if their conversation hadn't happened, they went into the kitchen and returned with trays containing macaroons, marzipan bonbons, strawberry sponge cake, and Hannah's favorite, a flourless chocolate torte. But Moe's reward was sweeter.

Once the dining room was back in order the following morning, the four females reconvened at the kitchen table for lunch quickly pulled together from the previous night's Seder leftovers. The men wouldn't be home from the synagogue's lengthy holiday morning service for a while, so the women could relax. To be honest, Hannah appreciated women being exempt from all the festival prayers at shul so she could stay home with her mother and aunt.

She was wondering how to find the Yiddish words for the technical and scientific terms she might need for the vaccine article, when her sister Rae announced, "Last night was our greatest Seder ever. To think that we actually had an immigrant family from Egypt at our table."

Hannah nodded. "It was a good one. Though nothing compares to the year the State of Israel was born, when we could say 'next year in Jerusalem' and know it could really happen."

"As much as I love coming to yours, Deborah," Aunt Elizabeth began, her low voice like a cat purring, "my best Seder was in the Yemeni refugee camp in Hadera, when I was blessed to see, with my own eyes, the ingathering of Jewish exiles happening in my lifetime."

Three faces turned to Deborah, who looked increasingly uncomfortable. After some hesitation, she said, "My best Seder will be the one after Hannah's wedding."

Hannah turned beet red. "Mama," she blurted out as Rae giggled. "You promised not to nag me about marriage."

"All right. My best Seder was long before the war, when I was a child, before the Cossacks sacked our village. Back then I was still religious."

Rae looked at their mother in alarm. "You mean you're not religious now?"

"Oh, I keep a kosher home and observe Shabbos and Pesach like a Jewish woman should," Deborah replied. "But I don't believe in God, so I don't pray."

Aunt Elizabeth took that moment to intervene. "Deborah, I can see you've been under a great deal of stress; your hair had hardly any gray in it last year. Why don't you get some rest and leave the cleanup to me?"

Hannah observed her mother closely. Mama's once raven hair was streaked with gray, and there were areas of white at her temples. She was still lovely, though her lips turned down a little at the corners, and small wrinkles lined her dark eyes. Aunt Elizabeth, whose hair had been gray as long as Hannah could remember, seemed not to have aged as much as Mama had.

When Deborah followed her sister-in-law's advice and headed up the stairs, Rae reminded them that her friend Roberta had invited her over that afternoon. She gave a beseeching look at Hannah, who waved her off, saying, "Have a good time. Don't worry about the dishes." At age fourteen, Rae was too young to hear what was causing their mother's distress.

Now alone with Hannah, Aunt Elizabeth turned to her with a frown. "Don't tell your sister, but your mother is not just stressed from preparing for Passover. The House Un-American Activities Committee, going after anyone with ties to Communism, has subpoenaed her."

Though Hannah had taken only a few bites, she immediately lost her appetite. "But Mama quit the Party and condemned them when Russia signed that nonaggression pact with the Nazis," she protested. "She's not a Communist now—they betrayed her."

"Nevertheless, the HUAC thinks she can inform on members who might have quit but still sympathize." Elizabeth sighed. "If she won't cooperate, they can threaten to deport her, like they did with your boss."

For a moment Hannah was too shocked to speak. "But—but," she stammered. "Dad stopped them, and Mama is a US citizen too."

"The McCarran–Walter Act allows the US to deport immigrants and even naturalized citizens who engage in subversive activities." Elizabeth's voice dripped with disgust. "So while Deborah is probably safe, her friends and clients are not. Especially if they can't afford lawyers."

"So the HUAC is pressing her to give them names?" Hannah was horrified.

Her aunt nodded. "We can thank Sam that so far she's only had to answer written questions. Others have been called to testify in person, and often lost their jobs as a result. Sam makes sure that she never lies and provides only minimal information, things the committee already knows. Still, she worries that the Justice Department will prosecute her as a lesson to Sam for successfully stopping them from deporting Moe Novick."

"No wonder Mama's upset."

Aunt Elizabeth put her dishes in the sink. "Unfortunately, we don't know how long it will take until the HUAC is done with her." Then, after yawning broadly, she too went upstairs to take a nap.

Hannah felt too agitated to do any vaccine research. But she couldn't just sit there with her stomach churning, so she washed the dishes as she waited for Dad to come home. He was the person to assuage her fears, in private.

Before a half hour passed, Hannah heard his footfalls coming up the stoop. She forced herself to wait until he was settled in the kitchen with a cup of coffee before she shared what Aunt Elizabeth had told them. "Is Mama going to be all right?" She made no effort to hide her fear. "Is it true that someone who'd been a Communist decades ago would still be suspect?"

Samuel frowned and sighed heavily. "Maybe not someone like Deborah, who denounced and renounced her affiliation. But those unfortunates who became Socialists or merely drifted away from politics cannot easily defend against accusations of being a Communist sympathizer. It doesn't help that she works at HIAS; many of the HUAC are anti-immigrant too."

"Is that why they're targeting her?"

"They're actually targeting me." His gravelly growl was like subdued thunder.

The only other time Hannah had seen him angry was when the Torah Academy had denied her the Rashi Award. Today his barely restrained fury made her shrink back in her chair. "That's what Aunt Elizabeth thought," she whispered.

"They know my wife is innocent, but they keep harassing me about her." He must have seen Hannah's reaction; his voice softened and his scowl eased. "There are only so many hours in a day, and the more of them I spend on Deborah's case, the fewer I have to defend my other clients."

"I've heard that these so-called anti-Communists are really anti-Semites." Hannah had difficulty keeping her voice calm. "A *Freiheit* reporter found that most of the teachers kept from working in the public schools because of alleged subversive activities were Jewish."

Samuel nodded. "Many of the radicals, Socialists, and labor organizers, particularly in New York, are indeed Jews."

"So they're easy targets."

"Lawyers can't help teachers or other government employees who lose their jobs," he said. "Though it looks like the Supreme Court is going to hear Harry Slochower's case."

"Harry Slochower?"

"He was a professor at Brooklyn College who invoked his Fifth Amendment protection against self-incrimination a few years ago when a congressional committee questioned his past Communist Party membership." Samuel finished his coffee and put down the cup. "Despite his tenured status, which required notice and a hearing before termination, the city fired him immediately."

"Thank Heaven Mama doesn't work for the government like other social workers do," Hannah said. Though their conversation disturbed her, she felt proud that her dad talked with her like an adult.

It was early Friday afternoon during Chol HaMoed when Nathan finally got to see Sharon and her new baby. Dark circles under her eyes, accentuated by auburn tresses pulled back in a ponytail, showed that she hadn't caught up on her sleep since her lengthy labor, not surprising since she shared a room with five other new mothers and their infants.

Nonetheless, she greeted him with a smile. "Nathan, I'm so glad you came back. I was afraid I wouldn't see you before Shabbos."

"How are you feeling? How's the baby?"

"It'll be a week or so until I'm up and about, but the baby is doing well, *keinehora*."

"A week?" That sounded like a long time.

"I was in the hospital eight days the last time."

Nathan saw her tear up and cursed himself for reminding her of the son who passed away. "I can stay as long as you want, just so I get home before sunset."

The last time they'd been alone together was a walk and talk in the cemetery a month after the boy died. There she'd shared the unhappiness and bitterness she still felt when the Hasidic women didn't accept her. It made Nathan uncomfortable, but there was nothing he could do but let Sharon pour out her misery uninterrupted. She might dress modestly and cover her hair when she visited her in-laws, but she'd always be an outsider in Benny's community.

She gestured for him to come closer and whispered, "Don't tell Benny, but I am so relieved I don't have to spend Pesach with his family. I think that almost made all the pain I suffered in labor worthwhile."

He looked at her askance, and she quickly added, "That was a joke, Nathan. Every minute I spend with my daughter makes giving birth to her worthwhile."

"Is it really so terrible to spend a week with the Stocksers?" He'd spent two months with them and had no complaints.

"It wouldn't be so bad if it were only that week. But in the five years I've been married, this will be the first Shabbos I'll spend with my parents." Her face fell. "I'll probably never have Shabbos dinner with my aunt and uncle again."

"You should talk to Benny. He's the one who can do something about it."

She shook her head. "It's too late. I made certain compromises to marry him, and I can't go back on them."

Nathan didn't see why they couldn't be renegotiated, but he was reluctant to start what would likely be a futile conversation. So he felt thankful when Sharon changed the subject.

"Benny said you approved the *Freiheit* article about you."

"It's coming out Sunday." He blushed thinking about the attention he'd get.

Sharon sighed. "I wish they'd write one about Benny and his work."

"About Benny's work? But there's such a terrible stigma against mental illness among Jews." He couldn't imagine any Jewish paper writing about a subject so taboo.

"You're right. Most of the religious ones believe it's God's curse for having sinned," she said. "The Haredi are terrified that even a rumor of a family member seeing a psychologist will make their children unmarriageable."

"It must be a challenge getting patients."

"That's putting it mildly." She sighed again. "Some of Benny's cases are very sad, but at least those children are being helped."

"He certainly helped your cousin Joey." Nathan had kept up his friendship with the young man, now studying astronomy at Berkeley. Without Benny's intervention, Joey Goren would have been institutionalized. *There, I said something positive.*

Sharon gave him a shy smile. "If Benny hadn't been treating Joey, I never would have met him."

Nathan wanted to further lift her spirits, so he grinned back. "And you never would have had your new daughter."

They could hear crying outside, and a nurse entered, carrying the unhappy infant. She turned to Nathan and declared, "You'll have to leave while Mrs. Stockser feeds her child."

"Have a good Shabbos." He couldn't escape the now wailing baby fast enough.

On the cab ride home, Nathan's mood darkened. If a couple so much in love as Benny and Sharon had marital problems, what hope was there for him to have a successful marriage? And if, as Benny intimated, he was searching for the mother's love he never had, what hope was there for him to ever fall in love? Maybe he should just give up his fruitless search and marry Barbara.

THREE

"HANNAH, WOULD YOU like to drive to the Mandels'?" Aunt Elizabeth asked as they walked toward the blue roadster. "You haven't had any practice since last summer." Without waiting for an answer, Aunt Elizabeth opened the passenger door and sat down.

At first Hannah had been surprised that her aunt, whose clothes were classic and practical, would buy such a sporty car. But then, Aunt Elizabeth, who had been a nurse in war zones all over the world, was in many ways the female personification of adventurous. Hannah had to admit that when she imagined what a great movie her aunt's life story would make, she pictured Katharine Hepburn, driving a convertible, as the star.

"I'd love to." Hannah was grateful for her aunt's presence. Her interview with Nathan had run in today's paper, and meeting his father would be less nerve-racking than if she went alone. Her own parents hadn't pressed her on how she'd learned so much about Talmud but only praised her writing. Just as they did when one of her Israel stories was published.

With any luck, Aunt Elizabeth would be in the spotlight at the Mandels' and Hannah merely the sideshow. "You're wearing your Israeli Defense Force nurse's uniform."

"A woman in uniform gets more respect than one in civilian clothes." Her voice hardened. "And in war zones, she's not subjected to the restrictions and indignities that local women suffer."

The weather forecast was unseasonably warm, so Hannah put the top down. She looked forward to the attention they'd receive, two women driving such a flashy vehicle down Eastern Parkway. Sure enough, the numerous envious—and some disapproving—stares from passersby filled her with pride.

Cars being relatively rare in Williamsburg, Hannah easily found a parking spot outside Nathan's apartment. Until now, she had been too exhilarated driving to worry about how she and Nathan would need to act to avoid betraying their Talmud study relationship. Hopefully, his father would be too engrossed in talking about Israel.

Which, to her great relief, he was.

Solomon Mandel obviously recognized Elizabeth's uniform because he greeted her with a broad smile. "Lieutenant Covey"—he reached out to shake her hand—"delighted to meet you."

"Please call me Elizabeth."

"And you should call me Solomon." He turned to Hannah, who was marveling at how different, and pleasing, the light-filled front rooms looked with the curtains pulled open. "So nice to see you again, Hannah. I want to compliment you on Nathan's interview and your story about the Dead Sea Scrolls. I used to think the *Freiheit* was nothing but a Communist rag."

"My dad used to think so too." She paused and grinned. "Until I started working there."

"I think the *Freiheit* now has the best Israel coverage of any paper in New York," Solomon said. "I'm impressed at how Zionist they've become since 1948."

He directed them to the dining table, where a vase of colorful spring flowers was surrounded by a variety of Israeli foods, their distinctive aromas carrying Hannah back to the Yemeni refugee camp dining hall where she'd eaten so many meals.

Solomon pulled out a chair for Elizabeth, after which Nathan hurried to do the same for Hannah. Elizabeth ran her hand over the chair's curved wooden back before sitting. "This is a beautiful walnut dining set, and comfortable as well."

"Thank you." He winced slightly. "It was a wedding gift from my late wife's grandparents."

Nathan looked at the furniture with new reverence. He sat there every day and never particularly noticed it. He had no idea that it was made of walnut, or more importantly, that it came from his great-grandparents. He did know that it had eight comfy chairs: two with arms now in Abba's bedroom and study, two without in his own bedroom, and four around the table. And that the darkish multicolored floral fabric hid a multitude of stains.

Solomon quickly turned to Elizabeth. "Tell me all about your time in Israel, start to finish. I understand from my son that you were there for over four years."

Elizabeth smiled at his enthusiasm. "It actually started with my service as a US Army nurse in Europe during the war." She helped herself to several of the dishes. "I won't spoil this lovely meal with a description of my experiences treating the concentration camp survivors. I expect you've heard enough about their deplorable condition."

Nathan and Abba both winced and nodded. Hannah, despite all her time with Aunt Elizabeth, had never heard her war stories, and she struggled with a jumble of divergent feelings—excitement and curiosity but also shame that she knew so little of her aunt's history.

"In the displaced persons camps, I heard about underground efforts to transport Jewish survivors, who, understandably, refused to be repatriated to their previous homelands, to the Holy Land," Elizabeth began. "Once I realized how desperately they would need nurses there, I was determined to volunteer."

"You were still in the army?" Solomon asked.

She nodded. "Plenty of troops remained in Europe, and the military had more important things to do than keeping track of nurses in the DP camps. They wanted those camps emptied as quickly as possible, and if that meant closing their eyes to groups facilitating transport to Palestine, so be it."

"When did you leave Europe, then?" Nathan quickly asked.

Hannah saw the distress in his eyes and recognized that he, too, wanted to get to the Israel part rather than dwell on what had happened in Europe.

"In 1947 I joined a ship full of young people, many merely children, but we were intercepted and forced back to Cyprus. I worked there as a nurse for a year, until Israel's independence. Then I helped assess the new immigrants' health at an old British Army camp near Haifa, which was appalling."

"Which was appalling?" Solomon interrupted. "The immigrants' health or the old army camp?"

"Both." Elizabeth scowled. "The British soldiers vandalized everything they could: furniture, doors, and windows, even the walls were smashed. As for the immigrants' health, what would you expect when large groups of malnourished people, some with contagious diseases, are crowded together in a camp with inadequate housing and poor sanitation?" She looked heavenward before concluding, "It is truly a miracle so few died."

The awe with which Elizabeth spoke that last sentence made it clear she attributed this to divine intervention. "I am a devout Christian whose beliefs sustain my mission to heal the sick. I expected no recompense in this life, but the Good Lord granted me the reward of spending Christmas in Bethlehem and Easter in Jerusalem." She sighed with pleasure at the memory. "I was also blessed to be able to visit Nazareth, swim in the Sea of Galilee, and bathe in the Jordan River."

Hannah gulped back her discomfort at her aunt's demonstration of religiosity. Nathan looked like he was going to ask her a question but then addressed her aunt. "So, your first year wasn't an unmitigated catastrophe."

Elizabeth looked at him sternly. "That came in 1949, when the Communist and Arab countries began expelling their Jewish populations. To quote Dickens, 'It was the best of times; it was the worst of times.' Worst because we were overwhelmed with patients from Yemen and Iraq, many of whom, because of the language barrier, could not communicate with Israeli medical workers. Thankfully, I'd learned Arabic while nursing in Ethiopia during their war with Italy." Her eyes shone as she continued. "Best of times because I could see with my own eyes, after almost two thousand years, the Ingathering of the Exiles."

Hannah's stomach tightened with anxiety that Nathan and his father would be affronted by Aunt Elizabeth's overt reference to an omen foretelling the Messiah's arrival, which her aunt saw portending the Second Coming. Nathan was already looking at her strangely, but thankfully Solomon Mandel didn't seem offended.

"Some of Israel's greatest supporters are pious Christians like yourself," he said. "And I should know," he added with a smile. "I sit on far too many boards of Zionist organizations."

Elizabeth, perhaps deciding she'd monopolized the conversation too long, gestured at her niece. "The need for help was so great that I had Hannah, who knew some Hebrew, brought to Israel, though it would only be for the summer."

Hannah was impressed that Aunt Elizabeth spoke of this feat as if she'd merely snapped her fingers to make it happen. She would have preferred to hear more of her aunt's story, but she accepted that it was her turn to join the conversation. "My aunt is being modest. It was her knowledge of Arabic that made her uniquely valuable and led to our being assigned to the Yemeni camps," she said proudly. "That and the fact that the Yemeni refused to let any male doctors or medics examine their women or girls."

"Not being a nurse or a medic," Nathan said, "what did you do for them?"

"I disinfected and bandaged small wounds, showed them how to shower with soap and running water, how to use a toilet, and other things we take for granted in the West." She chose not to mention that she also showed the women how to use sanitary napkins during menstruation.

"Traveling to Israel and back couldn't have left you much time there," Solomon said.

"I traveled by airplane, so it only took a few days."

Nathan's eyes opened wide. "Weren't you frightened?"

Hannah's mind revisited the initial terror on her first flight. "It was scary at the beginning, but exciting too. Once the plane was up in the air for a while, however, it got boring. There was nothing to see out the window and we couldn't get up except to use the lavatory."

"I hope you got a chance to travel around the country occasionally," Solomon said.

"Oh yes. Aunt Elizabeth insisted I take a day or two off every two weeks. That first summer I enjoyed playing the tourist, but the following years I went exploring with my immigrant friends." She inclined her head toward her aunt. "Aunt Elizabeth took me to Jerusalem's Old City, where the guards assumed I wasn't Jewish."

"So you saw the Western Wall?" Solomon's voice was full of awe.

"I even touched it, although I acted like it was nothing special." In truth, Hannah hadn't found the Wall particularly special. It was merely one more ancient wall in a city full of them. "Of course I had to visit the Christian shrines too, but my favorite part of the Old City was walking on the wall that encircles it. From up there you could see for miles."

"What else impressed you?" Nathan asked.

"Bathing in the Dead Sea, which really is so salty that you can float in it, and climbing up to Masada." For a few moments Hannah was back in time, triumphant at reaching the end of that grueling climb, then watching awestruck as the sun rose and illuminated the vast desert below.

Solomon turned to Elizabeth. "And you?"

"Besides the holy places, I enjoyed exploring the Crusader fortresses and hiking in the Galilee. Especially during early spring, when almond trees are in bloom and fields are covered with wildflowers."

Hannah had to interrupt. "But the most impressive thing about Israel was the many different peoples, all Jews. And despite all their suffering and deprivations, many had complete faith that this was the beginning of the messianic era in Israel."

"You were there through 1952." Solomon addressed the two women, who nodded. "How were things different when you left?"

"The main difference was that only one-tenth the number of immigrants arrived in 1952 as did in 1949," Elizabeth replied. "The other big change came at the end of 1950, when the IDF took over running the camps. They repaired the roads and brought in supplies regularly. They opened schools for all the children—girls as well as boys—and staffed the medical clinics."

Hannah's pride in her aunt's accomplishments would not let her remain silent. "When I arrived in 1951, Aunt Elizabeth was a lieutenant in the IDF, running several of those clinics."

"The powers that be thought it would give me more authority over the soldiers if I were an IDF officer rather than an American one," Elizabeth explained.

"They promoted you, a Christian woman, to an officer in the IDF," Solomon said. "Impressive."

"They knew what I could do." She was not boasting but being matter-of-fact. "The previous winter had been so disastrous that I used every contact I had in the US Army to get surplus tents and blankets shipped to Israel and my contacts in the medical world for antibiotics and other drugs."

"Good Heavens." Solomon stared at her in admiration. "Are you involved with the Covey Foundation that donated so magnanimously to the JDC?"

Her eyes narrowed. "That was supposed to be anonymous."

"Even anonymous donations are known to the executive board, although we do our best to keep them confidential," he said. "But now that you're sitting here at my table, please give me the opportunity to thank your family for its generosity."

Hannah tried to keep up with the conversation while Solomon and Nathan peppered Aunt Elizabeth with more queries as they lingered over coffee and Halvah. But her mind was filling with an increasing number of questions about the Covey Foundation.

She got her chance to ask her aunt about them as they approached Prospect Park on the drive home. "Aunt Elizabeth." She tried to sound nonchalant. "It's such a nice afternoon, and I'm still stuffed from lunch. Can we walk it off a little in the park?"

Elizabeth looked at her shrewdly. "I need to talk to you too."

"You never told me you gave money to Israel." Hannah knew this was a poor way to begin an interview, especially one about her aunt's wealth, but she was flustered.

"I was planning to tell you eventually, but there's no time like the present." Aunt Elizabeth turned to Hannah and asked, "What did your father tell you about our family?"

So the interviewer was going to be interviewed. "Let's see. Papa was born in New England and had an older brother who died. I saw a photo of his family in front of a big house," she began. "Mama told me they were

Episcopalians who didn't like him marrying a Jewish girl. She said they disowned him when he became a Communist and married her, so I figured he hadn't come from a poor family. I think they were in the lumber business."

"My father's family *was* the lumber business, or perhaps I should say the lumber *industry*." Elizabeth's cold voice gave Hannah the shivers. "Father was a ruthless entrepreneur who amassed more money than he and my mother could spend. To avoid taxes, he set up a charitable foundation, but it only disbursed funds to places like universities, museums, orchestras, and the like. Good causes that benefited Episcopalians like him."

Her bitter tone moderated as she continued. "When he died without any surviving sons, control of the foundation passed to Mother. I appealed to her Christian sensibilities, and slowly we began to fund charities like hospitals, youth organizations, and missionaries in poor countries. After Mother died, I began donating to Israel."

Hannah was stunned. "You run the Covey Foundation now?" It was difficult to imagine Aunt Elizabeth, who lived in a modest apartment in Boston, controlling any wealth.

"I employ experts to evaluate the many applicants, but yes, I make the final decisions." Her impenetrable expression invited no further questions on the subject.

They walked on quietly, arm in arm, listening to the birds. As the car came into view, Hannah asked, "What happened to the big house in the picture? We always go to your farmhouse in the summer." Hannah had formed such a strong bond with Aunt Elizabeth during their summers together in Israel that she began to spend each July with her aunt on Prince Edward Island after they returned.

"Mother donated it to the local historical society," Elizabeth replied. "If you want, we can see it when you come visit. Your father's room is the same as when he left home."

"Yes, I would like that." *Though it might be a bit intimidating.*

Sleep eluded Nathan as he pondered how an Orthodox girl like Hannah could have such a devout Christian aunt. He recalled how their schoolmates had teased her that first semester about being a shikse. Poor Hannah hadn't even known what the word meant, only that it was something bad. At the time he'd supposed they called her that because of her blond hair, so he'd defended her, declaring that her mother was Jewish, so she was too. But the harassment stopped only when her stepbrother, Dovid, intervened and threatened anyone who harassed his sister.

Until Nathan met Hannah's aunt, he'd assumed Michael Covey was Jewish. Yet Elizabeth Covey clearly wasn't. Had she converted to Christianity or was her brother the convert? If neither, which was likely, then Hannah's mother had married a—he couldn't bring himself to face the obvious. Though he knew that anyone with a Jewish mother was halachically Jewish, he was disconcerted that Hannah was only half-Jewish.

But why should that bother me? True, almost all Jews condemned intermarriage and many considered a child of such a union to be a *mamzer,* usually translated—incorrectly—in English as "bastard" because Jewish Law did not recognize the parents' marriage. Nathan was well aware that halacha did not consider a child born outside of wedlock a mamzer, and furthermore, according to the *Shulchan Aruch,* a mamzer can be produced only by two Jews. Yet he couldn't deny that the stigma such a child suffered was the source of his new uncomfortable feelings about Hannah. *Which I'll have to hide from her.*

Thank goodness Hannah's widowed mother remarried Samuel Eisin, a pillar of the Orthodox community, and had him adopt Hannah. Outside of a few coworkers at the *Freiheit,* probably nobody knew who her birth father was, and even those who did would have no knowledge of the man's religion. In any case, Nathan thought, why should it matter to him? *I'm teaching her, not marrying her.*

When Hannah entered the *Freiheit* offices Monday, Moe Novick, grinning ear to ear, hurried to intercept her. "Thanks again for the tipoff, Annie." He handed her some sheets of paper, typed in English. "Tomorrow, Dr. Salk will announce that his polio vaccine works."

She had read only the first paragraph when she looked up and exclaimed, "*Gottenyu,* is this Dr. Salk's medical report? How did you get it?"

"I have my contacts, remember?" He let her read for a few minutes before interrupting. "So, how long will it take you to turn this into a compelling Yiddish article? I want to put out an extra edition that hits the newsstands tomorrow afternoon."

She swallowed hard. Assuming one of the expert Yiddish editors would go over her work, she'd need to have a final draft typed when they returned from lunch. But what a scoop it would be when the *Freiheit* broke the story in Yiddish. She could feel her pulse racing. "I'll get right to it." *Thank Heaven I learned the correct Yiddish terminology over the weekend.*

Ninety minutes and several cups of coffee later, she had an acceptable first draft. Two hours later, when the editors left for lunch, she started typing her semifinal draft. She used a Yiddish typewriter so rarely that it seemed to take forever to produce an error-free version, but she managed to get it onto Moe's desk before the editors returned.

The atmosphere at work was electric with excitement when Hannah arrived the next morning. The linotypes were done and cut into small pieces, and everyone rushed to lay them out to fit their pages. Her jaw dropped when she saw all the additional articles, including a lengthy bio of Dr. Salk—hometown Jewish boy makes good—history of previous vaccines and how they were made, the difference between viruses and bacteria, and which diseases each caused. Plus there were photos of children wearing braces and one in an iron lung. When it was time, Moe turned the radio on so they could hear the press conference. Suddenly she, and the other reporters, realized that all their individual pieces had been written specifically for this day.

The layout was finished in record time, and Hannah went outside for some fresh air when the first run began. Then, as these were printed, she, along with the rest of the editorial staff, swung into action to find the inevitable typos and get them corrected. Only then would the presses start rolling in earnest. It was imperative that everything happen as quickly as possible so the special edition could hit the newsstands without delay after the radio announcement ended.

Hannah's eyes filled with tears of joy when she saw the giant headline "Salk Polio Vaccine Success" staring back at her in Yiddish. But they flowed unrestrained when she read the front page byline "H. M. Covey." Nearly everyone in the office was crying or looked about to. All of them knew, or were related to, someone affected by polio. Now the plague was over.

When Nathan and Hannah resumed their learning, he began by extolling her Salk vaccine article, his acclamation even more lavish when she explained that it came about because she first saw an Israeli news article. "My friend Benny Stockser's first child died of polio," he told her, "but their new baby will be immune."

Blushing at his praise, she changed the subject and told him how wonderful her Seders were because of their studies. "I understood so much more this year. I can't thank you enough for teaching me."

Nathan confessed that his Seders were boring. "It's just the same old men, although fewer of them these days," he grumbled. "Old friends and colleagues of my father, with their same old complaints. I wish we could go to Professor Goren's for Pesach, but it's too far for Abba to walk."

Hannah was momentarily too awed to speak. "You mean Isaac Goren, *the* Isaac Goren?"

Nathan nodded. "They invite us to their Seder every year, though they know we can't attend. We met them years ago, when we vacationed together near Peekskill in the summer. My father, of course, teaches with Isaac Goren at the Seminary. And their son Joey is one of my closest friends."

"Wow, Isaac Goren invites you to his Seder every year." She was so excited that, forgetting that a woman never removes her gloves in front of a man, she shoved them into her coat pockets before sitting down. "I've read all his books and can't tell you how much I admire his writing. He asks the same questions I have, about belief in God and the Bible's literal truth, and more, in such beautiful prose. No matter how difficult and complex the subject, he makes it understandable."

Nathan pretended not to have noticed her breach of etiquette, but his breath quickened as he watched her slip off her gloves. "I like his questions too. Tell me, do you like his answers?"

"Some of them," she admitted, reluctant to let Nathan know the extent of her apostasy. "But his great talent is making you think about his questions."

They spent the rest of the evening discussing Isaac Goren's works. They concurred that it was impossible to believe in a literal interpretation of the Torah in light of modern scholarship, but that didn't mean sensible people must abandon traditional Judaism. Certainly, a person could reject the dogma that God gave the entire Torah directly to Moses at Sinai, yet accept that the Torah was divinely inspired. Also that believing in God was not a simple choice between an anthropomorphic, omniscient, all-powerful deity versus a human concept, a mere noble ideal. There had to be a middle ground, but they couldn't decide what attributes it encompassed.

For Hannah, already thrilled to study Talmud with Nathan, discussing theology with him added immensely to her exhilaration. Especially when they agreed on so much.

For Nathan, sharing his doubts with someone who respected his opinions and didn't revile him as heretical was an unimagined pleasure. Only when the clock chimed nine did he realize how the time had flown. With chagrin he promised that, in the future, they would stick to discussing Talmud.

Confident they'd have other opportunities to debate theology during their Talmud studies, Hannah acquiesced. But on the subway ride home, she couldn't help but wonder how Nathan could be such an admirer of Isaac Goren's theology and still remain an Orthodox Jew.

The first Tuesday evening in May, Nathan was trying to restrain his annoyance as he again explained to a group of belligerent students how an observant Jew could reconcile the Talmud as both holy canon and containing variant texts without undermining halacha. Most *Freiheit* readers probably forgot the article about him once the special edition on the polio vaccine came out. Not at Spektor though. In general, the interview was well received, a testimonial to the school's excellence. But for the Haredi students, it was an assault on their deepest values.

When Nathan finally noticed the clock, he realized that if he didn't leave soon, he'd be late for his study session with Hannah. He'd never cut off a debate with students before, even the most closed-minded, but he did so now. It still took so long to extricate himself from their protests that he got to the subway platform just as his train pulled away. The next train was too crowded to board, so he raced back upstairs to hail a taxi.

Hannah was also running late. Her interview with a recent émigré from the USSR, Dr. Yakov Lewitsky, had not gone well. Two previous reporters had already met with Lewitsky. Both had returned empty-handed, complaining that the doctor was uncooperative and bad-tempered.

Praise for Hannah's recent articles had strengthened her position at the *Freiheit*. So when Moe asked her to interview Lewitsky, she approached this meeting determined to get his story. She already had in her notes that the medical scientist had barely escaped with his life when Stalin's death ended the Doctors' Plot persecutions. Scheduled to present a paper at a conference in East Berlin, he'd crossed into West Berlin before delivering it. Now he was fielding offers from America's most prestigious universities and research institutes.

Yet the man who opened the door was nervous to the extreme, his eyes constantly darting down the hall behind her. He appeared to know neither Yiddish nor English well enough to understand her questions, and Hannah, suspecting his ignorance was feigned, was furious she hadn't thought to bring a Russian translator. Her frustration mounting, she continued questioning him even when it meant missing dinner, but he only became more defensive and evasive.

Well, she wasn't going to be late to Nathan's. She would just have to forgo dinner and interview the doctor again another time. *And bring along Mama, who still used her native Russian working at HIAS.*

Hannah knocked on the door to Nathan's brownstone apartment a few minutes before seven. To her surprise, it didn't open. She knocked again, and when nobody answered, she peered in the front window only to see darkness. She walked down to the sidewalk and looked both ways, but no

Nathan. In different circumstances she might have waited for him on the stoop, but she didn't dare attract attention. Suddenly the solution came to her. There was only one subway he would have taken from Spektor. She could wait for him at the station, underground where nobody here would see her.

When the taxi dropped Nathan off twenty minutes later, there was no sign of Hannah. Hoping she'd merely taken a walk around the block, he set the Talmud volumes on the dining table and decided to eat later. He was too anxious to wait inside, so he paced back and forth on the sidewalk, desperate for a glimpse of her despite the increasing darkness. Finally there was nothing to do but trudge inside and reheat his dinner. He left the front door ajar, but didn't make coffee. Obviously, Hannah hadn't waited for him, and he couldn't blame her. The whole neighborhood would be gossiping if an attractive female stood around outside his door at night.

Then, suddenly, just as he got a plate from the china cabinet, there she was. Mortified at being late, Nathan apologized. But Hannah insisted it wasn't his fault. When their stories came out, they laughed in relief at how each had waited for the other in different places.

As they started reviewing the previous text, Nathan had just asked if she had any questions when his stomach growled. His face reddened with embarrassment and he said, "Excuse me. I got here too late to eat."

"I haven't eaten either," Hannah confessed.

Nathan grinned. "You know what it says in Pirkei Avot: 'No bread, no Torah.' And I happen to have enough bread, and chicken stew, for both of us."

The meal was quickly served, and coffee was ready in time for dessert. "You're a good cook," Hannah complimented him. "This chicken was delicious."

"We used to have a housekeeper when I was young, but these days Abba and I eat mostly at school. So I learned to make a few dinner dishes and you think I'm a great chef." Heart pounding at his audacity, he locked eyes with Hannah. "Why don't we meet earlier and eat together first from now on?"

She blushed and looked down at her plate. "I suppose we could do our review over dinner and have more time for the new material afterward."

"I have an idea," he added when they finished eating. "I'll give you a key so you can let yourself in if you get here before I do."

Taken aback at the intimacy this suggested, she took a while to reply. "That makes sense. I'll be able to avoid your neighbors' prying eyes," she finally said once she got over her surprise. "And if I'm going to have a key to your apartment, I think you should call me Annie like my friends and family do."

"Annie." He savored the sound of it. "What would you like for dinner on Thursday?"

"Surprise me," she replied. Then, because it was almost Mother's Day, she recalled that he never talked about his mother. Her own mother disliked the big *tzimmes* Jews made over Mother's Day, criticizing it as a fake holiday created by businesses to sell cards and flowers. It must sadden Nathan to have no mother to celebrate. They weren't strangers now, so she asked, "Do you have any favorite memories of your mother?"

"I was so little when she died that I don't remember her at all."

"Didn't your father tell you stories about her?"

Nathan's expression grew somber. "Abba didn't say anything about her until I was thirteen, when he gave me her Hebrew name and yahrzeit date so I could say Kaddish for her."

"That was all your father told you?" She couldn't hide her shock and incredulity.

"I tried asking him, but he always said I was too young to understand, that he'd tell me when I got older," he said plaintively.

"But you were never old enough," she gently concluded for him.

"I finally asked Abba when I graduated from yeshiva." Nathan's chin began to quiver, and he broke off to control himself. "But before he could tell me anything, he started sobbing so hard I couldn't bear it."

All Hannah could say was "How awful for you."

"Can you imagine watching your father cry, knowing it was your fault?" When she didn't answer, he sniffed a little and blew his nose. "I gave up after that. She was dead, after all. What else did I need to know?"

Hannah was appalled. *What else does he need to know? Doesn't he want to know where she was born and grew up, what kind of family she had, how his parents met?* But rather than asking Nathan anything like that, she said instead, "You don't have to ask your father to learn things about her." She drew upon her reporter's experience. "There aren't that many Jewish cemeteries in New York, and they should all be in the Yellow Pages. Just keep calling until you find the one where she's buried. It would have some information about her."

The next day Nathan called every Brooklyn cemetery in the New York City Yellow Pages, then those in the Bronx, followed by those in Queens and Manhattan. But none of them had a Mina Mandel in their records. No wonder Abba never took him to visit her grave; she was probably buried someplace too far away to visit. Maybe near where her family lived.

Still regretting how he'd made his father cry, he realized there was something he could do to make Abba happy. He'd propose to Barbara. He was twenty-six years old. It was time to settle down with a nice Jewish girl already. According to the shtetl stories, love would come later.

The following week, on a day that wouldn't interfere with Talmud study if the visit went late, Hannah and her mother stopped at a Russian bakery for an assortment of *vatrushka* on the way to interview Yakov Lewitsky. Deborah Eisin introduced herself in Russian and handed him the pastry box. When he remained mute, she explained where she worked and what she did there. Without going into details, she made it clear that she had no regrets leaving Russia for America.

Despite his silence, it was clear to Hannah that the unshaven man in ill-fitting clothes understood her mother. When Mama asked if he preferred to be addressed as Yakov, his Russian name, or Yankel, the same name in Yiddish, his face seemed to crumple.

"You may call me Yankel," he replied in Yiddish as he waved them in and deposited the pastries on the rickety dining table. "Please sit while I make some tea."

The sadness and defeat in his voice made Hannah fear that he might be about to harm himself. "No, no," she said, also in Yiddish. "Let us help you."

The tiny kitchen was furnished with a hot plate and a small icebox. Hannah brought the kettle to a boil while Mama took three teacups and small plates, none of which matched, from the cupboard to the table. Helpless against this feminine onslaught, Yankel sat down, examined the bakery box's contents, and waited.

Once the women were seated, Hannah turned to her subject and smiled. "Thank you for giving us some of your time."

He took a sip of tea and gazed at Hannah over the cup's rim. "What do you want to know?" His voice was shaking.

Before Hannah could answer, her mother interrupted, saying soothingly, "You're in New York now, Yankel. There's no reason to be frightened."

"My family is not in New York, and I do not know where they are or what has happened to them," he whispered. "I will be in no condition to work until I find them. That is why I do this interview, so someone who knows will read it and contact me."

Hannah, her sympathies roused, turned to her mother. "Mama, there must be something you or Dad can do for Yankel."

Mama became all business. Before the hour was over, she had all the information she needed. Locating and reuniting immigrants' separated families was part of her job, but she didn't always have good news for her clients.

"Dr. Lewitsky, I must be honest with you. While the odds are good that with time we can determine the whereabouts of your wife and children, they may not all be alive. Or they may be in prison." She stood up and brushed the crumbs from her skirt. "I will report back with our progress in no more than six weeks."

"*A dank, a sheynem dank,*" the weeping doctor gushed.

After her mother left, Hannah poured Yankel and herself more tea. "Tell me about your childhood, how you became a doctor and then went into research. Oh yes, and how you met your wife." Now that he was talking, that would be plenty for the first of a two-part article. Filled with satisfaction at having succeeded where her male colleagues failed, she took up her pencil.

In between cups of tea, Yankel provided the information Hannah summarized in her notebook. *Y grew up in a shtetl near Kiev. Excellent student, so allowed to continue studies at advanced school in Moscow. Fascinated by science, why people got sick, so studied medicine. Many Jews there, but all secular. Didn't like dealing with patients, and research was more prestigious. Parents arranged marriage with daughter of prosperous local miller, they had 3 children. Family had life of Soviet-style privilege, him working with little hindrance in his medical specialty of immunology. Sensed increasing anti-Semitism for several years.*

When he hesitated, Hannah went to the meat of her inquiry. "How were you caught up in the Doctors' Plot?"

"Early 1953 Tass reported terrorist doctors plotting to murder Soviet leaders by sabotaging medical treatment." He shuddered at the memory. "All around me doctors, most Jews, arrested. Another doctor in my building taken away, along with wife; their children left to fend for themselves. I was doing research, not seeing patients, thanks God, but still terrified I would be next." He gazed out the window. "Then Stalin died, irony because all best medical specialists in prison. Soon my colleagues released, but I know Jews never be safe in Russia."

"So you decided to emigrate to America?"

"Not only because of being Jewish. Russian government spending enormous sums to make bigger bombs and spaceships, with pittance for medical research." His voice hardened angrily. "I could have created polio vaccine before Salk if they gave me enough money. Instead, my daughter died and my son crippled."

"I'm so sorry," Hannah murmured.

"It is in America that best research is happening, where new treatments and cures are developed." His voice rose in vehemence. "In Russia, my intelligence would be wasted."

Hannah wrote that down and closed her notebook. It would make an excellent final sentence for part one of this touching story. Now if only Mama could find his family, and even better if his wife and children were alive and not in a Russian gulag. Then Yankel's story would have a completely happy ending.

FOUR

A WEEK LATER, during another excellent chicken dinner at Nathan's, Hannah was giving an enthusiastic description of life in Israel where Shabbat, not Shabbos, was the day of rest instead of Sunday and everyone from prime minister to garbage collector was Jewish.

"Things got really exciting once I started teaching the Yemeni English. Some of the men were learned Talmud scholars," she gushed.

Perhaps she was too enthusiastic because Nathan said, "I'm surprised you didn't stay."

She stopped in midsentence and considered what to say, how much to tell him about a memory that still pained her, one she hadn't even shared with Naomi.

Nathan interrupted her musing. "You don't need to tell me if it's a personal matter, Annie. I won't be offended."

But Hannah felt a need to tell someone. After all, she and Nathan had shared some personal matters. "I almost did stay after my second summer, after a Yemeni man and I fell in love."

Nathan stiffened. He wasn't expecting quite such a personal matter.

When he remained silent, she continued. "Zechariah was a Talmud scholar who knew little else, but he was so eager to learn about the world. He knew the Mishnah by heart, so I taught him English using that as our text. He wanted me to stay and marry him, and part of me wanted to, but I couldn't give up my writing." She looked up at Nathan, her eyes begging him to understand. "I was starting Columbia's graduate journalism program, one of the rare women they accepted, and the *Freiheit* had just published my first Israel interview."

"But you didn't marry him." He tried to appear nonchalant but broke out in a sweat.

She shook her head. "I told him I needed to think about it and went home to Brooklyn. When I returned the following summer, Zechariah was married to his sixteen-year-old cousin." She looked down at her plate so he wouldn't see her blinking back tears.

Nathan was astonished that the Yemeni man could let someone as lovely and intelligent as Hannah go. His anger grew at how much pain the man's rejection had caused her. He should say something, but he couldn't share any of that. Not when he appreciated their studies together so much that he was glad she hadn't stayed in Israel. So he asked if she'd studied any Talmud with the man.

"I tried to," she replied. "But it made him so uncomfortable, I gave up."

"That doesn't surprise me. He would have been taught that women are forbidden to study Talmud."

Hannah scowled. *Along with every other Jewish man.* Regretting that she'd said anything about Zechariah, she threw down the gauntlet. "I believe you are just the one to enlighten me why this is so."

Nathan slowly drained his coffee cup. They had pretty much finished with Pesachim, and he had planned to discuss what they should study next. So if she wanted to know why women were forbidden to study Talmud, then they'd tackle that subject.

"Most prohibitions against teaching women Talmud are set forth in medieval codes," he began. "But they originate from the same two sources, Sifrei Devarim and Mishnah Sotah."

Hannah leaned in toward him. "Since both are in Hebrew, I should have no trouble understanding them."

Nathan further closed the distance between them. "Sifrei Devarim says that 'Teach them to your *beneichem*' means 'to your sons, not to your daughters' because it states in Tractate Kiddushin that a father is obligated to teach his son Torah but not his daughter."

"*Beneichem* means 'children,' not just 'sons,'" she protested and quoted several instances in the Torah that proved it.

"Usually it does," he cautiously agreed. "But the Sages state that in this specific case it means only 'sons.'"

Hannah persisted. "Even if I were to accept that, which I don't, why can't a woman have someone else teach her?"

"The Sages disapprove of that as well." He knew she'd loathe what came next, but his integrity wouldn't allow him to leave it out. "Several say women lack the intellect to study Torah, that their minds are not settled or they're light-headed."

Lack intellect? Light-headed? Now she was angry. *I'm smarter than most Jewish men, yet they were commanded to study Torah, not me.* "Just because a father is not commanded to teach his daughter Torah shouldn't mean he cannot teach her Torah."

"Now we come to the Mishnah." Aware this next text would upset her more, Nathan tried to remain calm. "In Sotah, Ben Azzai says a father must teach his daughter Torah, and Rabbi Eliezer argues that a man who teaches his daughter Torah teaches her *tiflut*" (lewdness).

Hannah glared at him. "I know that Mishnah. It has to do with the adulterous wife who drinks the bitter waters. Normally divine punishment comes immediately, but if she has merit her punishment is delayed. That's why Ben Azzai advises a father to teach her Torah, so she'll acquire merit and people will know that if she isn't punished immediately it's on account of her Torah studies, not because the bitter waters don't work."

Before she could continue, Nathan finished what he knew would be her argument, for it was his as well. "So if a woman's Torah study gives her sufficient merit that the bitter waters don't affect her even if she has committed adultery, then teaching her Torah *would* be teaching her tiflut."

"In other words, teaching a girl Torah gives her permission to have an affair, so don't teach her anything," Hannah scoffed.

"Rabbi Eliezer also says it is better that words of Torah be burned than be transmitted to a woman." Nathan's breath quickened in response to her blazing eyes, but he had to finish. "And though halacha is never decided in accordance with Rabbi Eliezer in other cases, his prohibitive opinion here becomes Jewish Law."

"What?" Furious, she stood up and slammed her hand down on the table so hard the dishes rattled and Nathan drew back in alarm. "And because Jewish Law permits multiple wives and owning slaves, we must permit polygamy or slavery today?" His wide-eyed look of apprehension brought Hannah to her senses, and she sank back in her chair. "I am sorry. I shouldn't lose control like that. I got carried away."

Nathan gazed at her in awe; she was breathless and her cheeks were flushed. He hadn't met such a passionate Talmud refutation in years.

She saw the admiration in his eyes. *Please don't let him say, "You're beautiful when you're angry."*

He knew better than to praise her beauty at that moment. "Don't be sorry about being vehement in supporting your position," he said. "I'm proud of you, and I agree with you."

She looked at him in astonishment. "You approve of how I argued?"

"Great Talmud battles use words instead of swords, but they can still cut deeply."

Thus encouraged, she didn't give up. "When we were in grade school, girls learned Torah with Rashi's commentary the same as the boys. So it can't be forbidden to teach it to them."

"Yet Talmud classes were for boys only," he reminded her.

As Hannah calmed, her eyebrows rose as the import of what he'd said earlier sank in. "If Rabbi Eliezer's prohibition is halacha, then you're violating Jewish Law by teaching me." Her voice crescendoed with dismay. "How can you do that?"

He was warmed by her concern. "Don't worry. Some authorities say a woman may study those parts of Talmud that deal with the laws she must observe—kashrus and *niddah*, of course, plus Shabbos and other holidays."

She sighed with relief. "We've only been studying Pesachim."

"But other authorities, including some at Spektor, hold with Rabbi Eliezer, so we must continue to be discreet."

"Well, it's only a few more weeks." She tried to hide her regret and sadness.

Nathan felt as if she'd punched him in the stomach. He almost said, *You're going to stop studying with me?* But he caught himself and changed it to "You're going to stop studying Talmud?"

"I want to study as long as possible," she insisted. "But I go away for the summer, and I can't impose on you to keep teaching me next year."

He struggled to control his panic. "You've proven you're not light-headed. Now you're on the cusp of actually learning and understanding Talmud, not merely dabbling in it. But that doesn't mean we can't take a break in the summer, providing we continue in the fall."

"I do want to become truly learned in Talmud, and I will study with you as long as you're willing to teach me." She felt like she could burst with happiness. "You know, we needn't stop after Shavuos. I don't leave for summer with Aunt Elizabeth until July. We could meet at my house during the day; my parents will be at work and my sister and brother in camp."

That night Hannah relived their Talmud battle and concluded that the Sages' arguments against women studying Talmud were merely an excuse. It was a matter of power. If women didn't know how halacha was formulated and established, then they couldn't challenge it or change it. Yet she was learning Talmud. Not enough to gain access to those corridors of power long inaccessible to women, but with Nathan's help, she could look in through a window.

She'd never expected to keep studying with him, but she couldn't resist his offer to resume in the fall. Who would have imagined, back when her teacher told her girls can't study Talmud, that she would be studying it with one of New York's most learned scholars? And that she'd find her studies so exciting?

And that he would be so nice—and such a gentleman?

She kvelled at her good fortune. Her interview with Dr. Lewitsky had been a hit, and Mama had traced his wife and children as far as Odessa. All she'd told her parents so far was that she was taking a class on Tuesday and Thursday evenings, which was true. Now she'd be attending it in the fall as well.

Nathan was also having trouble getting to sleep. Until today, he hadn't considered his learning with Hannah to be more than temporary. Yet he'd been shocked, and dismayed, at her announcement of a summer break. He hadn't realized how much he would miss their semiweekly sessions.

Nathan knew he hadn't been forthright about the consequences should their studies be discovered. Though it was true that only a few rabbis at Spektor would uphold Rabbi Eliezer's ban on teaching women Torah, those were the men who wielded the power, most of whom already considered him a heretic for teaching text criticism. Though he had only taught Hannah from Tractate Pesachim, he wasn't merely instructing her on how to observe the holiday. They were delving into the dialectics of how the halacha was decided, which even lenient rabbis forbade teaching women.

He was in exactly the situation the Talmudic sage Rav Huna had warned about: "Once a man transgresses and then transgresses again, the deed will seem permissible to him." Rashi elaborated: "Once he repeats his sin and does not repent, he no longer recognizes he is sinning." But after consideration, Nathan decided he wasn't in that situation. He didn't consider it sinful to teach Hannah Talmud. So there was nothing to repent.

At least he didn't have to worry about his father. Abba didn't raise an eyebrow when Nathan said that after Shavuos he'd be doing some tutoring twice a week until it was time to leave for their Brighton Beach cottage in July.

When Nathan turned from Eastern Parkway onto Hannah's block for their first summer study session, it was as if he'd stepped out of a black-and-white movie into Technicolor. In Williamsburg, everything looked grayscale: the asphalt roads and concrete sidewalks, the faded brownstones, the Hasids' clothing. Even the cats were monochrome. But President Street was a riot of color with its bright green trees and lawns, hydrangeas blooming pink and purple, window boxes with vibrant yellow and orange flowers, a woman in a red dress watering her front garden.

He felt drab in his gray slacks and pinstripe shirt, a feeling that intensified when Hannah opened the front door and greeted him in a sky-blue shirtwaist that brought out the color of her eyes. Of course she wasn't wearing gloves, not in her own home. Her hair was pulled back in a ponytail. This was the first time since they were children that Nathan had seen her without a hat. Many blond children saw their hair darken with age, but Hannah's was still the beautiful golden yellow he remembered. He followed her through a light-filled living room to the adjoining dining room, where her notebook and volumes of Talmud were spread on the table.

Hannah must have noticed him gazing around. "Let me show you the nearest bathrooms before we start," she said. "One's upstairs between the two bedrooms, and the other is on the ground floor next to the laundry."

Reluctant to intrude into the Eisins' private space, Nathan said, "Downstairs will be fine."

To get to the stairway, Hannah led him through a large modern kitchen—at least twice the size of the one in his apartment—from which a wonderful aroma emanated.

Nathan's breakfast had been a bowl of cereal, and his mouth watered in response. "What are you cooking? It smells delicious."

"That's the *matzah brei* we had for breakfast. I'm sorry, but there's none left," she said. "I can offer you some coffee."

"I'm surprised you still have matzah around."

"My family loves matzah brei so much my mother buys enough to last us for months."

After they carried their coffee to the dining table, Nathan opened Tractate Rosh Hashana and turned to Hannah. "You've had two weeks to study the Mishnah's four chapters, but as short as they are, there's no way we can learn all their Gemara in ten sessions," he said. "So I'd like us to concentrate on the parts that are both important and not overly complicated. Any questions?"

She had one prepared already. "Since today's Jewish calendar is calculated so we don't need to witness the new moon to establish a new month, aren't the first and second chapters irrelevant?" When he nodded, Hannah continued. "But the end of chapter three, where they discuss how a man's intent determines if he has fulfilled the mitzvah of shofar, that sounds important."

"It is, and there is also a part of chapter four I want us to study together," he said. "But first I'd like you to read this." He handed her a page of stationery with his Spektor letterhead.

"What is it?" She teased him, happy to be studying together again. "A letter of recommendation?"

"I would gladly write you one, but I can't imagine who we'd want to receive it." He chuckled and continued. "This small piece of text comes from chapter one. It's my favorite to demonstrate how much we need Rashi. I've translated it into English, without the punctuation, so you can see how impossible it is to understand without his commentary."

Intrigued, and impressed with his fine penmanship, she read what he'd written. *They made Elul full does Babylonia recognize the favor we did them what favor Ulla said for vegetables and Rav Acha bar Chanina said for the dead what is between them between them Yom Kippur after Shabbos.* She had no idea what it meant.

Nathan smiled as her eyes squinted in confusion. "Turn it over and you'll see that, even with the punctuation, it's not much more understandable."

The second side read: *They made Elul full. Does Babylonia recognize the favor we did them? What favor? Ulla said for vegetables and Rav Acha bar Chanina said for the dead. What is between them? Between them Yom Kippur after Shabbos.*

"You're right. I still don't know what this means."

He opened the tractate to page 20a. "Then let's see what Rashi says."

He sounded like he was about to share a great secret, so Hannah hurriedly looked to the page's inner corner, where the great medieval scholar's comments were listed. "Aha, Rashi says *they* are the Sanhedrin in Jerusalem," she announced. "So when the Sanhedrin declared the month of Elul would be full, it meant Elul would have thirty days rather than twenty-nine."

Hannah had learned that, unlike the secular solar calendar where the months' lengths varied inconsistently, months in the Jewish lunar calendar alternated between twenty-nine and thirty days long. Which the Sages called deficient and full months.

"Very good. So as soon as the Babylonian Jews heard Elul would have thirty days, they knew the next day would be Rosh Hashana, the first of Tishri," he explained.

"I can see how helpful it would be to have a month to prepare." She felt pleased and proud that she'd understood Rashi. "Yet when the Gemara asks if the Babylonians recognize what a favor this is, they evidently don't know because they ask 'What favor?'"

When Nathan agreed, she read on. "To which Ulla replies it was for the vegetables, but Rav Acha says it was for the dead." She stopped and said, "I hope Rashi explains this."

"Indeed he does, but let's finish the text."

"'What is between them' asks what is the disagreement between Ulla and Rav Acha, but I don't understand how 'Yom Kippur after Shabbos' answers the question."

"What Rashi says about that"—Nathan's voice rose in excitement—"is the key to the importance of this discussion."

Hannah eagerly responded to Nathan's enthusiasm. "He says that by making Elul thirty days instead of twenty-nine, they pushed Yom Kippur ahead one day. Thus, instead of falling on the day after Shabbos, Sunday, it would fall on Monday."

"And Rashi explains Ulla's concern about the vegetables as . . ." He smiled and waited for her to continue.

His fervor was infectious, and she quickly read on. "Rashi says that if Yom Kippur were on Sunday, then vegetables would have to be picked on Friday to break the fast two nights later, by which time they'd be wilted." She nodded. "Having fresh vegetables would certainly be a favor."

"And what about the dead?" His eyes twinkled.

She looked at Rashi's comment and grimaced. "Even worse, if Yom Kippur is on Sunday, then anyone who dies on Friday cannot be buried for three days. Yuck."

He looked at her in triumph. "Which is why our modern Jewish calendar is arranged so that Yom Kippur, and Rosh Hashana, never fall on Friday or Sunday."

Astonished, Hannah pondered this new information. "I have noticed that Rosh Hashana and Yom Kippur come on Saturday more often than the odds of 1:7 should require, but I never wondered why," she admitted.

"Now you see how, even if you were fluent in Aramaic, the Talmud would still be a closed book without Rashi's commentary."

"Thanks so much for sharing it with me," Hannah said as she slipped Nathan's letter into her notebook. Then, after he left, she placed it carefully inside the box where she kept special memorabilia.

The two weeks passed quickly and too soon their studies drew to a close. On their last session, Hannah surprised a delighted Nathan with a large platter of matzah brei.

"This is great," he said. "I'd thank your mother except nobody's supposed to know I'm here."

Hannah chuckled. "You can thank me. I made it. I've helped her for years, so I figured it was finally time to do it myself."

"I tried to make matzah brei a few times, but it never came out anywhere as good as this."

"It was Mama's bubbe's special recipe. "I'm sorry I can't explain it or write it down. I'd have to show you."

"Well, I'm not sorry it took so long to learn these *sugyiot*," Nathan said. "But I still want us to get to the section in chapter four that deals with women blowing the shofar. What the Tosafos, particularly what Rashi's grandson Rabbenu Tam says, is four times longer than the Gemara."

"What page is it on?" she asked, keen to start on it. "My Hebrew should be good enough to understand it."

"Maybe not. There's Aramaic mixed in too," Nathan said. "But if you want to spend the summer on it, the page is 33a."

There was a lump in Hannah's throat as she realized they were saying goodbye, for months, but also possibly forever. What if his schedule changed and he couldn't teach her anymore? What if he didn't want to teach her anymore?

Suddenly she knew what would ensure she'd see him again. "If you want to spend the summer reading my Israel interviews and articles, I'll let you borrow my collection," she offered. They'd have to meet again, if only for him to return it to her.

Nathan's smile lit his face as he nodded in agreement. Hannah felt herself blushing in response and quickly pivoted to go upstairs. When she returned, she handed him the three-ring binder. Then they shook hands and bade each other goodbye for the summer. As Hannah closed the door behind him, she was acutely aware that this was the first time in years she had touched a man who was not a member of her family.

That Saturday night, less than twenty minutes after Nathan and his father said Havdalah, a taxi dropped him at the dance hall. Music poured from the door as he elbowed his way past the smokers crowding the entrance. Several recognized him and called out their welcomes, but he was looking for Barbara. He'd already procrastinated too long. If he didn't propose tonight, he'd have to wait until the fall, when her family was back from the Catskills.

No sooner had he reached the dance floor than Barbara's friend Shirley waved him over.

"Good to see you again, Nate."

"Nice to see you too." He looked around purposefully. "Is Barbara here yet?"

"She's powdering her nose, if you know what I mean."

"Already? Didn't you two just arrive?"

She chuckled. "This band is too good to miss. We've been here for hours."

"That's a long walk, or did you take the subway?" Nathan tried to sound casual. Taking a cab before sundown on Saturday would be violating Jewish Law, and some authorities would object to the subway even though it traveled on its own schedule and stopped for everyone.

"Don't be silly. A taxi brought us."

He said nothing as he led her through a couple of dance moves, but his silence may have given away his disapproval because she suddenly exclaimed, "Oh no, Barb made me promise not to tell you about that."

Before he could respond, she implored him, "You won't let her know, will you? Please."

The last thing he wanted to do was confront Barbara about desecrating Shabbos or how she intended to deceive him. "Don't worry. I won't say a word."

"Thanks. I knew you were a nice guy."

Desperate to get away from Shirley, Nathan was grateful when a slim girl approached him as the music slowed. "Hi, Susie, isn't this past your curfew?" he teased the teenager.

Susie Abrams, Joey Goren's favorite dance partner, giggled. "Even my parents know what a great band this is, so they let me come with my brother." She waved at a young man a short distance away, then asked, "When's Joey coming back from college?"

"He's on vacation with his parents, but I expect them home by the Fourth of July."

"I can't wait to go dancing with him again."

He tested her skill with some expert moves and was impressed as she easily followed him. "I'll ask him to call you."

"Do you know any aerials?" she asked.

Figuring she couldn't weigh more than ninety pounds, he nodded. "Shall we start with a couple of dips?" *Something easy.*

When those went well, he asked her which lifts she knew and successfully led her in the easier ones, being careful to warn her in advance which move he'd attempt next. It wasn't long before other dancers formed a circle around them to watch.

"Want to wow them with a throw?" he asked now that there was room for them to show off.

"Absolutely." She named a few she knew.

Nathan chose the least risky of them, and when that was successful, he alternated various aerials. To his relief, for he considered it a miracle that he hadn't dropped Susie or injured his back, the song ended.

At that moment, Barbara broke through the circle and put her arm around him proprietarily. "How come you've never done any of those moves with me, Nate?"

Susie returned to her brother while Nathan, fuming at Barbara's attempted subterfuge, was of a mind to answer *because you weigh too much*. But he replied instead, "You've never asked me to."

Then, because this would be the last time he'd see Barbara until after Labor Day, he smiled and twirled her into his arms for the next dance. Then, after the last set of the night, he accompanied her home rather than taking a separate taxi.

But once the cab had let her off and he was alone, he heaved a sigh of relief that he hadn't bought an engagement ring earlier. He wouldn't mind dancing with Barbara on occasion, but he wanted to marry a nice Jewish girl, not one who violated halacha with impunity as long as she thought he wouldn't know. Out of the blue, a thought came to him. Too bad Hannah was a career woman who wasn't interested in marriage. After all, why else would she have turned down a man she loved when he proposed to her?

Hannah and Aunt Elizabeth celebrated the Fourth of July in Maine, then took turns driving the rest of the four hundred miles to Elizabeth's farmhouse on Prince Edward Island. Hannah was disappointed that the Covey family home was closed over the long holiday weekend—the volunteer docents were home with their own families—but her aunt promised they'd visit the historic property on their return.

As much as Hannah looked forward to her first glimpse of the white clapboard house her great-grandfather had built at Durrell Point, she still felt overwhelmed by the area's strangeness, as if she'd entered a fairy tale. Here she was surrounded by flat green fields that met an endless blue sky instead of tall gray buildings that blocked the sun except at midday. Instead of the suffocating city air that stank of hot asphalt, here she breathed in cool clean ocean breezes. Here she could concentrate on her writing, the stories she wanted to tell, not those she was paid to tell.

But the most powerful contrast was the sound, or rather the lack of sound. Instead of Brooklyn's constant din, here there was a blissful silence broken only by occasional bird cries and the crashing of distant waves. Hannah was thankful she vacationed at Sea Gate following a month here, rather than vice versa. Sea Gate, with its honking horns, airplanes overhead, and neighbors' conversations coming through everyone's open windows, provided a transition between countryside quiet and Brooklyn's cacophony.

The blinding sunrise coming through her bedroom window the first morning shocked Hannah awake and left her muttering at her folly for forgetting, again, that with the nearest neighbor miles away, there was still a need for window shades. Keeping one eye closed, she stumbled to the bathroom, grabbed a large towel, and hung it up on the nails she'd hammered in the window frame two years ago for the same purpose. Then she fell into bed, turning her back to the east window, and sank into blissful sleep.

When she woke later to the smell of coffee, the sun was too high to shine directly into her room. This time, when she passed the sepia photo hanging in the stairwell, she stopped to examine it closely. It showed a mother and daughter, but even allowing for the passage of time, the girl was definitely not Aunt Elizabeth.

"Ah, here's my sleeping beauty." Elizabeth greeted her with a smile. "It will just be a minute while I reheat your oatmeal."

Hannah poured herself a cup of coffee, wistfully recalling how she and Aunt Elizabeth had shopped for dairy dishes the year they returned from Israel.

"Then you'll be able to keep kosher when you visit me in the summer, Annie," Elizabeth had said. "With all the fresh fish and eggs available, we won't need to eat meat."

Of course the dinnerware saleslady assumed this was a bridal gift for Hannah, and they hadn't disillusioned her. The Titania blue floral service for eight—Hannah had seen enough kosher dishes to know that those for dairy often incorporated a blue design—was shipped to Elizabeth Covey.

It was both a tribute to their unique relationship, the only Coveys left, and a poignant reminder that Hannah was still no closer to being a bride than she'd been back then. She had mixed feelings about getting married. Naturally, she'd looked forward to falling in love with a nice Jewish man and making a home with him, but not if it meant giving up her writing career. Making her goal more difficult, her beauty seemed more an impediment than a benefit. Most people assumed good-looking women had their choice of potential husbands, without realizing that many men, often the nicest men, were too intimidated to approach them. But the main obstacle was the actual path from meeting to marrying, the time when men wanted the milk without buying the cow.

"While you were sleeping in"—Elizabeth interrupted her reverie to put a small dish of blueberries on the table—"I made a quick reconnaissance of the forest and found these."

Hannah eagerly stirred them into her oatmeal. "I hope there's more where they came from."

"Don't worry. We should be able to pick enough to keep us in blueberries all month. But we'll need to drive if we want enough to make jam."

"I'd rather relax and start writing today. Maybe we can make jam next week."

"Then you won't mind if I go into town and buy groceries before the best fish is gone."

"Before you go and I forget again, who are the people in that old photo on the stairs? I assume they must be family, but they don't look like you or my father."

"The older woman is your great-grandmother Mary Taylor, and the girl is her daughter, Margaret, your grandmother, who was born and grew up in this house." Elizabeth smiled. "Your father and I take after the Covey side of the family."

Hannah recalled reading in her father's obituary that he had been the second son of George and Margaret Covey. The resemblance between him and her aunt had only grown stronger with time. Elizabeth had bobbed her hair during the war and kept that style even after returning to America. Now, with Elizabeth sporting slacks and short hair, Hannah swallowed hard when her aunt turned to the side. It was almost as if Michael Covey were there in the kitchen, not his sister.

"Aunt Elizabeth, Papa told me that your Grandfather John left this house and the land around it to you and him after your older brother died."

"That is true." She must have intuited what Hannah would ask next because she continued. "But now it all belongs to me. After you were born, during those hard Depression years, Michael asked me to buy out his share. I couldn't do it all at once, but we agreed for me to pay him over ten years, which enabled your family to live on his pitiful reporter's salary."

After washing the breakfast dishes, Hannah walked down the grassy hill to the beach. There was something about walking in this serene setting that always put her in a creative mood. As she strolled along the shoreline, ideas popped easily into her head—stories about the struggles and triumphs of families, wives and husbands, parents and children, sisters and brothers, couples searching for love, immigrants, and those left behind. Set in big cities, small towns, tiny *shtetlach*, during war and peacetime. The endless combinations would overwhelm some writers, but Hannah found them exhilarating, making each morning a new adventure. Later in the day, she would settle into her favorite chair on the porch, notebook on her lap, and write. Assuming things went as well as previous summers, she would have plenty of first drafts to edit when she returned home.

Those based on her Israel experiences would go to the *Freiheit*. As for the others, she had only vague ideas of how, and if, they might eventually be published. For now they would join boxes of what she called her "special writings" waiting patiently in her bedroom closet.

FIVE

NATHAN STOOD UP and waved as Lenny Weiss made his way down the steps to their seats above the right-field foul line. He hadn't seen his old friend in several months, since the bris of Lenny's second son, but they should have plenty of time to catch up during the doubleheader.

"How's it going?" Nathan shook Lenny's hand. "How's the family?"

"Great, keinehora. The baby's growing like a weed, and the older boy is finally out of diapers." Lenny grinned widely as he sat down. "To tell the truth, I'm happy with two sons, but Pauline wants to try again for a girl, and business is doing so well, I guess we can afford three kids."

"Glad to hear it."

"Yeah, with all the GIs using their benefits to buy houses out in the suburbs, furniture is selling like hotcakes," Lenny said. "Pop and I are opening another store down the block, just for modern stuff."

"The Star-Spangled Banner" interrupted Lenny's near monologue, and when they sat down, Nathan used the brief silence to address his friend. "I still can't thank you enough for getting me into dancing. You were absolutely right about never having trouble finding dates."

"Hey, if you hadn't helped me with math back at Spektor, I would have flunked out. Letting you in on my secret way to meet all the girls you want was the least I could do for you." He groaned as Cincinnati scored first. "But I hear you're too good a dancer, that all the girls want to be your partner." When the inning ended with the Dodgers down 0–1, he turned to Nathan and scowled. "So how come you're still single, Nate? I thought the Talmud was big on being fruitful and multiplying."

Nathan regularly pondered the same question. But he wanted to mollify Lenny. "For your information, I've been exclusively dating someone I met at a dance last fall."

"Good. It's about time," Lenny said.

The rest of the afternoon, Nathan was distracted by perturbing thoughts of Barbara. Why did it upset him so much, and still upset him,

61

that she violated the Sabbath to go dancing but not when his buddies went to baseball games on Saturday? Why hadn't he confronted her about it, and why was he so loath to do so? And why had he misled Lenny about their relationship when the vision of Barbara as his wife and mother of his children gave him no pleasure whatsoever?

The sun had barely risen when Hannah took the blue roadster's wheel and headed toward the ferry that linked Prince Edward Island with the mainland. From there it would be several hours to the Covey Family Historic Home near Bar Harbor.

Aunt Elizabeth was driving when they saw the first signpost, but instead of turning off to her childhood home, Elizabeth drove to a nearby hotel. "We'll likely be at the house all afternoon, so I arranged for us to stay here overnight," she explained. "Plus, I need to change clothes first."

To Hannah's surprise, her aunt donned an elegant cream-colored suit and matching hat, reminding her of an outfit Katharine Hepburn had worn in *The Philadelphia Story*. "You told me to pack a nice dress, but I didn't expect to need anything quite so fancy," Hannah apologized.

"The historical society ladies know I'm coming today, so I want to be prepared. Heaven forbid I disgrace the Covey name by appearing poorly attired. Mother would never forgive me." After Hannah changed clothes, Elizabeth looked her niece up and down, then removed her double-stranded pearl necklace and fastened it around Hannah's neck. "There, Annie, you look perfect."

"But what will you wear?"

"My usual." Elizabeth pulled the simple gold cross on a chain from her purse. "Let's exchange earrings too, so our jewelry matches."

Hannah took off her gold studs and put on Elizabeth's pearls. "These do make my dress seem more sophisticated."

Aunt Elizabeth was right about the luncheon being fancy. At least twenty middle-aged and elderly ladies, each immaculately attired, were milling around the foyer outside the formal dining room when Hannah and her aunt arrived. Immediately two women detached themselves from the group and hurried to greet them.

Introductions were made, following which Hannah took her place next to Aunt Elizabeth at the center of a long dining table set with ornate china, crystal goblets, and real silverware. Elaborate floral arrangements graced the table, and a magnificent chandelier hung overhead. The three-story brownstone the Eisins now occupied was grander than any of the rundown apartments Mama and Papa had been evicted from when Hannah was growing up, but the Covey mansion was another thing altogether.

"Everything is so grand and beautiful," Hannah said to the historical society president on her left. *Is it my imagination, or do the dining table and chairs look just like the Mandels'?*

The woman beamed at Hannah's compliment. "We host weddings every weekend in the summer."

The luncheon was a deliberate affair. First came a vegetable soup, followed by salad and a local fish appetizer. Elizabeth had just whispered, "Don't worry. We'll see the entire house even if we have to stay after closing," when the main course—lobster thermidor—was set before them.

Aunt Elizabeth saved the day by declaring, "I'm so sorry I didn't think to warn you, but my niece is allergic to shellfish."

Hannah watched with relief and awe as the president instructed the waiter to remove the offending dish and replace it with a larger portion of the fish course. Here, as in Israel, her aunt's understated authority was unchallenged. Aunt Elizabeth made no demands and never displayed anger, yet her expectation that her orders would be followed, her needs satisfied, and anything not meeting her standards remedied was always fulfilled. No wonder the army had promoted her.

The rest of the meal went smoothly, and by the time dessert and coffee appeared, Hannah recognized that the ladies' discussions, particularly complaints that the younger generation wasn't interested in preserving the past or upholding tradition, weren't much different from those at Sisterhood or Hadassah luncheons she'd attended. Like there, she listened more than she talked, asked questions, and would thus be judged an excellent conversationalist.

When all the women except the president and an assistant had finally left, Hannah couldn't wait for Aunt Elizabeth to show her the rest of the house.

The president, however, led Hannah into the wood-paneled library. "In 1876, our country's centennial, it was common for historical societies to commission a county history," she explained as she handed Hannah a thick, well-worn volume. "Prominent families who donated money for the endeavor were guaranteed their own stories included, as you can see."

Hannah's eyes widened as she read the Coveys' history. According to whoever provided this information, the immigrant ancestor had come to New England from France in the mid-1700s, and a son named George had fought in the Revolutionary War. The history was short on details for the next fifty years, until the decade of the Civil War. Now there was a wealth of information on the Covey men who had fought for the Union: their names, ranks, units, battles they fought, and dates of death. Those few who returned went into the lumber business and prospered.

Hannah was spellbound by all this new information. When she finally looked up, the president had another volume waiting for her, this one printed fifty years later.

"Keep in mind that some of the old stuff is more legend than reality," Aunt Elizabeth warned. "And naturally families provided only favorable information, never any scandals."

In the 1926 book, the Maine Coveys were down to one remaining family, that of George and Margaret, née Taylor. There was nothing about what happened to George's brothers or uncles. There were photos of the big white house, of three young Covey children, and praise for everything the elder Coveys did for the community. Hannah scanned the article again to be sure, but while the 1920 death of George Jr. was mentioned, the name of Michael Covey never appeared. Apparently, Papa was already the family's black sheep three years before he married her Jewish mother.

Hannah wished she had time to search this library, now the depository of the historical society's collection, to learn more about her ancestry. But a discreet cough by Aunt Elizabeth reminded her that they had the entire house to see and it was already midafternoon.

"We'll tour the rest of the rooms ourselves." Elizabeth's voice, while polite, had an undercurrent of insistence.

The president and her assistant returned to the dining room and made themselves busy supervising the cleanup. Elizabeth took Hannah by the arm and propelled her toward the foyer. "Let's go to your father's room first."

"I can see why they like to hold weddings here," Hannah said as they climbed the wide curved staircase.

"The family bedrooms are on this floor," Elizabeth said when they reached the landing. "The third floor was for servants."

The walls of the landing were hung with formal portraits of women and men Hannah assumed were family members. Judging by the subjects' clothing and sober expressions, only a few of the paintings dated from the current century. One couple did seem familiar, and when she stepped closer to examine them, the man's resemblance to her father became clear.

Elizabeth stopped next to Hannah. "Those are your grandparents, Annie."

The double doors to the master bedroom were open, allowing a view of the four-poster bed, bedside tables, and an enormous armoire in the same style as the furniture downstairs. Velvet ropes confined visitors to a path where they could see, but not touch, the furnishings.

Next they entered a boy's bedroom. The walls were festooned with Boston Red Sox memorabilia from their heyday in the 1910s: pennants, faded World Series tickets, photos of the team, and a poster of Babe Ruth. A small table next to the bed held a lamp and an antique radio.

Hannah's skepticism grew as she surveyed the decor. "Was Papa really such a baseball fan, or did the historical society provide the furnishings?" She'd never seen him display any such interest while she was growing up.

"Oh yes. Father often took us down to Boston for games, and there's no question that Michael enjoyed them the most." Elizabeth undid one of the velvet ropes. "You're free to go anywhere and examine anything while we're here, but I thought you'd appreciate your father's taste in reading material."

Having been an English major in college, Hannah was familiar with nearly everything in her father's bookcase. Children's novels such as the Peter Pan and Wizard of Oz series crowded the lower shelves, while the more adolescent fare of *Call of the Wild*, *Riders of the Purple Sage*, *Tarzan of the Apes*, and its ilk were above. At the top were some adult nonfiction that seemed to indicate a budding interest in society's problems: *The Education of Henry Adams*, *The Octopus*, and *The Jungle*.

As they walked through a 1920s bathroom into an adjoining bedroom, Hannah experienced a disquieting sense of déjà vu. Yet there was nothing personal about this room. A double bed matched a plain dresser and an end table in what was apparently a guest room. A framed mirror hung above the dresser and a nondescript landscape on the wall opposite the bed.

With a jolt of amazement, Hannah realized when she'd seen that painting before. She turned to her aunt and declared, "This is where I slept on our trip to the farmhouse, when I was so ill after Papa died." When Elizabeth nodded, she continued. "I dreamed a man and woman were looking down at me, but it wasn't a dream. They were my grandparents; I recognize them from their portrait in the hall."

"I'd hoped seeing you would lead to a reconciliation, but . . ." Elizabeth's words trailed off with a sigh as they walked back into the hallway, but Hannah understood what her aunt hadn't said. Her paternal grandparents could not accept having a Jewish grandchild.

The two of them left no area unexplored, including the servants' quarters upstairs and the basement below. When the sun finally dipped below the horizon, Hannah was buffeted by conflicting emotions: awe at the opulence of her surroundings and resentment at how her grandparents had disowned their son, and her, so completely. But these were overwhelmed by a need to understand how her father could have given up such luxury to live in squalor in New York and devote his life to defending underdog workers from people like his family.

That night, tucked in bed in the dark hotel room, she asked Aunt Elizabeth about it. "Before he left for Spain, Papa told me about being in Centralia during the Armistice Day Massacre and how that made him a Communist. Yet with your family being wealthy captains of the lumber industry, who would expect him to ally himself with Communists?"

"You were just a child, so he couldn't tell you the horrors he experienced," Elizabeth began. "Keep in mind that until Centralia, he was a spoiled, rich man's son who had no idea how his family's business treated its workers."

"I'm not a child now," Hannah insisted. "And after hearing the concentration camp survivors' stories, I doubt anything could be worse than their horrors."

"Michael wrote me about what happened, and in hindsight, it was clear he would make an excellent journalist." When Hannah started to interrupt, Elizabeth quickly added, "Unfortunately, I didn't save his letters."

Hannah couldn't help but sigh with disappointment. "What did he tell you?"

"Let me give you some background first. Back in 1919, Washington State was rough pioneer country with enormous timber resources. Thousands of World War I veterans flocked to mill towns hoping to make a good living. But lumber barons with their company stores exploited the loggers, working them long hours and then overcharging them for food, lodging, and liquor. In Centralia, the men rebelled by forming a union that demanded a forty-hour workweek and better conditions."

Hannah realized the consequences. "Which infuriated the lumber barons."

"Michael wrote that on Memorial Day a mob led by the head of a local lumber company raided the union hall, attacked the men inside, and drove them out of town. Refusing to be cowed, the union opened another hall, but the bosses incited the American Legion against them, calling them Bolsheviks."

"So Papa was already friendly with the union before the massacre," the reporter in Hannah speculated.

Her aunt nodded. "He wrote that the parade on Armistice Day started out peacefully. However, the Legion had changed the route to pass the union hall, where they planned a new raid. They didn't know the union had been warned and had armed themselves." Elizabeth glowered. "Sure enough, when the Legion stormed the hall, shots were fired and raiders soon lay dying on the street. One of them was your father's cousin, nephew of the lumber baron the union accused of instigating the raid. Michael saw him gunned down before his eyes."

"And then?" Hannah asked. Surely this should have made her father anti-union.

"The town went crazy. Vigilantes descended on the union members, beating them and throwing them in jail. Later that night, a mob dragged Wesley Everest, an IWW member who fired some of the fatal shots, out of jail. Then they castrated him and lynched him. Michael wrote that he'd seen men using the body for target practice. It was something he could never forget."

"Nobody could forget something like that," Hannah whispered, the hideous scene now etched in her memory. After Papa's death, she'd found the Dos Passos novel *Nineteen Nineteen* in the library but had been too young to understand much of it. She did understand where it said that a Centralia businessman had cut off Everest's penis and testicles before they hanged him. She couldn't forget it either, and she'd merely read about it.

"Later, Michael attended the proceedings when union members went on trial for murder." Elizabeth's voice was gruff with restrained fury. "Once lumber lawyers appeared as special prosecutors, it became clear to him that the Centralia Legion had been used by the timber barons to eject the union, whose men had fired in self-defense."

"So Papa came back with his eyes opened to the evils of capitalism," Hannah said firmly. "And horrified at his own family's part in it." *Now I understand.*

"Oh yes, and promptly told Father what he thought. At first he tried to convince Father to improve conditions for the loggers, but to no avail. They argued for days, Michael using language he must have learned from the lumberjacks." Elizabeth's tone made her disapproval clear. "I remember one particularly vicious quarrel when Father called Michael a Communist, to which Michael shouted back, 'And proud of it.' The next morning, my brother packed his bags and left. When I tracked him down in New York, he was working for that radical newspaper."

Hannah needed to process this. "Do you think he really was a Communist by then, or did he just say that to rile your father?"

"I don't know. But there's no question he was outraged by how the lumber companies exploited their workers and furious that his own father, who had the power to remedy the situation, refused to do so. He was also deeply ashamed of how his family's wealth and his rich man's son's upbringing were the products of these downtrodden men's labor."

Hannah made a shrewd guess. "It sounds like you shared some of his feelings, Aunt Elizabeth."

"True, but I became a nurse missionary for my penance." She chuckled softly. "Then, after Father died, I convinced Mother to treat the lumberjacks better—to pay them higher wages, care for any injured, and provide better housing while charging less for it. Soon the other companies had to follow suit."

Hannah was in awe of her aunt's goodness, but she had one more question. "Mama told me your parents disowned him, but it sounds like Papa rejected them first."

"The situation still makes me angry, and sad. Undoubtedly the rejection and disowning were mutual. Let's just leave it at that and say good night."

"Good night, Aunt Elizabeth. Thank you for taking me to your old house and explaining everything about Papa."

"Good night, Hannah. You're very welcome." After a short silence Elizabeth began her nighttime prayers.

Hannah closed her eyes and said the bedtime Shema, but she couldn't fall asleep. She kept wondering how much of Papa's decision to marry Mama had resulted from anger at his father, how much from love, and how much from the pregnancy that resulted in Hannah's birth seven months after the wedding. Whatever the reason, that choice ensured that the breach between Papa and his parents would never heal.

Two days later, Hannah kissed her aunt goodbye at Boston's South Station and boarded the train to New York. When she disembarked, she was surprised to see her mother waiting, and even more so when Deborah rushed up and gave her a big hug. Deborah had never been a demonstrative mother. Communism and Michael Covey had been her great passions, and Hannah could never decide which took priority. Without them, Deborah poured her devotion into her work. Most of the time, Hannah didn't mind; she relished her independence.

"We found Dr. Lewitsky's family, in Turkey of all places," Deborah gushed. "Using her maiden name, his wife went to family in Odessa, where they bribed someone to smuggle her and the children to Istanbul."

Unable to contain her excitement, Hannah hugged her mother tighter. "Where are they?"

"Somewhere on the Mediterranean, on their way to a port with a ship going to New York."

"That's incredible. I can't wait to see Yankel again."

Nathan watched Joey Goren wipe the sweat from his brow. "I'd forgotten how miserable the weather is here in the summer," Joey said. "Don't tell my parents, but I'll probably stay in California."

"It's not always this bad," Nathan said. True, New York had seen temperatures in the high nineties each day that first week of August, but that was ten degrees above normal. "Be thankful we're in Brighton Beach and not in the city."

"I'm thankful your father rents this cottage every summer, and I thank you for inviting me to visit."

Nathan appreciated that with two incomes, he and Abba could afford to spend the entire summer at the shore. "So, where are we going dancing tonight? Coney Island or the Baths?"

"Coney Island," Joey replied. "Susie wants to practice more aerials, and they have a bigger dance floor."

"I don't mind teaching you new moves, but can't we take a night off to dance just for fun?" Nathan teasingly complained. He suspected Joey wasn't as enamored of Susie as vice versa.

Joey's reply confirmed it. "I wouldn't mind more than one night off, with some opportunities to dance with new partners."

Each time Nathan saw Joey during a college break, he couldn't get over how much progress the tall, handsome twenty-year-old had made since those dark days in his early teens. Thank Heaven for Benny Stockser, who'd found the way to break through Joey's psychosis and was still treating him. Benny had been the one to suggest that Joey go to college far away from New York, in a town without a large Orthodox population. Nathan had done his part, taking Joey out dancing to make him comfortable with girls just as Lenny had done for Nathan.

"How serious are you about staying in California for grad school?" Nathan asked.

"Very serious. Berkeley and Stanford both have good astronomy and astrophysics departments," he replied. "Even better, nobody out there associates me with my infamous father. In fact, outside of a few people in Jewish studies, no one has even heard of Isaac Goren." He turned to Nathan and wiped his sweating forehead again. "But the best thing is the weather."

Joey was right about that. The second week of August saw the attack of Hurricane Connie, followed by Tropical Storm Diane a week later. Nathan utilized his hours confined indoors to read Hannah's writing collection, growing more impressed each day. Her interviews and accounts of life in Israel were not only informative, but many moved him deeply. All were difficult to put down.

It seemed that the skies had barely cleared when the city was scorched by another heat wave. Eager to escape the now stifling cottage after ten days imprisoned there by storms, Nathan put on swim trunks and a T-shirt and told his father he'd be back for dinner. Then he walked to the water's edge and headed west toward Sea Gate. There were so many families spread out on towels, blankets, and folding chairs that it seemed the hot weather had emptied all of Brooklyn onto the beach. From behind his sunglasses, he took in the scene, taking care to avoid the minefield of children's sand toys.

Nathan had been walking almost two hours when he was struck by the sight of a woman sitting under an umbrella, a dark-haired boy building a sandcastle nearby. The umbrella hid her upper body in such a way that all he could see was a pair of great-looking legs. Nathan had observed hundreds, perhaps thousands of women in bathing suits during his summers at Brighton Beach, but these shapely, seemingly disembodied legs stopped him in his tracks.

He was standing there in admiration when the boy walked over to the woman and pointed at him. To Nathan's horror, she stood up to look while he, utterly mortified, tried to turn away.

But it was too late.

Hannah Eisin, wearing only a one-piece bathing suit and a large sun-hat, was waving and calling his name. He had no choice but to approach, ashamed of ogling her, but also, now that he could see her in totality, appreciating her fine figure.

Hannah, astonished to find Nathan standing in front of her at Sea Gate, hurried toward him. "What a wonderful surprise. I hope the storms haven't spoiled your summer," she said when he was close enough to hear.

"They gave me time indoors to read your stories," he replied. "Which were excellent."

Flustered by his praise and sudden appearance, she changed the subject to Talmud. "Translating that Tosafos on Rosh Hashana 33a has been driving me crazy, but now you show up out of nowhere just in time to help me with it."

He tried to sound casual. "I'd be happy to."

She beckoned him toward the umbrella. "Perfect timing. I have my notes right here." Then, remembering her manners, she continued. "Nathan, this is my little brother, Jake. Jake, I'd like you to meet Nathan Mandel, that Spektor professor I interviewed."

Jake shook Nathan's outstretched hand and returned to his sandcastle.

Between the heat, his long walk, and now, confronted by Hannah in a formfitting pink swimsuit, Nathan needed to cool off. "Do you mind if I take a swim first?"

"You walked all the way from Brighton Beach?" When he nodded, she took a thermos from the beach bag next to her chair. "Here, have some lemonade. I could use a swim myself."

He gulped down the cold drink and hid his disappointment when she removed her hat and revealed not the unbound tresses he'd anticipated but a tidy French twist. When they reached the water, he dove right in. Hannah took her time getting wet but eventually joined him. When they got out, Nathan didn't put his T-shirt back on right away but waited until he was dry.

Then it was Hannah's turn to admire him, albeit discreetly. His skin was nicely tanned, and the amount of hair on his chest was enough to look masculine without being overly hirsute. Regular dancing kept Nathan's body, especially his legs, in shape, but six weeks of demonstrating lifts to Joey and Susie had honed his arms and chest to the point where he was more a Charles Atlas than a ninety-eight-pound weakling. She was careful to avert her gaze from the area covered by his bathing suit.

After he sat down on the towel next to her, she poured them more lemonade. She had just opened her Talmud notes when her sister ran up.

"Mama says lunch is almost ready. How soon do you want to eat?" Rae stopped short and stared at Nathan.

As Hannah introduced them, she realized she had to invite Nathan to lunch, even though that would bring him to her mother's attention.

For his part, Nathan was happy to accept; he was hungry.

"I'd better hurry back and tell her to set another place at the table," Rae said. "Good luck keeping him off her radar."

Once Rae was gone, he asked, "What was that about?"

"My mother is going to put you through the third degree," Hannah warned him.

"Don't worry. I'll be careful not to say anything that might give away our Talmud studies."

"Or that we've had any contact after I interviewed you."

"Speaking of Talmud, shall we see how far we can get in the Tosafos before your sister returns?"

Hannah consulted her notes. "After the Mishnah says we do not restrain children from blowing the shofar, the Gemara asks if women are restrained, even though there's a Baraita in the next line teaching that neither women nor children are restrained."

"Most scholars interpret the text not as a question but as a statement that women *are* restrained," Nathan said. "Yet I can see how, with no punctuation, you might read it as a question." He'd never considered it before, but it was obviously a question since the next sentence was the answer. Yet the Rabbis chose to restrain women from blowing the shofar. Why?

Before he could address that question, Hannah continued. "I won't argue the point since the important thing is that Abaye resolves the conflict by saying it is Rav Yehuda who teaches that women are restrained and Rav Yosi who teaches they're not. This is where the Tosafos gets interesting."

As she leaned over to point out the pertinent text, her swimsuit gaped open slightly. Nathan immediately looked away, but not before getting a bird's-eye view of her splendid cleavage. It was a few moments before he managed to catch his breath and stammer, "How so?"

Hannah was too intent on the point she wanted to make to notice his discomfort. "Rabbenu Tam says that even though other Mishnah disputes between these two sages are decided according to Rav Yehuda, here halacha follows Rav Yosi because he has *svara*, deep reasons," she replied, her breath quickening. "Then Rabbenu Tam brings proofs from other places in the Talmud that Saul's daughter Michal put on tefillin and Jonah's wife went to Jerusalem for the festivals." She hesitated before asking, "But these are both positive mitzvos done at a particular time, right?"

"Yes, and he says women may do them despite being exempt."

"But how can Rabbenu Tam decide that the law is according to Rav Yosi when Abaye implies you could follow either sage and others say Rav Yehuda's words take precedence over Rav Yosi's?"

Nathan could hear that she was applauding Rabbenu Tam, not criticizing him. "Rabbenu Tam is Rashi's grandson, and his rulings are still authoritative today," he explained. "By supporting Rav Yosi, he doesn't restrain the women in his community."

"Clearly, because next he says that women, despite being exempt, are even allowed to make the *broche* [blessing] on doing a time-bound positive mitzvah, just as Michal fulfilled the mitzvah and also made a broche." Hannah was both incredulous and excited. This meant women were permitted to do the men's rituals. And though women were not obligated, like men were, they could do them if they chose.

"It doesn't look like you need help translating Tosafos," he said, careful to sound impressed rather than annoyed. He didn't like how scholars had misinterpreted the Gemara by turning a question about women blowing the shofar into a statement forbidding them.

"That's because we've only done a few lines. This next part, about Rav Yosef and blind people, doesn't make sense," she complained. "So I'm probably not translating it right."

Despite Nathan's help, Hannah still wasn't confident that she understood the discussion by the time Rae came back for them. But he assured her he could stay for a few more hours after lunch.

Lunchtime was every bit as trying as Hannah had feared. Instead of just the usual tuna and egg salad sandwiches, there was lox, smoked whitefish, bagels and cream cheese, and coleslaw and carrot salad. There was even a platter of pastries. No sooner had they sat down and blessed the bread than Jake loudly asked why they were getting all this good food even though it wasn't Shabbos. Deborah beamed at Nathan and mumbled something about having the deli deliver something nice because of their guest.

Then, to Hannah's chagrin, her mother proceeded to grill Nathan about his work, his studies, and what he did in his spare time. Jake earned Hannah's undying gratitude when, upon learning Nathan was a Dodgers fan who had season tickets just like their family, he monopolized Nathan the rest of the meal, discussing baseball. Unable to compete with Jake's enthusiastic sports talk, Deborah turned her attention to Hannah. But she got nothing from her daughter to explain Nathan's sudden appearance except that he'd walked that way by chance, and Hannah thought it would have been rude to leave for lunch without asking him to join them.

It seemed forever until the two were walking back to the beach, and by then Hannah knew her mind was too vexed to study Talmud properly.

"Nathan, if you don't mind, let's just concentrate on fixing my translation," she said. "Once I have the words right, I can work on figuring out what they mean."

Normally study partners translated the text and hammered out its meaning a line or two at a time before going on to the next. But what Nathan and Hannah did could hardly be called normal Talmud study, so he replied, "Good idea. That way you won't go off on a tangent because the translation is wrong."

Hannah was relieved that limiting themselves to this task got them through the entire page before the day ended. Packing up her notebook, she said to Nathan, "If you want to take the bus, I can show you where it stops."

"I'd appreciate that," he replied. "It's a long walk back to Brighton Beach."

After walking in silence awhile, Hannah mustered her courage. "I apologize for Mama's exuberance; she's never had me bring home an eligible bachelor before." She grinned to mask her embarrassment. "In fact, I haven't dated anyone since college."

"What about Zechariah?"

"That wasn't dating, and besides, Mama doesn't know."

"If you think it would stop her from *nudzhing* you, you can tell her I have a girlfriend."

"Do you?" She was suddenly afraid he'd answer yes.

"Actually, I'm still seeing a girl I met dancing last fall." He started explaining how Lenny had mentored him at local dance halls. Then the bus drove up.

Hannah's heart sank. "I don't think we should meet at the beach again, or my family will wonder how well we do know each other," she told him. *Oh no, he does have a girlfriend, one he's been going with for almost a year.*

Only after his bus disappeared around a corner did she begin to cry.

Hannah's misery deepened when she returned and heard the rock and roll music blaring from the bedroom she shared with her sister.

"Rae, will you turn that record player down?" Exasperated, she yelled over the din, "If I have to suffer through 'Ain't That a Shame' one more time . . ." She left the threat unstated.

"But it's Pat Boone," Rae protested.

"You can hang all the posters of him you want in your room back home, but I'm sick and tired of being forced to listen to him whine about his tears falling like rain when I'm trying to translate this *Freiheit* article."

"If you're going to be such a grump, I'll turn it off."

To Hannah's relief, her sister not only did that, but she also stomped out and left her alone upstairs. Dad would be home soon, bringing new edits for her to proofread. Thank goodness she was able to work from Sea Gate in the summer. Each morning she walked to the newsstand to pick up that day's *Freiheit*, while Dad dropped off her finished work when he drove to his office.

Now, if only she could stop thinking about Nathan having a girlfriend and concentrate on her translating.

SIX

"ABBA," NATHAN CALLED OUT from the dining room. "Could you look at this Tosafos from Rosh Hashana and tell me if it means what I think it means?"

They'd just returned home from Brighton Beach, but he couldn't stop thinking about what he'd discovered helping Hannah.

Solomon Mandel went to the den, pulled out his dog-eared copy, and sat at the dining table. He turned to the page his son had open and read to where Nathan had his finger. "What do you think it means?"

"It seems to say that nine hundred years ago, women in Rabbenu Tam's community had aliyah to the Torah," Nathan said slowly. "And they're unsure if those women should make the broche since women are not commanded to learn Torah."

"I may have confirmation from another source." The older man scanned the shelves of two bookcases before exclaiming, "Aha, *Machzor Vitry*, there you are." He held the book aloft in triumph. "Let's see what Rashi's twelfth-century disciples have to say on the subject." Abba found the page and read it aloud. "You should know from Talmud that everyone in a minyan can be one of the seven *aliyos* of Torah—one of the seven who read from Torah on Shabbos—even women. Women are exempt from Torah study, but if called for an aliyah, they must do the blessing."

"I can hardly believe it, but it sounds like they counted women in a minyan too." Nathan's excitement growing, he recited from Tosafos. "If a woman receives an aliyah, she goes up for one of the middle Torah readings, when they do not make blessings. As the Gemara says in Tractate Megillah, 'The first reader makes the opening blessing, and the last to read recites the concluding blessing.'"

Abba turned to him. "I'd say your interpretation is correct. In those days, unlike today, they only said a broche for the beginning and final readings, not those in the middle.

"This is amazing. Nine hundred years ago, in France, women were counted in a minyan and read from the Torah on Shabbos, in public." Nathan didn't understand how Abba could be so blasé about this incredible discovery, but he knew Hannah would be thrilled.

His father nodded. "Apparently they did."

"Look down here." Nathan pointed lower on the page. "Rashi and Tosafos have two different versions of the text."

"Excellent." He bent over to peruse the section. "We must publish a paper on this."

As Nathan hoped, Abba was too elated to question how Nathan had discovered the variant texts. Which was just as well because he couldn't imagine an explanation that didn't involve Hannah.

Yet eager as Nathan was to resume their studies, he couldn't shake the vision of Hannah's bare legs under the beach umbrella or the glimpse of her bosom he'd gotten later. Especially after he went to bed. Night after night she appeared to him, wearing only that pink swimsuit, her breasts and legs begging to be caressed. Once she wasn't even wearing the swimsuit, and Nathan woke up with sticky pajama bottoms, as if he were still an adolescent.

It wasn't lost on him that he'd also dreamed about her that way when they were in school together, when he was going through puberty. Now he could only hope that once they were involved in Talmud study again, fully dressed, his carnal thoughts would be ousted by intellectual ones.

And if not, he would have to be very careful that she never became aware of them.

With her notebook balanced on a box of Russian pastries, Hannah knocked on Dr. Lewitsky's door the day after Labor Day. Over the summer, the *Freiheit* had received myriad letters complimenting her first installment about the doctor's trials and tribulations. Now Moe was eager to get the story's happy ending in print before Rosh Hashana. Hannah expected a change from the depressed and fearful schlimazel who'd been so reluctant to be interviewed, but what she saw when the door opened left her speechless.

The clean-shaven gentleman opposite her was well dressed and recently barbered. "Come in, come in," he welcomed her warmly. "Thank you very much for the sweets, but you see I have a large supply waiting on the table for us, with fresh coffee."

"You're looking well, Yankel." Hannah managed to find her tongue. It was astonishing how he now spoke perfectly understandable English.

He pulled out a chair for her. "Please pardon me, but I would prefer to be called James. Once my family and I are settled in San Diego, I will have the court change our last name to Lewis. Then we will be real Americans."

"You've found a position in California?"

"Yes. The ship bringing my family to New York will dock in a few days, and then we'll take the train across this great country." He kept talking as he poured them each a cup of coffee. "The people at Scripps have already found us a nice furnished apartment near the institute, but they assured me there are many new houses being built nearby."

"You're going to work at Scripps—that's wonderful." Hannah's readers would think it was wonderful too, although probably not that he planned to change his name. *Well, that part doesn't have to go in my article.*

"Excuse my poor manners. Would you like cream or sugar?"

Hannah helped herself to both and took notes as he excitedly described his first phone call with his wife, the details of her narrow escape from the Soviets, her years hiding in Turkey, concluding with how HIAS ultimately helped her and the children come to America.

At one point he was so overcome with his good fortune that he choked up. "The Scripps people say they will arrange for my son to receive the latest therapy for polio victims so he can soon walk without braces."

"I'm so happy for you," she said, and truly she was. When he'd composed himself, she asked, "Would it be all right if my paper sent a photographer to take you to the dock? It would really bring your story to life if our readers could see a picture of you being reunited with your family. We would send you copies."

Yankel—she couldn't see him as James—hesitated, but thankfulness or not wanting to appear ungrateful won the day. "After everything you've done for us, of course."

"Then we'll phone the drugstore for you tomorrow to make the arrangements?" she asked. Like many Brooklyn renters, Yankel didn't have a telephone in his apartment but used one at a nearby store.

When he agreed, Hannah drained her coffee cup and stood to say goodbye. He shook her hand vigorously and insisted she take the unopened box of pastries.

At the *Freiheit* office a few days later, draft article in hand, she met with Moe and the photographer. It had been an emotional reunion at the dock, and they wanted to choose photos that captured just the right combination of tears and joy.

Alone in her room that night, Hannah couldn't get Yankel's and his wife's ecstatic faces out of her mind. She berated herself, again, for allowing herself to fall for Nathan like the cliché student with a crush on her teacher. Of course someone as smart, attractive, and nice as Nathan would have a girlfriend, so it was impossible even if she dared to tell him how she felt.

But he doesn't know, thank Heaven. So she would just have to keep her feelings hidden, to bury them so deep he'd never suspect, because the day he did would not only be the end of her Talmud studies, but he'd probably never want to see her again.

The Saturday night between Rosh Hashana and Yom Kippur, Nathan's taxi picked up Barbara for their movie date. Unfortunately, the evening started downhill as soon as he gave her a kiss hello. She'd used mouthwash, but it didn't completely disguise the acrid taste of tobacco. Nathan had dated other girls who smoked and agreed with whoever said that kissing a smoker was like licking an ashtray. Feeling ill at ease, he agreed to see the new Hitchcock movie *To Catch a Thief.* But this was a mistake because beautiful blond Grace Kelly kept reminding him of Hannah.

He was still daydreaming about her when they arrived at the restaurant and it was too late to object that Barbara had asked for the smoking section. "When did you start smoking?" He tried not to sound too petulant.

"During the summer. All sophisticated girls in the Catskills do it," she insisted.

Nathan could barely taste his dinner with all the haze in the air, and he let his thoughts wander to the scenes of Grace Kelly racing her convertible through the twisty French Riviera roads. Except he imagined Hannah at the wheel and himself in Cary Grant's seat. He was thrust back to reality when Barbara lit a cigarette while the waiter got their dessert.

She must have noticed his being distracted because she frowned and said, "I don't know where your mind has been tonight, Nate, but now I need you to stop staring out the window and listen to me."

Apprehensive, he turned to face her. "I'm listening."

She took several puffs before speaking, which made him annoyed in addition to more worried. "We've been dating almost a year now, right?" When he nodded, she continued. "Where do you think we are on the path to marriage?"

Nathan didn't need to think about it, but he paused anyway. There was no answer that wouldn't upset her. "I don't think we're on that path," he finally admitted.

Barbara blanched and crushed out her cigarette. "Excuse me, but I'm dating to get married, and if you're not, then we shouldn't continue."

He watched helplessly as she put on her coat and headed for the door. He may not have wanted to marry Barbara, especially since she'd taken up smoking, but he liked her and wished he could have ended things better.

Thankfully for both Nathan and Hannah, once they settled back into their studies in the fall, they were able to act as if their meeting at the beach had never happened. He was disappointed that he didn't get to see her take off her gloves anymore; she always removed them in the vestibule before entering the apartment. He missed the small thrill it gave him to watch her remove them. But as he'd anticipated, she was delighted to learn that women in Rashi's community were counted in a minyan and read from the Torah in synagogue. She also had no trouble following his explanation of the variant texts and how he intended to teach about them.

The Thursday after Yom Kippur, however, Hannah noticed that Nathan seemed preoccupied, and as the evening wore on, he grew increasingly agitated. When he lost his place on the page for the third time, she finally had to say something. "If you're so distressed by the Yankees winning the first two World Series games, maybe we should just call it a night."

He was surprised at her perception. He'd been trying to push the horrific scene out of his mind. "I apologize, Annie, but this has nothing to do with baseball." He hesitated, for he wasn't sure what to tell her. Yet now that she knew something was wrong, it would be a relief to share the burden. "A terrible thing happened at Spektor today," he began.

"Go on." Hannah closed her notebook to give him her full attention.

"I went into the student bathroom, which I often use because it's closer to my classroom than the one for faculty, and there was Zelig, one of my Haredi students who's good in math." Nathan stopped to take a deep breath. "He was standing over the sink trying to cut his wrists."

Her eyes opened wide. "Gevalt."

"I ran over and stopped him, and thank Heaven he wasn't bleeding too badly. I didn't even think about it, just grabbed a bunch of paper towels, hustled him off to my office, and I called Benny. I had no idea what I'd do if he wasn't there, but they found him and he told me to keep Zelig with me until he arrived. He wanted to talk to Zelig in private, so I went back downstairs. He shook his head. "Heaven knows what my students thought; I could barely string two sentences together. When my class was done, they were gone."

"No wonder you can't concentrate on Talmud." Her heart was pounding. "Thank goodness you found the poor boy in time. Do you think Benny will call you tonight?"

"I don't know. Just because I found Zelig like that doesn't mean I have the right to know his problems."

A sick feeling began forming in Hannah's stomach as an inkling of Zelig's problem came to her. "What's his last name?"

"Fishkoff. Why do you ask?"

Before Hannah could reply, the phone rang and Nathan raced to answer it. He made no attempt to hide his side of the conversation, which consisted mainly of combinations of "Yes, I understand, good," and ultimately, "I'll talk to you tomorrow."

Heaving a sigh of relief, Nathan sank down onto his chair. "Benny says I saved Zelig's life, and he's arranged for Zelig to become his patient."

Hannah added her sigh to his. "You should absolutely be written into the Book of Life now."

They looked at each other in silence as the enormity of Nathan's actions sank in. Finally, he told her, "It's getting too late to study any more. If you're not busy Saturday night, how about I call you and we can make up what we missed tonight?"

"Oh, I'm not busy, not unless you call babysitting my brother while my folks go out busy." She didn't dare ask what had happened to his girlfriend that left him free on Saturday night. It was an effort to keep any hint of hope out of her voice and off her face.

Their extra Talmud study via telephone went well enough. Hannah's dad had all the texts she needed in his library, Rae was out with friends, and Jake was ensconced in a Hardy Boys mystery. At the end of the session, Nathan announced that he wouldn't be able to study with her Tuesday because, should there be a seventh World Series game, he and his father were going. Even if not, he and his buddies planned to get together for dinner to celebrate, or more likely, commiserate. But he would call her next Saturday night so they could study by phone again.

Hannah, still up when her parents came home from a Broadway show, saw they were in a good mood. When they praised *Damn Yankees*, a plan formed in her mind.

"What perfect timing," Hannah said. "To see it right while the Dodgers are playing them in the World Series."

Samuel smiled. "Especially since Brooklyn evened it up today."

"I've only gone to one Dodger game all season." Hannah tried to sound hopeful rather than like she was complaining. "Would you take me to Game Seven if there is one?"

"That's fine with me," Deborah said quickly. "I'm happy to stay home with Jake and watch it on television."

"He's not going to be happy, but it's only fair that Annie attend at least one World Series game," Samuel said.

"Thanks so much, Dad." Hannah gave him a hug.

"Don't thank me yet, Annie. There might not be a seventh game."

Hannah didn't articulate what she suspected they were all thinking. *And if there is, the Dodgers will probably lose and leave us saying, "Wait till next year," like always.*

But there was a seventh game. Hannah had never been to Yankee Stadium, and she couldn't help but stop in awe as she caught her first view of the interior. The place was enormous, with three tiers of seats that held almost twice as many people as Ebbets Field. Gazing around, she realized how foolish she was to imagine encountering Nathan there.

Warned by Mama that the number of ladies' restrooms was insufficient for all the women who'd need them, Hannah decided to use one before the game started. When she exited, whom did she see talking with Dad outside the men's room but Solomon Mandel.

"What a coincidence," he declared as they greeted each other. "Would it be all right with you if Samuel and I sit together so we can continue our conversation?"

Hannah couldn't believe her good fortune when her dad added, "I hope you won't mind sitting with Nathan Mandel instead of me."

"Of course not," she replied blandly, as if he were suggesting she have tea instead of coffee. Inside, she was turning cartwheels.

Nathan thought his eyes must be deceiving him when he saw his father walking down the steps with Hannah. She was dressed in one of her gray suits, but with a colorful floral-patterned blouse instead of one of her usual open-necked Oxford shirts. Her hair was hidden under a wide-brimmed hat that matched the pink flowers in her blouse.

"How nice to see you again." He reached out to shake her hand. He was determined to act as if they were merely acquaintances, but his pulse was racing.

Hannah didn't particularly notice his clothes. Like nearly every other man in the crowd, including her dad, Nathan wore a suit and tie topped with a fedora. "It's a pleasure to see you again," she said. *It worked. My plan actually worked.*

They were both relieved when Solomon Mandel returned to sit with Samuel. With the two fathers seated a good many rows below, Hannah and Nathan could watch the game in relative privacy.

When they were alone, not counting the sixty thousand people around them, Nathan turned to her in confusion. "I know your family has season tickets, but how did you end up here, next to me?"

She explained about meeting his father outside the restrooms and then continued. "For the World Series, my dad likes the whole family to go. So to give everyone else a better chance, I volunteered for the seventh game." She smiled. "And here I am."

Flustered by her sudden appearance, Nathan turned his attention to the field.

When the second inning ended with ten batters up and ten down, Hannah had to break the silence. "Do you think we'll get to see Koufax pitch? People at the *Freiheit* can't stop talking about him, the Dodger's first Jewish player, and a Brooklyn native too."

Nathan would have liked seeing a local Jewish baseball star, but he was not impressed with Koufax. "I know he's on the roster for this game, but I doubt he'll play. He's very wild, no control at all."

"What do the Dodgers expect from someone with so little experience?" She parroted her dad and brother's opinion. "They almost never let him play."

Before Nathan could answer, a man sitting behind them put in his two cents. Then two others joined in the debate. By the scoreless fourth inning, Hannah was sorry she'd brought up Sandy Koufax.

Until suddenly, it happened.

Campanella doubled, the next Dodger batter grounded out, sending him to third, and then Hodges singled, putting Brooklyn in the lead, 1–0. Nathan and Hannah were on their feet cheering, as were the many other Dodger fans in their section.

The next inning saw six batters up and six batters down. "I know it's better to be ahead by one than losing by one," Hannah said to Nathan, "but I'm more nervous now than before."

"I know what you mean," he said, keeping his eyes on the field. "It's like we're waiting for disaster to strike."

Instead, Hodges batted in another run on a sacrifice fly. For a little while it looked as if the Dodgers were going to break it open, but to their great disappointment, the inning ended with the bases still loaded.

Nathan swallowed his frustration. "At least we're ahead by two now," he consoled an equally disheartened Hannah.

She nodded, not daring to say aloud what she was thinking. *The Yankees still have plenty of time to score three runs.*

She was starting to feel excited that they might actually win it when the Yankees came to bat at the bottom of the eighth. Then, in only a few minutes, her heart was in her throat as two singles put men on first and third with Yogi Berra at the plate.

Crack! She, Nathan, and every Dodger fan in the stadium watched with a sinking feeling of déjà vu as the long fly ball dropped toward the left-field corner. The Yankee fans were on their feet, ready to cheer, as Sandy Amorós raced in for what seemed a futile attempt to make the catch while McDougald, representing the Yankees' tying run at first base, headed toward third. No one doubted that this ball was a sure hit that would ignite a late-inning Yankee comeback.

But without breaking stride, Amorós reached out at the last possible moment, and not only miraculously made the catch, but he fired the ball back to the infield, where it was relayed to first base to tag out an astonished McDougald.

For a very long moment, the stadium was silent. Then, as Yankee fans slowly dropped back into their seats, pandemonium broke out among Dodger supporters. They not only cheered but jumped up and down and hugged complete strangers. The woman next to Hannah did all of these, until Hannah, terrified the two of them were going to tumble into the row below, managed to extricate herself from the woman's embrace. But when she turned around, the next thing she knew, Nathan was hugging her tightly, and she was hugging him back.

Just as she began to appreciate her situation, Nathan abruptly let go and turned to watch the final Yankee batter strike out to end the inning. Hannah couldn't believe what a miraculous day this was turning out to be. Her crazy plan to see him at the World Series had succeeded beyond her wildest dreams, and now the Dodgers were three outs away from winning it.

Hannah's perfume still in his nose, Nathan considered apologizing for his presumptuous behavior. But she didn't appear aggrieved, so he took the coward's way out and decided that least said, soonest mended.

Finally, the last three Yankees were retired in the bottom of the ninth, handing the Dodgers the World Series win they'd waited so long for. Nathan and Hannah cheered heartily along with the other fans and vigorously shook hands, but they reserved their hugs for their fathers.

In a cab on the way home, Nathan's concern over whether he'd been too forward with Hannah kept him so preoccupied that his father had to tap his shoulder to get his attention.

"Nathan, did you have a good time with Hannah?"

"We just won the World Series, Abba. I had a great time."

His father sighed. "Of course you did. I did too."

Once inside their apartment, they went over the game's highlights and again appreciated how their seats above the left-field line gave them a perfect view of the game-saving double play, until eventually they fell into a contented silence.

Later, as Nathan undressed for bed, he noticed that his jacket still carried a whiff of Hannah's fragrance. So, telling himself he should let it air out, he hung it on the chair next to his bed. Which meant he could still smell it. Suddenly it occurred to him that his father changing seats had been in hopes of fixing him up with Hannah, just like when her mother served him that extra-special lunch at Sea Gate.

Thinking back to how it felt to hug her, and what she looked like in a swimsuit, he definitely found the possibility appealing. *Not that it matters what I think. Hannah Covey Eisin is a career woman who hasn't dated anyone since college.*

After three successive Saturday-night phone calls with Nathan, in addition to their regular Tuesday and Thursday study sessions, Hannah was filled with hope as she concluded that he wasn't seeing his girlfriend, nor dating anyone else. Nathan told himself he wasn't ready to get back into dating, especially since going out dancing again would risk encountering Barbara. Discussing Talmud on Saturday night was preferable to going to the movies or the theater alone, and if he tried to get together with Benny and Sharon, they would ask about Barbara.

So he could only sigh with resignation when Sharon Stockser called to invite him to dinner the following Sunday. "By the way," she added, "I heard you broke up with Barbara."

"Actually, she broke up with me," he said with irritation.

"Want to walk and talk about it?"

He kept silent rather than say no and invite further questions, but that didn't deter her.

"Very well. We don't have to talk about her, but I really need to talk to you about something else."

"Can't it wait until I'm there for dinner?"

"I need to talk to you about Benny."

The distress and urgency in her voice alarmed him. "Shall we meet in Prospect Park?"

"I'd prefer the cemetery." Sharon didn't need to specify which cemetery. Of course it would be where her son was buried.

The trees and bushes were a riot of gold, topaz, ruby, and garnet—with a few emeralds thrown in for contrast, but Nathan barely noticed the fall foliage as he rushed to the boy's grave. He met Sharon as she pushed a baby stroller along the nearest path.

Her eyes welled up almost immediately. "I'm so unhappy, but I don't know what to do. I love Benny with all my heart, but I can't live in his Hasidic world anymore. I was so naive, thinking I was going to be like Ruth—'Your people will be my people and your God will be my God'—but you can't imagine how it is for an educated woman like me. I thought they'd all be pious and spiritual like Benny, but that's only for the men. Women are totally consumed by who will marry their children, making a good *shidduch* for them. None of the women my age attend synagogue, except on *chagim*. I went on Shabbos after we were first married, but it was only a few teen-age girls and old ladies crowded into such a narrow space I could barely breathe. Well, I won't have Judy brought up like that—illiterate in English, attending terrible girls' schools that don't teach real history, just stories of miracle-working rabbis, with no women in their books at all."

She stopped to wipe her eyes. "All these years Benny and I have never spent a single Shabbos or Jewish holiday at my parents' house. Yet at his parents' I scarcely see him except at dinner Friday night, when he sits up front with the men in their black caftans, all rich prominent Hasidim so proud to eat at the rebbe's table. The entire day his mother hardly speaks to me. Hershel's new wife, Zisse, from Israel has never said a word to me; she acts so snobbish because she's descended from some illustrious tzaddik who did miracles in Poland a hundred years ago." She sniffed softly before adding, "The other women don't talk to me either, so they think I don't understand Yiddish and say bad things about me."

"Like what?" Nathan asked, ashamed of his ignorance. All those years he'd spent Shabbos at Benny's house and never took notice that the women weren't around much. He was pretty sure Benny didn't pay attention to their absence either.

"Like I'm to blame for Benny refusing to be the next rebbe, brazen for not covering my hair, and not a good mother—which is why our son died." With that, Sharon burst into sobs, leaving Nathan to awkwardly pat her shoulder in sympathy.

"You don't have any Hasidic friends?" he asked.

She pulled out a handkerchief and blew her nose. "There are a few women who ask me privately about the outside world and how they can learn good English so they can get better-paying jobs, but they never acknowledge me in public."

Nathan had heard enough. He stopped on the path and turned to face her. "Sharon, you have to tell Benny how you feel. That's the only way things can get better."

"I can't. Benny is who he is. His Hasidim are who they are." She sighed in resignation. "I agreed to compromise in order to marry him, so how can I ask him to change now?"

"But you can't go on like this. Your marriage will suffer."

She smiled wistfully. "Just talking to you about it and letting off steam has made me feel better. Promise me you won't say anything to Benny about it."

Nathan didn't want to keep something so important from his best friend, but Sharon insisted until he gave in.

"Now that I've told you my secret, tell me what happened to Barbara. I thought you two started out with such potential."

He didn't want to blame, or shame, Barbara for hiding her Shabbos violation. And her smoking seemed trivial to break up over. Yet his secret studies with Hannah were too heavy a burden to carry alone any longer. "Only if you promise not to tell Benny—or anyone else—either."

Clearly intrigued, she immediately replied, "I promise."

"Remember when we were first dating and it started out with great potential . . . until you met Benny?"

"Yes." Her soft voice was cautious.

"This time I met someone, who must remain nameless, because the relationship between the two of us is forbidden."

Her shocked expression made him realize that she thought he was talking about a married woman or a shikse. "I've been teaching her Talmud."

"I don't understand. What's wrong with that?"

"First of all, it is against Jewish Law to teach Talmud to a woman—not that I see anything wrong with it," he explained. "Second, remember the problem Eileen Farber had with that professor who wanted to date her and how things got so uncomfortable she finally had to drop his class?" When Sharon nodded, he continued. "So I can't tell my student how I feel, not when I know she can't find another Talmud teacher."

Now that her expression was pensive, Nathan said, "So you see why you can't tell Benny. I know he'd disapprove. And that's all I'm going to say."

As Nathan walked with Sharon to the cemetery gates, he slowly got the feeling that he'd been here years ago. He closed his eyes and vaguely recalled a scene with Abba, when he was a little boy and all the leaves were green. *Maybe my mother's grave isn't someplace far away.* The more he thought about it, the more he became convinced that she was buried here. Maybe the person he'd talked to on the phone back in May had been lazy or incompetent. More likely, he realized, the staff was too busy to help anyone who called just before Mother's Day. The cemetery office wasn't far; he'd likely get better assistance in person.

The man working there patiently combed through several large card catalogs but came back empty-handed. Yet Nathan wouldn't give up.

"I'm sure my mother is buried here somewhere," he declared.

The man looked at him with sympathy. "When did she die?"

"May 1931," he replied, wondering why that mattered.

The man turned to Nathan. "Your mother is likely buried in the old cemetery." When Nathan looked at him blankly, he explained. "There are actually two different cemeteries here. They used to be completely separate, but the old one filled up in the early thirties and the new one expanded until they abutted each other. The old cemetery has hardly any graves from this century, so their records, such as there are, were put in storage."

"Storage?" Nathan's voice rose in frustration. "How long will it take to get them?"

"Not long. They're in the basement. If you watch the office, I'll go look."

It seemed like hours that Nathan paced the room, but it was actually fifteen minutes later that the man came back upstairs wearing a triumphant expression. He handed Nathan a small card that read "Minnie Mandel, section 142."

His heart beating wildly, Nathan's feet flew until he was standing in front of an enormous pink marble tombstone. It was elaborately carved: Minnie Trachtenberg Mandel, b. 1902, d. May 9, 1931. Next to it was a small marker for Baby Girl Mandel, who had died one day later.

My mother died in childbirth. And for one day I had a baby sister.

Nathan was still sitting on the grass in front of the two graves, head in his hands and questions careening around inside, when a groundskeeper announced that it was closing time.

SEVEN

EVERY TIME NATHAN visited Benny and Sharon's fourth-floor walkup on the Upper West Side, he marveled at how they could live in such a cramped space, especially with a baby. Overflowing bookshelves covered every wall, and the bathroom was so tiny someone taking a bath could simultaneously rest one foot on the toilet and the other on the sink.

"I hope whatever I smell is what we're having for dinner," he said, sniffing the air appreciatively.

Benny gazed at his wife with pride. "Sharon is taking Italian cooking classes."

They took their places around the small Formica-topped dining table, and seeing little Judy sitting in a high chair, Nathan was reminded how quickly the last seven months had passed. Sharon brought out the meal. The main dish, sliced beef in a savory tomato sauce, was delicious.

And Nathan said so. "Where did you buy this excellent meat? I've never tasted anything better."

"We get it from the kosher butcher my parents use." Oddly, Benny appeared embarrassed.

"You schlep all the way to Williamsburg to buy meat?" Then Nathan remembered the big disagreement Hasidim had with other Orthodox Jews over kosher meat, something about the slaughter knife, with the result that Hasidim ate only at their own homes. "Oh, of course you have to."

"I don't mind the schlep," Sharon said. "It gives me an excuse to see my family in Crown Heights. Besides, the butcher not only gives us the best cuts, but he doesn't charge for them since Benny's the rebbe's son. It's supporting Torah scholars."

Now Benny looked even more uncomfortable. "None of my father's Hasidim charge him for anything. They say it's an honor to supply his needs," he explained. "The practice extended to me when I moved up here for grad school and continued when I married."

"At first Benny would go to Brooklyn for the meat, until one time he couldn't go," Sharon said. "I didn't want it to be a problem that they were serving a woman who didn't cover her hair, so I put on a scarf and it was fine."

"I doubt it was actually fine," Benny said. "I think the butchers were afraid my father would feel disrespected if they wouldn't serve his son's wife."

"It's too late to worry about it now," she said. "We've been getting meat there for so long that they'd probably be insulted if we stopped."

After the dishes were cleared, Nathan recalled that Hannah continued to ask about Zelig, but he still knew nothing more than that Zelig was back in school. "How is Zelig doing? Can you tell me anything to allay my concerns?"

"I apologize for keeping you in the dark, especially since Zelig gave me permission to tell you whatever you want to know. I should warn you, however, that it is quite disturbing." Benny looked at Sharon and tilted his head toward the bedroom.

"I need to put Judy to bed." Sharon picked the baby up and started walking away. "We can have coffee and dessert after she's asleep."

Nathan waited with trepidation until the bedroom door closed. Then he turned to Benny. "For Heaven's sake, what happened?"

"I won't beat around the bush. When Zelig was studying for his bar mitzvah, he was sexually molested by his tutor, a Hasidic rabbi." Benny's demeanor was of scientific detachment, but Nathan could see the fury in his eyes.

"Gevalt." He stared at Benny in horror. His immediate reaction had been disbelief, but Benny was telling the truth. "That must have been years earlier. Why attempt suicide now?"

"Try to calm yourself so you don't disturb the baby," Benny said softly.

Nathan relaxed his clenched fists. "Go on. I'll try not to interrupt you."

"Last year Zelig's younger brother, Beryl, died when a car ran into him, and it was judged an accident. Apparently, when boys that age play tag, they sometimes dare each other to run across the street without looking for cars," Benny began. "Then this year, when Zelig opened his High Holy Day prayer book for Rosh Hashana, he found a letter from Beryl."

"A suicide note," Nathan whispered.

Benny nodded. "Beryl detailed how that rabbi had molested him for years, even after his bar mitzvah, and had stopped only because Beryl was going on to yeshiva. Between being rejected by the teacher he adored and guilt over what they'd done . . ." Benny waited to let Nathan take in what happened. "It was too much pain for Beryl to live with."

"Gottenyu. A Hasidic rabbi." Nathan, unable to look Benny in the eye, rested his forehead on his hand. *It was horrific, unbelievably dreadful, and yet undoubtedly true.*

"This is not a new problem," Benny said. "The fifth Lubavitch rebbe, Sholom Dov Schneersohn, was sexually abused by his mentor. It only stopped when he married."

Nathan looked up. "How can you possibly know that?"

"The rebbe suffered such psychological trauma that he consulted Freud."

"Never mind them—what about Zelig? How is he holding up?"

"That note not only brought back all of Zelig's shameful memories, but he blamed himself for not warning Beryl about the tutor, for not interceding in some way to save his brother." Benny put his hand on Nathan's arm. "I can stop here if you've heard enough."

"No. I want to hear it all." *One boy was dead and another psychologically damaged because of this despicable man. How could it have happened?*

"Zelig and Beryl's father is a diamond merchant whose work often takes him overseas, which left the boys vulnerable to the tutor's attentions. After several sessions with Zelig, it is clear to me that while this pedophile's behavior is contemptible, he is clever in how he goes about seducing these susceptible youths. Oh yes, I'm convinced the Fishkoff boys were not his only victims."

"What did the man do?" Nathan couldn't bring himself to say "pedophile."

"First of all, being a bar mitzvah tutor gave him plenty of time alone with his students, who were just entering puberty but not yet thirteen—"

"Of course," Nathan interrupted. "They would be too young to legally bear witness against him in a Jewish court."

"Hasidic boys are entirely ignorant about sexual matters. So it is easy for the rabbi, somebody they would trust unconditionally, to rub up against them or place his hand near or on their groin, at first apparently by accident. If the victim is receptive, the pedophile grows bolder. He knows that between the boy's sexual pleasure and pride in their special, secret relationship, the boy will soon be in his thrall."

"Until the student realizes what they're doing is wrong."

"That knowledge only makes things worse for the boy," Benny said. "Now shame over enjoying his sinful behavior and fear that it might be exposed come into play."

"So he keeps it secret, exactly what the pedophile needs so he can keep on molesting others." Nathan's eyes flashed with anger, but he kept his voice down. "This man is a menace. He must be stopped."

"But how? Any Haredi family who dares accuse him will be ostracized for bringing shame on the community, for making a *shanda fur die goyim.* Their children will become unmarriageable."

"You could do it, Benny. You're a tzaddik. Your *yichus* and Talmud scholarship make you unassailable."

Benny was silent a long time. "I can't do anything with only one victim and his brother's letter. But if this pedophile has been active for years, which is likely, there would be other boys."

Nathan locked eyes with Benny. "Boys so tormented by their abuse that they require treatment by the eminent Hasidic child psychologist, Rav and Doctor Benjamin Stockser."

Benny stood up and headed for the minuscule kitchen. "Come, let's surprise Sharon by getting the coffee and dessert ready."

All that coffee probably made it harder to sleep, but Nathan tossed and turned much of the night raging over Zelig and other unknown boys who had suffered, and continued to suffer, from this scourge. He was still so agitated in the morning that, in desperation to talk about it and because Abba was already gone, he called Hannah. After all, she was always asking how Zelig was doing.

He let out his breath in relief when she answered the phone. "Annie, it's Nathan. Are you alone?"

"I am." Her throat tightened as she heard the upset in his voice. "What on earth is wrong?"

"I hate to bother you at home, but I don't want to take time from our studies tomorrow." He then proceeded to unburden himself about what Benny told him the previous evening. It took a long time, but Hannah didn't interrupt.

When he finally trailed off, she sighed softly. "I suspected it might be something like that." Actually, it was worse than she'd suspected.

"That's why you asked about his last name," he said, his mind functioning again. "You knew about the car accident."

"I did, but I wanted to make sure it was the same boy," she replied. "Listen, I can't talk long. I have a staff meeting."

"That's okay. I just needed to get this off my chest. I'll see you tomorrow night, like usual," he said. "I hope you like Italian food. I'll be trying a new recipe."

That evening Hannah rummaged through her file cabinet. She quickly found the small article in the *Freiheit* about Beryl Fishkoff being killed by a speeding car while crossing the street; it bemoaned his loss and went on to advocate more crosswalks and stop signs. It took longer to find the story she'd written years ago about the child molester at a Hasidic girls' school. Giving in to pressure from leaders in the community, the newspaper never published it, despite her many revisions. But Hannah still had all the versions, and she thought Benny Stockser should see them.

Perusing the articles now, it still galled her that the story had been Moe's idea in the first place. Clear as if it were yesterday, she remembered being called into his office and told to close the door behind her. Terrified that she was being fired, Hannah just stared at his wire-rimmed glasses until she grasped the assignment he was giving her.

There had been rumors of child molestation at a certain Hasidic girls' school, Moe informed her, but they were impossible to confirm. However, the school needed a new English teacher, and he wanted Hannah to take the position. She was the perfect candidate, he assured her, an observant unmarried woman with a college degree in English, one who was willing to accept the pittance of a salary they paid.

As Moe surmised, the school was thrilled to have her.

After teaching there a year, she had amassed more than enough evidence to confirm that the school's custodian was the culprit. She presented her case in various ways in the different versions of her article, but each was rejected. She learned only later that the custodian had a new job at a yeshiva in Lakewood.

Rereading her article and unable to stop thinking about the Fishkoff brothers, Hannah wanted to scream with outrage and frustration. She couldn't do anything to stop the abuse or to help the victims, but someone had to.

Maybe that someone is Benny Stockser.

Nathan was still preparing dinner when Hannah arrived on Tuesday. "You're early. Dinner won't be ready for a half hour."

She laid the large envelope on the counter where he couldn't miss it. "I can stir the noodles while you read. I thought Benny would find this interesting."

Hannah had drained the pasta and moved on to setting the table when Nathan looked up. "I bet he'll find it very interesting. How should I proceed?"

She'd already considered that. "Say you're still in contact with the reporter who interviewed you and you asked if the *Freiheit* ever investigated the kind of thing that happened to Zelig."

"Very good." He nodded in approval. "I'll be careful not to say anything to indicate the reporter's gender."

"Any questions?" she asked.

He thought of Sharon. "You taught at that Hasidic girls' school for a year. Are they as bad as I've heard?"

"It depends on what you've heard, but I was appalled," she said. "The morning religious studies were all taught in Yiddish. Even the older girls never studied the Torah's actual Hebrew text." She snorted in disgust. "The teacher didn't read them an accurate Yiddish translation of the weekly portion either, just told the story of what happened. But mostly there were lectures about the evils of secular books and magazines, movies, theaters, television, museums, et cetera."

"Aren't they required to have secular classes?"

"Oh, they're supposed to follow New York's regulations in teaching English, history, and science, but nobody from the state checks." She rolled her eyes. "Every book has words blacked out, and often entire pages are missing. The English textbooks have no stories about girls or women, or *chas v'chalila* [Heaven forbid], girls and boys together. The sixth-grade girls get history and science books written for third graders, but it doesn't matter because they don't need to know history or science. They're just killing time until they're seventeen, when a good girl gets married off to some yeshiva *bocher* she hardly knows."

Nathan shuddered. "I'm very glad you didn't go to a school like that, Annie." He couldn't imagine Sharon and Benny sending their daughter to one either.

Hannah grimaced in return. "You and me both."

Nathan didn't tell Hannah about finding his mother's grave until Saturday night.

"Have you told your father yet?"

"I hate to make him suffer."

"He's probably already suffering guilt at not telling you about her, plus anxiety that you could ask him at any moment."

"I supposed I could mention that I was at the cemetery and found her grave . . . and see how he reacts." Immediately as he said it, Nathan knew he was being a coward.

"She was your mother. You're entitled to know her history—it's your history too." Hannah realized she was close to yelling and softened her tone. "It's been over twenty years, and you're not a child anymore. You can do it," she urged him. "Think of it like pulling out a splinter."

When they eventually hung up, Nathan was filled with resolve. He recognized that he had confided in Hannah because he'd anticipated that she would react just as she had.

While Nathan procrastinated, Hannah utilized her experience at the *Freiheit* to locate Minnie Mandel's obituary. She was expecting the task to be time-consuming and disappointing, for even if the newspaper had announced her death, it was unlikely that such a young woman would rate more than a few sentences. So she was awestruck at the several columns it took up in addition to a photograph of Mrs. Mandel posing with several other women at some official function. Hannah easily picked Nathan's mother out before she read the caption; the family resemblance was that strong.

Like all lengthy obits, it began with the subject's birth. Minnie had been born in 1902 in Philadelphia to Arthur and Lilly Trachtenberg. Hannah skipped to the end, where, as usual, it concluded with a list of survivors. She was excited to see that, in addition to Solomon and Nathan Mandel were brothers Arnold, Barney, and Max Trachtenberg and a sister Dora Strauss. Hannah couldn't wait to share this trove of information with Nathan. The more she read, the more interested and impressed she became.

Minnie Mandel had been active in the Women's Branch of the Union of Orthodox Jewish Congregations. Crusading for better Jewish education for girls and women, she had helped write *Symbols and Ceremonies of the Jewish Home*, a guidebook about ritual observance for the twentieth-century homemaker, published in 1930. In addition, Minnie had worked to promote the Jewish dietary laws to modern American women. Apparently, there was no central kosher authority back then. Local rabbis, European immigrants for whom endorsing a particular product was a source of income, had a reputation for lax and even fraudulent practices. Frustrated Jewish women demanded better oversight, and Hannah didn't blame them.

So the Women's Branch lobbied until they finally convinced the food industry of the financial rewards of a standardized kosher market. Led by women such as Mrs. Solomon Mandel, the obituary pointed out, they then succeeded in consolidating kashrut oversight to the Orthodox Union, with the result that the barely noticeable seal of a *U* within a circle was to be found on an ever-increasing number of products.

Hannah reread the obituary, even more excited as an idea for a news story grew in her mind. Today's *Freiheit* readers, while aware of the ubiquitous OU symbol on their kosher foodstuffs, were unlikely to know its history. Surely they would be as fascinated with its origin as she was.

Minnie Mandel might not be alive, but other members of the Women's Branch probably were. Hannah could start with the women in Minnie's obituary photo and move on to older ladies in her synagogue. Some of them would remember those days, and if they hadn't been personally active in the kashrus oversight movement, they might lead her to those who were. Hannah's mind raced with exhilaration as she imagined writing the article.

So far in her career she had never suggested a story idea to Moe. She'd pointed out interesting articles in the Israeli papers and angled for interviews, like Nathan's and Dr. Lewitsky's, that Moe had already decided on. Taking the initiative on this would be a bold new step for her, but she had two things going for her. First, getting the story involved interviewing women, a task most male reporters eschewed. Second, she was pretty sure Moe would love it.

Hannah smiled the entire time it took to make a copy of Minnie Mandel's obituary. She couldn't wait to see Nathan's face when she gave it to him.

Despite Nathan's good intentions, it took a week before he found a time to broach the subject with his father, just as they were finishing their tea after dinner. He started by disclosing his talk with Sharon at the cemetery. She had made him promise not to tell Benny about her problems, but Abba wasn't Benny.

"I feared something like this would eventually happen." Abba shook his head. "As much as I commiserate with Sharon, I think the Talmud is right that a tanner should only marry a tanner's daughter or sister," he said. "I'm sorry Sharon got you involved. This is something they must work out together."

In the resulting silence, Nathan gathered his courage. "While I was in the cemetery, I saw my mother's grave, and my baby sister's." Abba's face paled, but Nathan looked him in the eye. "I'm a grown man now. I want to know the whole story."

"What do you want to know?" Abba finally asked.

"How did you two meet?" Nathan asked. He didn't just want to hear how she died.

"I met her older brother Shai first when we studied together at the yeshiva. I could tell by his clothes and demeanor that his family was well-off and had lived in America for years," he began. "I, on the other hand, was a poor orphan who had come to New York only a decade before. The cousin who'd sponsored me had died, leaving me no place to live."

"What?" Nathan exclaimed. "You were homeless."

"The yeshiva had a dormitory, and because I was a good student, they gave me a small stipend for food. Still, I was hungry much of the time." He paused and almost smiled. "Until Shai found out and insisted I share his lodgings, which included two rooms and ample meals. When he saw I had no place to go for holidays, Shai invited me to his home in Philadelphia."

"So that's how you met her?" Nathan nudged the topic back to his mother.

Abba nodded. "Your mother's family were prosperous department store owners who took pity on their son's penniless friend. It was the furthest thing from their minds, and mine too, that their young daughter would settle her heart on me. After all, I was ten years her senior. But apparently I was the only person who talked to her like she was an adult."

That explained the expensive tombstone, Nathan thought. Her family bought it. "Their last name was Trachtenberg?"

"Ah, yes, you read the tombstone." Abba's chin quivered, but then he composed himself. "Minnie had a large family, more Conservative than Orthodox, but I managed."

"How did you arrange to court her when you saw her only a few times a year in Philadelphia?"

"After high school, she moved to New York to attend Hebrew Teachers Training School. She roomed in the same boarding house as Shai, so we three dined together regularly," Abba replied.

It was apparent to Nathan that his father did not want to elaborate further on their courtship. "Eventually you married." Nathan encouraged him to continue.

"Yes, in 1922," he replied. "Though most of Minnie's family thought she could do better than a poor yeshiva student."

"But I wasn't born until 1929," Nathan said, blushing as he realized the intimate information his comment was asking about.

"Minnie was barren for several years, until a friend suggested she see an infertility specialist." Abba didn't seem embarrassed. "Obviously, the doctor's treatment was successful."

Abba hesitated again, making Nathan abruptly aware that his father had come to the time when his mother died. He wasn't sure he wanted to hear those details, but he did want to understand, now that he knew she'd come from a large family, how Abba became estranged from them. So he said, "Go on."

"It started out like other Saturdays, except that your mother, who was eight months pregnant, complained about nausea and a headache. I wanted to stay home with her, but she insisted I go to shul. The weather was so nice that I took a leisurely walk back." He closed his eyes for a moment. "I was on the second-floor landing when I heard a child crying, and when I reached our front door, the cries—your cries—coming from inside threw me into such a panic that my shaking hands could barely get the key into the lock."

Abba pulled out a handkerchief and blew his nose. "I'll never forget the scene. Your mother was lying on the bathroom floor having convulsions, and you were holding on to her, screaming. At first I was paralyzed. I had to get help, but I couldn't leave either of you alone. Nobody in our building had telephones back then." His words came faster. "I picked you up and started banging on doors until I found a neighbor who was home. She agreed to stay with you and Minnie until help came. Of course, on Shabbos nearly all the stores with phones were closed, but I finally found an open drugstore that called an ambulance."

"But it was too late," Nathan said softly. His chin began to quiver.

Abba's eyes moistened as he nodded. "She lived to reach the hospital but not much longer, and then they operated in hopes of saving the baby. But your sister was too small and survived only a few hours."

Determined to control his own grief, Nathan put his arm around his father's quaking shoulders and waited.

"Word must have spread because when I got home some people from my shul were waiting. A woman found a phone number for your grandparents, so when you woke up early Sunday morning, they were there, along with Shai. The rest of her family arrived by noon." Abba broke off and sighed deeply. "I was too distraught to do anything except care for you. Your grandfather arranged the funeral and paid for everything. We sat shiva in that apartment, and I didn't see any of them again until the unveiling at the cemetery. I'm afraid I lost my temper when I saw that oversized pink tombstone."

Nathan could not recall a single time Abba had gotten that angry. "Why? What happened?" The tombstone was ostentatious, but Abba had endured all sorts of hateful insults without losing his temper when his first book came out.

"Remember, this was the beginning of the Depression, when the only way I could keep my yeshiva going was to forgo my salary. Yet I had to pay a housekeeper to care for you. I made the mistake of complaining about them spending so much money on a hunk of rock for Minnie when her son was going hungry. That's when her parents and siblings let loose with a barrage of fury that her death was my fault, that I should never have left her alone.

And they were right. I still blame myself for her death, but I couldn't admit that to them."

Nathan wanted to console Abba, but his father's error in judgment had been too costly. "So you and her family never spoke to each other again?"

"It wasn't that abrupt, just a gradual losing touch at first. After your grandfather died and you inherited your mother's portion—which thank Heaven saw us through the Depression—I found us a new apartment." He looked around the room as if seeing it for the first time. "This place, actually. And though I was sure I'd sent them our address, when Shai died the following year, I wasn't notified. I found out only when a mutual friend asked why I hadn't attended his funeral."

Nathan could see why there was no love lost between Abba and his in-laws. He could also see Abba was growing weary. But he had one more question. "Do you have a photo of her?"

Without a word, Abba got up and disappeared into his bedroom. He returned with a framed wedding portrait and laid it on the dining table. "You can keep this one."

Nathan stared at the feminine version of his own face framed by a bridal veil and was shocked to realize that the woman who'd borne him was almost the same age in this photo as he was now. But she might as well be a complete stranger for all the memories the picture brought up. He didn't want to know her through his father's unhappy memories, but he didn't dare try to find his maternal relatives. *They didn't try to find me, so best to leave well enough alone.*

The following Tuesday, Nathan and Hannah finished studying the sober final chapter of Tractate Yoma, the one about atonement and repentance. Some sages said that Yom Kippur itself atoned for a person's sins, but the majority declared that a sinner must repent to receive atonement. All agreed that while confession on Yom Kippur atoned for sins against God, such as eating forbidden foods, for sins against another person, Yom Kippur did not atone until the sinner sought forgiveness and appeased his fellow. Then came pages describing the Sages' differing procedures for this, necessary because there was nothing on the subject in the Torah. Hannah found the sugya informative but not as compelling as those dealing with women.

Then Nathan brought the evening's studies to a close by sharing what his father had told him about his mother. Each detail brought him closer to tears, until he broke down completely while describing Abba's continuing guilt at being responsible for her death. "If only the Talmud taught us how to forgive ourselves," he finally whispered.

Hannah had never seen a man cry before. The embarrassed part of her wanted to give Nathan privacy, and the compassionate part longed to take him in her arms to console him. Yet she felt constrained from doing either. Helpless, she waited until Nathan regained his composure and presented him with his mother's obituary. Then it was her turn to blink back tears as his eyes shone while he read it.

"This is amazing, Annie." He looked at her in awe. "How can I ever thank you?"

"You can thank me by teaching me more Talmud" was what she said. But "by taking me dancing" was what she wanted to say.

EIGHT

SATURDAY NIGHT, when Nathan told Hannah how grateful Benny was for her unpublished *Freiheit* articles, she realized how else she might be able to help Benny, as well as the molested children. Zelig and Beryl couldn't be the only boys, plus there were students at the girls' school. Hasidic women, cloistered in their own female-centered community, cared more about their children than anything else, so there must have been gossip.

And when it came to what the women were whispering that nobody wanted to talk about, Hannah knew whom to ask—Yetta Feinstein.

Hannah had never heard of Yetta until a few years ago, on the Monday morning after the *Freiheit* rejected her article. Hannah was in the kitchen working on her third cup of coffee after a sleepless night fuming over her wasted effort, when the telephone's strident ring made her pick up the receiver if only to silence the jangling noise. But what she heard from the other end jolted her completely awake.

The woman's voice had the barest hint of a Yiddish accent. "May I speak with H. M. Covey?" The caller clearly expected her target to be available.

Hannah froze. She was H. M. Covey at the newspaper's office but never at home. She'd rejected her first reaction, which was to say the caller had the wrong number. "Who is calling, please?" she'd asked instead.

"This is Mrs. Feinstein, Yetta Feinstein. If Miss Covey is not available, she can call me at this number." She gave the number slowly and distinctly. "I would like to meet with her to discuss her recent investigation into child molestation at a local girls' school. It's a shame her story was killed."

Despite her astonishment, Hannah repeated the phone number and said she'd give Miss Covey the message. Then she sat down and started to think. Who the devil was Yetta Feinstein? How had she become privy to the articles Hannah had written and know they'd been rejected? How had she found out that a woman, Hannah Eisin, was H. M. Covey and then get the Eisins' unlisted phone number? Why would she want to meet Hannah?

Using her reporter connections, Hannah had no difficulty learning about the resourceful Yetta Feinstein. The formidable first cousin of a local rebbe's wife, Yetta had been widowed twice, each death leaving her wealthier than before. Since a woman who outlived two husbands was considered a killer wife, she was forbidden to remarry. It was common knowledge that neither of her arranged marriages had been happy, so it seemed to Hannah that Yetta, that rare Hasidic woman with both freedom and power, was more to be envied than pitied.

It was likely that Mrs. Feinstein had discovered the articles the same way other Orthodox authorities had—somebody at the *Freiheit* leaked them. But the only way to get an answer to the last question was to return the woman's call and agree to a meeting. Which back then, protective of her dual identity, Hannah had no intention of doing.

But now that there was a way to help molested children like Zelig and Beryl, Hannah wondered if Yetta Feinstein might be the key to getting Benny more patients. Thus she came to be sitting in an elegantly furnished second-floor brownstone apartment in Williamsburg, drinking tea with a stylishly coiffed silver-haired matron dressed in black.

"I appreciate your coming to see me, Miss Covey. I've been impressed with your articles in the *Freiheit*." Thankfully, Mrs. Feinstein did not ask Hannah why it had taken her so long to call. "I was disturbed, but not surprised, when I read your unpublished story. Something similar happened in my family."

"It must have been difficult for your daughter," Hannah replied. "I hope she wasn't too traumatized."

"The victim was my son, Feivel, and he has not recovered fully even though it has been seven years." She locked eyes with Hannah. "I've never told anyone about this, but I'm going to tell you. You know about these things—you'll understand."

Hannah tamped down her eager curiosity and put on her best listening demeanor. "Feel free to unburden yourself, Mrs. Feinstein. You can trust me."

The older woman refilled their cups and heaved a great sigh. "Feivel's father died when our son was little, so at first I was pleased when the Mishnah teacher took him under his wing."

Hannah had a bad feeling she already knew the answer, but she still asked, "Was the rabbi's name Brenner?"

"Oy Gottenyu." Mrs. Feinstein clasped her hand to her ample bosom. "How did you know?" Then she calmed herself. "You've heard about him—I won't foul my mouth by saying his name—from someone else."

It wasn't a question, but Hannah nodded.

"I had a daughter and then several miscarriages before my son was born, so the two of us were close," Mrs. Feinstein began. "But after that rabbi started teaching Feivel to *leyne* Torah for his bar mitzvah, I noticed my son acting different—secretive and withdrawn—and eventually got the story from him. I was so upset I went right to the rebbe, who promised to look into it."

"And did he?" *Finally I'll get a first-person report of a rebbe's reaction.*

"He certainly did." The woman's voice was hard and bitter. "He told me that my son had misinterpreted the teacher's affection. I came home and questioned Feivel thoroughly, then went back and was adamant that there was no misinterpretation. Next I was told that my son had been the aggressor and the rebbe wanted him to go to a new school," she continued. "Can you believe it? But I had *yichus*; my grandfather was the rebbe before this one. I said why should my Feivel have to make new friends at a different school when it was the teacher who should be punished?"

"So they moved the teacher someplace else." Hannah named Zelig and Beryl's school.

Mrs. Feinstein, likely understanding how Hannah knew this, frowned. "I didn't trust them. I suspected my son might not be the only one, so I did a little asking around and found other mothers like me. Eventually I heard that you were investigating the problem."

"Mrs. Feinstein, you are a very brave and loving mother to fight for your son like that," Hannah said, planning how she would bring up Benny Stockser.

"Please call me Yetta."

"And me Hannah." She hesitated before asking, "How is Feivel doing these days?"

"He seems all right, but I, his mother, know he isn't. With our money and status, he could marry any girl he wanted, but he refuses every match." Yetta shook her head helplessly. "Thank Heaven my daughter is long married already, so I don't have to worry about her."

"Yetta, I know someone who can help your son, and other children like him," Hannah said. "Dr. Benjamin Stockser."

"Reb Stockser's son, the one who wanted to study psychology?"

"Yes. He got his doctorate from Columbia and practices as a child psychologist. He has experience treating children who've been molested."

"You think my Feivel might benefit from seeing him?"

Hannah nodded. "You would be doing a great mitzvah if you could let other mothers know about Dr. Stockser."

"You can count on me to spread the word—discreetly, of course." Yetta's tone indicated their meeting was concluding. "In case you didn't know, it was due to my efforts that the school janitor you wrote about was transferred to a yeshiva in New Jersey, where he has no access to girls."

Hannah stood up and squeezed Yetta's hand. "On behalf of all those innocent girls, I thank you."

Hannah was both incredulous and envious when Nathan told her on Saturday why they wouldn't be able to study together the following Thursday. "You're having Thanksgiving at the Gorens'?" Not that she didn't have plans herself; Aunt Elizabeth always came down for the holiday, and Hannah looked forward to seeing her.

"My father and I have been going there every year since he started teaching at the Seminary, although some years it's at Isaac and Leah Goren's place and others at Dave and Sarah's, Benny's in-laws," he replied. "Now that Joey Goren can fly back from California for the long weekend, Thanksgiving is the one night a year I get to spend with all of them."

"How can Benny Stockser eat there?" Hannah asked. "Hasidim are so strict about their food."

"While the rest of us have kosher turkey, he has fish. But he doesn't object if Sharon eats like her parents at their house." Sharon had made most of the compromises Benny's father insisted on before they married, but Thanksgiving with the Gorens was one of the few Benny agreed to.

"How tolerant of him," she said sarcastically.

"A Jewish couple needs to choose how they will observe halacha. Not that they must follow it exactly the same way," Nathan added quickly. "One of the reasons my recent girlfriend and I broke up was that she deliberately violated Shabbos and then tried to hide it."

For a long moment Hannah was silent. Nathan had not only admitted that he was now unattached but had told her why. "You're right. A couple should decide this in advance," she said. "Although I don't know if I'd want to marry a man who'd agree to a kosher home but continued to eat *treif* outside."

Nathan felt a small thrill run through him. Hannah had just told him what kind of man she wouldn't marry and, by implication, the kind of man she would. Other than her Yemenite old flame, she'd never expressed any interest in marriage. After they hung up, he lay down and wondered if she'd even consider someone like him. And if so, how could he introduce the idea to her without scaring her off?

Later that night, Hannah pondered what she'd learned from that brief conversation. She now knew one of the reasons Nathan was no longer with his old girlfriend. *Which indicates there is another reason he isn't telling me.*

Nathan handed his coat to Sarah Goren, then turned around and stopped in his tracks. Sometime in the months since he'd last been to Sharon's parents' apartment, their heavy traditional furniture had been replaced with minimalist modern pieces. The living and dining rooms, now occupied by curved blond wood tables and chairs upholstered in neutral shades, seemed much larger. At the same time, Sarah's brightly colored abstract paintings appeared to jump off the walls.

"Wow!" he complimented her. "What a great change."

"I would have done this years ago, but it took a while to get Dave used to the new style," she replied.

"Plus a trip to Denmark," Dave Goren said as he came over to add his welcome.

"I like it," Nathan said. His and Abba's apartment would seem even darker and gloomier in comparison.

Nathan took his customary seat between Joey and Benny, noting with relief how comfortable the chair was despite what looked like insufficient padding. Benny announced that he had four new patients, two boys and two girls, which meant his reputation was becoming known in the community.

"Yes." He lowered his voice so only Nathan could hear. "Each has been molested, the girls by family members."

"I'm sure you'll take good care of them," Nathan said. Then he turned to Joey and asked about going dancing.

That began a lengthy discussion to determine where the best bands were playing. Joey wouldn't be back in New York again until Pesach, and Nathan wanted to make the most of his friend's one Saturday night in town. Fortunately, Shabbos ended by six this time of year, so they could get an early start.

When Benny left the table to use the bathroom, Sharon leaned across the now empty seat between her and Nathan. "I hope you can find time for another walk and talk next week," she whispered.

She sounded so frantic he couldn't refuse. "On Wednesday, at the cemetery?" It would also give him an opportunity to revisit his mother's grave, this time knowing more about her.

"I'll see you then," Sharon replied before returning her attention to little Judy in the high chair next to her.

Once the dishes were cleared, everyone nodded graciously as Benny and Joey excused themselves for some privacy in the den. At first Nathan tried to hide his discomfort as Abba vividly shared with everyone what they'd learned about Israel during their Pesach visit with H. M. Covey's aunt. But he relaxed and joined the conversation when he saw that the Gorens assumed Elizabeth Covey had come alone.

"So much has changed since I was last there after the war," Isaac Goren said. "There's going to be a big conference for Jewish scholars in Israel this summer. Leah will accompany me, of course, but I'd love for Joey to join us." He turned to Nathan. "Maybe he'd be more inclined to go if you came too."

"If anyone is going to be invited to present the latest research on Talmudic textual criticism—and that's a big if—my father is the greater authority," Nathan replied. Not that he was averse to visiting Israel.

"All the more reason for you to attend and support him."

Solomon Mandel rolled his eyes and said, "*Patsh zikh nit in baykhele ven fishele iz nokh in taykhele.*" (Don't pat yourself on the belly when the fish is still in the stream.) Then he added, "Even if a miracle should occur and I am invited to Israel, I'm not sure my doctor would permit it."

They all knew better than to compliment his current good health. "We don't need to make any commitments until after Pesach," Isaac said soothingly.

Nathan had no worries about running into Barbara at the dance hall; her family spent Thanksgiving with her grandparents in Baltimore. But though this was his first Saturday night out in months and the weather was excellent for late November, he was going only because Joey wanted him to. Even so, it wasn't long before the music's rhythm took hold and, once he'd demonstrated his prowess on the dance floor, he couldn't ignore the many attractive young women giving him encouraging looks.

The crowd, with a surfeit of college students home for the holiday weekend, was a bit juvenile for Nathan's taste. But it was ideal for Joey. While Nathan appreciated dancing again after his hiatus, he got more pleasure watching Joey and marveling at Benny's healing skills. The confident, poised young man had come a long way from the neurotic adolescent Nathan had first met six years ago.

Later, when the band took a break and women left to powder their noses, Joey returned to Nathan's side. "Would you mind if I saw one of these girls home?"

Nathan smiled. "Not at all. You're only young once. I can find my way home."

"You mean nobody has caught your eye?" Joey sounded incredulous.

"I'd like to play the field a bit longer," he lied. While it was true that he was having a good time, what he really wanted was to take Hannah dancing.

"You've been playing the field too long, if you ask me."

Nathan scowled at Joey's criticism. "I didn't ask you." Then his expression softened at his friend's dismay. "Believe me, nobody wants me to settle down more than I do."

In the end, despite Joey's high hopes, neither of them saw any of the girls home.

As Hannah hoped, Moe enthusiastically approved her idea of a story on the history of the OU hechsher. She promptly arranged interviews with the two women who'd appeared alongside Minnie Mandel in the obituary photo and began searching for others who might remember Nathan's mother. Within a week, she realized this would be a bigger task than she'd anticipated. Almost half the women she contacted not only remembered Mrs. Mandel but were eager to tell H. M. Covey about her.

After Hannah spoke with the two in the picture, she knew whom to interview next: Amy Davidson, Minnie's best friend. Luck was with her because Amy was a member of the Eisins' synagogue and was the congregation's librarian. Hannah met her in the library Wednesday morning.

"Hannah Eisin, what a pleasure to see you." Amy looked down at her watch. "I'm sorry, but I can't help you right now. I'm being interviewed by H. M. Covey at ten thirty."

Hannah smiled. The pride in the librarian's voice made it clear that this was an honor. "I hope you don't mind that I arrived a little early." She didn't have to wait long for Amy's eyes to open wide with surprise.

"Good Heavens, Hannah, I had no idea."

"Most people don't, and I prefer to keep it that way." Although at the rate she'd be interviewing women for this OU article, her pen name would soon be public knowledge.

"Of course, I understand."

They settled down in the library office, and Hannah brought out her notebook. She'd already heard how instrumental Minnie Mandel had been in getting major American food manufacturers to agree to OU oversight, but she let Amy talk with minimal interruption. Who knows what personal information the woman might inadvertently reveal about her best friend?

"We never could have done it without Minnie," Amy kvelled. "She spoke like an American, with hardly any accent, so she was the one who negotiated with the big food company men. And oy, were those negotiations complicated. But she was smart, Minnie was, and they soon knew they were dealing with a real maven."

"You must have been so proud of her," Hannah said.

"Can you believe that only a few years after she died, we could buy bread, soup, breakfast cereal, noodles, shortening, ice cream, and candy— even Pepsi-Cola—all certified kosher by OU? Your generation has it easy because so many things are labeled OU now. You have no idea how stressful it was to keep kosher back then, always having to tell your children they couldn't eat this or that."

"What else did Mrs. Mandel do?" Hannah encouraged her.

"Minnie didn't have children, so she had time to go with our rabbis to inspect the processing plants." Even though they were alone, Amy lowered her voice. "Between you and me, she knew more than the rabbis when it came to modern kashrus."

For a moment Hannah was confused. "But isn't Nathan Mandel her son?"

"Yes, but she didn't have him for a long time." Amy looked around surreptitiously and whispered, "And if it weren't for me, she wouldn't have had him at all."

"Oh?" *This is going to be really interesting.*

"I was the one to recommend that specialist doctor, who had no trouble diagnosing Minnie's problem." She hesitated before adding, "And explaining how to cure it."

Hannah looked at Amy with curiosity but said nothing. Experience had taught her that most people couldn't abide a lull in conversation. So if she waited long enough, they often divulged something significant to fill the silence.

"You promise you won't put this in your article or tell anyone I told you."

"Of course not." Hannah made a supreme effort to hide her impatience. "I'm writing about Minnie Mandel's role in the OU, not her medical history."

"Well, Minnie got her period about every twenty-three days, not once a month like most of us. The doctor, who knew she was Orthodox, explained that she wasn't getting pregnant because she must be ovulating during her seven clean days."

"Her what?" Hannah's voice rose with bewilderment.

"Of course you wouldn't know. You're not married," Amy said. "According to halacha, after a woman's period ends, she's supposed to wait seven more days with no blood, her clean days, before she goes to the mikveh and can sleep with her husband."

Hannah made sure she'd understood. "So by the time Minnie and her husband slept together again, it would be too late." She was annoyed, but not surprised, that sex was such a hush-hush topic. She almost missed that Amy had said "supposed to wait."

"The doctor advised her to wait just six clean days for a couple of months, and if that didn't work, then decrease the clean days to five for another two months, and so on." Amy smiled triumphantly. "Sure enough, in six months she's pregnant, and they had no trouble conceiving the second child."

"Did she have trouble getting rabbinic dispensation to go to the mikveh early?" Hannah asked. While Jews were permitted to violate halacha to save a life, would curing infertility qualify?

"Minnie said it *was* a matter of life and death, so what was there to consult a rabbi about, especially since she wasn't going to a mikveh anyway." Amy shrugged. "She was determined to have a baby, and she wasn't going to let any rabbi stop her."

"Wait." Hannah managed to hide her astonishment. "What do you mean she wasn't going to the mikveh anyway?"

"None of us went to the mikveh for long after getting married, not when we had perfectly good bathtubs we could use in the privacy of our own homes instead of those rusty old iron tanks down in some filthy tenement basement." Amy wrinkled her nose in disgust. "Our husbands didn't know or want to know what we did when our periods were over. All they cared about was how soon they could sleep with us again. Frankly, I think Minnie was one of the few who at least went to a Russian bath to immerse."

Amy's revelation was interrupted when a congregant came in needing help to find a book. Hannah sat down at one of the large reading tables and used the time to think about what she'd learned. The Torah said that a niddah immersed seven days after her period started, not seven days after it ended. And there was nothing about changing this in the Mishnah. *So how did halacha change?*

The congregant left with his book, which gave Hannah an idea. "Do you have any books about the laws of niddah?"

"Of course." Amy led her to a section in the back.

Hannah perused several and checked out three, including one that appeared to have instructions for installing a mikveh in one's home.

Knowing how Nathan felt about women who violated halacha in secret, Hannah recognized that she must now join the conspiracy of silence so neither he nor his father ever learned about his mother's actions.

That same Wednesday, Nathan and Sharon met at the cemetery. It added to his melancholy that the wilted leaves, those few still clinging to the branches, were a faded brown rather than the riot of autumn colors they'd walked under before. Sharon's voice shook as she began telling Nathan her tale of woe.

"Sukkos was a nightmare." She started with a new grievance. "Reb Stockser sets up a sukkah in the backyard, and it overflows with men at every meal. But while they're having a raucous time, the women spend the entire festival week cooking and cleaning up after them. Chas v'chalila I should want to eat in the sukkah so I could fulfill the mitzvah of dwelling there."

"Women are exempt from dwelling in the sukkah," Nathan started to explain.

"The way they yelled at me when I went in and picked up the *esrog* to smell it, you'd think I was violating the Ten Commandments." She stopped abruptly and turned to him. "Why can't Hasidic women observe Sukkos?"

Nathan took a deep breath. It was difficult enough explaining women's exemptions from time-bound positive commandments to Hannah, who studied Talmud. "The Talmud says that women are exempt from positive mitzvos that occur at a specific time, like sitting in the sukkah during Sukkos."

Her eyes narrowed. "I've read enough Torah to know that it says nothing of the kind," she protested.

"You're right. This exemption isn't in the Written Torah." He spoke calmly, trying to mollify her. "It's from the Oral Law."

She was quick with another objection. "But 'exempt' doesn't mean 'forbidden,' so why can't I go in the sukkah if I want to?"

Now came the difficult part. "Some rabbis interpreted 'exempt' as 'permitted,' but others disagreed," he said. "Women in these communities didn't fulfill time-bound positive mitzvos, so eventually, because of *minhag yisrael din hu*—a custom of Israel becomes law—it became forbidden for women to do them."

Sharon's gray eyes flashed. "That explains the Hasidic women's actions. But what does your special Talmud student say about this?"

He knew very well Hannah's protests on the subject, but he prevaricated. "We haven't studied this particular piece of Gemara, although we did have a lively discussion over why women are forbidden to study Talmud."

Her expression softened. "The two of you have been studying together almost a year, right? And you enjoy each other's company?" When he nodded, she continued. "Has it occurred to you that maybe, just maybe, your student could be in love with you too?"

Nathan's stunned silence answered her question.

She sighed. "You know, if I'd never met Benny, you and I would prob-ably be happily married now." Before she could say more, church bells chimed the hour, and she got ready to leave. "Benny will phone you about a night to celebrate Hanukah with us," she called out as they waved goodbye.

In a daze, Nathan found his way to his mother's grave. Until now, he had never thought of his feelings for Hannah with the label "love," but Sharon clearly saw something he hadn't even admitted to himself. *What I feel for Hannah must be love.* But he'd always assumed that when he finally did find love, there would be a mutual affection, like Benny and Sharon's. And that it would be a source of great joy.

Yet Nathan only felt more miserable. He wept quietly as he gazed up at the tall tombstone. Look at how love didn't always lead to happiness. Abba still bereft more than twenty years after Minnie died. Sharon desperately unhappy despite marrying her beloved Benny. Hannah giving up Zechariah in order to write and then seeing him wed to another.

And now, loving Hannah and unable to declare it, Nathan too suffered the wounds of Cupid's arrow.

A few days later Nathan received Benny's call inviting him to dinner on the Sunday during Hanukah. What he didn't expect was his friend saying, "I hope you will enlighten me as to what might have made my wife ask why women cannot study Talmud."

The next morning Nathan waited until Benny was at work before call-ing Sharon.

"I'm sorry, I thought I could just ask about women studying Talmud," she said. "But he immediately became suspicious, and you know how impossible it is to keep anything from Benny."

Nathan forced himself not to scream at her. "You told him I'm teaching a woman?"

"Yes," she admitted. "But he's not going to tell anyone."

There was nothing else to say. Nathan was too angry at Sharon's breach to continue their conversation, but eventually he calmed down. He'd learned his lesson. There would be no more cemetery walks with Sharon, especially if she was thinking she'd have been happier married to him.

Over several weeks, Hannah interviewed a dozen women for her article about the women behind OU becoming the preeminent organization and the most recognizable symbol in kashrus supervision. But it took more than twice that many interviews to confirm her unexpected discovery that

Minnie Mandel and Amy Davidson weren't anomalies. Orthodox women, even those who kept a scrupulously kosher home, had mostly abandoned the mikveh, immersing instead in swimming pools, so-called Russian or Turkish baths, but mainly in their own bathtubs. None had an in-home mikveh.

Not that Hannah would be writing about the fascinating finding. Indeed, the subject was never mentioned in public, and despite her considerable interrogation skills, nobody would say anything about observing the prescribed period of abstinence. It didn't matter that she was single; the topic itself was taboo.

"My friends can discuss their kitchen rituals endlessly and in great detail," one woman told Hannah. "But nothing that concerns the bedroom."

"It's too private to talk about," another explained. "And nobody wants to admit they don't fulfill that mitzvah."

Of course, Hannah thought. Any woman who didn't follow kashrus would quickly be found out and ostracized, but one could ignore niddah restrictions with complete confidence that no one else would know about it.

One woman bluntly stated what others hinted at. "Using a mikveh is medieval, a primitive relic left over from the olden days. It has no place in a modern Jewish woman's life."

Those few who went to the mikveh did so reluctantly, or even resentfully. "It's something a Jewish woman has to do," one said.

Another complained using a mixed metaphor: "A cross we have to bear."

Orthodox rabbis were apparently equally unwilling to talk about women's *personal* rituals, preferring to distribute pamphlets that extolled the practice but convinced few to adopt it. Many of Hannah's subjects still had the copy of *A Marriage Guide for Jewish Women* they'd received before their weddings, but few showed signs of use. One woman confessed that she kept hers only because she'd feel guilty throwing it out.

The more Hannah considered it, the more she understood and sympathized with these women. Even at best, visiting a mikveh was inconvenient, and unless they went to a Russian bath, they'd need to bathe in their own tub when they got home anyway. They would all know that secular, Reform, and most Conservative Jews didn't use a mikveh, with no apparent ill consequences.

Maybe it had become like playing the numbers. Sure, it was against the law, but lots of people did it clandestinely and nobody got arrested. Hannah even played occasionally when her favorite numbers runner, a woman, came by the *Freiheit* office. But they transacted their business in private in a nearby alley.

NINE

HANNAH WAS SITTING at her dad's conference table when the phone rang. Her sister-in-law, Naomi, sounded anxious. "You're still coming over for coffee this morning, right?"

"I'll be right there. I needed to finish something first." She couldn't admit the something was a line of Talmud she'd been translating, not even to Naomi.

"I thought you submitted that article about the OU hechsher already."

"I did. Moe wanted it for one of the Hanukah issues."

"I'll see you soon, then." Naomi hung up before Hannah could say more.

As she walked the two blocks to Naomi's apartment, Hannah wondered what her best friend was so eager to talk about. They had coffee together at least once a week while Naomi's older daughter was at school and the baby napped, when there was only the toddler to watch. But then, Naomi Eisin, née Helfman, Hannah's first friend, always wanted to talk about something. After Papa died, when Hannah and Mama moved into the same building as the Helfmans, Naomi would stop in every day. Their friendship blossomed when Hannah switched from public school to Naomi's Jewish school and they became classmates. Hannah was glad to help her with secular subjects while Naomi tutored Hannah in Hebrew.

Once Mama married Sam Eisin and he, with son Dovid, moved into their apartment, it wasn't long before Naomi set her sights on Hannah's new stepbrother. Hannah could see that Dovid, a yeshiva student whose head was continually buried in the Talmud, didn't stand a chance against the determined redhead who lived upstairs. She was happy to serve as Naomi's bridesmaid when the couple married during Dovid's last year at Spektor and was delighted when they moved in around the corner.

Hannah had accepted that their friendship would wane as she attended college and summered in Israel while Naomi had three children in six years.

But to Hannah's relief, they grew closer once she returned to living with her parents. Naomi was still a pleasure to be with, as friendly and good-natured as a puppy, with a talent for finding out what people were hoping to keep private and then telling everyone about it. Hannah wouldn't call Naomi a gossip. Naomi had only good things to say about others and never shared anything bad unless it was to let folks know that someone was ill or otherwise needed help. She didn't spread rumors, only information she knew was true.

So Hannah reluctantly hid her studies with Nathan from her friend. As her feelings for him grew, she would have liked to talk with Naomi about them, but sadly, she couldn't trust her to keep them secret.

As usual, the door was unlocked and Naomi was in the kitchen. "Avi and the baby are with my mother this morning, so we can talk in peace," she said, setting out the two steaming cups.

"So, *nu*?" Hannah realized her friend must have something important to impart to arrange for all three children to be away.

"Remember how I told you the neighbors were looking to buy a house out on Long Island?" She didn't wait for Hannah, who had a vague recollection of this, to reply but continued. "They gave notice and are moving out on January first. So I need your help, Annie."

"What for?"

"Every time I eat at your place, I wish I had a nice new kitchen." Naomi put down her cup and grinned. "Now, with a little assistance on your part, I can."

Bewildered, Hannah stared at her. "From me?"

"Once the next-door unit is vacant, we can renovate our kitchen and use the other one in the meantime." She was so excited she couldn't sit still. "Then, when it's finished, we can do the other kitchen too. Think of the fun we'll have, you and me, shopping together for appliances, cabinets, new flooring."

Hannah easily read Naomi's intention that the two of them could more readily convince Dad to finance the remodel if it were for both units. After all, his original intent in buying the duplex was for Dovid's family to live on one side and Hannah's on the other.

"Sounds good to me, but I think we should get Mama on our side first. Dad will find it hard to refuse all three of us, especially when we point out how it will bring in higher rent."

"You're actually going to help me?" Naomi gave Hannah a hug. "And I was so worried how I'd convince you."

Hannah wasn't surprised when Naomi wasted no time and came over that evening. Mama regarded Hannah suspiciously when the two made their appeal, but to Hannah's relief, Mama acquiesced without questions. "I expect the contractor will give Sam a big discount for doing both kitchens."

Dad nodded sagely as Mama outlined the proposal, and then he turned to Naomi, "While I agree that this would be a good investment, I must insist that I be the one to choose the contractors and deal with them."

Mama had the last word. "If Naomi wants her kitchen finished before Pesach, she and Annie should decide on every item the contractor will need well before he needs them. There will be enough other delays we can't avoid."

Hannah walked Naomi home, listening to her friend babble about how happy she felt. "I can't wait to finally have an automatic dishwasher," Naomi said as she hugged Hannah goodbye at her stoop. "Oh, Annie, I can't thank you enough."

On her way back, Hannah imagined how sweet it would be to marry Nathan and move into the new apartment. But then, realizing how pernicious dwelling on such a fantasy could be, she returned to reality.

The Hanukah candles were still burning at the Stocksers' and, his stomach comfortably full of Sharon's excellent latkes, Nathan leaned across the small table to address Benny. "Are you ready to discuss the legality of teaching a woman Talmud?"

Benny, grinning, looked eager for their dispute. "Since Sharon has expressed interest in the subject, I suggest we quote our sources rather than just name them."

Nathan smiled back. Benny had a photographic memory, which gave him an encyclopedic knowledge of not only the Talmud but also all the codes that came later. While this would normally give Benny an insurmountable advantage, he probably hadn't studied the laws of women studying Torah in years. Now, with so many women attending college and entering professions, there were new rulings, ones Benny might not be familiar with. And it was the most recent rulings that mattered most.

"I think we can concur that the disagreement starts in how the Talmud interprets Deuteronomy 11:19, 'And you shall teach them diligently to your sons—*beneichem*'—which Rashi informs us means *not* teaching your daughters," Nathan began.

Benny nodded and proceeded to sum up the pertinent texts from the Talmud. "In Kiddushin we learn that in regard to girls, since the father has no obligation to teach her Torah, she is not obligated to learn Torah either. And in Sotah, while Ben Azzai says a father should teach his daughter Torah, Rav Eliezer protests that it would be teaching her tiflut." He turned to Sharon. "Which can be translated as 'lechery' or 'frivolity,' but in either case, it is a bad thing."

"Rashi and Maimonides agree that women are not commanded to study Torah but are free to do so if they wish," Nathan countered. "The BaCH commenting on the RoSh declares that while there is no obligation to teach women Torah, there is no prohibition either. Furthermore, RaShaSh holds that since the Talmud informs us that, because there is no requirement to teach women, it can be inferred that a woman is obligated to study and teach herself."

Sharon nodded in agreement, but Benny shook his head. "The Birkei Yosef explains that Jewish law codes are unanimous that in this controversy between Ben Azzai and Rabbi Eliezer, we accept the opinion of Rabbi Eliezer as binding." He then began quoting from the *Shulchan Aruch* as if the page were in front of him. "Yoreh Deah 246:6 says that a woman who studies Torah receives a reward, but not like that of a man, because she fulfills the mitzvah while not obligated. And though she does earn a reward, our rabbis have commanded that one should not teach his daughter Torah, because the majority of women are not intellectually prepared to be taught, due to their minds' limitations."

Sharon scowled, but Benny kept reciting. "The rabbis said: One who teaches his daughter Torah is as if he taught her tiflut. With what is this stated? With regards to the Oral Torah. However, in regard to the Written Torah one should preferably not teach her, but if he did so it is not tiflut."

Nathan was well aware that the *Shulchan Aruch*, though written in the sixteenth century, was still the legal authority for Orthodox Jews. But some later scholars found ways to get around its medieval edicts. "*Igrot Ha-Reiyah* says the prohibition only applies to teaching, but she may learn by herself by listening to others. *Tuv Ayyin* tells us that Bruriah was taught because it was recognized that her heart was firmly set on study and because of her remarkable intelligence," he shot back. "*Torah Temimah* restricts the proscription to teaching a young daughter, whereas an older daughter who takes the initiative in Torah study may be taught by others."

"I will grant you that in certain cases it is permitted to teach women Torah," Benny acquiesced. "But Samson Raphael Hirsch says that women should not pursue advanced Torah learning and scientific study of halacha since such scholarship is the function of men." He frowned and locked eyes with Nathan. "Which is probably what you are teaching your student."

Nathan couldn't deny Benny's accusation, but he had two other twentieth-century scholars who disagreed with Hirsch. "Chafetz Chayim tells us that nowadays, when we find that young women regularly study secular subjects, it is certainly a mitzvah to teach them Bible and rabbinic ethics as in the Tractate Avot and so on. Otherwise they may stray from God's path and transgress."

"I am familiar with that argument," Benny said, clearly not convinced.

Nathan played his final card, an opinion so recent Benny hopefully didn't know it. "Malka in *Responsa Mikveh ha-Mayim* points out that modern women play a significant role in society: managing offices and businesses, filling the universities, conducting scientific research, participating in government and political affairs." He smiled at Benny and concluded. "He says that surely Rabbi Eliezer would now waive his ban on teaching women even the Oral Law so they might carefully observe all Torah laws affecting their activities and employment."

While Benny paused to consider this, Nathan congratulated himself for finding a text that stopped his friend in his tracks.

"Your unnamed student—I will call her Miss Plonia—is undoubtedly a modern woman of remarkable intelligence who has taken the initiative in Torah study," Benny suggested.

Nathan couldn't help smiling at Benny feminizing the name "Plony," which Talmud gives anonymous men, like John Doe in English. "Indeed she is, with a MA from Columbia."

With the debate slowing, Sharon interjected, "Wait a minute. It seems to me that no matter what all these rabbis say, the whole thing comes down to translating *beneichem* as 'sons' rather than 'children.'" She glared at Benny and Nathan, "Despite all the places in the Torah where *beneichem* clearly does mean children."

"You hit the nail on the head." Nathan had studied logic in college and knew Benny could not refute his next statement. "Any argument that depends on a false hypothesis cannot lead to a true conclusion."

"Logic has nothing to do with it," Benny insisted. "The majority opinion forbids teaching women Talmud."

"You do realize that we have just taught Sharon some of it."

"It is permissible to teach one's own wife if he deems her capable." Now Benny stared hard at Nathan. "However, even if it were permitted to teach Talmud to capable women, you have clearly violated halacha by being secluded with Miss Plonia—not once but many times."

Nathan shrugged. Benny was right about that.

Benny's expression softened. "Sharon tells me that you are in love with your student."

To Nathan's surprise, and embarrassment, tears welled in his eyes. "I'm afraid so."

"Of course you are." Benny spoke in his psychologist voice. "You could not have picked a better situation to make you fall in love. For months the two of you have been meeting secretly, in private, engaged in a forbidden and risky, albeit exciting, activity."

Nathan considered this for a while before sighing in agreement and quoting from Proverbs. "Stolen waters are sweet and bread eaten in secret is delicious." Then he brightened. "In which case, she should have fallen in love with me as well."

"I have been giving this matter some thought," Benny said. "You say you cannot approach her because you are the teacher and she would feel intimidated and pressured, which would ruin your studies?" When Nathan nodded, Benny continued. "However, what if she returns your affection but does not approach you because she is afraid you will be offended and stop teaching her?"

"She is a career woman who gave up the one man she loved for her profession and hasn't dated anyone else since college."

"But that doesn't mean she doesn't love you, Nathan," Sharon encouraged him. "Especially since she's so eager to study with you."

"I have a suggestion," Benny said. "Why not choose a section of Talmud that has to do with marriage? Maybe something from Ketubot? See what her reaction is."

During the lengthy cab ride back to Williamsburg, Nathan's pleasure at having bested Benny in their Talmud debate gave way to ire at how unfair some halacha was to women. It was forbidden to teach them Talmud, the cornerstone of Jewish learning, because they were "light-headed," yet Nathan had studied with, and taught, plenty of males for whom light-headed would be high praise. Even so, men were commanded to study Torah and women prohibited. And worse, it was downright cruel that halacha made divorce one-sided, forcing women to stay married to men they hated or who deserted or mistreated them.

He remembered Hannah's argument about slavery. A hundred years ago in America, there were laws making it illegal to harbor escaped slaves. Yet twenty years later, those laws were repealed and slavery prohibited. But according to Orthodoxy, God made Jewish Law, and no man possessed the authority to repeal it. Halacha was immutable. Nathan's anger slowly turned inward. Abolitionists protested against slavery, and some braver souls risked imprisonment, or worse, to run the Underground Railroad. But he was too craven to make his opinion public. All he could do was continue to violate halacha in secret.

But Nathan took Benny's advice the very next time he and Hannah studied together. It was still Hanukah, and she was in an excellent mood from the praise her OU article had received. Still, he was so nervous he had to keep his hand from trembling as he lit the candles. But just before Hannah left, he got up the courage to suggest that they study Tractate Ketubot next. He would let her know which sugya to prepare when they talked on Saturday.

As usual before beginning a new text, Hannah wanted to get a quick overview in advance. Her stomach tightened immediately upon reading the Mishnah. "A virgin is married on Wednesday and a widow on Thursday. The reason for the former is that courts convene in towns twice a week, on Monday and Thursday. So if the husband has a complaint concerning the bride's virginity after consummating the marriage on Wednesday night, he can go to court early the next day and make his claim."

She didn't need to read any more Gemara to know that she couldn't possibly study this section with Nathan. Not this one or any other having to do with a bride's lack of virginity.

As the time of their weekly Saturday-evening phone call approached, Hannah grew increasingly nervous about how she'd ask Nathan to study something else. She practiced several versions, but it only made her more afraid that he would want to know why. She couldn't blame her reluctance on modesty or embarrassment over the subject, not when they had already talked about child molestation. But she couldn't tell him the truth.

When the telephone finally rang, she startled as if touched by a live wire and didn't wait to exchange pleasantries. "Nathan, I have a favor I need you to do for me." She hoped her voice wasn't shaking so much that he would notice.

He knew immediately she was upset about something, but if she wasn't going to tell him what it was, he wasn't about to ask. Instead, he replied calmly, "I will if I can."

"Could we please study some other piece of Talmud?"

She had spoken so fast that Nathan had to ask her to repeat herself. Then, once she did, he slumped back against the wall as if the wind had been knocked out of him. So much for slowly probing to discover how she felt about marriage, not when she was so frightened of learning Ketubot with him.

"Nathan, are you still there?" she asked anxiously.

"Yes, I'm here. I'm trying to think of what we should study instead." But his brain seemed frozen.

Her sigh of relief came over the line loud and clear.

Suddenly he had it. "There's a sugya in Tractate Shabbos that, in the middle of debating what oils and wicks to use for the Shabbos lamp abruptly switches to discuss Hanukah," he said. "It's not as easy as other holiday tractates, but you should be able to handle it."

"I don't recall any Mishnah in Tractate Shabbos about Hanukah," she said slowly. She was pretty sure Hanukah wasn't mentioned in another Mishnah either.

"It's not. We only know about Hanukah from the Gemara," he replied. "Hold on while I look up exactly where to start."

Hannah closed her eyes and relaxed. She was saved. Nathan had agreed to her request without expressing any curiosity about her motive. A wave of gratitude washed over her.

He was back on the line in a few minutes. "The Gemara starts on the third line from the bottom of page 21a."

"Let me get Dad's copy and make sure I can find the place." She returned with the volume and scanned the page. "I see it."

"I think you'll find it very interesting."

"Now I have another request for you." *This is my opportunity to be bold, but will he appreciate my invitation or feel burdened by it?*

"I'm all ears, Annie." *Oy, what now?*

"My family is going to Florida for two weeks for winter vacation, and I was wondering . . ." She hesitated and then hurriedly concluded, "Maybe we could study together in the morning at my house, instead of in the evening at yours. And, if you have time, more than two days a week."

Nathan was so astounded he didn't know what to say.

When he remained silent, Hannah sweetened her offer. "I'll make matzah brei for you. You've been giving me dinner twice a week for months, so it's only fair I return the favor."

Nathan didn't need any extra incentives. "My father expects me to study with him on Shabbos, but I should be able to come over Sunday through Friday."

"Friday morning I need to be at work to get the weekend edition ready, but Sunday through Thursday should be fine. Does ten o'clock work for you?" The last two weeks of December were always slow at the *Freiheit*; she'd just have to wake early and pick up her assignments before Nathan came over.

"Ten is fine." He couldn't believe this was happening. She wanted to study with him five days a week; it was a miracle.

"I'm so excited that we'll be studying together almost every day. I really appreciate your letting me take up so much of your time."

When they finally hung up, Nathan felt whipsawed like when he'd begun to cross the street and, seemingly out of nowhere, a speeding taxi hurtled around the corner. He'd jumped back onto the curb in the nick of time and marveled at how quickly he had gone from terrified to relieved and jubilant. Hannah might not be interested in marriage, but she certainly wanted to study Talmud with him.

The day Hannah's family left for Miami, Brooklyn temperatures dropped precipitously. Bundled in his wool scarf and winter coat, Nathan told Abba that he had a student to tutor and would be home in the early afternoon. The weather stayed below freezing for two weeks, but Nathan sat with Hannah at her family's warm dining table, flames crackling in the fireplace and plates of matzah brei in front of them. One day she was wearing gray slacks and a fluffy yellow sweater that his hands longed to stroke. But he kept one hand following the text in front of him and the other tightly gripping his coffee cup.

Hannah was eager to learn how the Talmudic rabbis created the festival of Hanukah, for it obviously wasn't in the Torah. Her Communist parents ignored religious holidays, so it wasn't until she began attending the Torah Academy that she'd heard about Hanukah. After Mama married Dad, it quickly became her favorite. Everything about Hanukah happened at home, where girls and women participated equally with the boys and men. At the Eisins', there was fun for an entire week, with lots of singing, games, and lighting the menorah each night.

Oddly, Aunt Elizabeth was the one who told Hannah about the two Books of Maccabees in the Apocrypha, which contained the familiar tale of Judah Maccabee and his comrades defeating the Greeks and expelling them from the Holy Temple. To her surprise, and puzzlement, neither book mentioned the Hanukah miracle, where one small bottle of oil kept the Temple's lamp burning for eight days. Yet, according to what she'd been taught in her Jewish school, that miracle was the reason behind the eight-night candle-lighting ritual.

Sitting next to Nathan, she eagerly read the Gemara's debate over which was the mitzvah of Hanukah—lighting a lamp for eight nights or placing the lamp where passersby could see it to publicize the miracle.

"I love how Yehoshua ben Levi answers the question by pointing out that only the blessing for kindling the Hanukah lamp uses the word '*vetzivanu*'—commanded us. The blessing for seeing it does not," she enthused. "It's a great example of Talmudic logic."

"As well as one that doesn't rely on a biblical proof text," Nathan pointed out.

"Oh. Here's where he declares that women are obligated to kindle the Hanukah lamp, for they too participated in the miracle." As she read further, her excitement lessened until all she felt was puzzlement. "But nobody explains what the miracle was."

"Don't worry. The Gemara will do so eventually," Nathan assured her.

Each day Hannah asked him how soon they would study that part, but Nathan, enjoying her impatience, would only tease her by replying, "Soon."

It was almost New Year's Eve, when Nathan started grinning during a discussion over where to place the lamp, that Hannah knew her wait was over. Sure enough, in the middle of that debate, the Gemara abruptly asks, "*Mai Hanukah?*" (Why/what is Hanukah?) She could barely contain her delight when the question was answered by describing how, after the Hasmoneans vanquished the Greeks, they found all the Temple's pure oil defiled except for one small flask. But miraculously, its contents burned for eight days until new oil was obtained, and the festival was established in commemoration.

"Amazing," she gushed. "I've always wondered where the Hanukah story with the one day's worth of oil lasting eight days originated, and here it is in the Talmud."

"What's amazing is how little difficulty you've had understanding this sugya."

"That's because you're such an excellent teacher."

Nathan could feel his face warming in response to her praise. "I think you're ready for some advanced study," he said. "Let's go back to the broche for lighting the Hanukah lamp. Does the wording seem familiar?"

Eager to tackle a section he considered advanced, Hannah smiled. "It's almost the same blessing as for lighting the Shabbos candles."

"You're absolutely right." He was pleased and relieved that she'd recognized the similarity. "Now look at the Gemara's question that follows: 'And where did He command us?'"

She thought about this so long that Nathan began to worry he'd expected too much from her. He was about to offer a hint when she looked up at him, her eyes bright with comprehension.

"Of course. How can we bless lighting the menorah with 'vetzivanu' when there's no commandment in the Torah to do so?" she asked. The approval on Nathan's face told her in more than words that she was correct. When he confirmed this by gesturing for her to read further, she continued.

"Rav Nehemya says this is derived from the verse in Deuteronomy 'Ask your father and he will inform you, your Elders, and they will tell you.'"

What? How does that answer the Gemara's question?

Nathan knew she'd be perplexed. "This is one of the most important texts in the Talmud, where the Gemara questions how the Rabbis got the authority to enact new laws and call them mitzvos." He challenged her. "What do you think of Rav Nehemya's answer?"

They'd been studying together long enough that she could boldly reply, "That proof text about listening to what your fathers tell you is not very convincing."

"Agreed. But it's the best Torah text the Sages could come up with to justify their mandate."

"After the fact," she pointed out, disappointed that the Sages couldn't do better.

"The important thing, at least in my opinion, is that they're honest enough to question how they gained their authority. Not that they intend to relinquish it." He helped himself to more matzah brei and let her think about this for a while. "Now let's go back to blessing the Shabbos candles. Do you think that mitzvah is d'oraita or derabanan?"

"Hmm. I'm pretty sure there's no place in the Torah where God commands anyone to light a lamp for Shabbos," she said slowly. "So, like Hanukah, it must be derabanan."

He chuckled and shook his head. "While the Talmudic sages discuss various Shabbos rituals and their blessings, like Kiddush and Havdalah, for example, it never even hints at a special ritual for lighting the Shabbos lamp. Their main concern is that it be lit before sunset."

"But the Mishnah says women die in childbirth—"

"For neglecting the Shabbos lamp," he interrupted. "Which means either that she didn't light it in time, so her family has to eat dinner in the dark, or that she violated halacha by kindling a flame after Shabbos began. It doesn't say anything about it being a mitzvah. Rashi is the one who tells us that."

Intrigued, she found the corresponding commentary. "Rashi says, 'Regarding the Shabbos lamp, as it is written in Proverbs, "For the lamp is a mitzvah and the Torah is a light." By observing the mitzvah of kindling a lamp on Shabbos and Hanukah, one brings the light of Torah into the world.'" She stopped to think. "All right. Rashi calls it a mitzvah, but he doesn't mention a blessing. So where did the broche come from?"

"Where indeed?" Nathan echoed her question, then pointed to the Tosafos.

"Ah. Rabbenu Tam agrees lighting the lamp is a mitzvah and says one should make the blessing when doing it." She spoke slowly, laying out her logical progression. "So we know they're saying it in twelfth-century France. But he doesn't tell us what the blessing is." Her face fell with disappointment.

Nathan's doctorate in Jewish history had never been more useful. "The blessing, the same one we say today, first appears in a ninth-century Babylonian siddur, which instructs the shammes to say it when he lights the synagogue lamps on Friday afternoon."

"But what about saying it at home?" Hannah could see by his look of confidence that he knew the answer to this question as well.

"I looked in *Machzor Vitry*." He was delighted with both their discussion and her matzah brei. "It not only gives us the blessing to make when lighting the Shabbos lamp, but it explains why we can use the word 'vetzivanu' in this situation."

Hannah thought on this while they cleared the table. "Incredible. I always assumed the Shabbos broche is the original and the Hanukah broche the derivative, but you say it's the other way around."

"That's right. The Hanukah broche is hundreds of years older than the one for Shabbos."

They worked as a team in the kitchen, Nathan rinsing the dishes and Hannah loading the dishwasher. When the last item was inside, Hannah was overflowing with happiness. Nathan had not only shown her the Talmudic origin of the Hanukah lamp miracle, but he'd also shared the practically unknown history of the Shabbos-candle-lighting ritual and blessing. And under his guidance, she'd successfully negotiated what he considered an advanced Talmud text.

With a wide smile, she stretched out her arms and took a step toward him. "I can't thank you enough, Nathan, for all the amazing things you've taught me."

At first he was rooted to the spot. *Gottenyu, she wants to hug me.* But just as he began to raise his arms in return, the doorbell rang.

They both stepped back, and Nathan looked at her in alarm.

"Let me see who it is." She walked quietly to the living room, peeked out the window, and hastily returned. "Oh no, it's my sister-in-law, Naomi. If she finds you here, the whole world will know." Hannah spent most weekday afternoons with Naomi shopping for their new kitchens. Her friend was right about all the labor-saving devices to be found in a modern kitchen, and it took time to choose the right ones. *Why is Naomi here so early?*

He grabbed an armful of books. "Where should I go?"

"Upstairs. I'll get you when she's gone."

Nathan raced up the stairs and put the books on a table at the second-floor landing. Naomi seemed to be in a panic about some faucet being out of stock. Afraid they might come upstairs to the bathroom, he tiptoed up to the third floor. He could still hear the women's voices below, but he could no longer tell what they were saying. Still, to be cautious, he ducked into one of the rooms. He was slowly closing the door when he noticed the door harp and, just in time, grabbed the balls to muffle them.

He was in Hannah's bedroom.

Her purse and notebook were on the desk. He surveyed the sunlit room, taking in the twin beds, a framed photo of horses on a beach on the wall between them, and the full bookcases. He was impressed that, in addition to the classics one would expect from an English major, there were many of Isaac Goren's works.

Then he noticed a thick book on the bottom shelf with a brown paper cover like the ones they made to protect textbooks in school. Curious, he picked it up, opened it to the title page, and then nearly dropped it. It was Alfred Kinsey's *Sexual Behavior in the Human Female*, and it had obviously been well read. He was greatly tempted to open it to one of the many dog-eared pages but was afraid what might happen if Hannah caught him with it.

He quickly replaced it and, turning to a shelf that held photo albums, picked one at random. When he saw that it contained pictures labeled *Israel—1952*, he sat down in the very comfortable armchair near the window and opened the first page. Soon his heartbeat returned to normal.

He was perusing album *Israel—1954* when Hannah found him. "You can come back down now," she said, "but we can't study any longer today." She scowled with annoyance. "I have to go with Naomi to the plumbing store."

"I should be able to stay longer tomorrow if you'd like," he suggested. "Then we can finish this section."

"And have lunch together," she added.

Nathan took a deep breath. "But I won't be able to call you Saturday night. I'll be out dancing." As soon as the words were out of his mouth, he regretted them.

"Of course. It's New Year's Eve." She was silent for a while, her mind goading her to ask him which dance hall he was going to, to suggest that she could meet him there. But her courage failed. "My family is coming back on January second, so I expect we'll resume our Tuesday, Thursday evenings schedule then," she said instead, trying to hide her regret.

He too was feeling down, but he was determined to leave on a positive note. "I was so impressed at how easily you learned this sugya that I think you're ready to study the lengthy one in Tractate Kiddushin, where the Rabbis debate what constitutes a time-bound positive mitzvah and why women are exempt from fulfilling them."

She managed a smile and walked with him to the foyer. The magical moment when she'd almost hugged him had passed. The most she could do now was clasp his hands and shake them as she said, "I'll see you tomorrow, then."

On his cab ride home, Nathan mentally kicked himself for his rudeness. How could he mention he was going dancing on New Year's Eve and not ask Hannah to join him? *Why am I such a coward?*

On New Year's Eve Hannah agreed to go dancing with a couple of girl-friends from the *Freiheit*, but to her disappointment, they didn't encounter Nathan.

Nathan went out dancing Saturday and Sunday nights, though none of the women interested him. Still, he felt he needed to rekindle his social life.

On January 2, during a seemingly interminable wait to verify that all the kitchen items they needed were still available, Hannah was surprised by Naomi complaining about the unequal legal position of Jewish women. Her friend had never shown any interest in such religious controversies before.

"I heard Tateh and Dovid mention that after publishing nothing for eight years, Mordecai Kaplan has a new book out," Naomi began. "They were pretty critical, so I decided to read his previous one to see what they were so upset about."

Hannah admitted that she'd never read anything by the infamous Orthodox rabbi reviled for his naturalistic theology. Though she did admire him for giving his daughter a bat mitzvah thirty years ago.

"There was a lot I disagreed with and a lot I didn't understand, but I can understand why the Union of Orthodox Rabbis excommunicated him when he said the Torah was written by men, not God. Even so, I agree with Kaplan about the inferior status of women in Jewish Law."

"What does Kaplan say about women?" Hannah was curious about both Kaplan's opinions and Naomi's.

"First, he points out that traditionally, women are on the same plane as children, slaves, and people of unsound mind." Naomi's tone made her disapproval clear.

Hannah knew this from her studies. But she didn't want to argue with Naomi by saying that she too thought men, albeit divinely inspired, had written the Torah. So she asked, "How so?"

"Women are not counted in a minyan and are exempt from all sorts of mitzvos done at a specific time. They are not only exempt from Torah study, but the father who teaches his daughter Torah is regarded as if he'd taught her frivolity."

Hannah fought the urge to tell her best friend that she had actually been studying Talmud just a few days earlier. "I assume Kaplan objects to this view," Hannah said instead.

"Of course he does, but honestly, it doesn't really affect me. I'm sure God hears me, and my children, when we say the bedtime Shema just as well as He hears Dovid. And my father taught me Torah; he taught Torah to all the girls at school."

"But nobody taught girls Talmud." Hannah allowed some irritation in her voice.

"Believe me, after living with a man who spends every spare minute studying Talmud, I'm happy to be exempt." Naomi frowned. "But Kaplan reserves his greatest criticism for the Jewish woman's inferior marital status." She didn't wait for Hannah to speak but hurriedly continued, her voice rising with each complaint. "Whatever the wife earns or finds belongs to her husband, and if she dies during his lifetime, he inherits everything from her, while if he dies first, she inherits nothing."

"That's not the law in New York." *Maybe I should suggest to Nathan that we study what the Talmud says about marriage. He might get the hint. Plus, I'll learn something even more important and useful than the history of the Hanukah and Shabbos lights.*

"Thank goodness for that, but chas v'chalila a Jewish couple want to end their marriage." Naomi's eyes blazed with fury. "Only a husband has the power of divorce. He can divorce his wife without her consent or refuse her a divorce if she wants one. And if he deserts her or disappears, she's left in limbo—a married woman without a husband. It happened to a woman I know, whose husband never came back from the war."

Hannah was trying to control her anger when she had a horrifying thought. "It's a good thing my father wasn't Jewish. He was killed by a grenade, and they never found his body," she said slowly. "If he'd been Jewish, my mother would have been forbidden to remarry."

Shoppers were staring at them, so Naomi's voice dropped to a whisper. "Even worse is the poor childless widow who can't remarry unless one of her husband's brothers releases her. You know, from the laws of levirate marriage in Deuteronomy."

"They still follow that today? But it's absurd."

"You think that's bad—if the brother can't be found or won't do it, she's stuck."

Hannah was appalled. "Gottenyu, that's what happened to Miriam at the *Freiheit*," she blurted out. "She got married right after Pearl Harbor and didn't get a chance to have any children before he was killed. I heard her in the ladies' room telling an editor that her ex-brother-in-law was demanding too much money to release her. Our boss offered to help her pay, but she refused to be extorted."

Before Naomi could reply, a salesman confirmed that every item their contractor ordered had arrived. Then Hannah asked what Kaplan said to do about this.

Naomi sighed. "He doesn't expect Orthodox rabbis to change the law. He says Jewish women themselves must rise up and demand equality."

"That'll be the day." Hannah was too disgusted to say more.

They drove home in silence, but Hannah couldn't help thinking that less-observant women in those situations could marry a secular or Reform Jew. Or even a non-Jew.

TEN

RELUCTANT TO ADMIT how quickly Hannah had repudiated Benny's idea to study Ketubot, Nathan put off seeing his friend until late January, when Sharon practically had to beg him to come to dinner. But Benny was too preoccupied with his own difficulties to discuss Miss Plonia.

"I went into psychology expecting to help disturbed patients." His eyes blinked with anxiety. "I thought I had a unique insight into a child's suffering that could help me alleviate it."

"But you do," Nathan reassured him. Besides the twitching, there were dark circles under Benny's eyes. Only in the black days, when Joey was resisting therapy, had Nathan seen him so discouraged.

"I have several molested Haredi boys among my patients and now a few girls too," Benny said. "I begin by talking about why they're seeing me, what crisis prompted their parents to consult me. Most children, sooner or later, admit there is a problem, at which point we can move on to the delicate and difficult task of getting them to tell me what happened."

Benny grew silent, so Sharon addressed Nathan. "Molesters usually make their victims promise not to tell anyone or threaten them with dire consequences if they do."

Benny quickly responded. "I am confident that I can work with these children so they eventually will no longer feel guilt or shame, so they understand that what happened is not their fault and that they have not been tainted or stained in any way." He shook his head. "But first they have to trust me enough to confide in me, and few have made that breakthrough. Yet even assuming a breakthrough happens, I still have to help them manage their anger and sense of betrayal," he said. "But how can I do that when I cannot control my own?"

Nathan felt the pain he could see in his friend's eyes. "I think anger and betrayal are completely appropriate responses," he said.

"That may be true, but dwelling on them injures the soul," Benny replied. "After all, it is unlikely that an abuser will seek forgiveness. Though I would truly like to have one as a patient."

128

"I don't know which is worse for Benny," Sharon said. "That an apparently religious man can do these evil things or that pious people can let such abuse continue because they're afraid exposing it will bring shame on the community."

"You see how it is exactly my unique viewpoint that makes things difficult for me." Benny's voice rose in frustration. "I am the son of a rebbe, a tzaddik. How am I supposed to feel when I learn that this tutor has been active for many years and nothing was done except to move him to new schools, where he found new victims? How am I supposed to feel when I realize the *rabbonim* know about these abusers and place their well-being above that of the children?"

"I imagine your patients would take comfort that you also feel angry and betrayed by what happened to them," Nathan said. "Perhaps you could share your own efforts to deal with these feelings."

"Perhaps, but that would be sometime in the future." Benny leaned forward and turned to Nathan. "So, *nu?* How did it go studying Ketubot with Miss Plonia?"

"Not well, I'm afraid. It took less than a day after I told her we'd be learning Ketubot next that she phoned and asked me to choose another text." Nathan sighed. "So we studied the sugya on Hanukah instead."

"You didn't pick out a romantic section to start with. You merely told her the tractate?" When Nathan nodded, Benny rolled his eyes. "Any woman would have trouble with the beginning of Ketubot." He turned to Sharon and explained, "It deals with how a groom makes a complaint in court if he thinks his new bride is not a virgin."

"Oy," Nathan moaned. How could he have been so stupid? How had he not considered that she'd assume they'd start at the beginning? Why hadn't he looked at the text first? No wonder they didn't teach this piece of Talmud in yeshiva.

"But she's continued to study with you?" Sharon asked. "Right?"

"Yes." Nathan explained how they studied together every day for two weeks while her family was away, at her suggestion.

After grinning at each other, Benny and Sharon turned and smiled at him.

He smiled back. *Maybe there's still hope.*

Shortly before lunch Nathan's secretary knocked on his office door and, when she entered, he immediately wondered who had died.

"The dean wants to see you in his office at your earliest convenience." She looked down, where she was wringing her hands, and abruptly separated them. "He didn't say why."

Trying to appear unconcerned, Nathan slowly stood up and straightened his tie. Until that moment he had been in a good mood. As he'd hoped, Hannah made an excellent study partner for learning about women and time-bound positive mitzvos, forcing him to think deeply about the conflicts. He was very much looking forward to seeing her that evening.

Soon he was sitting opposite the dean, who glowered at Nathan like a principle with an errant pupil. Glare from the midday sun streaming in from the window behind the dean made Nathan even more uncomfortable.

"Rav Mandel, the trustees and faculty are pleased with your teaching. Even Rav Klein has no complaints." The dean's voice did not sound like he was pleased with Nathan. "However, there is a distasteful matter that has come to my attention."

Nathan swallowed hard. "Which is?"

The dean leaned forward and locked eyes with him. "We have received reports that an attractive young woman, apparently a shikse, regularly visits you alone in the evening for several hours at a time."

Nathan's heart was pounding so hard he was sure the dean must have heard it. After nearly a year during which he'd grown less and less worried about being caught with Hannah, the moment of denouement had come. He bristled and decided the best defense was a good offense. "I demand to know who has been spying on me and spreading such defamations."

The dean, apparently expecting Nathan to explain, or better yet, deny the reports, scowled. "I am disappointed to surmise that the rumors are true, and it is with great unhappiness that I warn you that this illicit relationship must end if you want tenure."

"There is nothing illicit between us." Nathan tried to keep his voice down, but his anger was too strong. "She is my student."

The dean's eyes widened in shocked dismay. "You are teaching a woman . . . Talmud?" When Nathan nodded, he cringed. "Oy gevalt! This is even worse." He motioned for Nathan to leave. "I must consult the other rabbis and our trustees."

Nathan was so furiously caught up mentally replaying the dean's accusations that he didn't see Rav Klein gesturing to him from the open door. Rav Klein, like all professors at Spektor, had office hours, but Nathan had never utilized them as a student and didn't know anyone who had. He hesitated when he heard the "Psst, psst" sound, then looked around in confusion. When he saw Klein's gnarled hand curling toward him, more of an order to come in than an invitation, Nathan almost bolted.

But that would be disrespectful. There was enough antipathy between the two already. He entered and gazed in awe at the overflowing bookcases that covered every wall of Klein's office, with the exception of a small space holding his framed smicha certificate. The window was closed tight against the early February cold, and Nathan nearly choked on the combined smell of cigarette smoke and musty old books.

"Mandel." Klein still addressed Nathan by his last name, like when he'd been Klein's student. "The dean told me—"

"I don't need a *musar* message," Nathan interrupted. "Save your breath."

"So, it is true you were teaching this young woman Talmud?" There was no censure in Klein's voice, only curiosity.

Dismayed at who else might know, Nathan stiffened. "And I intend to continue teaching her. She's brilliant, asks altogether different kinds of questions, and why should she be denied Talmud learning?"

Klein took a long pull on his cigarette. "My wife, *zichrono livracha*, had no brothers, so her father, Rav Shlomo of Boguslov, taught her instead. After we married she asked to study with me, and once I discovered her quick mind, I was pleased to do so. She looked at Talmud differently—not improperly, mind you. I found studying with her refreshing."

Nathan was so astonished at Klein's admission that it took him a while to realize the man was waiting for him to speak. "Yes, it is different, and refreshing, to study with a woman with a quick mind."

Nathan hadn't meant to let any emotion color his reply, but Klein must have heard or seen something. "This young woman, you have feelings for her?"

Nathan could feel his cheeks flush as his face answered the question for him.

"You know, Mandel." Klein flicked the ash from his cigarette into a cracked cup. "No one could criticize you for studying with your wife."

"But ..." Nathan launched into all the reasons he didn't dare expose his affection and lamely concluded, "I'm afraid she'll reject me and I'll lose her."

Klein snorted in disbelief. "You, who weren't afraid to use text criticism in your smicha exam, are afraid to let this woman know you care for her?"

Ashamed, Nathan stared at the floor like Rav Klein's students did when they couldn't answer his Talmud questions.

His voice softened. "Mandel, remember how I urged my students to make choices for Torah?" When Nathan nodded, he continued. "You must make a decision very soon, and I think you know which choice would be for Torah."

Nathan took a deep breath and quoted the Hasidic master Nachman of Breslov. "All the world is a narrow bridge, and the important thing is not to succumb to fear."

Klein put his arm around Nathan's shoulders and walked him to the door. "Good. You know what to do. Don't forget: *Gelt farloren, gor nit farloren; mut farloren, alts farloren.*" (Money lost, nothing lost; courage lost, everything lost.)

Recalling that Klein's wife and daughters had been killed by Nazi stormtroopers, after which he'd never remarried, Nathan went to teach his three o'clock class determined to finally declare his love to Hannah.

When Nathan got home, however, he was more distraught than determined. Each scenario he imagined ended in Hannah repudiating him. When she arrived and asked about his day, his stammering reply gave away his distress.

"Whatever is the matter? Your father . . . ?" She couldn't imagine what else could have upset him so much.

He reluctantly confessed his confrontation with the dean. "But I won't stop teaching you. I'd rather resign and go be a pulpit rabbi than allow them to decide who I can teach."

Appalled, Hannah jumped up and fumbled for her notes. "It's not your decision. I won't allow you to ruin your career over this." She headed for the door. "You've taught me for almost a year, which is far longer than I expected, and I will always be grateful."

In a panic, Nathan grabbed her wrist to keep her from leaving. "Wait. Rav Klein suggested another solution."

That stopped her. She was abruptly aware of Nathan's fingers, warm and firm against her skin. "What advice, pray tell, did Rav Klein give you?" she asked.

He took a deep breath and let it out slowly. "He recommended that we get married." There, he'd said it.

Hannah froze. "Are you proposing to me? To save your career?"

"Not for that." *Gevalt, I'm losing her.* "I want to marry you because you're everything I want in a wife. You're smart and courageous and beautiful."

She turned and put her things back on the table.

Nathan had seen enough romantic movies to know what to do next. He dropped to one knee and took hold of her hand. "Hannah Covey Eisin, I love you. Will you marry me?"

Her face lit with happiness. "I was afraid you'd never ask."

Nathan couldn't believe his ears. "Does that mean yes?"

"Yes, Nathan Mandel, I will marry you."

Overcome with joy, and relief, Nathan didn't need a movie to direct his next move. He took her in his arms and kissed her. In his years of dating, he had kissed many girls good night after the requisite three dates. But never had he experienced anything like the passion in this one.

Hannah could count on one hand the number of men she'd kissed, yet she instinctively recognized that Nathan was a very good kisser. She reveled in the feeling of his lips on hers.

For a while time was suspended, and when their lips parted they continued to stare at each other in amazed wonder. Until they smelled something burning.

"Oy vey, the chicken." Nathan dashed to the kitchen and turned off the stove. Right behind him, Hannah poured water into the smoking pan. Soon they were eating the burned chicken without complaint, pausing to gaze at each other and grin.

Nathan was the first to break the silence. "You said you were afraid I'd never ask you to marry me. How long have you been waiting for me to do it?"

"I realized I was falling for you that day we met at the beach." *Had it really been five months ago?* "It was all I could do not to cry right then when you said you had a girlfriend."

"I'm sorry. I never imagined it would matter to you." His feelings toward her had changed at the same time, but he wasn't going to share how seeing her in that bathing suit had affected him. Not when he was trying to find an excuse to kiss her again.

"I wasn't sad for long," she continued. "After you told me you'd broken up with her and were taking a break from dating, I began to hope you might like me better."

"I did. In fact, the reason we broke up was that I could not get you off my mind." He shook his head in chagrin. "But you told me you hadn't dated anyone since college, so I thought you were a career woman. I was afraid to even ask you out."

"I am a career woman, and I intend to keep writing after we're married," she said. "But I stopped dating after college because the boys there only wanted one thing."

Of course Nathan wanted that too, but he chuckled and said, "Fortunately we've managed to get engaged without dating at all."

"We are actually engaged, aren't we?" she murmured in wonder.

"I certainly hope so. And with your talent as a wordsmith, it would be a shanda if you stopped writing." He put as much enthusiasm into his reply as he could, and Hannah's smile lit her entire face.

After clearing the dishes, which took longer because they kept stopping to steal kisses, they returned to the table to study. But they continually paused to gaze at each other.

Finally, Hannah gave up. "So, when do you want to get married?"

Nathan didn't need to think about it. "Tomorrow."

They both laughed until Hannah calmed enough to say, "Seriously, my family will want a big wedding, and there isn't enough time to organize one before Pesach."

"After Shavuos, then," he agreed. Legend had it that a plague had killed many of Rabbi Akiva's students between the two holidays. To memorialize their deaths, no Jewish weddings were held during those seven weeks.

Hannah rewarded him with another smile. "As soon as possible after Shavuos."

"I don't care if we marry in a wedding hall or a synagogue, whichever place can make it happen sooner."

Before they could discuss any details, the clock tolled once. Hannah stood up in alarm. "What? It's nine thirty already. I've got to go." Obviously, they'd missed the nine o'clock chimes.

"As long as it's this late, can't you wait a little longer until my father gets back so we can tell him together?" Nathan asked. "He'll be here any minute."

"I suppose so, but I should call home and tell them I'll be late."

He led her to the telephone and waited anxiously.

"Hi, Mama. . . . No, nothing's wrong. I'll just be a little late, that's all. . . . Don't worry. A girl in my class got engaged and we're celebrating. . . . I'll be fine. I'll take a cab, not the subway. . . . See you soon."

"A girl in your class got engaged and you're celebrating?" He looked at her in admiration and amusement.

"When I started studying with you, I told them I had a class that met on Tuesday and Thursday," she explained. "I wanted to say something, but I wouldn't lie."

"Your mother needn't worry about you traveling alone at night. Now that we're engaged, I'll be seeing you home."

Just then they heard a key in the front door lock. Solomon Mandel entered and was hanging up his coat when he turned and saw Hannah and Nathan standing next to each other, a bit closer together than mere acquaintances.

His eyes widened in surprise, but before he could speak, Nathan said, "You remember Hannah Eisin, Abba. Well, we've decided to get married."

Solomon looked in astonishment from Hannah's smiling face to his son's, then rushed to embrace him. "Mazel tov! Mazel tov! Come, let's have a toast."

"We don't have much time. Hannah has to get home."

"All right, when you're back." He hesitated and looked up at Nathan. "Before you go, tell me, have you chosen a ring?"

"We only just decided tonight," Nathan admitted.

"Please wait a little." Solomon disappeared into his bedroom and returned with a small box. "This was your mother's." He handed it to Nathan. "I've always hoped you could use it."

Nathan took out the ring, a sapphire surrounded by diamonds in a Victorian setting.

"It's beautiful," Hannah said, holding out her left hand for Nathan to slide it onto her ring finger. "It fits perfectly."

"Thank you, Abba. Thank you." He hugged his father again. He could scarcely believe that only a few hours ago, he'd been afraid he might never see Hannah again. Now she was wearing his engagement ring.

"Nathan," she said softly, reluctant to interrupt the emotional scene. "We should go. It's late." Then she turned to his father. "Now that we're almost family, please call me Annie."

The taxi was nearly at President Street when Hannah exclaimed, "Oh no, I left my Talmud notebook on the table."

"If you can live without it for two days, I'll bring it with me Saturday night." When she looked at him questioningly, he said, "Now that we're engaged, shouldn't we start dating?"

She giggled and asked, "What did you have in mind for our second date?"

"Our second date? Did we date already and I missed it?"

"At the World Series." She giggled again. "I'm pretty sure our fathers set us up. So it was sort of a blind date."

He knew exactly what to do for their first real date. "Dinner and dancing, of course. Assuming you know how to dance."

"I learned how in high school." She hesitated briefly. "I even went out dancing with some girlfriends New Year's Eve, hoping I'd run into you." She couldn't get over how long they'd been in love without the other knowing it.

Nathan was marveling at that too, when an alarming thought interrupted his pleasant reverie. "What are we going to tell our parents about how this came about? I can't see giving credit to Rav Klein."

"Mine know I take a class on Tuesday and Thursday, so I'll tell them you are the teacher," she said. "And that we wanted to keep our feelings about each other private."

"That's certainly true." Then a more alarming thought occurred to him. "Hannah, do you think your dad will be upset that I didn't ask his permission first?"

She scoffed. "This is the twentieth century, not the eighteenth, and we live in New York, not some Polish shtetl. I'm old enough to make my own decisions."

Nathan's reassured feeling disappeared when the cab pulled up to her house. The first floor was blazing with light. "It looks like we may be crossing that bridge sooner than expected."

Hannah squeezed his hand. "Don't worry. They'll be thrilled."

After they came in, Hannah left Nathan in the entry hall while she peeked into the living room. There they were—her dad, mother, and sister, all wearing robes over their pajamas and nightgowns. She took a deep breath and beckoned Nathan to join her.

"Mama, Dad, you remember Nathan Mandel."

That was as far as Hannah got before Rae cried out, "Look, Annie is wearing a ring."

Face flaming, she glared at her sister. "Rae, let me reintroduce you to Nathan Mandel, my fiancé."

Deborah burst into sobs and ran to embrace her, but Samuel looked askance.

"I apologize for not consulting you first, sir." Nathan tried to sound contrite. "But our engagement was rather sudden."

"It couldn't have been that sudden," Samuel pointed out. "My daughter has a ring."

"Sam, stop cross-examining Nathan like a trial lawyer," Deborah scolded him. "Our twenty-six-year-old daughter is finally getting married, and you know we couldn't ask for a finer son-in-law."

Hannah had the last word. "Dad, don't be so old-fashioned. Nobody needs to ask a father's permission anymore, only the woman's." She smiled fondly at Nathan. "And I have most definitely given Nathan mine."

Samuel reached out and shook Nathan's hand, then led him to the liquor cabinet. He poured out five drinks and held his glass up high. "A toast to the happy couple."

Everyone chimed in, "Mazel tov!"

Deborah didn't waste any time. "Nathan, you and your father must join us for Shabbos dinner."

"I'd like to, but my father can't walk that far," he replied. "And I'm taking Annie out on Saturday."

"Sunday, then," she said. "You can confirm the time when we see you Saturday."

"When were you thinking to get married?" Samuel asked.

"The soonest we can after Shavuos," Hannah replied.

"If you don't mind, I'd like to ask Rabbi Katz to check the shul's calendar when I go to minyan tomorrow morning."

Hannah and Nathan looked at each other and nodded.

"If I have good news, I'll call you."

Deborah elbowed her husband. "We should get to bed. You have an early court appearance tomorrow, and Rae has school." She clearly wanted to give Hannah and Nathan the opportunity to say their goodbyes in private.

Minutes later they were alone in the entry hall, locked in an impassioned embrace.

Nathan waltzed into the apartment to find his father perusing Hannah's notebook.

"I couldn't help but notice the Talmud sitting out and concluded that you'd been studying Kiddushin tonight," Abba said. "Yet these notes, not in your handwriting but written by someone who is clearly well versed in Talmud, forced me to conclude that you were not studying alone."

"I admit it." Nathan saw no reason to hide the obvious from his father, not now. "Annie and I study together, even though it violates halacha and I would be in big trouble if it were to become known. So we kept it secret; even her parents don't know."

"How long has this been going on?"

"Abba, we'd already been studying for months when you arranged for us to sit together at the World Series."

His father chuckled. "I guess the danger is over now that you're getting married, but I'm not happy that you hid something so important, and so risky, from me."

"You would have tried to dissuade me, and I didn't want to fight with you," Nathan explained. "By the way, the ring you gave me for Annie looks more expensive than you could have afforded. How did you get it?"

"I didn't buy it. Minnie's bubbe gave us hers," he replied. "She wanted Minnie's ring to be just as nice as her other granddaughters'. Minnie told me her bubbe was pleased to have a *chacham* in the family of merchants."

Nathan kvelled at the compliment to his father. "Before I forget, the Eisins want us to have dinner with them Sunday."

"I'm looking forward to it." Solomon yawned. "Now I need to get some sleep."

Nathan hugged Abba good night and got ready for bed. But sleep eluded him as he relived the details of this most amazing day—especially his and Annie's first kiss.

Hannah was too happy and too wound up to sleep. She couldn't stop fingering her ring as tangible evidence that she really was engaged. After much tossing and turning, she got up and, hoping an empty bladder would enable her to sleep, went to the bathroom.

Minutes later, Deborah softly knocked on her door. "I heard the toilet flush and figured you were awake." She sat down on the other bed. "Can we talk?"

Hannah wasn't going to sleep anyway. "Sure."

"Do you truly love Nathan, or are you marrying him because you're twenty-six and he's the best you've seen since college?"

"Mother! How can you ask such a question?"

"I'm sorry if I offended you, Annie. I'm just thinking of my own experiences," she replied. "Adam Blum wanted to marry me in Vienna, but I said no because I wanted to leave Europe and come to America, and I guess also because I didn't love him enough to stay. Then I met your father and fell hard. It was against everything I'd been taught . . ." Deborah stopped to think. "Perhaps partly because it was forbidden, we had a whirlwind romance and, believing in Communism and free love, we moved in together. When I got pregnant with you, we married."

"What about Dad?" Hannah asked. Papa had told her that all three men had loved Mama, but she'd chosen him.

"I was terribly lonely after your father died, and Sam had been a widower for years. I knew he was a good man who loved me and would treat me well. It's not the youthful passion I had for your father, but I've grown to love Sam more and more as the years have passed."

"Don't worry, Mama. The answer to your question is yes to both parts."

"Good. I hope he approves of your working," Deborah said. "I made it clear to Sam that I expected to continue at HIAS as long as they needed me."

"Nathan knows how important my writing career is."

"I'm glad. What worries me now is that so many couples want to marry right after Shavuos that our rabbis and all the nice locations will be taken."

"Well, there's nothing we can do about that tonight."

Hannah's mother kissed her good night and went back downstairs, leaving her daughter no less agitated than before. Hannah kept feeling her new ring to prove it was real, but as she focused on remembering Nathan's kisses, her thoughts became increasingly carnal. The Kinsey book had been educational, and it wasn't long until her hand reached down between her thighs to bring her relief.

The next morning Hannah pulled the pillow over her head to shut out the light and muffle the noise. The telephone had woken her before seven, and she'd managed only a little more sleep until the calls seemed to come nonstop. *Who are these people who feel entitled to call so early in the morning?*

She could hear excited female voices below, both Mama's and Naomi's, but there was an older woman's voice too, probably Tante Essie Helfman, Naomi's mother. Tante Essie was actually Dad's aunt, his father's youngest sister, but everyone called her that. Hannah sighed and pulled on her robe. She might as well go down, but she wasn't going to get dressed first.

She reached the second-floor landing and heard her mother on the phone below. "Yes, it's true. Hannah is getting married to Nathan Mandel on June third. . . . I know. It's amazing luck that Rabbi Katz had a cancelation for a wedding originally planned for that Sunday. . . . Apparently, somebody in the bride's family was ill, so the couple married sooner but neglected to take the old date off the shul calendar."

Deborah looked up, saw her bleary-eyed daughter at the kitchen doorway, and ended the call. "I'm sorry, Hannah. I know you had a hard time sleeping last night, but I knew the first call had to be from Sam." She hugged Hannah and whispered, "I hope that date works for you . . . to go to the mikveh first."

Hannah hadn't thought about that. She did a quick mental calculation; she usually got her period in the middle of the month, so June 3 should be okay. "It will be fine."

"Don't blame me for spreading the news so fast," Naomi interjected. "I came right over after Mama called me."

Tante Essie kissed Hannah on both cheeks. "Mazel tov, my darling Annie. Mazel tov. Bernie stopped back in after minyan, so I just had to call Naomi," she explained. "He told me Sam was so happy and excited, it wasn't long until everyone at shul heard the news."

As proof of that, the phone rang yet again. Deborah answered, confirmed the engagement, and accepted congratulations, then did her best to cut the conversation short and go back to making Hannah's breakfast.

Naomi took the opportunity to hug her friend next. "Oh, Annie, I'm so happy for you." Then she wagged her finger. "So that's why you were so agreeable to remodel the kitchens. Well, they should have it done long before June."

"Never mind that," Deborah said. "I want to see Annie's ring up close."

A still sleepy Hannah dutifully held up her finger to resulting oohs and ahs. "It belonged to Nathan's mother." She found it hard enough to believe that she was truly engaged, and now there was a wedding date on the calendar.

Essie sighed contentedly. "To think that Bernie had Nathan and you in his sixth-grade classes when you two were just children."

Deborah set down a plate of toast and eggs. "You should bring some pastries to the office and celebrate, Hannah. Your colleagues will be upset if they hear the news from someone else."

Nathan was opening the door to his office when his secretary, looking even more worried than the day before, rushed out to meet him.

"Samuel Eisin called for you," she blurted out. "Twice."

"Can you put a call through to him right away, then?"

He'd no sooner hung up his coat than his phone rang.

It was Samuel Eisin's secretary. "Mr. Eisin had to go to court, but he left a message for you, Rabbi Mandel." She paused, and Nathan could imagine her smiling. "He said for you and your father to put the afternoon of Sunday, June third, on your calendars."

Nathan couldn't help letting out a whoop, and the woman continued. "Congratulations from Mr. Eisin's entire staff."

His own secretary, no doubt alarmed by his shout, stuck her head in. "Is everything all right?"

"Couldn't be better, but I've got to see Rav Klein." He raced out the door, chuckling at how he was probably the first person at Spektor eager to see the irascible Talmud professor.

He could see cigarette smoke curling out of the half-open office door, so he knocked gently and walked in.

Klein stood up immediately. "*Nu?* You have news?"

"You may congratulate me on my engagement. The wedding is on June third."

"Mazel tov. And what is the name of your fortunate bride?"

Nathan told him, and Klein's expression grew thoughtful. "Hannah Eisin. Is she by any chance related to Samuel Eisin?"

"Yes, his daughter."

Then, to Nathan's astonishment, Klein started laughing so hard he choked on his cigarette. Alarmed, Nathan pounded him on the back, and when that didn't help, Nathan grabbed an empty coffee cup on the desk and ran to get some water. Klein hacked and coughed and finally drank the water.

Thus cured, he grabbed Nathan's arm. "Come, we must tell Rabinovich."

Upon hearing the news, Rav Rabinovich also burst out laughing. "So, Avram, which of us should tell the dean?" he asked, still chortling.

"I understand that you're happy for me," Nathan interrupted. "But what is so funny?"

The two sages exchanged surprised looks. "Samuel Eisin is a Spektor trustee," Klein replied.

Nathan's shocked expression told them everything. "I think we'd better both go see the dean," Rabinovich said. Then he turned to Nathan. "The dean sent a letter to the trustees yesterday afternoon, demanding an emergency meeting to discuss your situation."

"Now he is going to send out another one," Klein declared.

Rabinovich looked at his watch. "Don't worry, Nathan. Avram and I will take care of this. You go teach your class."

Nathan walked in to see his students suddenly stop talking and look guilty. Clearly, the gossip about him and a mystery woman had spread.

"I understand there have been rumors about my meeting regularly with an unknown beautiful woman." He tried to make his expression stern. "You should get your minds out of the gutter. I have merely been having dinner with my fiancée, Hannah Eisin. And yes, she is Samuel Eisin's daughter."

Sure enough, some students looked chagrined, and others elbowed their neighbors, but soon all were shouting, "Mazel tov."

An hour later, Rav Rabinovich came in, smiled at Nathan, and waited by the door for the class to be dismissed. But Zelig stayed after to talk. "Congratulations, Rav Mandel," he said. "And thank you for arranging for me to meet Dr. Stockser. He's an amazing therapist—he's helped me a lot."

Nathan shook Zelig's hand. "I'm pleased to hear that. I still worry about you."

"Don't worry too much. I'll still be seeing Dr. Stockser after I graduate." Zelig gave Rav Rabinovich a wary look. "I'd better go."

"I hope to see you at the wedding—June third at Congregation Israel."

Rabinovich waited until Zelig was in the hall. "You can have a good Shabbos rest tonight," he said. "Things will be fine. The dean is sending another letter, special delivery."

Nathan let out his breath. "Good Shabbos to you too." Now he and Hannah needed to decide how to deal with her dad when he received the letters.

But nobody answered the phone at the Eisin residence.

ELEVEN

THE *FREIHEIT*'S FRIDAY ritual of frantic yelling and typing, when the staff had to finalize that day's paper in the morning and the weekend edition in the afternoon, abruptly ceased when Hannah entered with the bakery box.

Before she could say anything, one of the men stood up. "Hey, Annie, what's with the goodies? You getting married or something?"

Hannah held up her ring finger. "As a matter of fact, I am." She paused for effect. "On Sunday, June third." Thank goodness Mama had suggested bringing pastries. Now everyone would know in one fell swoop.

She was immediately swarmed by the five other female employees, newspaper writers being that minuscule group of men who did their own typing. She reluctantly extended her left hand, submitting to what seemed to be a universal women's ritual. How odd, Hannah thought, that though women didn't usually examine other feminine jewelry, they seemed to be fascinated by engagement rings.

"Who's the lucky fellow?" Moe had to shout over the din as the men assaulted the pastries.

The room quieted as she replied, "Nathan Mandel."

Moe grinned and smacked himself on the side of the head. "Oy. I knew I shouldn't have sent you to write about him," he joked. "Now I'll lose one of my best employees."

"I don't intend to stop working just because I'm married." Yet he was right. With so much wedding planning to do and only a few months to do it, it was unlikely she'd have time to do translations, editing, and interviews in addition to her Israel stories.

"Yeah, like you'll have time to write once you have all those little Mandels pestering you night and day."

"It will be some time until there's a bunch of little Mandels," she protested, simultaneously warming to the image.

A female voice rang out with "Where's the wedding? Your dad's synagogue?" When Hannah answered in the affirmative, her colleague said, "I hope I get to cover it."

It hadn't occurred to Hannah that her marriage would be newsworthy to the Jewish community. "That's up to Moe, but I'll send you all invitations."

After the excitement died down and she completed the work she had to get done that morning, she sought out the paper's photographer.

"Do you still have the picture of Nathan you took for the article about him?"

He smiled. "Because you want a copy?" When she blushed and nodded, he said, "I need time to find it. Come back after lunch."

Hannah impulsively decided to get her hair done so she'd look especially nice for her dancing date with Nathan. "I'll be back to proofread the weekend edition. Then maybe you could take a photo of me to give to him."

The first run had begun when she returned, and she promptly joined in to find the inevitable typos and correct them. Only then did the presses start rolling in earnest. On Friday afternoon it was imperative that everything happen as quickly as possible so the weekend edition hit the newsstands well before sunset brought in Shabbos. Even so, this the season of short days, Hannah barely made it home in time.

Hannah could hear the phone ringing when she unlocked the front door, the large envelope with Nathan's photo tucked under her arm. Probably just someone else calling with congratulations, but she answered it anyway, just to stop the noise.

"Thank goodness I got through before Shabbos." Nathan summarized what happened that morning. "Honestly, I had no idea your dad was a Spektor trustee. Abba cautioned me not to get involved in school politics, so I make every effort to avoid those people."

"Eventually I did realize you were ignorant of his position." She tried to process what he'd said. "I liked that you hadn't taught me because of it, so I didn't enlighten you. I'm sorry. It never occurred to me that it would be a problem." *This mess is my fault, a direct result of my determination to study Talmud with him. But what can I do to fix it?*

"Listen, your dad has two letters coming from the dean." He tried to speak calmly, but his heart was in his throat. "The first is a complaint about me—about us, actually—calling for an urgent trustee meeting. The second, sent special delivery, canceled the meeting and apologized for the false alarm. I don't know the details."

"Oy vey. Hold on while I check the mail." After a minute, she was back. "Both letters are here, but I don't know if Dad will have time to read them. Sometimes he doesn't get to Friday's mail if he comes home too close to sunset."

Hannah was immediately tempted to throw both letters in the trash, but that would only delay the inevitable confrontation. Her next thought was to lie about the illicit meetings, but that would mean Nathan lying too. No, she would not be dishonest, nor ask Nathan to be. However, they needn't disclose everything.

He must have read her mind. "We need to agree on what to say so our stories don't conflict. We'll admit we've been studying Talmud here in secret, but I'd prefer to leave out Rav Klein's assistance."

Hannah sighed in resignation at how she'd abruptly become the center of attention today. "And when anyone asks why we waited to announce our engagement, we can say something like we knew how we felt about each other in the fall but didn't want to make things public yet and lose our privacy."

"Very good," he said. "Not untrue, but not quite the whole story either."

"I need to talk to my parents before Dad reads the letters."

"Abba found your notebook, so he knows we study together," he said. "He's expecting to discuss things further tomorrow."

"I guess it's okay for you, and him, to read my notes."

"He did read some of them while waiting for me last night. He was impressed with your learning, by the way."

Hannah heard the front door open. "Mama just came home. I've got to go."

"Don't hang up." He took a deep breath. "We'll get through this—don't worry. I love you."

Hannah felt her worries dissolve. "I love you too." While she knew he loved her, hearing him say it was another thing. Thus fortified, she headed to the kitchen to get her mother's advice.

Hannah's declaration of love still in his ears, Nathan began reading her notebook.

With great chagrin, Hannah showed her mother the letters and confessed that her semiweekly class with Nathan had consisted of only the two of them, that they met at his apartment, and they usually had dinner alone together first. "In December, when you were all on vacation, we studied here every day." *There, it was out in the open.*

Deborah frowned and carefully slit open the envelopes. "We must tell Sam everything tonight, and since the letters are no longer sealed, he can read them without violating halacha. We'll just have to wait and see what he says."

Their conversation ended when the doorbell rang. Hannah jumped at the noise, then, with some trepidation, went to answer it. "Mama, look, Nathan sent flowers." Her anxiety lessened, she brought them into the kitchen.

"How sweet of him. Why don't you put them on the dining table so we can all enjoy them?"

All through dinner, Hannah kept up her spirits by looking at the vase of colorful blooms and reminding herself who sent them. It made avoiding her parents' eyes easier.

After they'd eaten, Samuel read and reread both letters without interruption, then handed them to Deborah, who eagerly perused them and then sighed with relief.

To Hannah, the silence seemed to go on interminably, until her dad looked at her.

"I don't think we need to worry, Annie. With both Rav Klein and Rav Rabinovich on Nathan's side, I probably won't have to do a thing," he said. "But if necessary, I'll talk to the other trustees."

Deborah passed the letters to Hannah, who took them as if they were bombs ready to explode with any errant move. However, her anger at the first one melted after she read the second. "At least the dean had the decency to apologize for acting hastily before knowing all the facts," Hannah admitted.

"And conciliatory to suggest that Nathan was trying to be chivalrous and protect your privacy by not telling him about your engagement," Sam added.

"I doubt any of the trustees care that a woman studies Talmud," Deborah declared.

Samuel locked eyes with his wife. "Deborah, this could be the opportunity we've been waiting for so Spektor will finally open the women's college."

"What!" Hannah almost shouted. "A college for women at Spektor? How is it possible that I haven't heard about it?" Her excitement obliterated her earlier anxieties.

"There have been top-secret discussions for over a year, and I think this situation with you and Nathan is the perfect impetus for why such a school is needed."

"It's a shanda that observant girls go to Barnard, Hunter, or Brooklyn College, where they study secular subjects with nonobservant men and graduate with no more Jewish knowledge than they started with," Deborah said. "Meanwhile, enlightened young Orthodox men go places like Spektor, where they meet no girls at all."

He chuckled. "We must see to it that the new school for women offers an impressive variety of MRS degrees."

"Sam, I'm serious."

"I am too. It's vital for our religion's survival that modern Jewish young women be educated at a college where they have a large selection of appropriate potential husbands."

Hannah finally found her voice. "So that's the underlying reason for your women's college?"

Sam shook his head. "Don't misunderstand me. The official reason—the most compelling reason—is to give Orthodox young women a college-level Jewish education," he explained. "But we need to make sure potential donors understand the very important auxiliary reason."

"Is this too secret to tell Nathan?" Hannah asked. "I can ask him not to tell anyone else."

"Tell him all you like, but also tell him to keep it under his hat," Deborah replied.

"I'll have to resign as a Spektor trustee," Sam said. "Having my son-in-law on the faculty would be a conflict of interest."

Deborah smiled. "How convenient. Then you can devote your attention to establishing the women's college."

Hannah's anxiety abated by her parents' astonishing news, she wished she could share it with Nathan and ease his worries too. But there could be no phone calls during Shabbos, and the Mandels lived too far away to walk. Well, she'd be seeing him in twenty-four hours.

Anticipating the worst about the letters' contents, Nathan waited impatiently as Abba led the blessings that welcomed Shabbos. The two men had a Friday-night ritual where they shared over dinner what transpired at each of their schools that week, Abba going first.

When Nathan didn't respond with any questions or comments, Abba stopped talking and said, "I guess with a wedding to plan, you're not thinking about what's happening at Spektor."

Nathan startled and looked at Abba in alarm. "What do you mean 'what's happening at Spektor'?"

"Nothing specific. It's just that you're so subdued for a newly engaged man."

"Actually, something did happen at Spektor." Ashamed to meet his father's gaze, Nathan proceeded to inform Abba how teaching Talmud to

Hannah had gotten him in trouble that morning. "According to Rav Klein and Rav Rabinovich, I shouldn't worry though."

"No wonder the kitchen was always so clean when I came home on Tuesdays and Thursdays," Abba gently joked. "You're probably right that Klein and Rabinovich will protect you, but if not, the Seminary will be delighted to have you on their faculty." Then his expression sobered. "I'm serious about your teaching there. You won't have to worry about anyone tattling to our dean about your so-called misbehavior."

Thankful his father hadn't scolded him, Nathan added, "And with our wedding scheduled for June third, people will assume we've been engaged for months already."

"You were fortunate to get such a desirable date." Abba frowned. "What really upsets me is knowing that our neighbors not only spied on you and Annie but reported it to Spektor in such unsavory terms."

Until that moment Nathan hadn't given any thought to who had denounced him. "I can't wait to move out of here." He shuddered. "Until then I'll be wondering *was it him?* about everyone I see in the building or on the block."

"I've been wanting to leave Williamsburg for years. It's gotten so Hasidic, I feel like an outsider," Abba said. "But now that you're getting married, have you given any thought about where you'll live?"

Nathan had thought about it. "Ideally, I'd like to live in her neighborhood, just south of Eastern Parkway in Crown Heights. That way we'd be close to her parents, so we can visit on Shabbos without having to stay over, not like Benny and Sharon. Also, I could walk to Spektor."

"It would certainly be nicer than our current locale, as well as convenient to the Seminary and the Gorens." Abba nodded slowly. "I hope you don't mind if I start looking for a small apartment near them."

"But you're going to live with us," Nathan protested.

"I'd be happy to live with you, but it's not your decision alone. Annie must not only agree, but I don't want her feeling coerced or obligated to do so."

"Of course." *Oy, something else to worry about.*

Saturday morning Nathan woke up to the astonishing reality that he and Annie would be getting married in just four months. His life had been completely upended as he had gone from seemingly unrequited love to full commitment in one day. Maybe that explained how he could have been so befuddled as to say Abba would continue to live with him before checking with her.

It was too cold to walk to shul, so Nathan and his father *davened* at home. Before turning to Talmud, Abba said, "I'm impressed with Annie's notes, cryptic as they are, and I'd like to get to know her better by you and I studying the same piece of Talmud that you two are on." His eyes twinkled. "I assume you're familiar enough with her arguments that you could take her side in the discussion."

"I'd be happy to."

They opened their Talmuds to the Mishnah in Tractate Kiddushin, which began by teaching, "Women are exempt from all positive time-bound mitzvos." This was defined by the examples of "residing in a sukkah and taking the lulav during Sukkos, and blowing the shofar on Rosh Hashana, which are fulfilled only at a specific time of year."

Before Abba could continue reading, Nathan brought up Hannah's difficulty. "The Torah doesn't separate positive mitzvos into two categories, so why does the Mishnah differentiate between time-bound and non-time-bound mitzvos?" he asked. "What purpose does this serve, other than making women exempt from the former?"

"That does seem to be its only purpose," Abba admitted. "By exempting slaves along with women, the reason seems to be that neither group controls their own time. Slaves are ruled by their masters and women by their husbands."

"But the Mishnah says *women* are exempt, not wives. Surely the Sages were aware of widows and divorcées," Nathan objected. "At least the Gemara does recognize a difficulty when it asks if this is an established principle, since there are the mitzvos of eating matzah on Pesach, rejoicing at festivals, and assembling after the sabbatical year. Each is a positive time-bound mitzvah, yet women are obligated in them."

"Rabbi Yohanan answers that we do not learn practical halacha from a general statement," Abba replied, "because a general statement in a Mishnah is not all-inclusive. There will be exceptions, and even when specific exceptions are given, there could be others too."

"Such as observing the mitzvos of Shabbos, Yom Kippur, Hanukah, and Purim," Nathan pointed out. "In fact, women are obligated to more positive time-bound mitzvos than they are exempt from."

"That may be true, but it doesn't negate the general principle."

Frustrated, Nathan took a different tack. "If you argue that a woman's responsibilities for running a household and taking care of children might interfere with her fulfilling a positive time-bound mitzvah, why is she obligated to light Shabbos candles during a short window of time on Friday afternoon yet is exempt from residing in the sukkah when she has an entire week in which to do so?"

"You know the Gemara doesn't address this," Abba chided him. "Let's read on and see what Abaye and Rava have to say."

To Nathan's surprise, since the two Talmudic sages normally disagreed on everything, both argued that women should be obligated to reside in a sukkah, albeit for different reasons.

"Abaye says the commandment to reside means just as a man and his wife live together in a residence, so too a man and his wife are obligated to reside together in a sukkah," Abba explained. "Rava compares Sukkos to Pesach, both of which are seven-day festivals that begin on the fifteenth day of the month. Just as women are commanded to eat matzah on Pesach, though it is a time-bound mitzvah, so too women are obligated to fulfill the mitzvah of residing in the sukkah."

"I think both men are right," Nathan said.

"Other sages must have agreed, because the Gemara then switches position to suggest obligating women in all time-bound positive mitzvos by deriving from the mitzvah of rejoicing on a festival, to which women are commanded," Abba said. "Still, some argue that this mitzvah does not apply directly to women. Rather, a woman is rendered joyful by her husband."

"That's absurd." Nathan rolled his eyes. "The Torah specifically states, 'You shall rejoice in your festival, with your son and daughter . . . and the widow'—who obviously has no husband. The Gemara is grasping at straws when it explains that other men must ensure that widows rejoice."

Nathan and his father spent the rest of the afternoon slogging through the more than twenty remaining arguments, each more inscrutable or convoluted than the last, none of which they or the Gemara found convincing. "It is clear to me," Abba said as the debate drew to a close, "that there were powerful voices among the Talmud's editors who thought women should be obligated to positive time-bound mitzvos."

Nathan agreed. "Since they couldn't find a way to overturn the Mishnah entirely, the best they could do was nullify it piecemeal."

When they finally finished the sugya, Nathan sat back to go over it again in his mind. Until a disturbing thought intruded. "You know, Abba, the Talmud lumps women together with slaves because neither has control of their time." He was careful to choose the right words, ones Annie would have said if she were there. "But women are like slaves in a more important area of Jewish Law. Women are acquired in marriage by their husbands just as slaves are acquired by their masters. Yet though slaves with sufficient funds can buy their freedom, a woman cannot divorce her husband. She must wait until he dies or divorces her to be free." Once the words were out of his mouth, Nathan was aghast at how unfair this was to the woman. And he said so.

"You're right, it is unfair," Abba said. "In New York State, however, it is just as onerous for a husband to divorce his wife as it is for her to divorce him."

Nathan glowered. *At least the New York legislature can vote to change the state's divorce law. But no rabbinic court can change Jewish Law.*

That evening, Nathan felt only eager anticipation when he saw all the lights on at the Eisins' brownstone. Samuel opened the door, thanked him for the flowers, and grinning, told him Annie wasn't quite ready.

"By the way, I can assure you there won't be any trouble at Spektor over you and my daughter studying Talmud." Samuel's expression became serious. "However, I must insist that you study here from now on."

Nathan nodded. It gave him the creeps to imagine a shadowy voyeur watching Hannah walk up his street and let herself into his apartment. "You won't get any argument from me. I can walk over from Spektor after my last class." He looked up when he heard footsteps upstairs, but it was Rae.

"Annie knows you're here," she said, "and will be down any minute."

He turned back to Samuel. "My father says June third is fine with him and to let us know what we need to do."

"We'll need your preliminary guest list so we can set a budget. Also, you and Annie should make an appointment with the rabbi . . ." He stopped when Nathan's attention became focused on the landing where Hannah had made her appearance.

Her blond hair hung over her shoulders, and she was wearing a full-skirted royal-blue dress with a scalloped neckline cut just low enough to give a glimpse of her swelling breasts. Nathan, who had never seen her hair down before, stared, stunned, as she descended the stairs. She was gorgeous, and he thanked his good fortune that he would soon be wed to such a woman.

Hannah blushed at his adoring admiration and rewarded him with a dazzling smile. For once it didn't bother her when a man appreciated her beauty.

Half an hour later, as they made their way to a table in the crowded restaurant, Nathan noticed the many eyes following them. Though he had dressed in his nicest suit for the elegant establishment, he felt schlumpy in contrast to his lovely companion. But he soon had other things to think about.

She reached out and put her hand on his. "I'd like to talk about where we're going to live." When he told her what he and Abba had discussed, she sighed with relief. "How convenient that Dad has a duplex around the block currently being renovated." Her voice got more enthusiastic as she continued. "It's similar to our brownstone: three floors with a kitchen, dining room, and living room on the first floor, two bedrooms plus the master bedroom and bath on the second, with more bedrooms and another bath on the third. The ground floor has its own front entrance and opens out on the backyard." She squeezed his hand in excitement. "We could have the workers enlarge the ground-floor bathroom for your father so he'd essentially have his own apartment downstairs."

"You want Abba to live with us?"

She looked at him in disbelief. "Of course. We can't have him living alone, not since he's lived with you your whole life. And especially not at his age."

"I can't tell you how grateful I am," he said. *I didn't even need to ask her.*

"Listen, why don't you and your father come early on Sunday, and we can see the place before it gets dark?"

Their meals arrived, and as they waited for dessert, Hannah leaned forward. "What I'm going to say is absolutely confidential," she whispered. "Don't tell anyone."

Nathan's eyes opened wider and wider as she explained about Spektor's budding women's college, but he remained silent until she finished. "If I could keep our Talmud studies secret, I can keep this incredible news secret too." He smiled and added, "Now I won't feel guilty when your father leaves the board of trustees."

Dessert arrived, and he waited to take a bite. "I'd like to get to the dance hall in time for the first lesson. That way we can practice together before it gets crowded." And he would have time to gauge how good a dancer she was without too many onlookers.

Hannah caught the hint of anxiety in his voice and hoped her novice dancing ability wouldn't disappoint him.

It was her turn for anxiety when, as soon as they checked their coats, the female dance instructor called out, "Nate, I am so glad to see you. My partner is sick, and I'd really appreciate your help teaching tonight."

"Normally I'd be happy to assist you, Gwen, but I'm here with my fiancée and need to concentrate on her."

"Please, just with some of the more complicated moves?"

"It's all right," Hannah said. "Then I can watch you dance." To her relief, she managed to follow Nathan's lead for the beginning foxtrot lesson.

He smoothly led her from the forward basic position into the back basic, then added left and right turns, which she followed without too much difficulty. "You dance well for someone who hasn't dated since college."

She felt sufficiently comfortable to talk to him while they danced. "Okay, I went to a few dances during college and sometimes with friends from the *Freiheit* after that, but any skill I have tonight is because you lead so competently."

Nathan thanked her for the compliment, but Hannah wasn't trying to flatter him. She couldn't explain how, but she moved exactly the way he wanted her to.

At the end of the class, Gwen called him up to demonstrate a complicated routine, one the beginners could aspire to in the future. Hannah watched with awe and astonishment as the two danced through a series of moves with names like twinkles, pivots, grapevines, and curved feathers. *Will I ever be able to dance so perfectly?*

As Nathan politely walked Gwen over to meet Hannah, Gwen nudged him and said, "Now I know why I haven't seen you or Barbara here in months."

Nathan introduced the two women, and while they made small talk, he wondered if Barbara was avoiding his favorite dance hall because she didn't want to run into him.

As soon as Gwen was out of hearing, Hannah asked him, "How did you learn to dance like that? It was poetry in motion."

Nathan explained how his expertise came from years of effort. "The intermediate swing lesson is next," he said. "Shall we try it?"

"Absolutely. I want to learn all the difficult steps so I can dance with you as beautifully as Gwen does." *And so you won't be disappointed and think I'm a klutz.*

Thankfully, another of Gwen's partners showed up for that class, so Nathan could devote himself to teaching Hannah. Again, she had little trouble following his lead, but things weren't so easy when the band started playing for general dancing.

"I don't understand." Her voice was tense with frustration. "We danced fine together in class, but now I keep messing up."

"In class, we already knew what steps we were going to do." Nathan tried to reassure her. "I'll try to be more forceful in leading you, and we'll only do the moves you learned tonight."

That worked better when the band played foxtrots or waltzes, but Hannah had a hard time with the lively swing music. "I have enough trouble when we're in dance position. How can I follow you when our only contact is my hand in yours?"

He needed to think of something soon, before she grew too discouraged. "I have an idea. If you don't mind my holding you a bit closer, let's see if you can sense my lead through my torso, not just my hands and arms."

"Of course I don't mind. I'd love for you to hold me tighter."

Most girls, even longtime partners like Barbara, didn't like being pressed against him like that, but Hannah snuggled up to him cheek to cheek. Her perfume, which he'd merely detected whiffs of earlier, now flooded his senses. "Relax and concentrate on the song's rhythm," Nathan instructed her. "Don't try to anticipate me. Just let your body move in tandem with mine."

When the band began playing, Hannah shut her eyes and focused on the music. She had never been so close to another person, let alone a man, for so long, with everything from shoulders to thighs touching. Next thing she knew, her feet were taking steps without volition, as if Nathan were propelling them instead of her. She felt like she was flying in a dream, pulled and pushed by an invisible force she couldn't resist. Not that she wanted to resist.

"That was wonderful," she whispered when the song ended. Her heart was pounding, but not just from exertion.

They weren't able to replicate that success with every dance, but it happened often enough that Hannah wasn't discouraged. Nathan made swing dancing easier by telling her which move they'd do next. "Eventually you'll be so familiar with them that I won't need to warn you."

By the end of the evening, which was actually well into Sunday morning, Hannah was urging him to show her more difficult moves, not just the ones from class. *Who'd imagine a Talmud scholar could be such a great dancer?*

For his part Nathan was relieved and impressed at how much she'd improved in one night. He was also thankful that Barbara wasn't there, although other dancers who knew him were. He no longer worried about his appearance; his dancing skill more than made up for his unfashionable attire. But best of all was the marvelous feeling of Hannah in his arms.

"I can't wait to go dancing again next Saturday night." She sighed as they cuddled together in the taxi's back seat.

They would have spent longer kissing good night if the driver hadn't been waiting to take Nathan home, but eventually they parted. Hannah glided upstairs as in a dream, dance music in her head. Nathan couldn't have named any of the songs they'd danced to; her scent lingered on his clothes, and his mind was occupied with thoughts of her warm body pressed against his.

A series of chimes woke Nathan on Sunday, but he was still astonished when his bedside clock displayed twelve. Gottenyu, he had to tell Abba about getting to the Eisins' early. And he needed to call Benny. He threw a robe over his pajamas and stopped in the kitchen.

Abba was sitting at the table, which was laden with bagels, sliced tomatoes, cream cheese, plus lox and smoked whitefish. He looked up from the Sunday paper at his bleary-eyed son and smiled. "You must have had a good time last night. You still weren't home when I got up to use the toilet at two."

"You should have woken me. We need to be at the Eisins' in a few hours." He poured himself a cup of coffee and explained about the duplex on Union Street.

"*Az a leyb shloft, loz im shlofn.*" (When a lion is sleeping, let him sleep.) "You didn't even stir when Benny called."

"You didn't tell him about Annie?"

"I left that to you."

Nathan held his breath until Sharon picked up the phone. "Is Benny there? I have some good news for you."

In less than a minute Benny was on the line. "So, *nu*? Is Spektor giving you tenure?"

"Even better. I'm getting married."

There were squeals of delight from Sharon and enthusiastic mazel tovs from Benny. "I assume things worked out with Miss Plonia," he said, followed by Sharon's excited voice. "Do you have a date yet?"

"Her name is Hannah Eisin, and the wedding is June third," Nathan replied. "And I expect Benny to be my best man."

TWELVE

SUNDAY AFTERNOON, Hannah insisted on preparing dinner, allowing her mother and sister to merely assist by chopping the vegetables. As Hannah seasoned the brisket with onion soup mix dissolved in diluted burgundy, she regaled her skeptical helpers with descriptions of Nathan's amazing dance prowess.

Finally, in exasperation, she gave up. "You will just have to join us sometime and see for yourselves."

"Not a bad idea," Deborah said. "It's been entirely too long since Sam and I have gone dancing."

"What about me?" Rae asked plaintively.

"Maybe Nathan can take us somewhere college and high school students go."

Talk of dancing ended when Jake yelled from the living room, "They're coming up the stairs. They'll be here any minute."

"Keep your apron on until after they come in, Annie," her mother advised. "Make it obvious that you're the cook."

"I'll watch the oven," Rae offered. "I've already been to the duplex this week."

Introductions and congratulations were so enthusiastic Hannah doubted that anyone noticed her apron. Thankful the afternoon weather wasn't too cold, she took Nathan's hand and eagerly led the way around the block.

Nathan was pleased to see that, though the trees and most bushes had lost their leaves, the flora on the Eisins' street looked well maintained. Especially when compared with his neighborhood, where the Hasidim didn't care if the plants lived or died. Which meant they mostly died. The houses they passed here had tidy planted areas in the parkway and nicely landscaped front gardens.

"Everything looks barren now," Hannah said. "But next month the hyacinths and crocuses come up as forsythias and magnolias begin to bloom."

They turned onto Union Street, and Hannah could see Naomi waving from her front stoop halfway down the block.

"Goodness," Solomon Mandel exclaimed when they arrived at the address. "I believe I could walk from here to the Seminary in less than twenty minutes."

"It's only a ten-minute walk to Spektor," Samuel said.

Moments later, Naomi and her husband, Dovid, welcomed them into their warm half of the duplex. "Perfect timing," Naomi declared. "They installed the new floor on Friday. Next week they'll paint, and as soon as it's dry, we can move our kitchen things back in. I can't wait."

After Hannah introduced Nathan and his father to her stepbrother's family, they all admired the newly enlarged kitchen with its turquoise vinyl floor. "At first I was skeptical whether turning the kitchen and den into a so-called family room would be worth the inconvenience," Dovid said. "But opening up the wall between them is an enormous improvement. Naomi will be able to watch the children while she's cooking or washing the dishes."

"No more washing dishes for me." Naomi pointed proudly to the built-in dishwasher. "I already tried it out, just to make sure it works, and I don't know how I lived without it before."

"I was skeptical of this entire enterprise." Samuel smiled at his wife. "But Deborah was right to convince me to finance it."

"I assume we will have similar improvements on our side," Nathan said, trying to imagine him and Annie in such a modern space. It was difficult enough to fully grasp that they were getting married in just months.

Hannah nodded. "I haven't chosen the pattern for our family-room floor yet. Now that we're engaged, I'd appreciate your involvement, Nathan. After all, you'll be looking at it for years." She could hardly believe that she and Nathan would soon be decorating and furnishing their first home together; everything had happened so quickly.

"Sure, if you want me to," he replied. "But I know nothing about flooring." Still, he could see what she liked and try to steer her away from anything too ugly.

Solomon chuckled as he turned to Samuel and Deborah. "My son is getting domesticated fast. Only engaged a few days and already he's been roped into redecorating."

"I'm happy to do it." Nathan teased his father back. "Why should women have all the fun?" At least he'd be spending time with Annie, and who knows, it might be fun.

"Ready to see it?" she asked.

He didn't need to pretend enthusiasm. "Sure, let's go."

Hannah led them up the broad stairs to the brownstone's front door. A separate set of stairs on the right descended to the ground-floor entry. They came into an anteroom where the beveled leaded glass doors let in the waning light, then into the foyer. A long stairway ascended on their left, and a wide arched doorway opened to the empty living room on their right. She turned on the lights, and Nathan looked around in awe. This one floor was bigger than his entire apartment in Williamsburg. A hall continued to the rear, and he followed Hannah to the kitchen door.

"You'll really appreciate what they did next door when you see what it originally looked like." She opened the door for him.

Nathan gazed at the narrow galley kitchen lit by a flickering fluorescent ceiling fixture and a small amount of daylight from a window in the back door. Refrigerator and sink were on the left wall, the stove on the right next to a small table flanked by two chairs. "Amazing," he exclaimed. "Who would have imagined that removing the upper wall behind the stove and opening it to the other side would make such a difference?"

"Also enlarging the counter around the stove so people can eat on it," Hannah said, savoring the pleasurable thought of her and Nathan having morning coffee there.

They walked into what would be the family room, then through the dining room to go upstairs. The largest bedroom faced the street, with bay windows overhanging those in the living room below. Hannah couldn't let her eyes meet Nathan's, while he didn't dare let his thoughts dwell on what the two of them would be doing in this boudoir in a few short months.

Off the big bedroom was a full bathroom that opened to the hall as well. There were also two rectangular rooms overlooking the backyard. The third floor was similar to the second, except that two smaller bedrooms replaced the large one.

Finally, they went down to the basement. The small clerestory windows dimly lit the large area, so Hannah flipped on the switch. Nathan sighed with disappointment when the two overhead lights provided only marginal extra illumination. Unlike Dovid and Naomi's ground floor, which had been converted into an office for Dovid and a playroom for the children, here the floor was concrete and the perimeter walls unfinished. The only "finished" room was a small half bath next to the laundry area at the base of the stairs. The big oil-fueled furnace took up as much space as a small car. He didn't want to look a gift horse in the mouth, so he said nothing. *Making this place livable will be an undertaking.*

Hannah tried to be upbeat. "Demolition will be minimal, and adding more lighting should be easy, Nathan. Your father will be able to lay out his apartment however he wants."

"With the caveat that the new laundry room and full bath should be located where the current ones are," Samuel added.

"Considering that this space is nearly as large as the apartment Nathan and I now occupy, there should be plenty of room for me," Solomon said. "I could have an office and maybe a modest living room in front, with my bedroom and study in the rear with some new good-sized windows for natural light."

"That sounds perfect." Hannah appreciated how much privacy she and Nathan would have despite his father living with them.

"I'd like for Nathan and Hannah to decide how to fix up my rooms. I have better uses for my time than choosing curtains and flooring." Solomon paused and added, "My only request is that the bathroom be primarily white and include a shower."

Hannah looked at her watch. "I need to get home to finish dinner. But the rest of you are welcome to stay here awhile longer."

"I'll go back with you," Deborah said, and the men followed.

As soon as the front door opened, the air was flooded with the savory aroma of beef brisket.

"I was about to call Naomi to see what happened to you," Rae said. "Jake is starving."

Everyone was quickly seated, and dinner was served. Other than effusive compliments on Hannah's cooking, silence reigned until Solomon cleared his throat and asked if they'd told Elizabeth Covey yet. Samuel shook his head, while Hannah and Deborah guiltily admitted they had not.

Nathan looked at his father. "Why do you ask?"

"I am pleased to announce that my son and daughter-in-law will likely have our Brighton Beach rental to themselves this summer." Solomon beamed with pride. "I have been invited to spend a few months in Israel, starting at the end of June. During that time I will attend two conferences, meet with other scholars, and maybe teach a little."

"That's wonderful, Abba, but . . ." Nathan's father had rarely been sick since he began teaching at the Seminary, but several months traveling overseas would be stressful and tiring, especially for a man who'd suffered two coronaries.

"Don't worry. I have already gotten a clean bill of health from Dr. Grossman." Solomon turned to Hannah and continued. "Equally important, I plan to visit archaeological sites the Covey Foundation is funding and report on others that might be worth supporting in the future."

Nathan gulped. "Could it be an ethical problem for the Covey Foundation that you and Elizabeth Covey would be related?"

Samuel shook his head. "It's a family foundation under Elizabeth's complete control. One would expect it to sponsor charities that she, and other family members, consider worthwhile."

"Nathan, do you have any great attachment to Brighton Beach?" Deborah asked. "If not, Sam can find a cottage in Sea Gate for you and Annie, so we can all visit on Shabbos."

Nathan shrugged. "We used to summer in Peekskill, but we've stayed in different beach places after 1950."

Deborah burst out, "Gottenyu, were you there in 1949 during the riots?"

"Unfortunately, we were." Solomon grimaced. "Who could imagine that the hatred and rioting preceding Hitler's rise in Germany would happen here in America?"

Nathan clenched his fists at the memory. "And not in the Deep South, but in Peekskill, right outside New York City."

Hannah couldn't restrain her journalist's curiosity. "What happened? What was it like for you? I was in Israel that summer, so I missed it."

"Peekskill in August was actually two communities." Solomon sounded like a teacher beginning a history lecture. "One made up of summer people and weekenders, mostly Jews from New York City like us. The other of Gentile year-round residents, more conservative and working class. We'd been renting a lakeside cabin every summer for almost ten years—"

"For the last four, we always attended the Labor Day concerts to hear Paul Robeson, Woody Guthrie, and Pete Seeger," Nathan interrupted. He'd avoided thinking about that summer for six years and needed several deep breaths to calm his anger.

Solomon took advantage of the lull. "In 1949 we were surprised, and horrified, to see hostile locals protesting the Robeson concert by insulting Jews and Negroes."

"It was bad enough when they started shouting, 'We're Hitler's boys, here to finish his job,'" Nathan broke in again. "But things really got out of hand when a bunch of drunks physically attacked the audience. The violence was horrible, but I gave as good as I got," he said with pride.

"The organizers canceled the concert, but undeterred by the violence, they rescheduled it for a few days later." Solomon looked proud as well.

"But the locals were undeterred," Nathan protested. "We saw signs like, 'Communism Is Treason. Behind Communism Stands—the Jew!' and 'For My Country—against the Jews!'" He shuddered at the memory. "Someone burned a cross on a nearby hillside, terrorizing both summer and local Jewish residents."

"They still held the second concert?" Hannah's eyes were wide as she tried to imagine Nathan in a physical fight and failed.

"Yes, and more than fifteen thousand people came up from New York." Nathan's voice rose with excitement. "We were protected by thousands of Robeson's own guards, plus volunteers and a contingent of police."

"You cannot imagine my relief that afternoon when the concert ended peaceably." Solomon ended the sentence in a forceful exhale.

"But the day didn't end peaceably." Nathan's voice rumbled ominously. "As the audience dispersed, vehicles were directed onto a narrow forest road. Abba and I were with Dave and Sarah Goren, and we knew something was wrong because that wasn't the usual route to the city. Fortunately, Dave gave his summer address, and thinking we were locals, they let us go."

"It was like living through a pogrom." Solomon's expression was grim. "Dave appeared calm, but Sarah was petrified. I could tell Nathan was angry and defiant, but we made him control himself."

"The next day we heard that hordes of men had been waiting in the woods along the road," Nathan growled, his anger rekindled. "At first they screamed anti-Semitic and anti-Negro expletives. Then they threw stones, smashed car and bus windows, and eventually overturned many vehicles."

Hannah's insides curdled as she imagined being in one of those cars.

"We'd already paid a deposit, so we returned the following year," Solomon said sadly. "But it wasn't the same. In town the locals stared at us with open enmity."

"I heard one man, the son of a policeman, brag that the riot was all arranged by the Ku Klux Klan and the police." Nathan's voice was bitter.

Solomon sighed with resignation. "After that, we rented places at the beach."

Deborah nodded. "I don't blame you. I endured quite a bit of that myself while Annie was growing up."

Hannah, reluctant to relive her wretched childhood, turned to her dad. "Let's call Aunt Elizabeth before it gets too late."

While they were on the phone in Samuel's office, Nathan was captivated as Deborah explained how she'd been a Communist organizer for years, until Russia and Germany signed their nonaggression pact. "That's when Moe Novick and I parted ways."

"There's no getting around the fact that many of those early idealistic Communists, Socialists, and trade unionists were secular Jews," Solomon said. "Which led to all of us being tarred with the same anti-Semitic brush."

To Nathan's relief, Annie returned to the dining room with a large smile on her face. "Aunt Elizabeth is delighted," she announced. "She plans to come down the week before Pesach so she'll have time to get to know Nathan better."

Samuel reappeared a few minutes later. "Solomon, my sister-in-law would like to speak with you briefly before you go."

Abba finished his glass of wine and followed Samuel out.

Nathan stood up. "I'll get my coat." When Hannah accompanied him into the hall, where they could say goodbye privately, he told her, "Benny and Sharon want us to come to dinner, this week if possible."

"Tomorrow would be too last minute, but Wednesday is fine." She squeezed his hand. "I'd rather not schedule anything for us on Tuesday or Thursday."

Samuel and Solomon walked into the foyer, then turned so their backs were to their children in the hall. "We have to go." Nathan gave Annie a long kiss. "I'll see you here on Tuesday."

As Samuel drove them home, Solomon asked if he and Nathan might move in before the wedding, so he could look for a new shul in the neighborhood.

"I have no objections," Samuel said. "Although you should probably wait until the kitchen is finished."

"I'd feel uneasy moving in too soon, like it would be tempting fate," Nathan said. "But I can see the advantage of Abba living on the second floor temporarily, or at least staying over on Shabbos."

Samuel nodded. "Once the ground-floor work gets started, he can keep an eye on how it's progressing."

Monday morning Hannah knew she had to tell Moe that her current responsibilities at the *Freiheit* couldn't continue. He must have realized this too, because he beckoned her into his office as soon as she put her briefcase down.

"I figured you'd be resigning eventually, but I hoped it wouldn't be so soon."

"I'm not resigning." *Not yet*, she thought, thankful he'd been the one to bring up the subject. "But between planning a wedding now and running a household later, I can't work so many hours anymore, and definitely not on Friday afternoons."

He sighed with relief. "It should be no trouble finding someone with your English proofreading skills."

"And getting someone else to translate Yiddish into English shouldn't be too difficult either these days," she added.

"But I'd like you to keep translating the Hebrew articles."

"Of course." Reading the daily Hebrew papers was one of Hannah's favorite parts of her job. "And I have enough Israel interviews to keep the *Freiheit* supplied for at least a year."

And until then, rather than running all over town for interviews, she'd concentrate on the writing she could do at home. An image of boxes of stories in her closet waiting to be finalized warmed her inside. She was weary of being a journalist, tethered to the truth and assigned to write what others wanted. She needed freedom to write fiction. With mixed feelings of sadness at leaving and joy at her exhilarating future, Hannah put the Hebrew newspaper in her briefcase and gave Moe the contents of her in-box to distribute to others. She wasn't going to wait who knows how long until he hired her replacement.

Wednesday evening Hannah borrowed her dad's car to drive her and Nathan to dinner at Benny and Sharon's. "What did you think about studying at my house last night?" she asked cautiously. It wasn't like they had a choice.

"Studying in your dad's office was okay. It was private enough, and he had the texts we needed," Nathan replied.

"I miss eating together by ourselves."

"I do too, but it's only for a little while longer," he said. "I like that you can drive me home." They'd had more than enough privacy in the big car.

Hannah was glad it was too dark for him to see her blushing.

They drove in silence until it was time to find a place to park. "I'm nervous about meeting Benny," she admitted. "I don't want to say anything that offends him, but teaching in that girls' school gave me a poor opinion of Hasidim. Plus, it will be awkward that you and I know about Sharon's unhappiness while he doesn't."

"She doesn't know I told you about it either."

"Oy, Nathan, keeping secrets like that only causes trouble later," Hannah said. "I was thinking to try to persuade her to have lunch together regularly, to get to know each other better since our husbands are best friends. Then maybe I can convince her to talk to him."

"You're good at having people confide in you. And once she does, maybe you'll be able to convince her to tell Benny."

It seemed a good omen that she found an empty spot right in front of Benny's building.

Though Nathan had warned Hannah how tiny Benny's apartment was, she had to hide her shock when she saw that it was even smaller than the ones she'd grown up in. At least Benny and Sharon had heat. Her parents' landlords had turned theirs off after realizing their politics. Twenty years later, she still hated the cold.

After introductions, the four of them squeezed around the Stocksers' dining table, made more crowded by the baby's high chair. Hannah and Nathan couldn't help but exchange surreptitious grins when Sharon served beef brisket prepared almost identically to what Hannah had cooked on Sunday.

"Excellent brisket." Nathan gave Hannah's hand a quick squeeze under the table. "How did you know it was my favorite?"

Benny opened the conversation with a question for Nathan. "So, how did you two meet?"

That was an easy one for him. "I've known Hannah longer than I've known you. We went to grade school together."

"You've maintained contact all that time?" Sharon asked.

"We lost touch for several years, until out of the blue, the *Freiheit* sent her to interview me."

Benny looked at Hannah in sudden recognition. "You wrote that unpublished article Nathan gave me." He leaned forward eagerly. "I have so many questions about your research."

"Not now," Sharon cautioned him. "Not over dinner."

"It would be better when I can bring my notes with me," Hannah said. *And when I'm prepared to discuss such an odious topic with a man I just met.*

Benny sighed and switched to an innocuous subject. "How did you decide to become a journalist?"

"My father was one, and I wanted to follow in his footsteps. I enjoy writing and seem to have a talent for it," she began. "My first published story was about a Polish teenage boy who lived through Auschwitz, the only person in his town to survive the war. I interviewed him when I was still in high school." She waited for the others to take this in.

"It must have been devastating for you to learn about such things first-hand when you were young," Benny said. "And for the boy to have experienced them."

She didn't disagree, but after four summers working with refugees in Israel, she was inured to stories from concentration camp survivors. "I wanted to interview Jews, to tell their stories, so I majored in English at Barnard and took German in order to improve my Yiddish," she said. "One of my early stories came from a Russian defector from the KGB who had done unspeakable things during Stalin's reign. I was his escort when he lectured at Columbia, where I was a grad student. Somehow I got him to admit to things he'd never told anyone else."

"You write all those wonderful articles about Israel too," Sharon said. Her voice was a mix of admiration and envy. "I majored in English at Brooklyn College, but I merely studied writing rather than doing it."

"Tell Benny and Sharon about Israel," Nathan urged Hannah. He didn't want Sharon mired in even more regrets.

When Hannah finished answering their questions, it was little Judy's bedtime. Despite his wife's disapproval, Benny persisted. "How did you research that article?"

She knew which article he meant. "I was an English teacher in a Hasidic girls' school for a year." She turned to Sharon. "Let me keep you and the baby company."

Nathan offered to help Benny clear the table and make coffee. "We'll have dessert all ready for them."

As soon as the bedroom door closed, Benny confronted Nathan. "You never told me your Talmud student was so good-looking."

Nathan smiled and quoted from Tractate Berachot. "Three things lift a man's spirit: a beautiful home, a beautiful wife, and beautiful clothes. And soon I'll have two of these." He explained about the duplex Samuel Eisin was providing for them.

"That is close to where Sharon's parents live." Benny sounded wistful. "Well, at least I have one—a beautiful wife—and I would rather have her than the other two."

When Hannah returned, she took the opportunity to turn the tables on Benny. "I've met many fascinating people, people with unique and amazing histories, but I admit that few are as unusual and intriguing as yours." She looked directly at him. "Excuse my chutzpah, but *nu*, how is it that a Hasidic yeshiva bocher, son of the rebbe and heir to his dynasty, gives it all up to become a clinical psychologist?"

The room was silent except for their breathing as Benny considered her question. "That is a long story."

"I never expected otherwise," Hannah encouraged him. "Take your time."

"I remember being maybe three years old," he finally began. "I would go to shul with my father, and sometimes I would see him crying. But when I asked him why, he replied that our people were suffering, which even being a precocious three-year-old, I did not understand."

"Benny is being modest," Nathan interrupted. "Precocious, brainy, gifted . . . none of these describes his mind." He wanted an example that didn't involve Talmud. "We met when we were both fifteen and he was reading seven or eight books a week outside of schoolwork. But he didn't just read them; he memorized them and fully comprehended what he read."

"I got bored studying Talmud." Benny shrugged. "And the English stuff they made us read at school wasn't interesting."

"So you used to be a precocious Hasidic child with a loving father." Hannah wanted to keep Benny on track. "What happened?"

"I have always had a loving father and I am still a Hasid," Benny said vehemently. Then his voice softened. "Things changed when I was about five. I remember a time when I finished a book about a Jewish man who suffers all sorts of misfortunes as he tries to get to Israel. I was so proud. I had read the entire book by myself, and I remembered every word. But when I showed off my achievement, my father was angry. Of course, I had no idea why." Benny ignored dessert but poured himself another cup of coffee. "He stopped replying to my questions, telling me instead to look into my own soul for answers. Eventually, he never talked to me at all, leaving me miserable and confused by his rejection. I had nightmares for years. I hated his silence."

"Why do you think your father stopped talking to you?" Hannah asked. *How could a father do that to his child?*

"I know why, because years later he explained it to me," Benny declared. "It is a Hasidic practice called raising a child in silence. So the child will grow up to be a tzaddik."

"A tzaddik?" Hannah wanted to hear Benny's definition.

"A child is born with a tiny spark of goodness, the soul. This spark must be nurtured, for it is easily extinguished. Great intellect can extinguish it, and then you are left with someone who is all mind but no compassion." Benny took a deep breath. "My father believed I would understand the anguish of others through my own pain, and in that way I would find my soul. He told me a tzaddik must know how to suffer for his people, to carry their pain as his own burden."

"But you studied Talmud together. You weren't raised in total silence," she said.

"As Nathan can tell you, our Talmud debates were open warfare. I poured all my anger and resentment into those battles."

Sharon ended the stillness that followed his confession. "None of you have touched your cake." Nathan and Hannah hastily took a bite, but Benny sat brooding.

Hannah adroitly changed the subject. "What got you interested in psychology?"

He perked up. "I was fifteen, and it was only a few months before I met Nathan. I was sneaking into the public library and reading all sorts of books, hiding in the stacks so my father would not find out," he said. "I discovered one on psychology and began learning about the unconscious and subconscious, how they influence our actions and dreams. I was enthralled at how complicated people are inside, what goes on in their heads that they are not even aware of. I taught myself German so I could read Freud."

"Studying Freud at fifteen must have been a challenge," Hannah said. That was putting it mildly. She couldn't imagine how a Hasidic teenager could understand Freud.

Benny closed his eyes and sighed. "The more I read, the more it upset me. Freud was a genius with great insight into man's nature, but he tore man away from God. Yet I couldn't ignore what Freud wrote."

There was silence at the table until Nathan broke it. "That summer you told me you didn't want to take your father's place."

"I realized my father was trapped—he was born trapped. I admired him, but I also pitied him. I did not want to be trapped like that." Benny shuddered. "I was desperate to escape, but I was afraid. To put off the inevitable, I majored in psychology at Spektor."

"What were you afraid of?" Hannah asked.

She thought he'd need time to think, but he answered immediately. "Of my father's anger, of his disappointment, of letting him and our community down."

"What happened when your father learned about your plans?"

"By the time my father knew I wanted to be a psychologist, which was months before I told him, he was confident I would be more than a tzaddik for our people," Benny replied. "He said I would be a tzaddik for the world."

Nathan nodded. "Reb Stockser also said the world needs a tzaddik."

"After what happened in Europe, it probably does." Sharon's expression hardened. "But my children won't be raised that way."

During the drive back, Hannah kept thinking about what it meant to be the world's tzaddik. It sounded so Christian. Aunt Elizabeth would say that Jesus's suffering and sacrifice are the means by which God saves humanity from sin. Finally, she asked Nathan, "How can Benny, or any one person, carry the burden of the world's suffering?"

He shook his head. "I don't know. I don't understand or condone this raising a child in silence business." His voice was harsher than when he'd recounted what happened at Peekskill. "What I saw was Benny's father mentally torturing him in order to nurture this so-called holy spark. I don't think it did the world any good at all."

"It wasn't just Benny who got tortured by his father; you, his best friend, suffered too," she said softly.

When Hannah got home there was a message from Nathan with Benny's phone number. Would she please call him at her earliest convenience to set up a meeting?

Well, the tzaddik to the world didn't waste any time.

THIRTEEN

"I TALKED TO BENNY this morning," Hannah told Nathan as she drove him home after their next Talmud study session. "He wants me to come to his Columbia office to discuss child sexual abuse in Haredi communities."

"If you're comfortable with that, you don't need my permission."

"I know, but I don't want to hide my meeting Benny from you," she replied. "Not like Sharon hid her meetings with you from him."

"So, when are you going to see him?"

"I'm not sure. It's such a schlep from Brooklyn on a weekday. I'm already having lunch with Sharon at her parents' place on Wednesday," she said. "Then you and I need to meet Rabbi Katz at our synagogue about the wedding, decide on a band for the reception, and choose the flooring for the family room and your father's apartment. And that's on top of the newspaper articles I'm supposed to write."

"You don't have to see him. I expect it would be disturbing to have that kind of discussion with a stranger."

"No, I have to see him. This is important. Benny is in a unique position to help these children." Anger and helplessness welled up inside her at the thought of what they'd suffered. "If there's any way I can be of use, I'll do it."

"So what do you think of my best friend?"

"He is amazing." She started with the good things so as to not hurt Nathan's feelings. "Brilliant and charismatic . . . and not bad-looking." His eyes narrowed with jealousy, and she quickly continued. "I feel sorry for Sharon being married to him."

He looked at her in surprise. "Why?"

"I completely sympathize with her Hasidim problem. I'd feel the same," Hannah declared. "Plus, Benny is so serious. He didn't smile once while we were there, not even at his daughter, and I doubt he laughs or has fun. And he talks so formally. He never uses contractions."

"That's very perceptive," Nathan said. "Benny started teaching himself English by reading a translation of the Bible, then continued with reference books in the library. I doubt he heard anybody speak English when he was growing up."

"By the way, Dad's planning to take you clothes shopping as an engagement present. I hope you're not offended."

"Not at all. He very tactfully pointed out that I still dress like a yeshiva student. And buying me the groom's traditional gift of a Talmud set would be like *firn shtroy keyn mitsraim*" (carrying straw to Egypt). Nathan chuckled, but he hadn't forgotten the disparaging looks he'd received at the restaurant on their first date.

The following Wednesday morning Samuel picked up Nathan and drove them to Dobney Clothiers-Haberdasher. Nathan, who'd worn the same size for years and bought clothes off the rack on the rare occasions he needed new ones, was excited and intrigued at the idea of shopping at a store devoted solely to menswear. The moment the outside door closed behind them and the street noise disappeared, Nathan felt like he'd entered a bank or a library. Men's suits in somber colors hung on racks along the walls, while folded shirts filled glass cases next to displays of ties and handkerchiefs. It was overwhelming and a bit intimidating.

A short, impeccably dressed man greeted them. "Mr. Eisin, a pleasure to see you again." He shook Samuel's hand before turning to Nathan and scrutinizing him from head to toe. "This must be Rabbi Mandel, the future son-in-law."

"Meet Saul, proprietor of this establishment. He will be outfitting you personally." Samuel made it sound like an honor, but Nathan felt it was more like a lamb being introduced to the best butcher.

Saul walked around Nathan twice. "I'm confident we can do better than this." He made a small gesture, and a tailor appeared who separated Nathan from his suit jacket, then set to work measuring his neck, shoulders, and arms.

The tailor whispered numbers to Saul and led Nathan to a private room in the back. There he divested Nathan of his shirt and pants before taking more measurements. The room's three walls were mirrored, and Nathan tried not to cringe at the multiple views of him in his socks and underwear. He was determined to give a good impression, showing neither embarrassment nor ingratitude. After what seemed like an eternity, but was probably less than ten minutes, there was a soft knock on the door.

Nathan called out, "Come in," and Saul entered, carrying several suits on hangers. Samuel followed and took a seat.

Saul held out a gray jacket. "Let's try this winter one first." The fabric was heavyweight but not uncomfortably so. Nathan had barely turned around once when Saul waved his hand in dismissal. "See how the collar doesn't lie smoothly across your upper back. We can rule out this manufacturer's suits; none will fit any better."

Nathan thought it looked fine, until the tailor took away the offending garment and offered another jacket, this one navy blue. Nathan could tell that it fit better, but Saul and Samuel rejected it as well. Nathan began to fear that nothing would meet their exacting standards, including himself.

"This is the time-consuming part, trying on one jacket after another," Saul explained encouragingly. "Until we ultimately find the company whose cut fits you best."

"Then you can try more of their clothes, knowing they will require only minimal alterations," Samuel said.

"Alterations?" Nathan asked. His previous suits only needed the pants hemmed.

"Oh yes." Saul handed Nathan another winter coat, a dark gray pinstripe, but this time he did not dismiss it. "Even a suit that fits as well as this one can be made to fit perfectly."

Finally Nathan got to put on some pants, but to his disappointment, the pair that matched the coat was too loose.

Samuel must have seen his face fall. "Don't worry, Nathan. Pants usually have to be altered, and Saul can tell you it's easier to take in a waist that's too big than to enlarge a tight one." He nodded at Saul. "We'll keep these."

While the tailor chalked various marks on the fabric, Saul and Samuel went looking for more clothes of the same brand. Nathan had to concede that the fabrics here were far nicer than anything he presently owned. When they were done, Samuel had also ordered a lightweight navy suit for the spring, a herringbone sports coat, two pairs of slacks, gray and steel blue, as well as some shirts and ties that Nathan could take with him.

"Everything will be ready to pick up in two weeks," Saul assured him.

"Can one of the outfits be ready sooner?" Nathan got up the nerve to ask. "I'm taking my fiancée out next Saturday night."

"I can have something for you before noon that Thursday." Saul smiled and lowered his voice. "Maybe you'll like some of our clearance items. Most of my customers aren't so slim and trim as you. Our spring sale starts March first."

Nathan thanked Samuel effusively for the engagement gifts. Now that he recognized the difference between truly fine clothes and those he currently wore, he intended to buy more when he came back.

As Samuel dropped Nathan off at Spektor, Hannah was arriving at the Gorens' for lunch with Sharon.

"Come in the kitchen and meet my mother." Sharon took Hannah's coat and scarf.

An older woman with short dark hair sat opposite little Judy's high chair, feeding the girl. "I am so pleased to meet you, Hannah. I'm Sarah Goren."

"Please call me Annie," Hannah said. "Nathan told me his family and yours used to vacation together in Peekskill."

"That was years ago. Now we go to the Catskills," Sarah replied. She deftly landed a spoonful of something orange in her granddaughter's mouth without the child grabbing the spoon away. "You two enjoy your private lunch. When I'm finished here, I'll give Judy her bath and put her down for a nap. Once she's asleep, I'll be in my studio."

Sharon led Hannah into the dining room, where lunch was laid out.

"Your mother has a studio?" Hannah asked. Her own mother was one of the rare married women who worked outside the home, and here was another one.

"Yes. She's a painter and teaches art at Brooklyn College." Sharon waved her arm around the room. "Nearly everything you see on the walls is her work."

Hannah gazed at the art in awe. "I like the modern furniture and light wood floors; they really highlight her paintings. Is she the decorator too?"

"I guess you'd call her the decorator, but she doesn't do that for a living."

Hannah stopped in front of a large painting over the couch. "This one is lovely. Even though it's abstract, I can tell it's a landscape."

"The farther you step back, the more you can make out the different trees and bushes. That's why it needs to be hung in a big room," Sharon explained. "But we should eat before the soup gets cold. The paintings aren't going anywhere."

Back at the table, Hannah reminded herself that her goal was to have Sharon confide in her, not discuss art. They had both been English majors, so reviewing their most and least favorite literature was productive. Of course Sharon had read her uncle's books, so Hannah maneuvered the discussion to Isaac Goren's view that one could be an observant Jew and still question Orthodox dogma.

This proved to be the opening Hannah wanted. "You're so enlightened, Sharon. It seems unlikely that you would even meet a Hasidic man, let alone marry one."

"We never would have met if it weren't for my cousin Joey." Sharon hesitated, and Hannah waited patiently while her quarry decided how much to say.

"Joey is more like a little brother to me," Sharon continued. "His father, Uncle Yitz, and my father are brothers, and each had only one child. We've always lived in the same building, so Joey and I would see each other nearly every day. During the summer, when his parents traveled, he'd stay with us. We didn't go to the same school though. Unfortunately, Uncle Yitz made the mistake of sending Joey to a Haredi yeshiva—not that he knew it was a mistake at the time."

"Unfortunately?" Hannah wanted to hear more about this.

"Have you ever checked out any of my uncle's books at the Brooklyn Library?"

When Hannah shook her head, Sharon brought over a beat-up volume from a bookcase in the corner. Scrawled in Yiddish in large black letters across the title page was "This is the book of an apostate. Those who fear God are forbidden to read it."

Hannah was shocked. "Who wrote this?"

Sharon shrugged. "Some crazy Haredi who hates Isaac Goren and thinks it's okay to deface library books. It's the same in every copy of my uncle's books. Ask Nathan."

"They must feel terribly threatened by his words to attack him that way."

"They didn't just attack him. They attacked his son. School was hell for Joey. Each time someone said 'Goren belongs in Gehenna' or 'Goren is a *rasha*,' it was like saying that about him. And the more upset Joey got, the more they bullied him."

"The poor boy."

"Joey hated his father for causing him all this misery, but he loved him too, so he kept his anger bottled up inside."

"He started acting out?" Hannah suggested.

"Yes. He'd go into terrible rages over nothing. Or wreck property or start fires . . . destructive things like that. He was constantly getting into fights. I was dating Nathan at the time, and he told us about Benny."

"You were dating Nathan?" *He never told me that.*

"We'd only dated a few months when I drove Benny up to Peekskill to meet Joey. And . . ." Sharon blushed and broke off.

Hannah grinned. "And it was love at first sight."

"Only on my side. I didn't know what hit me. I couldn't stop thinking about him."

"How did you get him to reciprocate? Hasids don't date; they're not even allowed to touch someone of the opposite sex."

"At first I volunteered to drive Benny to see Joey for treatment. Benny wanted to learn as much as possible about Joey's childhood and what might be troubling him. Since I knew my cousin better than anyone, we began meeting for coffee."

"And you questioned Benny as well?"

"Yes. I wanted to know him better too," Sharon admitted. "Once I realized how innocent he was about the world, and also how curious, I suggested some educational outings."

"Like what?"

"Nathan's father was teaching a four-week course on the history of Israel, so we attended that together. It was quite informative and gave us a lot to talk about afterward."

Hannah's eyes opened wide. "I took his class too, before my first summer in Israel. It *was* informative."

"When the class finished, I invited Benny to several plays, always well reviewed and with a serious human interest story."

"You discussed those at coffee afterward too," Hannah said. Enticing an innocent Hasid like Benny would be like taking candy from a baby for sophisticated Sharon.

"By that time it was apparent we were dating, and I suggested we go out with Nathan and one of my girlfriends," Sharon said. "Not that I have any girlfriends now."

"No?"

"My old girlfriends didn't feel comfortable with my being so religious, but I don't fit in with the Hasidic women either."

"It must be lonely for you." Hannah hoped Sharon would divulge her grievances.

Apparently Sharon realized she'd revealed too much, because she brought the subject back to double-dating with Nathan.

"Even though my relationship with Nathan never advanced beyond being friends, I felt guilty for dropping him so abruptly. I kept hoping I could fix him up."

"I'm glad you didn't."

"Evidently you two were *bashert*. Although I'm not sure I believe in that kind of heavenly meddling."

"I certainly don't, although sometimes I have to wonder."

They laughed at their contradictions, and as their mirth calmed, Sharon added, "You know Hasids don't ask anyone to marry them. Matchmakers arrange everything. After we'd been going out for several months, Benny asked what my intentions were."

Hannah had to smile. "Like in those English romances where the heroine wonders if her beau's intentions are honorable?"

"Exactly. By that time I understood him well enough to know there could be no games or subterfuge. So I told him directly I wanted us to marry."

Hannah had probed enough for now. "I'm impressed with your mother's art. Do you think she'd mind showing me her studio?"

"Are you kidding? She'd love to."

Sharon was right. Sarah Goren was delighted to show Hannah her recent works, her current work, and every piece of art in the apartment, each with an explanation of what it represented.

The following Wednesday morning Hannah and Nathan met at the Eisins' synagogue, Congregation Israel of Brooklyn, for their premarital appointment with Rabbi Katz. But there was a delay.

"I'm so sorry," the secretary said. "Rabbi Katz is visiting a congregant in the hospital and hasn't returned yet."

A young man's voice called from an adjacent office, "Can I help them?"

"They're here for a premarital with your father," she admonished him.

The young man, whose yarmulke covered only a small portion of his prematurely bald pate, broke into an astonished smile. "Nathan Mandel, what a nice surprise." Then he turned to Hannah. "Nathan and I were at Spektor together for three years. I may be two years older, but he was two years ahead when it came to Gemara, so we were Talmud classmates. Now I'm auditing his text criticism class."

"Good to see you, Louis." Nathan reached out and shook his colleague's hand. "Annie told me you were the rabbi here."

"I'm the junior rabbi here. My father is *the* rabbi." His voice revealed the faintest hint of annoyance. Then he smiled. "But I'm sure I can give you a synagogue tour as well as he can."

Nathan took Hannah's arm. "Let's go, then."

Of course, Hannah was perfectly capable of giving Nathan a tour of her synagogue herself, but she let Louis do the talking.

Nathan had known that, compared to his tiny neighborhood *shtiebel*, any synagogue with an official name would be larger. But Congregation Israel was enormous. Nathan tried not to gape as Louis led them along wood-paneled hallways where corridors and doors opened in all directions. After passing meeting rooms and social halls of assorted sizes, they arrived at the imposing main sanctuary.

"We can seat nearly a thousand people here," Louis said.

Hannah could see Nathan looking around, not only in awe but also purposefully. "We don't hide our women behind curtains or walls." She proudly pointed to a waist-high partition down the middle of the center section. "Men sit on either side of the right aisle and women on the left. Families with small children often like the very center seats, on either side of the *mechitza*, where they can feel more together. Those who want to avoid the opposite sex take places near the walls."

"Where does your family sit?" He hoped it would be somewhere he'd feel comfortable.

"My mother feels uneasy among the men, so she sits on the left side," Hannah replied. "Rae and I sit in the center toward the back, while Dad and Jake sit in the center next to the aisle."

"I guess that's where I'll sit," Nathan said. Between davening at Spektor or the shtiebel, he'd never seen a woman at services. He had no idea if their presence would distract him from prayer, but he'd have to get used to it.

They were on the steps to the bimah when they saw the secretary beckoning from the door. "I don't think she appreciated us wandering around and keeping her precious rabbi waiting," Hannah whispered to Nathan.

Louis must have heard her because he laughed and said, "It's a good sign for your marriage, Nathan, that your fiancée doesn't put rabbis up on a pedestal."

"Have you done any of these premarital counseling sessions?" Hannah asked as they returned to the office.

Louis shook his head. "My father does all of them."

"But how can you learn if he doesn't show you?" Nathan muttered. Then he turned to Hannah. "Would it be okay if Louis sat in on ours? After all, he has to start somewhere."

"I'd appreciate it very much." She didn't like Louis being excluded either.

The senior Rabbi Katz was on the phone, but they only had to cool their heels a few minutes before he welcomed them in. Nathan felt at once the charisma and authority that made this man so admired in the Jewish community. Cognizant that these were not among his strengths, Nathan was grateful he had not taken a pulpit. But he used what little authority he could muster to have Louis included in their meeting.

At first Nathan thought Rabbi Katz was addressing all the questions to him because Hannah had grown up at the synagogue and he was the unknown quantity. After ascertaining that both Nathan and Hannah were halachically Jewish with no impediments to prevent them from marrying under Jewish Law, the rabbi asked how they'd met, how long they'd dated, what role they expected the synagogue to play in their family's life, and other routine questions. Nathan tried to deflect some of these toward Hannah, but the rabbi always returned to question Nathan.

Finally Rabbi Katz seemed satisfied. "It's a pleasure to counsel a mature couple, one so well matched and compatible. I'm sure Rabbi Mandel is an expert on Jewish marriage law, but it is my responsibility to ensure you understand the laws of New York." He looked at them sternly. "Getting married is easy—it's only a matter of applying for a license and having your blood tested—but getting divorced is very difficult. Unlike Jewish Law, where a man can divorce his wife for any reason, the only grounds for divorce in New York is adultery, which must be proven in court. And since Jewish Law does not allow a woman to divorce her husband, even if she obtains a legal secular divorce, she is still considered married to him until he either dies or gives her a get."

Hannah was aware that some couples went to Nevada for "quickie" divorces, but this wouldn't suffice for Jewish couples. "But what about the Jews who aren't religious, who get married and divorced in the courts without a rabbi?"

Rabbi Katz looked like he'd tasted something rotten. "That situation does not concern us here, but I'm sure Rabbi Mandel can explain the complications. It's a shame more Jews don't consider the potential consequences before they marry." He stood and walked them to the door.

After he shook Nathan's hand, Rabbi Katz handed Hannah a booklet, almost as an afterthought. She immediately recognized it as one she'd seen at the library about using the mikveh. He did not suggest she call him if she had any questions.

Hannah, more frustrated and disappointed than enlightened, wasn't thrilled when Louis walked them out. She wanted to share her feelings with Nathan in private.

Still, she was pleasantly surprised when Louis sounded critical as he asked, "What did you think of my father's premarital session?"

Nathan prevaricated. "I don't know what to think. I never went to one before."

"You didn't look happy, and Annie seemed downright dissatisfied." When neither of them replied, Louis tried again. "I personally was disappointed. Even though Annie grew up here and her family practically built the shul, his talk seemed rather impersonal and perfunctory."

"He could have been more *hamish*," Hannah said. "And not so focused on the groom."

Louis nodded. "My wife has been telling me for years that my father's premarital advice doesn't speak to today's young women."

"Do you think he automatically disregards the woman or that he thinks weddings are so bride-oriented that he needs to address the man?" Nathan asked.

"I don't know, but there's a favor you can do for me," Louis began. "Actually, for my shul and probably for others too. I'd like to improve the premarital session, make it less intimidating and more focused on learning."

"I agree it needs improving, but I'm so busy these days," Hannah replied.

Louis gave Nathan a hopeful look. "If you help me, I think my father would be more open to making changes."

"I'd be glad to, but it would have to wait until after the wedding."

"If you aren't busy for lunch, maybe you could at least get me started today."

Hannah looked at her watch. "I can't join you. I have lunch with Sharon on Wednesdays."

Nathan didn't have class until 3:00 p.m. "I'm free for lunch." He turned to Hannah. "Is it okay if I come for dinner tonight so we can start planning our wedding?"

"Of course." She blew him a kiss and set off to Sharon's.

"Let's go." Louis threw his arm around Nathan's shoulders.

Louis was familiar with the restaurants within walking distance of the synagogue, so Nathan let him lead the way. "I readily admit to being an indifferent Talmud student." He waved away Nathan's expected objection. "No, it's true. I wanted to be a modern American rabbi, not like the old Polish shtetl rabbi who can spout lots of Talmud but knows nothing else. I like being involved with my congregants' lives—counseling people, visiting them in the hospital, administering to their spiritual and educational needs," Louis explained. "And that includes the women."

Nathan looked at his colleague in admiration. Until that moment, he'd never wondered what the Spektor students might be missing in their rabbinic education, never realized how unprepared they were for serving a modern congregation. He suddenly felt ashamed of his ignorance.

"If my father hadn't been rabbi here, I would have gone to the Seminary," Louis confided. "But I needed smicha from Spektor to get an Orthodox pulpit."

"I understand," Nathan said sympathetically. He had a lot to think about.

Their soup came quickly—Louis also knew which restaurants had the fastest service—and they ate in silence. When Nathan was done, Louis leaned forward and said, "I can't thank you enough for letting me audit your class. I've read your father's books, but it's much better to learn text criticism in person."

Nathan agreed and, after deciding to meet again in the fall and go over Louis's premarital counseling ideas, they split the bill.

Hannah hadn't planned on discussing the mikveh with Sharon, but that turned out to be the key that unlocked her trove of grievances with Benny and his community. When Hannah complained that the only attention the rabbi paid to her was to give her a booklet, Sharon countered that she hadn't received any premarital preparation at all.

"Unless you consider his father's list of demands to be preparation," Sharon said bitterly.

"Demands? What did he insist you do?"

"Among other things, I had to spend all the chagim with them, buy meat from certain stores, and wear clothes that fit their definition of modesty. It was also imperative that I use only specific *frum* mikvehs." Sharon grimaced. "I protested to Benny when I saw they were all in Brooklyn, but his father only grudgingly approved one in the city, on the Lower East Side."

"You schlep downtown every month?" Hannah was incredulous.

"Not every month. Sometimes I'm in Brooklyn when it's time." She shuddered and didn't mince words. "But it doesn't matter. All their mikvehs are the same nasty stews."

"I don't think that community has the same cleanliness standards as modern New Yorkers." Hannah recalled how the older generation of women had reviled the unsanitary mikvehs of their time. Evidently things hadn't changed much.

"It wouldn't matter if they did. Between all the health department regulations and crazy rabbinic rules, mikvehs cost a fortune to build. So they keep the old ones, which are used by both men and women. Naturally, they're filthy and stink from yeshiva students." Sharon began to cry. "But I have to go. I can't drag Benny into sin by not immersing in a kosher mikveh."

Hannah put her arm around Sharon's shoulder. It wouldn't comfort her to explain that the New York City Health Department required the mikveh water to be changed only every thirty days and that inspections happened even less often. "At least you can take a proper bath when you get home."

"Thank Heaven for that." Sharon blew her nose on a tissue. "But even worse than their mikvehs is having to spend every Shabbos and all the chagim with Benny's family."

With that Sharon launched into the litany of grievances Hannah had already heard from Nathan. Hannah's heart went out to her. Hannah had taught at the Hasidic girls' school long enough to know how insular the women in that community were, how much they feared and distrusted the outside world. They would never accept Sharon. But she felt compelled to offer some advice. "I don't think it serves you well to hide how much Yiddish you know just so you can catch them criticizing you."

Sharon sighed. "It was clever at the beginning but I don't see how I can suddenly show that I understand everything without making the situation worse."

"The one who can improve things for you is Benny. Tell him how you feel."

"I can't burden him with my tsuris." She began to cry again. "He's too burdened already. So many molested children to treat, but most academics think this kind of abuse is rare and thus not worth studying. Then, after Benny does study it, the subject is so abhorrent that nobody will publish his research. He's truly brilliant, but how can he make tenure if he can't get his peers to review his work? I know how these things go; my parents are both professors. It's not fair."

Hannah agreed and wished she could help. But Sharon was the one who should talk to Benny. Not her and not Nathan.

Thankfully, Sharon changed the subject. "Enough sadness already. You and Nathan are getting married in three months. Tell me something funny about how you got together."

"Well, I had a crush on him back in grade school. I used to ask him for help with math even though I didn't need it." Hannah chuckled at the memory. "And our fathers tried to fix us up by having us sit together at the World Series, not knowing we'd already been studying together for over six months."

When Nathan got to the Eisins' after work, he was relieved to learn that Hannah's parents had already done most of the wedding preparations—they were the hosts after all. He and Hannah still had to choose a band, which he hoped they'd do that weekend. Since they had over an hour until he needed to go home, they walked to the new apartment. The kitchen was gutted, the new plumbing and electrical lines visible. Hannah wanted a bright sunny family room, so they'd agreed on a yellow color scheme. The contractor had left countertop and flooring samples for them to consider, but it was now too dark to see them well.

So Hannah brought up a question she had after reading the premarital pamphlet. "I borrowed a few books about niddah from the shul library, and some of the advice seemed strange."

"Like what?" Nathan had studied Tractate Niddah and knew what the *Shulchan Aruch* said on the subject, so he felt confident he could address her concerns.

"One book said to wear white underwear during the seven clean days while another recommended colored undergarments." Obviously the first would make it more likely to see any small stains, which would restart the seven-day count and prolong the couple's abstinence.

"Many legal debates end with both a lenient and a strict ruling," he explained. "Both are acceptable, although I usually prefer the lenient interpretation."

"Thus no white panties and slips for me." She smiled seductively and was amused to see him blush in response. "While we're on the subject, one booklet said that if the woman sees a blood spot she can't identify, she should take the garment to a rabbi to examine."

With Hannah looking at him doubtfully, Nathan wrinkled his nose in disgust. "That is definitely *not* part of today's rabbinic curriculum."

That settled, she told him about her lunch with Sharon. "I don't have much hope that she'll confide in Benny as long as his job situation is so unsettled."

Nathan put his arms around her, and she laid her head on his shoulder. He couldn't help feeling guilty at his good fortune compared to his friends' concurrent misery.

FOURTEEN

IT WAS A QUARTER PAST TEN when Nathan walked up to Dobney's, where a modest sign in the window announced WINTER CLEARANCE BEGINS MARCH 1. Nathan headed for the register, preparing to ask if his clothes were ready, when Saul appeared.

"I like a prompt customer." He shook Nathan's hand. "Come with me to a fitting room to try on your new suit."

Nathan, who'd expected to pick up the clothes and leave, followed meekly. He was pleased to see the navy outfit waiting for him, along with the sports coat and two pairs of pants. He was even more pleased to see how good he looked in them. Apparently Saul was satisfied, because he brought in another batch of clothes.

"I chose these from our clearance items. They should fit with minimal alterations and are more affordable than our regular items." He held out a beige jacket. "Every well-dressed man should have a classic camel-hair sports coat. It resists water, will keep you warm in the coldest weather, and should last for years if you care for it properly."

Nathan had never felt such a luxurious fabric, and it did look very nice on him. Then he saw the price and blanched. Since his new clothes were an engagement gift, Samuel Eisin had paid for everything without Nathan seeing the tags. Of course men's clothes at a place like Dobney's would be more expensive than at a department store, but he was still shocked.

"I think this is a bit over my budget." Nathan reluctantly took off the coat.

"But the sale price is 50 percent off, and you can pay in installments," Saul encouraged him. "It's not like you'll find another such top-quality jacket, one you'll still be wearing when you're a full professor, at this price. Think of it as an investment."

Nathan didn't care what people at Spektor thought. He wanted to look good for Annie. "All right, I'll take it."

There was no question he'd need a new wardrobe if he wanted to avoid any more judgmental looks when they were out together. So with Saul's help, Nathan added the practical purchases of another suit, this one with two pairs of pants, and a handsome raincoat with a removable lining.

"By the way," Saul added. "You should try the barbershop down the block. Your haircut is a little dated, and your beard could use a trim."

Nathan, who'd half-heartedly patronized the same Hasidic barber since high school, didn't need any encouragement. He stopped in, told them Saul had sent him, and made an appointment for Friday.

Climbing the stoop to Annie's home Saturday night, Nathan's stomach fluttered with nervous anticipation. With his stylish haircut and wearing his new navy suit, he knew he looked different. *But will Annie notice the change? How will she react?*

Abba had noticed, but he had not been impressed. He'd looked Nathan over, then quoted Pirkei Avot. "Look not at the vessel, but at what it contains. There are new jars full of old wine and old jars that do not even contain new wine."

Nathan thought of replying with the Talmud quote about the spiritual benefits of beautiful home, beautiful wife, and beautiful clothes, but he didn't feel like disputing his father. So he merely said, "I'll be home late. Don't wait up." Now, eager to have Annie in his arms again on the dance floor, he rang the Eisins' doorbell.

Rae let him in and exclaimed, "Wow, you look different." She quickly added, "I mean you look good."

Nathan tried to pretend he was insulted, but his frown gave way to a smile. "Thanks for the compliment."

Deborah hurried out from the kitchen, a scowl on her face. "I know you meant well, Rae," she chided her daughter. "But what you said implies that Nathan didn't look good before."

Samuel followed his wife at a more sedate pace, and his face lit with pride. "Very impressive, Nathan. Wear your new wardrobe in good health."

But the best was when Annie stopped midway down the stairs, and her eyes opened wide as she gazed at him with obvious pleasure. Finally she turned to Samuel and smiled. "Thank you, Dad. What a wonderful engagement present." Once in the taxi, she gave Nathan a kiss before saying, "You do look very nice tonight."

"You look very nice too, tonight and every night."

This time the looks they got at the restaurant were all approving. On the dance floor, Annie's skill had improved to the point that he rarely needed to tell her which move was next. They agreed that the band was first-rate and, after confirming that the band knew plenty of klezmer tunes, hired them for the wedding.

All in all, it was an excellent evening.

The following Tuesday Hannah's anxiety grew as she saw the Columbia Department of Psychology building looming ahead. She clutched her briefcase tighter and took a deep breath. She'd put off meeting with Benny Stockser long enough. *Time to get this over with.*

She found his office door ajar but knocked anyway. "Come in," he called out, and she did. Benny, dressed in a dark suit and tie, sat behind his desk. Diplomas and professional memberships lined the walls, while a landscape that Hannah recognized as Sharon's mother's work hung above a plush couch. The bookcases held only psychology texts, not Judaica. Down in the bottom corner, almost hidden in a shadow, she recognized the twin Kinsey Reports.

He did not rise to shake her hand but merely said, "I appreciate your finding time for me. Please have a seat."

She sat opposite him. "You requested this meeting. What do you want to discuss?"

"Your articles were carefully written in the third person, suggesting that all your information came from others. But I surmise that some of it was obtained firsthand."

She explained how she'd worked undercover as an English teacher at the Hasidic girls' school. "Everything I wrote about I either witnessed myself or another teacher told me."

"Good. Before I can treat my patients, I need to gain their trust so they will confide in me," he began. "If I show that I understand what happened and that they are not in any way at fault so they should not feel ashamed, it will help them overcome their fear of breaking a promise of secrecy."

She sighed as a feeling of sympathy for the children washed over her. "Of course any perpetrator would insist that his victim must never reveal what he did."

Benny nodded. "I know how the bar mitzvah tutor targeted boys, but it would help if I understood how this particular molester, who preyed on girls, operated. So I would appreciate you telling me what you personally know about his activities. It may make you uncomfortable, but I need you to be as frank as possible."

Just what Hannah had feared, but she was determined to help his patients. "Let me clarify that I actually interrupted the custodian twice when I searched for girls who were late to class, and several girls innocently told me what happened when I asked about him."

"Good. A reliable witness."

"The girls told me he got them alone in his basement office, so I knew where to look. Both children I saw were on his lap, their skirts arranged so their tushes and thighs were in direct contact with his groin area. I couldn't tell if their underpants were down or if his *ayver* was exposed." It was easier to use the Yiddish words, and hopefully she'd managed to keep from blushing or looking flustered.

Most men talking about this would smirk or snigger, but Benny's voice was unruffled. "So there was no penetration?"

"Not that I observed or heard about. I did hear that there was semen on a girl's underwear or skirt on occasion."

"I have learned that the majority of pedophiles have a particular age range that most arouses them. If the child's youth and innocence help hide their activity, so much the better," he explained.

"There was one girl who did suspect something was wrong. She came in late, so agitated she couldn't pay attention, and I asked her to remain after class." Hannah's stomach tightened as she recalled the incident.

"Please continue."

"When everyone was gone, I asked if anything was wrong. At first she just shook her head, but when I gently persisted, she started to cry and said she'd promised not to tell anyone." Hannah felt her own eyes moistening. "I reminded her that I was an outsider, that I didn't know anyone in the community to tell."

Benny leaned forward to catch each word. "What did she say?"

"First he enticed her onto his lap by offering to read her a special story. But when he started pushing up on her, she didn't like it and wanted to leave. Then he held her down tightly and wouldn't let go, even when she complained that his arms were hurting her." Hannah's cheeks were wet as she continued. "The poor child described his harsh breathing and strange sounds and how frightened this made her. Finally he let her get up, but only after warning her to never tell anyone, that no one would believe her and it would only get her in trouble." When Hannah finished, she was sobbing.

Benny handed her a box of tissues. Hannah looked up and saw trails of wetness on his cheeks. He appeared to be in pain.

He blew his nose and thanked her. "I apologize. I did not realize it would be so difficult for you."

"How can you listen to all these children's stories and not be an emotional wreck afterward?"

"Who says that I am not?" He paused and calmed himself. "By the way, this school custodian was unusual in that most child sexual abuse is committed by a man in the child's inner circle: a stepfather, a close family friend, an uncle, or an older cousin."

"Someone with unlimited access to the child whom nobody imagines would do such a thing." Hannah couldn't hide her disgust. "Someone who is supposed to love the child and have her best interests at heart."

"Because the family has such an enormous incentive to avoid a scandal, they deny the abuse happened or, failing that, keep it secret." Benny sniffed twice. "Which only further injures the child by fostering shame and self-loathing. Unfortunately, it appears that many pedophiles were themselves abused as children."

Hannah blinked back more tears. "You've almost made me feel sorry for them."

"We need to pity them. They still have a soul. One of my goals in treating these young victims is to break the cycle so they do not grow up to be child molesters."

"But somebody has to stop pedophiles from perpetrating more harm," Hannah said. "If this were any other crime, it would be the police's job." She saw Benny was about to speak and headed him off. "I know, families aren't likely to turn in one of their own. The same goes for Jews reporting their rabbis."

"That is true, but what I was going to say concerns the halacha of *mesirah*, which prohibits informing on a Jew to the secular government. While I, and most Jewish authorities, say this does not apply to killers, armed robbers, and other violent criminals, some question whether one should inform on pedophiles unless they are actually raping children."

"What halacha says about mesirah won't matter to families in denial that one member has molested another," she protested, her anger growing. "Even if they believe the child, the best you can expect from them is to try to keep the pedophile away from his victim."

"The best I expect from them is to treat both parties," he countered. "But family abuse is different from what the Fishkoff boys suffered. It is unlikely their tutor would come to me for treatment unless he were coerced, and even then he would undoubtedly resist therapy."

She snorted her antipathy. "Meanwhile Rabbi Brenner's victims, boys rather than girls, would be the future abusers."

"How did you get his name? I did not think Nathan knew."

"Beryl Fishkoff's obituary mentioned the yeshiva he'd attended. Whoever answers the phone there gave me the name of their bar mitzvah tutor." She then told him about Mrs. Feinstein.

"So that is how her son came to me, and why my practice grew after I began treating him." He gazed at Hannah with respect. "I thank you for your recommendation, especially since Mrs. Feinstein pays me generously to see other children too."

"She is still furious at the rabbonim for merely moving the problem to a new school."

"I am also angry about that." Benny looked at his watch. "Please excuse me, but I have a patient coming soon, and I have monopolized enough of your time."

Hannah headed for the door, which was still ajar. "I wish I could say it was a pleasure talking with you, but I hope I've been of some help." It took almost an hour of walking around the peaceful Columbia campus for her to calm down.

The next day, when Hannah had lunch at Sharon's, their conversation took an unforeseen turn. Nobody was with them, but Sharon leaned closer and whispered conspiratorially, "Though it's traditional for a father to teach his son about marital relations, Benny doesn't trust Nathan's father to instruct him properly. He intends to teach Nathan himself."

Before Hannah could say anything, Sharon's expression grew wistful. "You should know that Benny asked me if I was a virgin."

"He did?" Hannah almost choked on her soup. "Whatever for?"

"Believe me, the first thing out of my mouth was 'Why do you want to know?'" she replied. "Now, I admit I wasn't naive when it came to sex. I'd read *Lady Chatterley's Lover* and *Ulysses*. The reason I was still a virgin was that I hadn't met any man I wanted to sleep with until Benny."

"So, what did he say?" Hannah tried to sound nonchalant.

"He was very sweet about it. He said he knew I was a modern woman and didn't want to make any assumptions. Then he launched into this long legal explanation about how a virgin bride who bleeds on her wedding night is considered niddah. Jewish Law allows the couple to complete the first sex act, but afterward they separate for four days—or longer—until she's not bleeding anymore, and then for another seven clean days."

Hannah had read about that. "But what if her hymen is already broken, from horseback riding or some other injury?"

"Unless the bride has been married before, newlyweds, when she doesn't bleed, are supposed to act as if she did so there won't be any embarrassment," she replied. "Benny was pleased that I was a virgin, but he asked so he could be prepared on our wedding night."

Hannah rolled her eyes. "Why is it so important to men that they marry a virgin? Can you imagine if men had to prove they were virgins before marriage?"

"I suspect it's biological, like dogs marking their territory," Sharon said. "They don't want other dogs on their territory and will even fight to keep them away."

"Maybe they want new things—like preferring a new car to a used one or new clothes instead of secondhand?" Then Hannah shook her head. "But women want new clothes too."

"Or maybe it's like not wanting to eat something that has a bite taken out of it or a lollypop someone has already licked." Sharon frowned. "Except that women are usually more fastidious about food than men."

"You know . . ." Hannah spoke slowly as she organized her thoughts. "The reason anyone cares about a woman being a virgin is that there's a physical way to ascertain it. Nobody can tell if a man's a virgin or not by examining him."

"There's nothing we can do about that. It's how our bodies were created. But lots of men believe a virgin bride will be more faithful, that a woman who did it with someone else before marriage will also do it with other men afterward."

"That's absurd," Hannah snapped. "Those men are insecure and afraid of competition. If the bride has no other men to compare her husband to, then she won't know how competent he is in bed."

"Oh, she'll know." Sharon smiled. "Benny was a virgin too, but he was more than competent. He'd read so many books on the subject that he knew exactly what to do."

Hannah forced herself to smile back. "I've only just met Benny, yet obtaining this kind of information from books seems exactly what I'd expect him to do."

That night, gazing at Nathan's photo on her nightstand, Hannah wondered whether she should tell him that she wasn't a virgin. But the last thing she wanted was to dredge up those old memories. Maybe it would be best if she didn't tell him anything and then act surprised when she didn't bleed?

The next night she worried she wouldn't be a good enough actress, and Nathan would be angry that she'd hidden her defect from him. She could say she'd been injured; it wasn't like she'd be lying. It wasn't until Tuesday that she realized he might ask how.

It took her a long time to fall asleep, and then, just before dawn, she was jolted awake in terror. Her nightmare had seemed so real because it had been real—eight years ago. Everything she'd tried so hard to forget had come back as if it were yesterday.

Steven had taken her to a frat party, assuring her there was no need to worry because it was a Jewish fraternity. Except the punch tasted funny, and soon she felt so woozy that Steven helped her upstairs to lie down. But once the door was closed, he started fondling her and removing her clothing. He ignored her protests, and afraid to make a scene and shame herself by calling for help, she gave in and lay still. His breath, hot in her face, stank of alcohol, and she hoped it would be over quickly. The pain was sharp but blessedly short, and then, to her enormous relief, he soon rolled off and didn't move. The party was going strong downstairs, music playing and people laughing, so close but also a million miles away.

When he began to snore, she grabbed her panties from the floor and raced to the bathroom. There she rinsed away the blood on her legs and tidied up as well as she could before slinking down the stairs and out the front door. Thank Heaven nobody noticed her leaving, or at least nobody tried to stop her.

Walking to the dorm, all she could think was what had she done to deserve this? Was her sweater too tight or her lipstick too red? Back in her room, she stuffed the outfit she'd worn into a bag for Goodwill. Then she washed again, every square inch of skin he'd touched, crept into bed, and wept. But nothing could wash away the shame she felt.

The next morning he brought her flowers, lots of yellow chrysanthemums. Apparently he'd called earlier and somebody told him she wasn't feeling well. *Not feeling well?* She never wanted to see him again. She almost had her roommate tell him that, except then she'd have to explain why. So she went downstairs to confront her nemesis.

Steven shuffled his feet in embarrassment and said, "I'm sorry you're ill. I'm pretty hungover myself." She remained silent, so he added, "I was so drunk last night I don't remember how I got up to my room. But I promise it won't happen again."

She couldn't believe it. He had ruined her life yet had no recollection of what he'd done. He would never even feel guilty.

His anxious voice cut through her shock. "Shall I come back tomorrow, or do you want to call me when you're feeling better?"

"I'll call you when I'm better," she'd lied.

Upstairs she ripped the yellow mums into shreds until there was only a pitiful mound of yellow petals and torn green stalks. *Damn him! Damn that spiked punch! He'd better believe it won't happen again.* She stomped on the remains of his bouquet, threw them in the trash, and then flushed them down the toilet because she couldn't even stand the sight of them in the garbage can.

Yet what Hannah told Steven wasn't really a lie because the only time she felt better was when she got her period a few days later. But then the nightmares started. A few times a month for the rest of her freshman year, then, when she moved to a different dorm the following year, maybe every month or two. After her summers in Israel, they subsided to once or twice a year, usually in the fall, when yellow mums were unavoidable.

She had never told her mother what happened. Hannah still remembered that day during the year she said Kaddish for her father, when she was about nine. The word "pogrom" had come up, and Mama mentioned that soldiers had hurt her very badly and killed her sister. Their grandfather had died trying to protect them.

Eventually Hannah came to understand that those Cossacks had raped Mama, who'd been fourteen at the time. So she certainly didn't want to force her mother to relive those horrific memories.

This morning was her first bad dream since she'd begun studying with Nathan. She lay in bed, heart racing, knowing she had to tell him she wasn't a virgin—better tonight rather than wait for him to ask her—even if it meant he'd never want to see her again. Decision made, she didn't even try to quiet her sobs.

But Thursday was Talmud study, and she couldn't bring herself to tell him with all her family around. Friday evening was Shabbos, and Saturday night they went dancing as usual. Except it wasn't as usual. She couldn't concentrate on his lead and kept making mistakes. She even stepped on his foot with her high heels. Hard.

"Ow." Nathan couldn't help it. It hurt. "What's wrong, Annie? You seem distracted."

"Everything is fine." She immediately rebuked herself for her cowardly lie. "I'm just stressed by all the wedding plans." That much was true, since there likely wouldn't be any wedding and all their plans would have to be canceled.

Limping, he walked her off the dance floor. "I know it's early, but maybe we should call it a night."

Hannah had her chance when she dropped him off and he said, "You haven't said a word since we got in the car. Are you sure nothing's bothering you?"

"I'm fine," she bristled.

Their good night kiss was so perfunctory that Nathan had to conclude that not only was she definitely not fine, but she didn't want to talk about whatever was bothering her.

Hannah didn't know whether to feel relieved or rejected when Nathan didn't call her on Sunday, only that she felt wretched. She went to her room early but paced the floor until her parents were in bed and then crept downstairs to use the phone. Now that he knew something was wrong, she couldn't stand waiting any longer to get this over with and behind her.

It took several attempts, during which she put the receiver back in its cradle before she finished dialing, until she let the call go through.

He picked up on the first ring.

"I need to talk to you right away," she blurted out. Then, before he could even ask what was wrong, she continued. "Meet me in Prospect Park, at the Botanical Gardens Flatbush entrance, tomorrow morning at eight. It's urgent."

"Eight a.m. at the park? It's supposed to snow tomorrow." He couldn't hide his alarm. He could tell by her voice that something terrible had happened.

"I can't tell you over the phone. But it won't take long."

"Can't we meet somewhere indoors, have breakfast together?"

"No," she insisted. "I need someplace private." Then, before he could question her further, she hung up.

Nathan slept badly that night, waking several times to check the clock. Finally, at six thirty, he figured he might as well get up. It was snowing outside, so he decided to wear both his camel-hair sports coat and lined raincoat. If he were going to be miserable, it wasn't going to be because he was cold. Just in case, he phoned Spektor and canceled that day's office hours.

Nathan was half expecting to see Hannah waiting when he approached the Botanical Gardens entrance. But the snowfall was light enough to show that he was alone. Normally he'd have delighted in the scene of bare branches silhouetted against fresh snow while snowflakes swirled around him. But he kept his eyes focused in the direction from which he expected her to appear.

Shortly after eight, a figure emerged in the distance, and he hurried to intercept it. It was Hannah, but when she didn't rush into his arms but slowed her pace instead, he stopped and waited for her to approach him. With great trepidation, he also waited for her to speak first.

Hannah wanted this fiasco to end as soon as possible and didn't waste time on pleasantries. "I thought you should know I'm not a virgin." She looked at the ground rather than see his reaction. "So I'll understand if you want to cancel the wedding."

Nathan was rendered speechless. *For this I've been waiting outside in a snowstorm?* He tried to think of a better response.

Until she began to remove his mother's ring.

"Annie." He grabbed her hand to stop her. "I don't want to cancel our wedding. I love you. And whether you're a virgin or not doesn't change that."

This was the last thing Hannah expected to hear.

When she didn't respond, he asked, "Was it with Zechariah?" Then, after she shook her head, he said, "Then I assume it happened years ago," to which she nodded.

"You don't have to answer, but I'd like to know one thing. Is the man someone we're likely to run into later?"

She made a noise that sounded like choking and laughing, then shook her head and whispered, "He's dead."

Gevalt, Nathan thought. *The man must be someone from college she's never forgotten. Maybe that's why she hasn't dated since then.* Believing he should show some sympathy, he said gently, "You must have loved him a great deal."

The fury in her voice shocked him. "I hated him. I still hate him."

"Would it help to tell me what happened?"

No, it's too shameful. So she replied, "It was a long time ago. It doesn't matter anymore."

"It seems to me that it does matter, a lot."

"I can't tell you. You'll despise me."

"No, I won't. I love you."

Hannah gazed up at him, his expression so concerned yet also confused. She didn't go into details, just the basics of a frat party when she was a freshman, spiked punch, not feeling well, so a boy took her to his room to rest, then at this point she could no longer restrain her sobs.

"Gottenyu, Annie." He didn't want to use the word "rape." "It must have been awful for you."

"I've said this much—let me finish." Hannah looked off in the distance. "The following year he was killed in a car crash, but I was still afraid to date anymore." Now she was sobbing, and Nathan offered her a handkerchief.

He saw that she was shivering too. "You're cold," he said, putting his arms around her to warm and comfort her. She didn't pull away, and he struggled to control his feelings. He was so overwhelmed by anger, protectiveness, and desire for revenge that he didn't know what to say.

"I didn't dress for the snow," she replied. "I didn't plan to be outside so long."

He removed his raincoat and draped it around her shoulders. "I did. I had no idea how long we'd be out here." Thankfully, his camel-hair jacket was as warm as promised.

She looked up at him, and there was still anxiety in her eyes. "Are you angry?"

"Of course I am. I want to knock that guy's block off, but it's too late."

"I mean are you angry with me?"

"Never." Nathan put all his strength into his reply. "You were young and innocent. He got you drunk and forced you. I know it doesn't make sense, but I feel guilty that I couldn't have stopped him somehow." Even in Nathan's heavy coat, Hannah was still shivering, but at least she was no longer crying. "Do you think we could go somewhere warm?" he asked. "Preferably with food, since I was too worried to eat first."

"I've been worried since last Wednesday, when I had lunch with Sharon. She told me how Benny asked if she was a virgin."

"So that's what brought this on."

She nodded. "Now you can understand why I didn't want to study that piece of Talmud from Ketubot."

He sighed. "I only chose that one because Benny recommended we study some Talmud on marriage to see how you responded."

"You must have been devastated." When he shrugged, she looked into his eyes. "You're sure you still want to marry me?"

"More than ever," he replied. She was so beautiful, melting snowflakes darkening her eyelashes. He took her arm and started walking. "So, where shall we have breakfast?"

They went to the diner where she'd first interviewed him. Giddy with relief and eager to move on to a happy subject, they energetically discussed the apartment renovation; the new kitchen and family room would likely be finished by Pesach. They discovered they both admired Sarah Goren's paintings and modern furniture.

Then, after they'd devoured their eggs, toast, and corned beef hash, washed down by many cups of hot coffee, Hannah said, "As long as I made you cancel your appointments, can we do something fun together today?"

Nathan had a stroke of genius. "Let's go furniture shopping. One of the friends I share Dodger season tickets with has a store near here that specializes in modern stuff."

Her face lit up. "If we buy our beds, you and your father can stay in the duplex over Pesach and be close enough to have Seders with us."

When they got out of the taxi, Lenny welcomed them with enthusiastic congratulations. "You lucky dog," he whispered to Nathan, while Hannah made a beeline for the bedroom section. "You didn't tell me your girlfriend was such a hot chick."

Nathan said, "Just as lucky, we saw the final game of the World Series together."

Lenny punched his shoulder gently. "And you're even luckier because I'll give you a special price on our display sets for a wedding present."

"Thanks, that's very generous of you."

"Just returning the favor. Because you don't go to ball games on Shabbos, I got to see Sandy Koufax pitch two entire games the end of last summer. I tell you, that guy is amazing. Fourteen strikeouts against Cincinnati, including Gus Bell four times, plus shutting out Pittsburgh."

Nathan was in too good a mood to argue. "It's a shame he's so inconsistent."

"He needs more experience."

"And a good pitching coach."

"True," Lenny said. "But Koufax is caught in a vicious cycle. They won't let him pitch until his control improves, but the less he pitches, the worse his control."

"Hey, we're here to buy furniture, not criticize the Dodgers." Nathan turned to look for Hannah. "Let's see what my fiancée is up to."

They caught up with Hannah, who was examining some twin beds that fit together with one headboard. "My parents bought a set like this when they got married," she said. Nathan nodded to show that he understood its purpose. Which was to facilitate them sleeping separately while she was niddah.

Lenny encouraged the two of them to bounce on various mattresses as well as lie down on them. This brought on fits of embarrassed giggles, which subsided when he pointed out the display items on sale that included matching bedside tables and dressers. "I can have them delivered this week, and if anyone is moving in soon, you should get a dining set too."

Hannah eagerly headed for that area, leaving Lenny to elbow Nathan suggestively and say, "Before you finalize your choice of mattress, you might want to do a little bouncing on your hands and knees."

Nathan complied, but not before giving Lenny a dirty look. When he joined Hannah, it was clear she'd already chosen her favorite—a round wood table with a white laminated surface and matching chairs with white Naugahyde seats.

"These will lighten up the kitchen and go with our yellow color scheme." She beamed with a joy that Nathan knew was about more than matching furniture.

Lenny closed in for the sale. "This particular style comes with six chairs and an insert to make the table larger."

Hannah, her excited happiness growing, turned to Nathan. "Maybe we should look for a nice couch and chair for the family room. Your father should have someplace comfortable to sit."

When they were done, they had bought the table and chairs, a seven-piece bedroom set, along with a couch, chair, lamp, plus side and coffee tables for the family room. Nathan swallowed hard when he saw the bill but quickly realized this was exactly the kind of thing he'd been saving for. It was a commitment to his and Annie's future together, and it made her happy.

"Don't tell anyone what you paid here," Lenny warned them. "I don't want other people thinking they can get these prices."

Thus reassured, Nathan turned to Hannah. "What do you want to do now?"

"Let's go to the movies. I haven't seen *Carousel*, and it's playing at the King's Theatre."

"Perfect activity for a snowy day. I saw the play back in 1949 and really liked it." He hadn't liked his date that much though.

The matinee started less than a half hour after they arrived. Nathan put his arm around Hannah's shoulders, and they snuggled as close as they could with the armrest between them. With all the emotional upheavals they'd experienced that day, their cheeks were so wet by the final "You'll Never Walk Alone" that they needed both Nathan's handkerchief and one from Hannah's purse. They walked out of the theater slowly and stood silently watching the falling snow for several minutes.

There wasn't time to have lunch before Nathan's first class, but neither wanted to leave. Finally a taxi slowed in front of them, and they waved it over. At Hannah's house, Nathan retrieved his coat she'd been wearing and kissed her goodbye. They would have embraced longer, but the cab was waiting.

After their last kiss, Nathan whispered, "Since we're sharing secrets, you should know that I still am a virgin."

Nathan was so exhausted he went to bed right after dinner. But he spent a restless night trying to understand why men considered virginity so valuable. More importantly, why he was disappointed, and felt guilty about being disappointed, that Annie wasn't a virgin—not that he wanted her to know that. It didn't make sense. After all, she hadn't willingly relinquished her virginity; it had been stolen from her. Yet Nathan couldn't help fuming that the frat boy had also stolen it from him, to whom it should have rightfully belonged.

At the same time he accepted that he would have been disappointed, albeit not so angry, if Annie had lost her virginity in a consensual encounter. Then again, would he have felt disappointed if she'd been "wounded by wood," as the Talmud called a woman whose hymen had torn by accident? He didn't know. One thing he did know was that he didn't like how he felt, especially when he compared it to how Annie must feel.

Yet he had to admit it was a relief that Annie shouldn't bleed or have pain on their wedding night. And no matter how poorly he performed their first time, it wouldn't be as bad for her as before. On the other hand, being raped had obviously traumatized her. He'd have to be gentle and go slowly.

Hannah also went to bed early, and alone there she cried all the tears she'd suppressed during the day: tears of fear, of shame, of relief, and of joy. She'd been sure that the moment she told anyone her secret, her life would be ruined. Now she was grateful beyond belief that Nathan still loved her and hadn't rejected her. But she couldn't shake feeling damaged and guilty that somehow it had been her fault; if she'd only taken more care, she wouldn't have gotten herself into that predicament.

FIFTEEN

HANNAH SET OUT for Sharon's in a good mood. Aunt Elizabeth was coming on Friday to spend two weeks with them. The new furniture had arrived, and it looked even nicer than she'd imagined. She and Nathan had finally concluded the lengthy Talmud section on women and time-bound positive mitzvos, and she felt confident that she understood it. She was also excited, and a little nervous, about meeting theologian Isaac Goren when they had dinner at his home on Sunday, along with Sharon, Benny, and Nathan's father.

When she arrived at Sharon's for what was now their usual Wednesday lunch, Hannah was surprised, and a bit dismayed, to find an older auburn-haired woman smoking a cigarette in the kitchen. Hannah's initial curiosity at how an enlightened woman like Sharon could make a life with a Hasid like Benny was blossoming into friendship, but their talks had been private.

The stranger only increased Hannah's unease when she introduced herself. "I'm Leah Goren, Sharon's aunt. I've been eager to meet you."

"Pleased to meet you." Hannah tried not to feel intimidated, but this woman was the wife of Isaac Goren. From what Hannah had heard about them, Leah Goren was the writer responsible for turning his ideas into words on a page.

Sarah Goren ushered them into the dining room. "Sunday night will be a houseful of people, and I thought Hannah's first meal with Leah should be more intimate."

"Hannah is a writer too," Sharon said. "She has a master's in journalism from Columbia and works for the *Freiheit*. Her articles appear under the pen name H. M. Covey. That's how her romance with Nathan got started."

Hannah sighed with resignation as more people learned her pseudonym. Though it was probably hopeless to think it would stay secret after she interviewed so many women about their mikveh use.

Leah looked at Hannah with respect. "Yitz and I were so impressed with your interview of Nathan that we sent a copy to Joseph and saved two for ourselves."

"Mrs. Goren." Hannah wanted to address Leah but was interrupted when both older women, each a Mrs. Goren, broke out in laughter. Hannah felt uncomfortable calling women of her mother's generation by their first names, but obviously that presented a challenge here.

Sharon chuckled. "Until we married, Benny had the same problem. I still can't bring myself to call Nathan's father Sol like my uncle does."

"Mrs. Goren." Hannah grinned as she looked from one woman to another. "What does Nathan call you? I'll do the same."

"Just Sarah," replied Sharon's mother.

"And Leah," said her sister-in-law.

Once they were all seated, Hannah began again. "As one writer to another, Leah, how does it work to collaborate with your husband? Does he write and you edit, or do you each do both?" Hopefully, Leah would not find her questions too intrusive.

Leah answered without hesitation. "We've worked the same way since the beginning. First he explains, in some detail, a concept he wants to get across to the reader. Then I rephrase it, and he corrects me, and I rephrase it differently, and so on until he's satisfied that what gets written down is exactly what he means." Her voice was full of pride as she concluded, "Of course, I also keep track of the deadlines and deal with the publisher. Yitz has the lofty ideas, and I take care of practical matters."

Hannah was astonished at the extent of Leah's contribution to her husband's works. Like most married authors, Isaac thanked his wife in his books' acknowledgments. Yet he never divulged how much of the text everyone praised was due to her efforts. Maybe it was rude, but Hannah had to ask, "You don't resent him getting all the credit for your beautiful prose?"

She gave Hannah a condescending smile. "We are a team. He appreciates all my efforts, and when reviewers extol his writing, we both know who created it."

Hannah sighed. Leah sounded like one of the many "little women" she'd interviewed whose efforts and talents made their husbands' success possible. Before she could say anything more complimentary, Sarah added, "Even more amazing is that Leah disagrees with nearly everything Yitz writes. She's a fervent atheist, while he's somewhere between an agnostic and Spinozan pantheist."

"That describes Yitz, all right, but I'm not so much an atheist as someone who refuses to believe in any religion that is willingly blind to facts and accepts nonsense as the ultimate truth instead." Leah then challenged Sarah. "It's not like you and Dave share the same belief in God."

Sarah passed around a platter of poached salmon. "I admit it. He and Yitz grew up in an enlightened Orthodox family. Their parents were shocked when Yitz turned down Harvard for the Seminary. They followed Jewish Law because it was their tradition, and though they would say of course they believed in God, they didn't give much thought to the nature of God's existence."

"Is that what you do?" Hannah asked.

Sarah shook her head. "My family came to America from Russia when I was little. They were ardent Socialists who abandoned shtetl Judaism as soon as they landed in New York. We were still Jewish; we spoke Yiddish and didn't eat treif, but only my father went to shul, and that was once a year. Nobody in my family talked about God, and as far as my mother was concerned, religion did more harm than good." Her expression was serious. "I'm not an atheist. I don't know if God exists or not, and I don't care. But Dave and I do agree on one thing: what counts in this life is what you do, not what you believe."

Hearing how similar Sarah's history was to her own mother's—ardent disbeliever happily married to an Orthodox man—Hannah looked at the woman with new respect.

"When it comes to religious differences, I'd say that Sharon and Benny take the cake," Leah said. "He's probably the only one of the eight of us who has absolute faith in a personal God. Not to mention all that other Haredi rubbish."

"There is beauty and comfort in that kind of faith." Sharon spoke with confidence, not to argue with her aunt.

Sarah turned to Hannah. "If it's not too personal a question, how do you and Nathan differ in your religious beliefs?"

Hannah, fascinated at being a fly on the wall, had figured she'd be questioned eventually. She chose to talk about Nathan first, while she sorted out what to say about herself. "Nathan and I have been studying Talmud together for just over a year, and sometimes we digress into theology and the nature of divinity. Nathan is struggling with his beliefs. He has the same questions as Isaac Goren but doesn't like his answers, so he's still searching for what makes sense for him. More and more he reads the Torah not in a literal way, like he was taught, but as parable and legend.

Nathan doesn't doubt God's existence, but that doesn't mean he believes in a personal God who searches all hearts and understands every plan and thought."

"What about you, Annie?" Sharon seemed genuinely interested in Hannah's beliefs, not just ensuring that she wasn't left out of the discussion.

"I'd say my beliefs are evolving." Hannah realized that for her religious journey to make sense she would have to start with her childhood. "My parents were committed Communists, so I grew up with no religion at all. My father rejected his Protestant family's beliefs, and my mother abandoned her Orthodox Judaism years before I was born." *There, now they know my father wasn't Jewish.*

"So Samuel Eisin . . . ?" Leah left the question unsaid.

"My father died in the Spanish Civil War, and my mother married Samuel a few years later," Hannah explained. "I transferred from public school to the Torah Academy."

"Where Nathan also attended," Sharon added. "So they knew each other from back then."

"Suddenly I was living in an Orthodox Jewish home, studying at an Orthodox school, and going to an Orthodox synagogue," Hannah continued. "I missed my father terribly, but I liked my new life better than my old one. In particular, I loved how much everyone valued education. Nobody at the Torah Academy made fun of me for being smart." She halted for emphasis. "Nobody talked about believing in God, either, so I didn't think about it . . . until I went to Israel."

"That's where you got the information for your *Freiheit* articles," Sarah exclaimed. "They're excellent."

"Thank you. In Israel I saw firsthand what the Nazis had wrought. I met people who'd lost their faith completely and others whose faith was undimmed. I also met people who refused to let their faith fade; doing so would be tantamount to giving the Nazis a posthumous victory." She shook her head in wonder. "In Israel it was easy to have faith; everything around you is a miracle."

"So now you believe in God?" Sharon asked.

"I don't know. Sometimes I do and sometimes I don't, and when I do it's not always the same God," Hannah said. "I remember some older survivors in Israel arguing about God's existence, and somebody declared that the only thing all Jews believed about God was that there is, at most, one God. Everybody laughed, but I thought his statement was profound."

Leah smiled. "You'll get no argument about that from me." Her expression became serious as she turned to Hannah. "Enough about God, let's talk *tachlis*. How much do you plan to keep writing after you're married? I've often wondered if Joey's problems would have been less severe if I'd given more attention to him and less to Yitz's work."

Hannah explained how she'd already cut back her hours at the *Freiheit*. "Except for special cases, I won't be doing interviews for them anymore either. I intend to do other kinds of writing at home, on my own schedule."

The sun was low on the horizon when Elizabeth Covey honked her horn outside the Eisins' brownstone. Hannah, who'd been watching from the window, raced outside to move her dad's car a few feet and thus free up space for her aunt to park.

Hannah gave Elizabeth a relieved hug. "We were worried you wouldn't get here before dark."

"With everyone in a hurry to get home before the snowstorm hits, the traffic was terrible."

Normally Hannah and her aunt had a little ritual where Elizabeth insisted that as a nurse who had to lift and move patients every day, she was perfectly capable of handling her suitcases herself. But this time she let Hannah carry them up the three flights to their shared bedroom while she stayed downstairs.

"Do you mind if I take a little rest?" she asked Deborah as she sank onto the couch and put her feet up. "I'm exhausted from the drive."

Deborah and Hannah exchanged uneasy looks. "Rest as long as you like, Elizabeth. We'll have dinner when you're ready."

Hours later, the Shabbos candles had burned out and only Hannah, Deborah, and Samuel were still downstairs with Elizabeth. He had just stood up and stretched when Elizabeth cleared her throat. "I hate to ruin your Sabbath," she said. "But there's something I must tell you while it's just the four of us."

Samuel sat back down and took Deborah's hand while Hannah tried to hide her trepidation.

"I won't beat around the bush," Elizabeth said in her brusque nurse's voice. "The doctors say I have leukemia and likely less than a year to live."

When Deborah gasped in dismay, Hannah started to cry uncontrollably.

Elizabeth tried to console them. "I may not see an entire three score and ten years, but the Lord has given me close to that. I have lived a life of service to Him, privileged to become a nurse and utilize my skills to help desperate people in some of the most war-torn places on earth." She smiled wanly. "The Lord has blessed me to not only see the Ingathering of Exiles in the Holy Land but to participate in it. And He blesses me even at the end, for He has given me time to see my niece wed and put my affairs in order."

"That is a blessing," Deborah said with resignation.

"I have also been blessed with a financial reward such that I am able to benefit the less fortunate. But we will not discuss fiscal matters until after the Sabbath," Elizabeth concluded.

Upstairs in her room, Hannah couldn't hide her shock. "Aunt Elizabeth, are the doctors sure? Have you gotten another opinion?"

"Annie dear, I've consulted Boston's best specialists." With that, Aunt Elizabeth opened her suitcase and took out copies of *Brides* and *Modern Bride* magazines. "Something for you to enjoy with your mother and sister."

Elizabeth's ploy to distract her niece while she unpacked succeeded, and she had to tap Hannah's shoulder after she put the empty suitcases under the bed.

Hannah followed her aunt's gaze to where a fat manila envelope sat on her pillow. "Is this for Shabbos, or do I have to wait until tomorrow night to open it?"

"It contains the most recent Covey Foundation reports. Personally, I think these records, detailing which charities received our grants and how they used the proceeds, are more appropriate Sabbath reading than those magazines, where nearly every page advertises extravagant wedding merchandise." Elizabeth tsked her disapproval. "Please don't share these reports with your family though."

Hannah nodded. "I'll keep them up here."

After Elizabeth went to bed, Hannah was too distraught to sleep. She went to the window to watch the streetlight illuminating the falling snow, normally a soothing activity. Still wide awake sometime later, she opened the envelope and pulled out records going back five years. She started with 1955 and saw that the Covey Foundation primarily supported medical centers and schools, prominent among them children's hospitals and the Hadassah-Hebrew University Nursing School. There were donations to colleges, religious and secular. Also to Girl Scouts, Camp Fire Girls, and girls summer camps Hannah had never heard of, plus various refugee agencies, including the one that employed Deborah Eisin. As expected, there were reports from archaeological expeditions in Israel, including one that mentioned Professor Solomon Mandel.

Hannah forced herself to stop thinking about Aunt Elizabeth dying. But after her aunt passed away, Hannah would be the only Covey left. Her wealthy grandparents may not have given her an inheritance, but their foundation would need somebody to manage it after Aunt Elizabeth couldn't. She put the reports back in their folder and stared at the swirling snowflakes as questions filled her mind.

First came the scary ones. The Covey Foundation surely employed professionals, but what responsibilities would Hannah have to assume? How much of her time would it take? It was a good thing she'd already cut back her work at the *Freiheit*. As it was she didn't know how she'd juggle these new duties with her writing, plus being a wife and eventually, a mother.

What if she didn't want any extra duties?

Then Hannah began to contemplate the pleasant possibilities. She would get to decide how the Covey funds were allocated, and she could support the charities she preferred with amounts beyond her wildest dreams. She could hire all the household help she needed to ensure she had time for her writing. Eventually her children would follow in her and Aunt Elizabeth's footsteps.

When Hannah woke up, her aunt's bed was empty. A glance at the snowdrifts outside confirmed that the family would be spending Shabbos at home, so she brought the bridal magazines downstairs, where her mother and sister promptly took them off her hands. Hannah put some smoked fish, bagels, and cream cheese on a plate and made herself a cup of tea from the Shabbos hot water urn. Soon the four women were huddled around the kitchen table, magazines spread open before them.

The first things they looked at were wedding dresses. "Hannah is getting married in an Orthodox synagogue," Deborah reminded them. "Her dress must have sleeves."

"But can they be see-through like this?" Rae pointed to one with sheer sleeves and shoulders.

"I suppose so," her mother replied, clearly not enthusiastic. "As long as the bodice isn't too low cut."

"I think lace sleeves are more attractive," Elizabeth said.

Until that moment Hannah hadn't even thought about walking down the aisle. The bridal gowns were lovely, but she couldn't see herself in any one in particular. "The important thing for me is that I am able to dance in it. So no slim skirts, no floor-length ball gowns, no long trains, and no tight sleeves."

"Tea length, then." Elizabeth nodded approvingly. "It is, after all, the most appropriate style for a daytime ceremony."

Considering the mansion where her aunt had grown up, Hannah expected she'd seen enough society weddings to know what was appropriate.

Thankfully, Hannah agreed that a tea-length dress with lace sleeves was nicer. But that still left myriad designs to choose from.

"Let's start at the beginning again and dog-ear any page with that kind of dress on it," Rae said eagerly.

Hannah smiled at her sister's enthusiasm. Of course this was an excuse to leaf through the magazines again, but it was still a pleasant way to spend a snowy Shabbos. Hannah finally offered an opinion. "I don't like the short sleeves as much as the three-quarter or wrist length."

"But long sleeves don't seem to go with a midcalf skirt," Deborah pointed out. Then she frowned at the next page. "This backless style exposes too much bare skin. It's a shame so many ads don't show both sides, especially since the back of the dress is what everyone sees during the ceremony."

"No matter how pretty it appears on the page, the test will be how it looks in person," Elizabeth declared.

"I thought we'd do some preliminary shopping later this week, then come back to see Hannah's favorites during Chol HaMoed." Deborah looked outside and added, "Weather permitting."

Hannah reached for *Brides* magazine. "I'd like to read some of the articles."

Elizabeth stayed her niece's hand. "Let Deborah do that first. I'd like to speak with you privately."

They climbed the stairs to Hannah's room, where Elizabeth picked up the envelope Hannah had left on the bed. "Have you read the reports?" When Hannah nodded, she continued. "You must have questions."

"This is such a huge responsibility, and I have no experience with charities. I would need to learn so much." As Hannah thought aloud, her fear grew. "You're so competent, Aunt Elizabeth. Everyone runs to do what you want, but I don't know how to make people listen to me. Then, even assuming I learn what to do, how can I do this in addition to being a wife and, hopefully, a mother?" She began to cry. "I won't have any time for writing."

Elizabeth put her arm around her niece's shaking shoulders. "I don't think this is anything you can't handle. The foundation employs numerous professionals, from accountants to researchers, as well as clerical workers—most with years of experience. I meet with the administrators only twice a year to ensure we all know how the foundation's projects are progressing. I've had no difficulty performing all my foundation responsibilities without neglecting my nursing duties, even during wartime." She lifted Hannah's chin so their eyes met and smiled. "Your family could help you, and hopefully the Lord would bless you so a younger generation would eventually take over."

Aunt Elizabeth is dying. There would be no more shared summers on Prince Edward Island, no more driving around town together, no more learning firsthand about life in other countries . . . no more stories about her father's youth. As the years passed, Aunt Elizabeth had become almost a second mother to Hannah, albeit one who praised rather than criticized her. How sad that Nathan had grown up with no mother while she'd been blessed with two.

"But once people know I'm running a charitable foundation, I'll be inundated with appeals, even demands, for assistance," Hannah protested.

"True, but I'm confident you can be strong and insist that requests go through normal channels." Elizabeth's eyes searched Hannah's face as though trying to see inside. "Is there another, more critical reason, that makes you so reluctant to take on the role?"

Hannah let her grief spill out. "It hurts too much to even think about a time without you, when I have to take your place." She threw her arms around her aunt and hugged her gently.

The two embraced until Elizabeth let go and said, "You're getting married very soon, and I want to celebrate with you. Save your mourning until I'm gone." She gave Hannah a smile. "I thought you might like to honeymoon at the family farm before it becomes a Girl Scout camp. You can take home the dairy dishes, flatware, pots, and pans as my wedding gift. In fact, you are welcome to any of the house's contents."

Hannah managed a small smile and said, "Thank you so much, for everything."

"Now you can go downstairs and read all about etiquette and planning for your big day."

It was snowing so heavily Saturday evening that Hannah wasn't surprised when Leah Goren called to postpone Sunday's dinner. She very much wanted them all to meet before Pesach, so could Hannah come the following Friday instead? Joey would be home from school, and Nathan could share his room overnight.

Hannah accepted eagerly; it would be her first Shabbos dinner with Nathan. A few minutes later they were on the phone, reluctantly canceling their usual Saturday-night date. "Now that the apartment is somewhat furnished, Abba can move in Friday and stay the entire weekend. Then he'll already be there Monday for the first Seder," she suggested. "It would be nice if you could spend Shabbos afternoon with us." She couldn't wait to see him again.

Nathan hesitated. He didn't see Joey often, and soon enough he'd be spending most Saturdays with Hannah's family. "Would it be all right if Joey came too?"

"Of course. I'd like to meet him."

"We could all go out dancing next Saturday night."

"I doubt Aunt Elizabeth would go dancing, though." Hannah decided that when she ultimately shared Elizabeth's illness with Nathan, it would be in person, not over the phone.

"Weather permitting, I'll be over on Tuesday for Talmud. Tell your aunt I'm looking forward to seeing her again." Actually, he was nervous about seeing her again now that he was her future nephew. "I love you."

It made her heart melt when he said that. "I love you too."

When Shabbos ended, it was time for business. Rae and Jake went downstairs to watch television, leaving Hannah in the living room with her parents and aunt.

"Annie, your grandfather left Elizabeth a good deal of money when he died," Samuel began. "She came to me for advice, so I suggested she invest in the same real estate development company I did. And we've done very well in the building boom after the war."

Elizabeth turned to Hannah. "My share goes to you, including the duplex you'll be living in."

"I can't thank you enough," Hannah said. "But I doubt I'll need income beyond my salary from the Covey Foundation."

"You should take your share of the income anyway," Deborah declared. "To support your writing career."

"Gottenyu." Hannah's eyes widened. "What am I going to tell Nathan—and when?" *What if he expects to be the breadwinner and manage the purse strings? What if he worries people will view him as a gold digger?*

Elizabeth spoke up immediately. "Please don't say anything until after I leave. I don't want Solomon fawning over me and treating me like an invalid, not yet."

"I don't want to keep this a secret too long," Hannah said. "I say we tell him as soon as possible after Pesach."

"Speaking of Pesach, I have no objections to Nathan and Solomon staying in the new apartment whenever they like," Samuel said. "It will be convenient to have them within walking distance."

After dinner Saturday, Nathan presented his father with Hannah's suggestion that they move in on Friday.

Abba agreed immediately. "This way I can start visiting the local shuls."

"Maybe you should try Congregation Israel?"

"It's not for me." Abba shook his head. "Though I know that occasionally I must attend services there."

Nathan had not expected a different response. "Please understand that I will not be joining you. I want to pray where Annie does."

"I understand." He saw Nathan about to speak and quickly added, "Of course weddings are different; there men and women sit together, dance together."

"What am I going to do about Benny?" Nathan asked. "I can't imagine him not being my best man, but I don't know if he'd attend a wedding where men and women mix together."

"Do you think he'll agree to come to your *aufruf* at the Eisins' shul?" Abba asked.

Nathan stopped to think. "He and Sharon could stay with her parents that weekend, or with us. I'm going to call him right now. With this weather he's probably still at his parents'."

He was correct and was relieved when Benny agreed to attend both ceremonies. But he was irked at the lack of enthusiasm in Benny's voice.

The storm ended Monday, and by Wednesday the roads and sidewalks were cleared. Thus Hannah was able to join Sharon for their usual lunch. To her dismay, however, no sooner were Judy napping and Sarah ensconced in her studio than Sharon started crying.

"I hate going to Benny's parents for Shabbos, and this time I had to stay an extra two days because of the snow," she wailed. "Benny's downstairs in shul all day with his father and the men, while the women sit around judging me for wearing the wrong clothing and talking too brazenly." She reached for a tissue and blew her nose. "More and more, I stay in our room with a book."

Sharon obviously needed to vent, so Hannah spoke sympathetically. "I understand your feeling criticized. When I taught in that Hasidic girls' school, it took months before I could identify the difference between the women's clothes that distinguished the various sects, and I saw them every day."

"Benny is a completely different person over there, starting by changing into Hasidic clothes, including that horrid underwear." She saw Hannah's look of confusion and explained, "It covers him from waist to knees, spe-cially designed so he can urinate without touching himself."

"What?" Hannah exclaimed, then recalled that for Hasidim, there is no atonement for the grave sin of *wasting sperm*. "But Benny is a child psychologist. He's read Kinsey. He knows masturbation is normal."

"But he wears it anyway." Sharon lowered her voice. "Between that vile underwear and the walls being so thin I'm sure everyone can hear us, it's impossible to get in the mood for lovemaking." She sighed, and then her expression hardened. "He expects us to go to his parents this Friday as usual, even though Aunt Leah has you and everyone else coming to her for Shabbos dinner."

"I'm sorry you two won't be there."

"Not as sorry as I'll be. Before we got married and I agreed to spend Shabbos with his family, I had no idea how awful it would be. I thought it would be joyous, with lots of singing, but women aren't allowed to sing when men are there. I don't know how I'm going to survive another eight days there for Pesach."

"You've never stayed home on Shabbos?" Hannah was appalled. "Surely one of you must have been sick sometimes."

Sharon's face grew pale. "The first time I stayed home on Shabbos was when Eli was ill, and I began looking forward to him getting sick near the weekend so I could stay with him," she whispered. "Then he got polio."

"Oh no." Hannah knew Sharon had lost her first child in infancy because Nathan explained how they'd meet at the baby's grave. But she didn't know the circumstances.

"At first . . . at first, I was glad when he was sick. Not that I ever imag-ined it was polio." Sharon had to stop speaking, she was weeping so hard. When she finally found her voice, Hannah cringed at what came out. "That's why my son died—God punished me for wanting him to get sick."

Hannah put her arms around her sobbing friend and held her tight. What could she possibly say to console Sharon and lessen the woman's guilt?

Eventually Sharon sniffed back her tears. "I've never told this to anyone."

"Not your mother, not Benny?"

"Especially not him."

They finished lunch in silence, and neither ate dessert.

SIXTEEN

LATER THAT AFTERNOON, Hannah called Sharon with news she hoped would cheer her friend somewhat. "You're the closest thing to a sister Nathan has, so I'd like you to be a bridal attendant. We're going to look for my dress tomorrow if you want to join us."

"I'm honored, but it depends if my mother can babysit. I'll let you know."

The next morning Sharon called with her regrets, leaving Deborah, Rae, Naomi, and Aunt Elizabeth to do the preliminary shopping with Hannah, who was as nervous as she was eager. Everyone said a woman's wedding gown was her most important item of clothing, and thus anything less than perfect was unacceptable. So armed with magazine ads, they would start at Martin's Department Store and finish at Kleinfeld, famous for its large selection of special-occasion dresses.

Hannah wished they could have waited until her period ended, but they had delayed long enough. Again she was grateful to whoever invented tampons. No matter how strong her flow, a tampon and pad together meant she didn't worry about leaks or stains, which would be mortifying on the white bridal gowns. She was also relieved that, assuming her period came on time the next two months, she would finish her clean days in time to use the mikveh before the wedding.

When they reached Martin's, Deborah identified herself to the bridal department saleslady as the bride's mother, produced the photos, and stated that everything must be ready by June 1. In less than ten minutes Hannah had a dozen lacy dresses to choose from, and it was time for the exciting part, the actual trying on. But some of the prettiest gowns were so uncomfortable, even while performing simple dance moves, that Hannah promptly rejected them. Her family all preferred a sweetheart neckline to one straight across, but these displayed varying amounts of cleavage. So how much was too much?

"Obviously, any dress where Hannah's bra is visible is too low cut," Deborah said.

"But you'll be able to see her bra straps through the lace on all of them," Elizabeth pointed out.

Naomi examined the remaining gowns. "Some of these have built-in bras. Maybe Hannah should try those on next."

Now the saleslady entered the fray. "I suggest we ask the lingerie department to send over some strapless bras from the bride's current manufacturer in her size."

Hannah provided the information, though she was skeptical how well a strapless bra would stay in place with the energetic dancing she expected to do. Out of curiosity, she tried on a gown with a built-in bra. It looked nice, but the bra didn't fit right, and some of the others didn't fit either.

The saleslady arrived with an armful of strapless bras and a new suggestion. "Our bridal department provides alterations if the wedding date is over a month away," she said. "Find the bra that fits you, and we can sew it in. And if none of these gowns suit you, we can shorten one with a long skirt."

"Wow. We might be here all day," Rae blurted out, clearly relishing the prospect.

"Let me try the ones we have here already," Hannah said. Unless she found an absolutely perfect dress here, she still wanted to see what Kleinfeld offered.

Everyone left the dressing room so Hannah could find the best strapless bra. She was fascinated with the push-up varieties, though she doubted her mother and aunt would approve. Still, she chose one with a small lift. Returning to the remaining dresses, Hannah was soon down to two, one with lace she preferred and a neckline her mother deemed sufficiently modest, the other with a slightly lower neckline whose lace was pretty but not her favorite. Adding to her disappointment, both were merely fancy white dresses, neither of which entranced her into feeling like a real bride. *What is wrong with me?*

They ended up buying the bra and promising to return. The saleslady gave them her card, and it was off to Kleinfeld. There Deborah would find a better selection of mother-of-the-bride outfits, while Naomi and Rae looked for bridesmaid dresses. Unlike Martin's, the entire store was devoted to women's evening and cocktail attire. But its bridal section was smaller.

After learning the wedding date, the next question the saleslady asked was "What is your color scheme?"

"It won't be pink or lavender." Hannah gestured to Naomi. "Two of my bridal attendants are redheads."

"I suggest the turquoise family, darker for the mothers of the bride and groom." She turned to Hannah. "Have you chosen your wedding dress? We will want to match the style."

Hannah admitted she had not and showed her the magazine photos. The saleslady nodded and disappeared, returning shortly with an assistant pushing two clothing racks, one with wedding gowns and the other with fancy dresses in shades of turquoise, teal, and aqua.

Hannah tried on a few, including one identical to a gown she'd liked at Martin's only more expensive, but again they were merely white dresses, nothing special. "I'll get mine later," she whispered to her mother. "Now I can help the rest of you." Maybe seeing her family in their wedding finery would make her feel more enthusiastic.

"I don't mind a little lace," Deborah said, "but two of our attendants will likely want an opaque bodice and sleeves."

"I have to cover up," Naomi said. "Dovid will expect me to."

This must have been a common request in Brooklyn because several styles were identical except for the amount of skin visible through the lace.

"You choose first, Mama," Hannah said. "You know what mine will look like."

Deborah chose one similar to what Hannah had liked earlier, in a shade of turquoise that would look good on red-haired Naomi. Rae was so thrilled to be a bridesmaid that she loved all her choices, but Naomi preferred to wait and see what Sharon wanted. Elizabeth, true to her taste for classic tailored clothes, selected an elegant teal suit slightly darker than Deborah's dress. They would go back to Martin's for Hannah's wedding gown during Chol HaMoed.

Hannah hoped Sharon could escape Benny's family and join them.

Friday afternoon Hannah was waiting when a taxi delivered Nathan and his father, along with their suitcases, to the Union Street apartment. Uncomfortable at showing him too much affection in front of his father, Hannah gave Nathan a gentle welcoming hug. "Leah Goren called to say that Joey is home, so you two can go over anytime you'd like."

"You can go now, Nathan," Abba said. "I'd like to unpack and explore this place a little first."

"I'd rather not leave until you and Hannah can come too," he replied. "And I want to change clothes."

"I need to get dressed too. Why don't you show Abba around downstairs and come get me in an hour?" She waited at the stoop and added, "There are towels in the bathroom and some food in the kitchen. Naomi and Dovid say you can use their phone."

When Nathan turned on the new ground-floor lights, his father gazed in awe at how the apartment had progressed in six weeks. "What a difference all this light makes, now that the walls are plastered," Abba said.

"Wait till you see the bathroom," Nathan said. "The workers completed it quickly so they could use it instead of going upstairs."

As soon as they reached the bottom of the stairs, Abba hurried to the nearest door, but the room was empty except for a large sink. "It doesn't look done to me."

Nathan laughed. "You're in the laundry room. Eventually there will be a washing machine and dryer, plus counters for folding clothes and cabinets for storage."

Abba opened the adjoining door and sighed with satisfaction at the white porcelain sink and toilet surrounded by the white tiled walls and floor. "Just what I wanted." He pulled aside the shower curtain to reveal a gleaming white bathtub with shiny stainless-steel fixtures. "Do you think I could use it today?"

"Why not? If anything's not working right, we can let the workers know Monday."

None of the Gorens had seen Nathan in his new clothes and haircut, and only Leah and Sarah had met Hannah, so Nathan wasn't surprised when their entrance caused a stir. He could tell that Hannah was intimidated by Isaac Goren, while Joey was clearly shy around her. But by the time everyone was seated and done singing "Shalom Aleichem," the atmosphere was considerably more relaxed.

Hannah had anticipated being questioned by the male Gorens, who would understandably be curious about Nathan's bride-to-be. She was looking forward to questioning Isaac Goren about how his views differed from Mordecai Kaplan's. But Abba insisted she describe her years in Israel, following which Isaac talked about his earlier trip there. During dessert Hannah was back in the spotlight, and she was candid about her secular childhood and her parents' backgrounds. Increasing her disappointment, this opened a political discussion.

"Speaking of Communists," Dave Goren began. "The Supreme Court is hearing final arguments in the Harry Slochower case."

"The decision looks to be close," his wife, Sarah, added with some enthusiasm.

"Did you know him at Brooklyn College?" Abba asked them.

Dave and Sarah exchanged looks. "Not Harry so much as Bernard Grebanier, an English professor I knew well enough to despise, him being the one who accused Harry of being a Communist," Dave replied. "Bernard himself had actually been a Party member, but only briefly in the 1940s."

The last topic Hannah wanted to discuss was how former Communists were being persecuted, but she had to defend her mother. "Mama quit in 1939, when Russia signed the German nonaggression pact. She considered that act a complete betrayal of the cause."

Sarah nodded her approval. "Harry didn't deny being sympathetic to the Communists, but he was able to continue teaching when the college couldn't substantiate Bernard's charges."

"The entire English department knew Bernard pointed the finger only at Harry, and others, to deflect criticism of his own Communist past. Everyone lived in fear of him denouncing them next." Dave's voice hardened. "Then, when Harry was called before a Senate committee about his 'subversive activities,' he dared to invoke the Fifth Amendment."

Hannah's hands clenched at the mention of congressional committees, but she forced herself to remain calm and not enter the fray.

"Unfortunately, New York City requires that employees who take the Fifth be discharged," Sarah explained. "And when they fired Harry, he sued."

"And lost. So he appealed, and lost." Dave spoke with admiration. "He appealed all the way to the Supreme Court."

Hannah was thankful that the painful subject was drawing to a close, but before she could ask Isaac any questions, the conversation segued into a debate over what might have happened if Henry Wallace hadn't been dumped from the Democratic ticket in 1944. She gazed at Nathan helplessly as any hope of discussing theology evaporated.

He apparently got the message. "Enough of politics already, it's Shabbos. Let's have some more *zemiros*."

He immediately launched into "Yom Zeh l'Yisrael," and Hannah realized this was the first time she'd heard him sing. He was no Mario Lanza, but he had a nice baritone voice and could carry a tune. She still couldn't ask her questions, but celebrating Shabbos with song was better than wallowing in politics.

Yitz Goren then began "Tzur Mishelo," the song that introduced the Birkat Hamazon, the Grace after Meals. Everyone, including the women, joined in enthusiastically, and this was followed by a good hour of singing. The evening finally ended when the clock chimed eleven and Abba declared that he wanted to get up early to attend services.

Hannah understood why Sharon missed her family's Shabbos dinners.

When the three got to Union Street, Nathan told his father he'd walk Hannah home before returning to the apartment.

"What's the matter?" he asked her after they'd gone half a block in silence. "Didn't you like my singing?"

She knew he was joking, but she barely managed a smile. "I'm sure everyone else found the Slochower story interesting, but it brings back memories of how terrified my mother was that she would be called to testify before Congress."

"But she wasn't called, right?"

"Not so far." Hannah sighed. "In a way that only makes things more frightening because we never know whether she suddenly might be."

He put his arm around her. "Oy. You must have been sitting on *shpilkes* for years."

"I really wanted to talk to Isaac. I have so many questions about what he's written," she confessed. "I assumed more of the Shabbos conversation would involve religion."

"I've never been there for Shabbos before, but I expect the Gorens are probably tired of talking about work all week."

"Of course you're right." Her disappointment lessened considerably. "Teaching and writing about theology is their job, and they'd naturally want to talk about something else tonight." She'd have to find a way to chat with Isaac in private.

Sunday morning Hannah borrowed her aunt's car to drive Nathan, his father, and Joey Goren to the Mandels' Williamsburg apartment to get their Pesach dishes, cutlery, pots and pans, and other kitchen items. Prominent among these were beautiful sets of china and silverware.

"These came from my mother's family," Nathan whispered to Hannah as they carefully packed the delicate pieces. "There used to be more wineglasses, but Abba never replaced the broken ones."

Once at the new apartment, Naomi volunteered to help put away the kitchen things. "Look at this beauty." She held up a large soup tureen decorated with birds.

"It is lovely, isn't it?" Hannah agreed. "We won't need to register for Pesach dishes as wedding presents."

Naomi turned it over and gasped. "This is Homer Laughlin China . . . and they have a full service for twelve." She turned her attention to the flatware. "Gottenyu. This is sterling, not silverplate."

"Nathan told me his mother's family was wealthy."

"He wasn't kidding," Naomi said in awe.

They worked silently for a while until Naomi cleared her throat. "I need to tell you something that's been bothering me."

Hannah steeled herself for her friend's grievance. "Do I need to sit down?"

"That's not necessary." When Hannah remained standing, Naomi took a deep breath and let it out slowly. "We've been friends for a long time, Annie, and it really hurt my feelings that you didn't tell me about what was happening between you and Nathan, that I had to learn about your engagement from Tateh."

Hannah was filled with shame, but she didn't regret her actions. "We were afraid to tell anyone, even our parents and our closest friends." She then explained about them secretly studying Talmud, which led to them falling in love.

"So that's what you and Nathan were doing at your house in December while your family was in Florida."

Hannah nearly dropped the soup bowl she was holding. "How do you know about that?"

"I was suspicious that day when you took so long to open the door and then hurried to get rid of me. So I walked to the corner a few times until I saw Nathan come out, look around, and get in a taxi." Naomi appeared utterly unrepentant. "The next morning I saw him arrive, and the morning after that."

Hannah was speechless. *Is Naomi the one who tipped off Spektor?*

"What's the matter? Why are you looking at me like that?"

Hannah shared the dean's accusation but not Klein's help.

"Well, I didn't tell anyone," Naomi declared.

Hannah immediately felt chagrined. Of course Naomi couldn't have been the source. Nathan had been accused of meeting a woman at his own apartment. "I'm sorry I hurt your feelings, Naomi, but I'm glad you told me so I could explain."

"Is it still a secret?" Naomi asked.

"At least a dozen people know we studied Talmud together, so I suppose you can tell Dovid and your parents. But I'd rather it not become public knowledge."

"I understand."

"Speaking of secrets, what mikveh do you use?" Hannah asked. Naomi's mikveh had to be near where they lived.

Naomi hesitated so long Hannah was sure her friend was like the other women she'd interviewed last year. But eventually Naomi said, "The closest one, on Eastern Parkway, across from the library. It's not great; you have to bring your own towels and hair dryer. Still, it's clean and relatively convenient." She sighed. "What would really be convenient is to have a mikveh in my own house."

"You're my oldest friend, so I'll tell you a real secret." Hannah proceeded to share what she'd learned from her interviews. "Most Orthodox women don't use them at all," she summed up.

Naomi's jaw dropped. "So everyone just assumes they do." She hesitated and then asked Hannah, "What are you going to do?"

Hannah answered truthfully. "I don't know."

"But he's an Orthodox rabbi; he'll expect you to follow halacha."

Hannah knew her friend was right. "I'm hoping I'll be lucky and get pregnant right away. Then I won't have to worry about being niddah for a long time."

"I hope you do too." With her usual lack of tact, Naomi concluded, "Most of our old classmates got married and started having babies right out of high school. You'll have some catching up to do."

They were almost finished when Rae arrived and announced that lunch was ready. "Mom is making sure we'll all enjoy our last taste of hametz today . . ." Rae trailed off as Nathan and Joey came downstairs, and she stared at the attractive young stranger.

Nathan introduced them, and Naomi insisted she'd finish up so they could go eat.

Once at the Eisins', Rae and Joey ate quietly but occasionally glanced at the other, only to look away in embarrassment when their eyes met. To Nathan's surprise, but not to Hannah's, when he offered to stay and help the women prepare for Pesach, Joey volunteered as well.

Filled with boisterous children—Dovid and Naomi's three, plus those of the immigrant families Deborah assisted—the Eisins' first-night Seder was truly festive for Nathan. And not just because finally, not being the youngest, he didn't have to ask the Ma Nishtana (Four Questions). Most people around the table were strangers to him, except for Aunt Elizabeth, who sat between Hannah and Abba. How different this night was from last year's small Seder, attended by only a few of Abba's scholarly friends. At first

Nathan was astonished at how surprisingly well Abba got along with Moe Novick, his father's other seatmate. But their mutual love of Israel gave the two men much on which to agree. With so many immigrants present, the Seder was a true celebration of freedom, and Nathan was sorry when the evening came to an end.

Hannah, who'd considered the previous Seder her best ever, couldn't believe how things had gotten even better in a year. Last year, she'd just begun secretly studying Talmud with Nathan; now they were engaged to be married. Tonight, seated next to him and holding his hand under the table, she could freely give voice to all the interesting things she'd learned from Tractate Pesachim. Just as sweet was watching Mama truly enjoy herself for the first time in years. The HUAC threat had passed, and just as Mama had nearly given up hope, her wayward daughter was finally getting married.

The next night, Nathan enjoyed Abba's eagerness to walk to Yitz Goren's for the second Seder. Nathan would accompany the Eisins to the Helfmans', and while he knew it was silly, he still felt awkward celebrating Pesach with his grade-school teacher. Again there were many children, but this time Nathan sat between Hannah and Dovid. The wine was stronger, and the company grew more animated as the evening progressed.

Somewhere between the third and fourth cup, Naomi turned to Nathan and shot him a mischievous grin. "Did you know that when Hannah and I were in school together, I would inscribe 'Mrs. David Eisin' in my notebooks while she wrote 'Mrs. Nathan Mandel'?"

Hannah's face flamed as the room erupted in laughter. Thankfully, Nathan had not consumed so much wine that he was in danger of disclosing that in school he too had imagined being married to Hannah, although his thoughts had focused on the activity they'd be engaging in after the wedding.

When everyone finally calmed down, Naomi turned to Nathan again, this time with a serious expression. "Your Pesach place settings are beautiful; Hannah said they were your mother's."

"Yes, they were."

"What was her name? I mean her maiden name."

"Minnie Trachtenberg."

Naomi looked at him shrewdly. "Where was she from?"

Nathan had no sooner replied, "Philadelphia," than Naomi yelled across the table to her mother, "Mama, didn't Tante Rachel marry a Trachtenberg from Philly?"

Tante Essie replied, "She did, but don't get excited. Lots of Trachten-bergs live there."

Still thinking about Naomi's first question, Nathan lowered his voice to talk to Hannah. "I had no idea you had a crush on me in grade school."

She gave him a wicked grin and leaned so close they were almost touching. "You never wondered why someone as smart as me needed so much help with algebra?"

He pressed his leg against hers. "I certainly appreciated it, but you were the prettiest girl in school and I couldn't believe you'd be interested in me."

It was long past midnight when the Seder concluded after a lengthy stint of singing and drinking while Nathan and Hannah played footsie under the table. They walked hand in hand to her home and indulged in a great deal of good-night kissing. After Nathan made it back to the apart-ment and crept into bed, he gave no further thought to the Helfmans hav-ing some Trachtenberg relatives in Philadelphia.

Two days later Hannah was back at Martin's Department Store, accom-panied by her mother, aunt, sister, and two red-haired friends. She had resigned herself to not letting perfection be the enemy of excellence when it came to wedding gowns. Besides, it was more important that Sharon's first meeting with her female family went well.

Deborah gave Sharon a welcoming hug. "I'm very pleased to meet you. It's a wonderful coincidence that your family lives so close by."

In the week since their previous visit, the saleslady had found a dress with Hannah's favorite lace and sweetheart neckline, only with long sleeves. Hannah admitted that it fit well and looked very nice, but accepted that it was still just a fancy white dress.

"Since we're going to sew in your bra, we can easily shorten the sleeves too," the saleslady said.

"Then we'll take it." Guilty at not feeling more excited, Hannah started to get back into her street clothes.

The woman stopped her. "We still need to select your veil." Then she turned to Naomi and Sharon. "How closely do you two ladies want your dresses to match the bride's?"

It was a subtle way to ask how much skin they wanted to display. Naomi replied that she wanted something more modest, but Sharon sur-prised them.

"I dress like a Hasid too often as it is," she declared. "I'd like lace and a low neckline too."

Elizabeth supplied the skirt of her new suit for the saleslady to match the color, and they waited until she returned with an armful of lacey veils and a rack of aquamarine dresses.

"I don't care if the bridesmaid styles aren't exactly the same," Hannah said, trying to enjoy the happy mood as the trying on began. "As long as the colors match."

One hour later, the three attendants' dresses chosen, they all watched eagerly as Hannah considered the various veils. She decided on the one with lace that matched her gown even before she put it on, but she still modeled several for her family and friends' pleasure. She saved her favorite for last, and when the saleslady finished pinning it in position, the dressing room was filled with female sighs. The billowing veil did something the white dress alone did not, and in a transformation as breathtaking as a peacock's tail opening, Hannah saw a bride in the mirror.

She gulped in amazement. *Gottenyu, this is really happening.*

Tears filled Deborah's eyes as she gazed at her daughter. "Oh my," she began and then could say no more.

Elizabeth reached out and squeezed Deborah's hand. "What a beauty you and my brother produced."

"Until this moment, I couldn't let myself believe Annie was finally getting married," Naomi said.

"I can't wait to see Nathan's face when she walks down the aisle," Rae declared.

"I'm sure he'll think she was worth waiting for," Sharon said.

Hannah was too overcome with emotion to speak at all. She and Nathan were really and truly going to get married.

At the same time Hannah was choosing her bridal outfit, Nathan was back in Williamsburg. After a week in the new apartment, Abba asked him to bring over more of his things so he could stay for another Shabbos. "Here's a list of what I need."

Nathan had filled one suitcase with the clothes Abba wanted when the phone rang. "Mandel residence," he answered.

An unfamiliar male voice asked for Nathan Mandel.

"Who is calling?" Nathan said slowly, unsure he wanted to talk to this stranger.

There was a deep intake of breath at the other end of the line. "Barney Trachtenberg, from Philadelphia."

"This is Nathan." *No, it can't be.*

But it was. "Say hello to your uncle Barney. Your mother was my little sister."

For a long moment Nathan was unable to speak. "Hello. It's good to hear from you," he finally said, immediately feeling stupid for such an inane reply.

"I can't tell you how glad I am to hear your voice. Everyone will be delighted that I found you."

Everyone? "How many relatives do I have down there?"

"My sister Dora and brother Max are still with us. And you have ten first cousins."

"Wow" was all Nathan could say.

"Also, since your grandparents had eight siblings, there are at least thirty second cousins," Barney added. "Cousin Marsha will be writing you with all the details."

Nathan gathered his wits and gave Uncle Barney his address.

"Excellent. You'll also be receiving an invitation to a family wedding on Lag b'Omer. We very much hope that you and your fiancée will attend."

Nathan realized the Helfmans had not only found his family but had also supplied some information about him. "I'll have to ask her, of course, but I don't see why not."

"Good. You should come early for Shabbos dinner and the aufruf."

"My fiancée and I are *shomer* Shabbos," Nathan began, but his uncle interrupted.

"I understand, but you'll stay with Dora in the old family house near the shul. She keeps kosher." Barney stopped to catch his breath. "Wait until I tell her that I actually spoke with you."

After Barney hung up Nathan stared at the phone for a long time. For twenty-five years his father had been his only relative, and now, out of the blue, he had dozens. People he should have known since childhood, weddings and bar mitzvahs he'd missed. His throat tightened until he thrust away those regrets and focused on telling Annie that, in less than a month, they'd be going to a wedding in Philadelphia, meeting his large family, and learning so much more about his mother.

While spending an entire weekend together.

His opportunity came that evening, as they prepared to study Talmud, and her response was as enthusiastic as he'd hoped.

"Incredible." Her smile lit her entire face. "To think that you've had a big family all these years and never knew it. Naomi will be thrilled."

"Do thank her for me," he said. "Now I need to decide how and when to tell Abba. At best he'll have mixed feelings."

"Maybe wait until you get the letter from your cousin."

Nathan nodded slowly. "I could show it to him with the wedding invitation."

The matter settled, they turned to their Talmud texts, the first and last tractates, Berachot and Niddah. "When I asked you where it came from that instead of immersing seven days after their menses start, like the Torah says, women now delay for seven clean days after it ends," Hannah began, "I thought there would be something in the Talmud more definitive than Rav Zera saying: The daughters of Israel imposed on themselves the restriction that even if they observe a drop of blood the size of a mustard seed they wait seven white days."

She was eager for Nathan's explanation, but he only said, "Go on."

Her voice rose in disbelief. "So despite Rava's vehement opposition to changing a Torah law for a mere custom, this has become halacha?"

"We don't know how it happened, but in the twelfth century, Maimonides writes that this stringency found favor in the Sages' eyes and they gave it legal status." He saw her eyes narrowing and quickly added, "He also writes that the decree that a *ba'al keri*, a man with a seminal emission, may not say the Shema until he immerses was revoked because the men did not follow it."

"The Torah says that a ba'al keri must immerse, same as a niddah." Her voice rose as she stated her objection. "But the Sages changed the law so he only washes with water while she not only still has to immerse, but she waits an extra week to do so?"

"You're right. When it came to immersion, the Sages were lenient with the men and strict with the women, though both men and women are restrained by the seven-clean-days limitation."

"Not when men could have more than one wife," she shot back. "Plus, they can visit all the harlots they want." It took a great deal of restraint to keep from pointing out that if a decree is revoked because nobody follows it, then modern women shouldn't have to immerse either. Because chas v'chalila she should explain how she knew this.

Nathan sighed. "No sage today has the authority to change halacha." *Not that this stopped the Reform movement from voiding the entire concept of purity and impurity.*

Hannah was still angry enough that she needed to have the last word. "Unless it's to make the law stricter."

He remained silent. He wasn't about to say what had just entered his mind. God didn't give the Sages authority to make and change halacha; they took it upon themselves and people followed. *Or not.* Which is why Jews had divided into denominations.

The first thing Hannah did the next morning was call Naomi. "You'll never guess what happened." She was so thrilled she couldn't keep her voice down.

"What? What? Tell me," Naomi insisted. Hannah's excitement was contagious.

"Guess who called Nathan yesterday?" Hannah didn't wait for Naomi's response. "Barney Trachtenberg, his uncle from Philly."

"Wow. That was fast."

"So it was you we should thank. I thought so."

Naomi chuckled. "You're very welcome."

"This will make a huge difference in Nathan's—in our—lives," Hannah said. "How did you make it happen?"

"First I called Aunt Rachel, who gave me her sister-in-law's number. Then I looked up Solomon Mandel in the phone book so I had Nathan's number. Finally I called the sister-in-law, told her I was trying to connect Nathan with his mother's family, and gave her the information I had," Naomi explained. "That's all."

"That's all? Are you kidding? It was enough that Nathan and I are invited to a weekend in Philadelphia next month for a big Trachtenberg wedding."

"Ooh, will you and Nathan be staying in the same house?"

"Yes, with his aunt." Hannah shared her enthusiasm. "We'll get to spend an entire three days together."

"That's wonderful. And it took just two phone calls." Naomi sighed with delight. "Now Nathan can reclaim his mother's side of the family, and they can reclaim him."

"Listen, Naomi, don't say anything to Nathan's father yet," Hannah warned. "Nathan needs to be the one to tell him."

Saturday night Elizabeth stayed home with Jake so Hannah and Nathan, along with Samuel, Deborah, Rae, and Joey, could go dancing. Comfortably seated in Samuel's sedan, they drove to a dance hall popular with students. Most high schools and colleges didn't have classes this week, so the place was packed.

Once inside, Nathan took Hannah's hand and confidently led her onto the dance floor. Two months of his expert tutelage had done its job, and a crowd soon gathered around them. Hannah was filled with pride as she saw her parents, competent dancers themselves, watching her and Nathan command the room's attention.

After a few songs, they changed partners so Nathan danced with Deborah, Samuel with Rae, and Hannah with Joey. This was the first time since becoming engaged that she'd danced with anyone other than Nathan, and she realized how much she depended on his lead. With Nathan her body effortlessly sensed what to do, but she had to concentrate to follow Joey.

When the band played a foxtrot, Samuel cut in, saying, "I need to practice with my daughter for the wedding reception."

Hannah had no difficulty following him. "Rae and Joey seem to be enjoying themselves," she said. She was twelve years older than Rae, and her role in her half sister's life had mostly been that of a babysitter and occasional roommate. Now Rae was becoming a peer.

He looked over just as Joey lifted Rae up, and she squealed in delight. "Yes, they are. But she's only fifteen. That's too young to date anyone, let alone a college student."

Hannah defended Rae. "They're just dancing, not dating. Besides, he's going back to California in a few days."

Samuel turned to watch Nathan and Deborah. "I would never have expected a Talmud scholar to dance so well, and certainly not one who teaches at Spektor."

Hannah sighed. "Isn't he amazing?"

Samuel took in the lovestruck expression on her face and smiled. "Most definitely."

SEVENTEEN

THE WEEK PESACH ENDED, Hannah was astonished to get a phone call from Isaac Goren, inviting her to a "walk and talk" to answer her questions. "I have some questions for you as well," he told her.

"I should have time on Thursday afternoon," she replied. "I have an article to finish for the *Freiheit* by Friday, but it's nearly done." Thankfully, she had already completed four Israeli interview articles, sufficient to keep Moe happy until she returned from her honeymoon.

"Excellent. My doctor recommends taking a stroll after lunch. Shall we say two o'clock?"

The Gorens' apartment was on the way to Prospect Park, and Hannah rang the doorbell just as church bells chimed the hour. Five minutes later they were walking east on Eastern Parkway.

"Many people are like me, raised Orthodox but now searching for a way to reconcile keeping traditional Jewish observance with a skepticism of the literal meaning of the Torah," Isaac began. "I'm curious how someone raised completely secular but is now Orthodox deals with those difficulties."

Since studying Talmud, Hannah had wondered about this too. "Maybe because I majored in English, it seems clear that the Torah was written by men—some divinely inspired—who lived in ancient times," she replied, thinking of Kaplan's explanation that God didn't give Jews the Torah; rather, the Torah gave Jews God. "I've also studied enough Talmud to know that rabbis regularly reinterpreted the Torah to make its laws appropriate for their lives, both eliminating old rules and adding new ones."

"So why follow Orthodox halacha?"

"That's what my family, and my community, does. Though to tell the truth, if my family were Conservative Jews, I'd probably be one too. Society needs structure and rules to function, and I think Jewish Law does this well." She would not admit how much studying Talmud and reading Kaplan's books had led her to question Orthodoxy, but she hoped Isaac

Goren could help her find more meaning in Judaism. "Why do you follow it, if you don't believe God commanded you to do so?" she asked instead.

He evaded her question. "I prefer not to use the word 'believe' when talking about God. It implies something magical or supernatural, like believing in ghosts or tooth fairies. My views about God are still evolving. These days I'm moving toward the view that He created the world, a world with both physical laws and moral laws, and then left us to our own devices."

Hannah heard the uncertainty in his voice. "But?"

He sighed. "But while visiting Israel, I experienced a sense of something, or someone, both immanent and awesome."

"I had that experience too." She sighed at the memory and then asked, "Jewish men are obligated to pray, but how do you pray if you don't know who you're praying to or whether anyone hears you?"

"All modern Jews struggle with that, but it doesn't stop me from praying."

Hannah noted that he hadn't actually answered this question either, but she still admired his reply. "I learned back in grade school that Israel means 'one who struggles with God.' So you're in good company."

"How do you pray?"

"The first time I went to shul, I liked the singing," she replied. "Then, after my father was killed, I spent the summer with my aunt, who prayed every day. With her I felt the comforting embrace of a presence. I didn't understand who it was or where it came from, but it was all around, like the air. When I came home, I said Kaddish for my father at shul and at school."

He looked at her in awe. "They permitted you to do this?"

"They told me not to, that girls don't say Kaddish, but another student, a boy, was saying it, so I did too. And nobody stopped me." Back then she was being rebellious. Now she was proud of her actions.

"Nathan was in school with you then, so he knows you're not afraid to challenge authority."

"He's not afraid either. That's why he agreed to teach me Talmud." She paused before adding, "And why he read all your books even though his teachers put you in cherem."

"You two are a good match," Isaac said. "I'm very fond of Nathan, and it pleases me immensely that he's marrying an intellectual equal."

Embarrassed by his praise, Hannah returned to the subject of God. She would soon be a rabbi's wife; she needed to be more assured about her beliefs. Kaplan's view that God was the power that brings salvation didn't resonate with her; for her God was more an entity than a process. "I like your idea that since God obviously made the world with physical laws like gravity, why shouldn't God have given us moral laws as well."

"It would explain why people have a strong, almost innate, need for justice and fairness, and why everyone agrees that some actions are good and others evil," he said. "But though God is powerful enough to create the universe, He is not omnipotent."

"So, no miracles?" she asked.

"None that break physical laws," he replied. Then he shook his head and sighed. "But it is difficult not to see the establishment of the State of Israel as a miracle."

"So do you observe Orthodox halacha?" she pressed him.

He took a deep breath. "I'd have to say I prefer the Conservative approach, that halacha should adapt to modern society and change as the lives of Jews change."

Like the Talmudic rabbis changed halacha after the Temple was destroyed, she thought. Then she remembered what Kaplan wrote about women's inferior position in marriage. "Does Conservative Judaism have any remedy for the estranged wife whose husband won't give her a divorce?"

"It does now," he said proudly. "In 1953 my colleague Rabbi Saul Lieberman created a new clause for the Conservative ketubah that, should the couple obtain a civil divorce, requires the husband to give his wife a get so both can remarry according to Jewish Law."

They walked in silence for a while, Hannah wondering how Nathan would react if she asked for such a clause in their ketubah and what she would do if he refused to add it.

"I hope I've answered all your questions," Isaac eventually said.

"Nobody could answer them all, but you were very generous with your time. I thank you."

"Thank Nathan. He said you wanted to talk religion with me." He cleared his throat and then continued. "There is a different subject I want to broach with you, that of my son, Joseph."

"What about him? I only just met him."

"I'm concerned that he seems to be infatuated with your sister. He's never had a girlfriend, and in many ways he's immature for a twenty-year-old."

"Nathan told me that Benny has been treating Joey for over five years."

A shadow passed over Isaac's face. "My son's mental health is more fragile than it appears. I don't want to see him hurt."

"My little sister is as innocent as your son, and my dad is equally concerned that Joey is too old for her."

"Then let's all hope this puppy love is a sweet experience for both of them," he said with resignation.

The following Saturday, Nathan and his father were back at their old apartment, sorting and packing books. They'd given the landlord notice; that night would be Abba's last in Williamsburg.

"For years I've wanted to move to a nicer neighborhood, closer to the Seminary. I'm so tired of this rundown old street; just walking out the door makes me depressed and angry." Abba added the last volume of Talmud to his box. "I've waited a long time to see spring flowers in window boxes again."

"It seems presumptuous for me to move into the new place so soon," Nathan said. "I feel like it would be tempting fate." Yet it was also irrational to feel comfortable moving his father into the new home but not himself.

"Strange how old superstitions have such power," Abba said.

Nathan was examining a row of books, trying to decide which ones Abba could take and which he still needed here, when there was loud banging on the front door.

Abba looked up in surprise. "Who could be making all that racket on Shabbos?"

His question was answered when Benny's voice yelled to let him in.

"It's open," Nathan called out. Then his jaw dropped. Benny looked terrible; his hair was a mess, and dark circles rimmed his red and swollen eyes. "What the—"

His face a mask of fury, Benny lunged at Nathan, but Abba came between them.

"Sharon is gone." Benny's voice was rough and hoarse. He'd obviously been crying. "She took the baby and all their things and moved back to her parents."

Nathan and Abba exchanged shocked looks.

Abba asked, "What happened?"

Benny's eyes narrowed as he handed Nathan a folded paper. "You tell me. I spent all day Friday at their doorstep, but Sharon would not talk to me."

It was from Sharon. She wrote that she loved Benny but couldn't live with him this way anymore, that Nathan could explain why. Nathan reread the letter, his anger growing that Sharon, who'd made him promise not to tell Benny anything, now, without warning, wanted him to explain why she'd left.

Nathan fought to restrain his tumultuous feelings while Benny stared daggers at him. "Sharon told me how unhappy she was back in autumn," he began. "I wanted to tell you, but she made me swear not to."

"You, my best friend, were meeting with my wife, in secret." Benny screamed so loudly Nathan was afraid the neighbors would be at the door at any moment.

"We were never secluded. We only met a couple of times, at your son's grave."

That silenced Benny, who looked so miserable Abba took him in his arms and pulled him close. "I am so terribly sorry."

Despite being much taller, Benny put his head on Abba's shoulder and sobbed.

"Nathan told me about Sharon months ago, but I never promised not to tell you," Abba said. When Benny quieted, Abba slowly and honestly explained Sharon's suffering. It took a long time, as he tried to answer Benny's questions too.

"I urged her to tell you herself, but she refused," Nathan reiterated. "She said you had enough problems."

"I had no idea the other women treated her badly. I thought she would be honored as the rebbe's daughter-in-law." He closed his eyes and shook his head. "No wonder nobody was sympathetic when I came alone for Shabbos, hoping for comfort and advice. The shammes said everyone knew the marriage would never work, so now I could divorce her and marry a good Hasidic girl."

"Divorcing a woman is not so easy here in New York as it is in Jewish Law," Abba pointed out.

"Good." Benny's voice was determined. "Now I have a chance to fix this."

"I suggest you reconsider what compromises she made to marry you and which ones are most or least important now," Abba continued. "Also what compromises you're willing to make. For example, if you want to spend holidays with your family and she with hers, then maybe you should live in a neighborhood in walking distance of both."

"But she refuses to talk to me," Benny insisted. "I called her parents; that is how I knew she was there. They said she would not speak with me." His chin quivered. "If only she had told me, instead of suffering in silence for so long."

"Write to her," Nathan told him. "Send her a letter every day."

The sun was setting when Benny announced, "I will not go back for Havdalah. Not after everyone treated Sharon so badly."

"You can stay here in my room," Abba offered. "I was going to move out tomorrow, but I'll take a taxi and leave tonight."

Nathan waited impatiently for Shabbos to end, then rushed to phone Hannah. "I hate to do this, but I have to cancel our date." He'd gotten only a few words of explanation out when she said she'd be right over.

A half hour later, she was racing up the stairs. She stopped and looked at Benny, dressed in his Hasidic Shabbos outfit, in shock. "Look at the two of you. What a difference."

Benny stared at Nathan for a while before declaring, "He may have a different haircut and new clothes, but this is how I have always dressed for Shabbos."

"According to your wife, your clothes aren't all you change for Shabbos," Hannah accused him.

"What do you mean?"

Hannah turned to address all three men. "I've been having lunch with Sharon every Wednesday for weeks, including the week before Pesach. I knew she dreaded those days with Benny's family, but I never imagined she would leave afterward." She stared at Benny sternly. "She went shopping with us for wedding dresses during Chol HaMoed and seemed fine. Something must have happened since then."

"Nothing happened," he declared.

"Nothing you know about," she corrected him, then proceeded to share Sharon's dashed hopes. "When Sharon married you, she imagined it would be like in the Book of Ruth: 'Your people will be my people and your God my God.' Now she doubts your people will ever be her people, not when girls are taught censored Bible stories instead of how to daven. Not when she wore the wrong socks and the women looked at her like she was wearing a bathing suit to shul."

"I did not know—" Benny began, but Hannah cut him off.

"Of course you couldn't know the women view her with envy or contempt. Hasidic men and women are seldom in the same room with each other."

Benny, looking crushed, put his head in his hands, and Hannah realized she'd been critical enough. "Sharon knows she needs to tell you about this, Benny, but she wanted to wait until your situation at Columbia wasn't so difficult."

Nathan and Abba eyed him questioningly and Benny shook his head. "My area of research is considered taboo or occurring rarely, both of which limits funding so severely that my receiving tenure is no longer assured."

Abba put his hand on Benny's shoulder. "And I thought teaching Talmud text criticism was controversial."

"Benny's not telling the half of it," Nathan added. "Trying to treat these traumatized patients, yet forced to concede that men honored in his own community have injured them with impunity, is pouring salt in his wounds."

"Sharon knows you're suffering," Hannah said softly. "She didn't want to add to your burden, but something made her break." Then, deciding there were too many secrets between them, she told him about the guilt Sharon carried over their son's death.

Nathan had to do something. It was partly his fault things had gone this far; he should have made her tell Benny—or told Benny himself. "I'm calling her parents. Maybe she'll talk to me."

But Dave Goren said Sharon wasn't talking to anyone. Nathan then asked how she was and added how concerned he and Annie were about her, until Hannah gestured for the phone.

"When can Benny see his daughter?" she asked Dave. "I understand that Sharon can't see him just yet, but surely she doesn't mean to keep Judy from him." She turned to the men and announced, "He says to hold on." After what seemed like an eternity, she hung up and heaved a sigh of relief. "Benny can see his daughter on Thursday morning."

They finished packing Abba's books, after which Hannah drove him and the boxes back to Union Street. Nathan loaned Benny a pair of pajamas and could see that Sharon was right; he did wear that weird underwear.

"Why do you still wear those? You're married now," he asked.

"Habit, I guess," Benny confessed. "But now that I know how Sharon feels about them, today is the last time."

"I have a feeling not all your compromises will be so easy."

"I have a feeling you are right."

Once home in bed, Hannah tried to process what happened. She was thankful Sharon's misery was no longer a secret from Benny but horrified that it had burst out in such a traumatic fashion. Despite their love for each other, could the couple overcome all they'd suffered and reconcile? Certainly Nathan would want them to, but she wasn't sure Sharon could be open about her needs or that Benny would make the necessary changes.

Hannah was abruptly aware that tonight was a lesson for her and Nathan, too, to prevent something like this from happening to them. Things had worked out well when she'd told him about being raped rather than trying to keep it secret. So she must continue to be forthright and open with him, never hiding things from him—no matter how painful.

Thursday night, before Hannah and Nathan studied Talmud, they called Benny for an update. "I took Judy to the park, but Sharon stayed in her room." They could hear his heavy sigh over the phone. "She returned my letters unopened."

The only good news was that the Supreme Court had ruled in favor of Harry Slochower by a vote of five to four. "The privilege against self-incrimination would be reduced to a hollow mockery if its exercise could be taken as equivalent either to a confession of guilt or a conclusive presumption of perjury," the court's ruling read.

That decision, following Senator McCarthy's censure, lifted any cloud still hanging over the Eisin household. With the HUAC focusing on Hollywood rather than ordinary citizens, Samuel was confident that Deborah was no longer in any danger of being subpoenaed. Now she was free to concentrate on Hannah's wedding.

Despite all the upheaval, Nathan still needed to tell his father about his Trachtenberg relatives, and Hannah couldn't put off giving them the sad news about Aunt Elizabeth. Pointing out that, except for Pesach, Solomon Mandel hadn't dined with the Eisins in months and now he was living around the corner, Samuel invited him and Nathan to dinner on Sunday. Nathan decided to stay over at the apartment that night and show Abba the Trachtenberg wedding invitation in private.

Nathan realized something important was coming when Rae and Jake carried their desserts downstairs and Hannah clutched his hand under the table.

As soon as the children were out of earshot, Samuel took a deep breath. "I hate to interrupt all our wedding planning with bad news, but Elizabeth Covey has been diagnosed with leukemia." He waited until the guests' sounds of dismay ended. "While we expect her to attend the wedding, her doctors give her less than a year to live."

Nathan stared at Hannah in shock while Abba took out his handkerchief and blew his nose.

"Aunt Elizabeth told us when she came down for Pesach," Hannah said. "But she didn't want you to know until after she'd left."

Nathan squeezed her hand gently. "I'm so sorry. I know she means a great deal to you." Now that he'd expressed his sympathy, Nathan didn't know what to say next. His mind was a whirl of questions, most of which seemed crass and avaricious. So he remained silent.

His father was not so reticent. "What will happen to the Covey Foundation?"

Samuel and Deborah looked at Hannah, who'd anticipated the question. "Aunt Elizabeth asked me to take over its administration," she replied. "While the foundation employs many professionals, I hope Nathan will help me as well."

"Of course I will," he said promptly, though he had no idea what that would entail. Now he had even more questions.

One question Samuel did answer for Nathan. "The bulk of Elizabeth's estate goes to the foundation, but Annie, her only living relative, will still inherit a substantial sum."

"I always thought those 'I've got good news and bad news' anecdotes were jokes," Nathan told Abba on their way to the apartment. "But tonight it was real."

"So how do you feel about marrying an heiress?"

"I'm glad we got engaged before I knew she was wealthy. I would hate for Annie—or anyone—to think I'm marrying for money." He thought some more and added, "Still, considering how guilty I felt letting Samuel buy me those expensive new clothes, I'm not sure how to handle this."

"Keep in mind that *tsu hoben gelt iz a guteh zach; tsu hoben dai'eh iber di gelt, iz noch besser.*" (To have money is a good thing; to have a say over the money is even better.)

Nathan nodded. "She does want me to help run her charity."

"Remember how hard it was in the Depression?" Abba asked. "*Es iz nit azoi gut mit gelt vi es iz shlecht on dem.*" (It is not so good with money as it is bad without it.) "Think of all the people you two can help."

They walked the rest of the way in silence, Nathan worried that he didn't deserve such a bride: smart, beautiful, and rich. In stories, too much good fortune always seemed to extract a high price.

When Abba turned on the hall light, Nathan pulled the wedding invitation out of his coat pocket. "I got this in the mail during Pesach."

"Gottenyu" was all Abba could say.

Nathan explained how Naomi had found his Trachtenberg relatives, after which Uncle Barney had called and Cousin Marsha had sent the invitation. He did not share the long letter she'd included in the envelope. "They're eager to see me."

"You're going." It was a statement, not a question.

"Yes. Annie and I will go down on Friday and come back Monday afternoon in time for me to teach."

"You didn't need to wait so long to tell me."

"I'm sorry. I didn't want to upset you."

"Compared to Elizabeth's illness or Benny and Sharon's estrangement, this hardly qualifies as upsetting." He put his hand on Nathan's shoulder. "I hope you're not disappointed when you meet them."

Nathan smiled with relief. "I hope they're not disappointed when they meet me."

A week later, when Nathan arrived for their Tuesday Talmud session, Hannah had good news. "Sarah Goren called and said she'd persuaded Sharon to meet with both of us tomorrow. Evidently I convinced her that Sharon had an obligation to you because of your earlier involvement."

"I'm relieved, and anxious, at the same time."

"So am I. Now I need to reassure her that I'm on her side."

When they arrived at the Gorens' the next day, Sharon looked even worse than Benny. She was wearing a housecoat and hadn't bothered to put on lipstick or even brush her hair.

Nathan thanked her for seeing them, and when she didn't reply, Hannah said gently, "Pesach must have been awful for you."

"Going shopping for wedding dresses with you was like a parole from prison," Sharon began. "When I returned to the Stocksers' house, it was like being locked back in a dungeon. At Martin's, the clothes were colorful and vibrant, but what everyone wears at the Stocksers', even at shul, is drab and dreary. I tried to attend the festival services, but the women's section is so claustrophobic it's difficult to pray, and the few ladies squeezed in there gave me strange looks when they heard me davening in Hebrew."

"But holidays there have always been like that," Nathan said. "Something new must have pushed you over the edge."

"Judy came down with diarrhea the night we went shopping," Sharon replied. "She refused to eat matzah, and I couldn't give her oatmeal or toast, so it got worse. I hadn't brought enough diapers, so I had to constantly wash the dirty ones myself."

Hannah wrinkled her nose. "That must have been an ordeal."

"I finally bought some bananas for Judy since everyone says they're good for the runs." Sharon shuddered. "When I came in and put the bananas on the kitchen counter, Benny's mother let out such *shrayen* you'd think I'd brought in a suckling pig." She looked at them plaintively. "How was I to know Vinitzer Hasidim don't consider bananas kosher for Pesach because they didn't eat them back in Russia?"

"Was that the final affront?" Hannah asked.

When Sharon hesitated, then blushed and looked at the floor, Hannah motioned for Nathan to give them privacy. Sharon waited until he closed the door to her mother's studio behind him.

"I started my period on the first day of Pesach, the first time since my pregnancy with Judy. I'd begun to hope I was pregnant again, so not only was I terribly disappointed, but I wasn't prepared with any pads. It was mortifying, and I didn't know the right Yiddish words, but I had to ask Hershel's wife to find me some."

"How awful," Hannah commiserated with her. "I often get the blues when my period starts, even though I know the sadness will soon pass."

"I would have been miserable anyway, but this made everything worse." Sharon hesitated and took a deep breath. "Then I realized that my clean days would be over on Friday, which meant I'd have to go to that disgusting mikveh near the Stocksers while I was there for Shabbos."

"So that's why you left on Thursday." Hannah understood that Sharon, perhaps unintentionally, had employed an Orthodox wife's ultimate bargaining chip. Benny would not be able to so much as touch her until she'd immersed in a mikveh.

Sharon, her eyes downcast, nodded.

When Sharon said nothing more, Hannah asked, "Can Nathan come back now?"

Nathan had been stewing in Sarah Goren's studio at being excluded, which made him short-tempered. When he came back in, he lay Benny's letters down on the table in front of Sharon. "In case you've forgotten, Benny was traumatized by his father not speaking to him when he was young. I don't understand how you can refuse to communicate with him when you know how silence tortures him."

Sharon began to weep more loudly, but Nathan continued. "If you love him, as you say you do, please read his letters."

He handed her the letters and she took them. "Benny has at least taken one step in your direction. He will no longer wear that Hasidic underwear you detest."

"He is willing to make more compromises," Hannah added. "I know it's painful for you and you're scared, but you must be strong and tell him what you need and what you find intolerable."

"It will hurt him so much." Sharon sniffed back tears.

"He's hurting pretty badly now," Nathan said.

"All right, I'll read his letters. But I can't promise to answer them . . . yet."

Hannah hugged Sharon goodbye. No matter how much she loved Nathan, she would never tolerate such mistreatment.

Walking to Spektor for his afternoon classes, Nathan felt some relief that they might be making a little progress. But he couldn't imagine how Benny and Sharon could get back together if she wouldn't see him.

The next day Nathan didn't get to the barbershop until after eleven, when it was already filling with workers on lunch break. Resigned to wait, he thumbed through a pile of magazines, resisting the tempting *Playboy*s and picking up *Sports Illustrated* instead.

But suddenly the fellow next to him, exclaiming, "Man, oh, Manischewitz, check out the blond in this month's issue," stood up and unfolded the May centerfold. There was a raucous response from the barbershop patrons, and Nathan's faced flamed. Yet he couldn't look away. The attractive young woman was indeed a blond, but while she wasn't completely naked, she wasn't wearing much—merely a black bikini bottom and black high-heeled slippers. She gazed out at the reader, her breasts minimally obscured behind her crossed arms, with a bashful smile on her face.

"Hey, put that down." The barber pointed at Nathan. "This fellow is a rabbi."

With a chagrined expression on his face, the man immediately folded up the magazine and sat down. The other patrons quieted and stared at Nathan warily.

Nathan had to lessen the men's embarrassment. "Don't worry about me. I've seen lots of naked women in paintings at the Met."

When it was Nathan's turn on the chair, the barber spoke to him quietly. "That was a nice thing you said. Listen, I know you're getting married pretty soon. I've got an extra copy you can have. It has a funny article on training your first wife."

Nathan took the *Playboy* with mixed feelings. He didn't want to slight his barber, but he was curious too. He couldn't deny it was exciting to imagine Annie without clothes on.

At Pennsylvania Station Friday morning, giddy at the prospect of spending so much time with Nathan, Hannah eagerly reported how many RSVPs had come in. "Getting the mail is so exciting these days." Then she sobered. "I hope Aunt Elizabeth will be well enough to attend."

Once they boarded the train and found their seats, Nathan realized he should say something sympathetic. "I'm really sorry about your aunt."

"She's such a good person. She truly is." Hannah sighed. "With all the nursing she's done in so many dangerous places, I suppose it's a miracle she's lived long enough to die in bed."

They said nothing until Hannah recalled her resolve to be open and honest with him. She snuggled closer to Nathan and lowered her voice. "I'm not sure I like being an heiress."

Nathan was shocked. "What's not to like? I'm worried everyone will think I'm a gold digger."

"Do you think you are?"

"I may sound stupid, but even after learning about the Covey Foundation last year, I never imagined you'd have any involvement in it," he replied. "Your father had been disinherited, and I assumed you were too. I figured there were other Coveys still around besides your aunt."

"So this is as much a surprise to you as it is to me."

"You just found out? You weren't hiding it from me?"

"Aunt Elizabeth only told us at Pesach how sick she is. And before then, I had no idea she was planning to leave the Covey Foundation in my care." She shook her head in bewilderment. "I think I'm still pretty much in denial."

Nathan squeezed her hand in sympathy. "Why don't you like being an heiress?"

"Ever since I was little, I've been treated differently because I was blond and pretty. Girls envied me, nice boys avoided me, and other boys . . . well, they weren't so nice," she replied. "Being rich will be worse. Everyone will envy me, and lots of people will try to take advantage of me."

"That didn't occur to me. I was mainly thankful that we wouldn't have any financial problems, like the years it took my father to pay off the medical bills for his two heart attacks."

"You aren't ashamed about not being the breadwinner?"

Nathan waited until the train's horn quieted. "I admit I feel a bit of a drone to be living on my father-in-law's dole in his apartment. But I'm not sure I could support all of us on my salary alone once Abba retires and we have children, *borech Hashem*."

"Do you think we could keep my wealth a secret?" When he looked at her askance, Hannah quickly added, "I don't mean a secret from each other.

I can't hide how I look, but couldn't we live a rather modest life so nobody except our family knows we're more than comfortably well off?"

"I don't see why not, especially since very few people will associate the Covey Foundation with Mrs. Nathan Mandel."

Pleased at how soon she'd be Mrs. Nathan Mandel, she smiled up at him. "I'm glad I brought this up. I had no idea you thought I'd been hiding being rich from you."

They watched the countryside pass by through the window until Nathan thought of something else. "I assume your dad told you we've chosen the men's wedding clothes," he said. "But he might not have said that Abba is paying for them. Abba dislikes being beholden to your father even more than I do."

"Did you buy a tux for this wedding?"

"I didn't need to. Dovid gave me his. He said he's put on so much weight since he married Naomi that he doubted it would ever fit again. It only needed minor alterations."

Nathan had hoped that Hannah would say something about her niddah status by now, but he could no longer delay asking her. "Annie . . ." He looked around and started again in a quieter voice. "It's a little over a month until our wedding, and I wondered . . ." He knew he was blushing and hurriedly concluded, "Will you be able to immerse in time?"

Hannah fought down her annoyance. Men were so squeamish about menstruation they could barely mention the subject. No wonder many were ignorant of what their wives did. "I've already made an appointment at a fancy modern mikveh in the city for the Thursday before our wedding." She looked at him and frowned. "I hope you're not like Benny and think only certain old-fashioned mikvehs are kosher."

"Not at all," Nathan replied quickly, eager to end the awkward discussion. He'd learned what he needed to know. "I don't care which mikveh you use."

When the conductor announced, "Next stop, Trenton," Hannah noticed Nathan checking his watch for the third time. After a few minutes, she couldn't sit there in silent anxiety. "I understand that Benny and Sharon are carrying on a regular correspondence these days. Have you seen any of their letters?"

"No. Have you?"

She shook her head. "I know they're discussing concessions and compromises, even if she doesn't talk to him."

"Benny spends every Shabbos at my old apartment so he can walk to his family's shul without staying with them," he said.

"I'm glad you're not alone on Shabbos."

"It's strange having Shabbos dinner with Benny, just the two of us."

"He doesn't go to his parents' even for Shabbos meals?" she asked in amazement.

"It's not only how they mistreated Sharon." Nathan lowered his voice. "It's also the refusal of the rabbonim to deal with the child molesters in their midst."

"Benny and Sharon may not be talking to each other, but the two of them will have to see each other at our wedding."

"Maybe we can figure out a way to get them reconciled by then."

When Hannah heard Philadelphia was the next stop, she squeezed Nathan's hand.

Nathan squeezed hers in return. Why was he so nervous? He had nothing to prove to his maternal relatives. He was a professor with a wonderful fiancée. But this unexpected opening to connect with his mother's family after twenty-five years felt like being at bat with the bases loaded in the bottom of the ninth.

He didn't want to strike out.

EIGHTEEN

AS SOON AS Nathan and Hannah stepped off the train, he saw them: a gray-haired couple and a younger auburn-haired woman. The trio immediately started waving, and the older woman, despite needing a cane, hurried toward them.

"Nathan," she called out as they approached. When he turned in her direction, she took a few more steps and cried out, "Oh my God, you look just like her." Then she began to sob.

Nathan froze. *The dice have been thrown. There is no going back now.* He relaxed slightly when Hannah took his hand and gently squeezed it in support.

The redhead fumbled in her purse for a handkerchief and handed it to the older woman. "Here, Mom, you don't want to look all tearstained when you meet your nephew."

The man reached Nathan first. "Nathan Mandel." He thrust out his hand to vigorously shake Nathan's. "Barney Trachtenberg. It's a pleasure to meet you at last." He did not reach for Hannah's hand but turned to her and gave a slight bow. "And you too, Miss Eisin."

Nathan's throat was so constricted he could barely speak, but he managed further introductions and learned that the women were his cousin Marsha Blackman and his aunt, Dora Strauss.

"All the cousins call me 'Auntie Dora.'" She smiled at him through wet eyelashes.

By the time Barney's spacious Chrysler Imperial delivered them to Auntie Dora's house, including a short detour past the synagogue, Nathan was feeling more curious than nervous. Even compared to their Union Street brownstone, he found the Trachtenberg residence enormous, the most luxurious feature being that every room had at least one sizable window and corner rooms had two or more.

Walking up the broad front steps to the wraparound porch, Hannah experienced a sense of déjà vu. When she entered the foyer and gazed up at the grand curving staircase, she knew why. The similarity between this mansion and the Covey historic home was unmistakable. The high ceilings, marble fireplaces, dark wood floors, crystal chandeliers, and large windows all displayed the homeowners' wealth and prestige.

Cousin Marsha led her and Nathan upstairs, where he would have the room with twin beds that Max and Barney had once shared. After leaving Nathan to unpack in what she called the boys' room, Marsha took Hannah to an obviously feminine bedroom.

"This used to be Aunt Minnie's room," she began. "Being the youngest, I stayed in the nursery off my parents' room for years. Aunt Minnie died when I was seven, and I was too afraid of ghosts to sleep in her room." Marsha shrugged off her childish fears. "After Zayde died, I shared Bubbe's room downstairs with her."

Hannah did a quick calculation and realized she was only five years younger than Cousin Marsha. She looked forward to staying in Nathan's mother's room, especially if the woman's belongings were still there. "I'm fine sleeping here," she told Marsha.

Barney called out at the bottom of the stairs. "We need to go, Marsha. You'll have time to gab at dinner."

Once Nathan and Hannah changed out of their travel clothes and came down to the kitchen, Auntie Dora shared the home's history with them over lunch. "The house was built more than a hundred and fifty years ago, but my father bought it in the 1880s and started modernizing it." Dora sighed. "Back then there was no finer neighborhood for Jews than Strawberry Mansion."

"It's a beautiful home," Nathan said. He didn't say that it seemed very old-fashioned.

"But it's expensive to maintain, especially the high taxes and heating costs," Dora explained. "The younger generation prefers modern houses in the suburbs."

After lunch, Dora suggested they take a walk along the river in Fairmont Park while she took a nap. "Because of my knee, I only live on the first floor, so if you prefer, you two can have fun exploring the second and third floors," she said. "If you see anything you'd like for your new home, especially on the third floor, where we store things we don't use anymore, you are welcome to it. That way there will only be less to deal with later."

Hannah offered to clear the table, and when she picked up Dora's plate, the elderly woman grabbed her left hand and peered at it. "So that's what happened to Bubbe's ring."

"I gave it to her when we got engaged," Nathan explained, a bit defensively. "My father said it was my mother's."

Auntie Dora turned to Hannah. "I'm glad to see it on your finger, dear." She slowly stood up and hobbled to her room, mumbling, "Thank goodness it wasn't buried with Minnie."

Hannah shivered. "I'd like to walk in the park while it's warm outside."

Nathan put his dishes in the sink. "Let's go by the shul first. I need to leave my tallis there for Shabbos."

"How will you get it back?" Orthodox Jews were forbidden to carry anything on Shabbos.

"I'll bring it with us after the wedding."

It was only a short walk to the synagogue, an impressive edifice built in the previous century. Nathan had no trouble finding the wall of cubbyholes for tallis storage, and he placed his bag in one of the many empty compartments. *Do so few men wear a tallis here, or do they violate halacha by carrying it with them?*

He said nothing of his misgivings as he and Hannah strolled hand in hand along the river. It was a beautiful day; birds were singing and the spring flowers were in full bloom. They grilled each other on the names and relationships of his extended family until the temperature dropped and they headed back. By that time, Nathan had relaxed considerably.

"Cousin Marsha told me some of your mother's belongings might be in her bedroom, where I'm sleeping," Hannah said as they approached the house. "Let's look there first."

They could hear Auntie Dora's snores as they passed her door and tiptoed upstairs. Hannah opened her suitcase and turned to Nathan. "I'll check the closet and drawers as I unpack."

Normally Nathan would be tempted to pull Hannah into his arms any time they were alone together, but being in his dead mother's childhood bedroom quashed that inclination. "Give me a little time to put away my things," he said.

Before Hannah could finish emptying her luggage, she was distracted by the large bookcase. Some of the novels, such as *The Wonderful Wizard of Oz*, *Peter Pan*, and *The Scarlet Pimpernel*, were ones she'd seen in her father's boyhood room in Maine, which was not surprising since he and Nathan's mother were born the same year. But she was surprised at an entire shelf of Zane Grey's Westerns. There were books of interest to girls: the Anne of Green Gables trilogy, *A Little Princess*, and *The Secret Garden*. There was also more adult fare: Willa Cather's Great Plains trilogy, *Harriet—The Moses of her People*, and, intriguingly, Margaret Sanger's *Family Limitations*. She was about to pick up the latter when she heard Nathan's footsteps in the hall.

She grabbed an armful of clothing lying on the bed and opened the closet door just as he came in. "Her clothes, or some woman's clothes, are in here." Hannah put her dresses on the empty side and gently inspected the items hanging opposite. "They could be hers—the styles look prewar."

Nathan gave the contents of the closet a cursory look and headed to the bookcase, while Hannah examined the dresser. The top drawers were empty; the lower ones were not.

"Oh no, these cashmere sweaters are beautiful, but so many are moth-eaten." She held up a large black binder. "Nathan, look at this. It's a photo album."

He was next to her in an instant, and, all else forgotten, they sat down to peruse her find. "I think this is Auntie Dora's family." He pointed to a large formal portrait. "See, an older couple with four boys and two girls, dated 1910."

"It probably belonged to a woman," Hannah said. "The labels are in feminine handwriting."

"So the little girl would be my mother." He stared at the photo with a mixture of fascination and sadness.

Hannah waited until Nathan finally turned the page. It soon became apparent that the photos were all of Dora's family, starting with the earliest and progressing forward in time. When they got to one dated 1916 of young people sitting around the dining table downstairs, Nathan exclaimed, "The man on the left, I think he's my father."

"I don't know—he's got a beard," she said. "Let's go down to the dining room. The light is better there."

They sat at the big table close to the windows and scrutinized each picture. All had dates, and the man they thought was Nathan's father appeared in more of them as the years advanced. They got their confirmation from Max Trachtenberg's 1918 wedding photographs, several of which had shots containing the man identified as Sol Mandel.

Nathan was impatient to see the rest, but Hannah kept a slow pace. "I've noticed that your mother appears in every picture, and I think I recognize a dress from her closet," she said. "Look, here's one where the label says 'me,' not Minnie."

Nathan took a quick intake of breath. "So this is her album, not Auntie Dora's."

His assessment proved correct when photos began to have a New York locale in 1920 and some had only Sol—no longer identified with his surname—and her brother Shai in them, not her. There were pages of her 1922 wedding, with Sol no longer bearded, then significantly fewer until they got to 1929.

"Nathan," Hannah gushed. "These baby pictures are of you."

When he remained silent, she turned and saw he was shaking. She couldn't tell if he was crying or enraged, but she couldn't ignore him. "Are you all right? Maybe we should stop if this is upsetting you."

He didn't answer but abruptly turned to the last page. It held two pictures—one dated December 1930 that showed Minnie and a snow-suited toddler making a snowman and the other from February 1931 with the same toddler blowing out candles on a cake. The latter was labeled "Nate's second birthday."

When Hannah put her arm around his shoulder to comfort him, he flung it off, hissing, "How the hell did this end up here, hidden in a drawer, when it belongs in Brooklyn?"

Suddenly they heard footsteps and, startled, turned to look. It was Auntie Dora, carrying a cup and saucer in each hand. They had been too occupied to notice her earlier.

"I've brought you some tea." She came closer and spotted the open album. "How thoughtful, Nathan. You brought Minnie's photo album with you."

Nathan got up and faced her, his countenance dark with anger. "I didn't bring it with me." Hannah cringed at the cold fury in his voice. "We found it in her room, in the back of a bottom drawer, wrapped in an old sweater."

"Oh no." Cups and saucers crashed to the floor. Then Auntie Dora rallied as comprehension suffused her face, followed by shame. "At the end of Minnie's shiva, your father let us remove her clothes and other personal effects. Mama must have taken it then."

Confronted with his aunt's apparent innocence, Nathan took several deep breaths to calm himself. He didn't want losing his temper to ruin the weekend before it had even begun. "So nobody's seen this for twenty-five years?"

Ignoring the spilled tea and broken china, Dora sank into a chair. "Mama used to spend hours in Minnie's room with the door closed, especially after Papa died."

Hannah stood. "Let me clean this up, and then we can go through the pictures together."

"Wait." Dora turned to Nathan. "My parents were terribly angry when Minnie died, especially Papa. The expression on your face just now, it was exactly how he looked at your father that entire week. For a moment I thought I was seeing his ghost."

Now it was Nathan's turn to look ashamed. "I'm sorry. I didn't mean to frighten you."

"You have every right to be distraught. This photo album should be yours." Thankfully, Auntie Dora was someone whose upsets slid away like water off a duck's back. "And now you've found it."

Then Dora saw the pictures they'd been looking at. Her chin quivered, and though she tried to compose herself, she was soon weeping. Then Nathan's arms went around her and they wept together. Hannah couldn't watch without being overcome with grief as well, but she held back and cried quietly by herself as Minnie's son and sister consoled each other. She couldn't recall Nathan this enraged before. Today he was justified, but she hoped she wouldn't be at the receiving end of such a scary episode in the future.

The air redolent of chicken and dill, Shabbos dinner at Auntie Dora's was more rambunctious than Pesach at the Eisins'. With the many cousins of all ages talking at the same time, interrupting one another and switching conversations, it was all Nathan could do to follow any one discussion. At first everyone was eager to talk to him, but few were interested in what a Talmud professor did, and nobody wanted to talk baseball with a New Yorker. That was fine with Nathan; he wanted to learn more about his mother. Yet except for his two uncles, both of whom were reluctant to talk about her, everyone was too young to have known her.

Hannah, the only blond in a roomful of brunettes and redheads, had hoped to sit back to observe the family revelry, allowing Nathan to be the center of attention. Her job, she reminded herself, was to be there for him. But once word came out about her summers in Israel, she was showered with questions. During the brief moments of quiet, she tried without success to get anyone to talk about his mother. But they wanted to know about Israel. So she found herself answering the same questions and telling the same stories until the last guest had gone home.

Then, as she and Nathan dragged themselves up the stairs, he affirmed what she suspected. "I guess my mother was the black sheep of the family," he whispered, his voice heavy with disappointment. "The closest I could get to learning anything concrete was when Uncle Max told me, '*Achre moys k'doyshim.'"* (After death a person is holy, meaning, one shouldn't speak ill of the dead.)

When they arrived at the synagogue Saturday morning, there was barely a minyan in the enormous sanctuary. Hannah was the only woman present, and to Nathan's consternation, there was no mechitza. They stood in the back until an older man came over.

"You're here for the aufruf?"

Nathan nodded. "We're family. Where should we sit?"

"In the first few rows. Take an aisle seat if you're having an aliyah." When Nathan appeared bewildered, the man must have assumed Nathan needed instruction because he added, "Having an aliyah means you'll be called up to say the blessings before and after the Torah is read."

Nathan knew this, but he said nothing. When they reached the fifth row, he reluctantly sat next to the aisle. Apparently, Hannah was supposed to sit right beside him, and as soon as he opened the siddur, he knew why. This was a Conservative synagogue.

"Would you like me to leave some empty space between us?" she whispered.

He recognized that it would look strange. "I'm fine like this," he lied. Yet he was fine to sit next to her on the train or in the theater. Furthermore, even at Orthodox weddings, men and women sat together at both the ceremony and reception. Why was it different at services?

Eventually the pews filled with people, most of whom appeared to know one another. Men and women sat together indiscriminately, so Hannah scooted over a little closer to Nathan. From the first time she attended the Eisins' shul as a child, she'd disliked how they made men and women sit separately. Now she could sit together with Nathan like a normal couple. She was glad to see that her full-skirted dress and matching jacket fit in with what the other women were wearing and that her hat was similar to theirs as well.

To her surprise, the Conservative prayers were not quite the same as at her Brooklyn Orthodox synagogue. The first difference came early in the morning blessings, where the Orthodox English page had men thanking God for "not making me a woman," the Conservative men thanked God for "setting upon me the obligations of a man." Yet the Hebrew in both books was the identical "not making me a woman." Both had women thanking God for "making me according to Thy will."

The next difference was more substantial and one Hannah welcomed. This siddur omitted the lengthy section in Orthodox liturgy that described the ancient animal sacrifices and looked forward to resuming them in the rebuilt Temple in Jerusalem. Later prayers dealing with sacrifices changed the Orthodox phrase *"na'ase ve'nakriv"* (we will present and sacrifice) to *"asu ve'hikrivu"* (they presented and sacrificed).

Making a guess, Hannah turned to the Friday-evening service and looked just after the last of the psalms that welcomed Shabbos. As she hoped, also missing was Bamah Madlikin, the piece of Mishnah from Tractate Shabbos that taught "For three transgressions women die in childbirth: being careless regarding laws of niddah, separating challah, and lighting the Sabbath lamp." She couldn't imagine why the Orthodox put that odious text in their prayer book, but they likely assumed the women were home preparing for Shabbos when it was read in shul and therefore wouldn't see it.

On their walk back, Hannah asked Nathan how he could pray for the return of animal sacrifices. "Women aren't obligated to pray, so I don't say the parts I disagree with."

He was silent for a while, then shrugged. "It's traditional, although most Orthodox men don't know Hebrew well and say the words without understanding what they mean."

"But you do."

"I guess it was wishful thinking for all those centuries after the Temple was destroyed and there was no possibility of sacrifices being resumed. But now that Israel is established as a Jewish state, I suppose it could happen," he said slowly. "I never thought about it before, but I can't imagine participating in such disgusting rituals today."

Hannah heard the reluctance in his voice and didn't press him further. The weekend was stressful enough already. "I asked Cousin Marsha to come over this afternoon to see your mother's pictures. She wants to see the remaining clothes too."

"I hope you don't mind if I take a nap instead," he said. "Auntie Dora invited us to the rehearsal dinner tonight."

"But we're not in the wedding party, are we?" She hoped they weren't.

"No, but she didn't want to leave us home alone and thought we'd find the rehearsal instructive."

"I suppose so," Hannah said. "Especially since we won't be having a rehearsal ourselves." It was an Orthodox tradition that the bride and groom didn't see each other during the week preceding their wedding, although some women did attend the aufruf.

Nathan's discomfort increased when they arrived at his aunt's and Cousin Marsha handed him his tallis bag. "I noticed that you left it at shul, so I brought it back with me." She sounded proud of her good deed.

Though his cousin had violated the Sabbath to carry it, and again by riding in an automobile to deliver it to him, Nathan had to thank her. But then he reminded himself that Marsha was a Conservative Jew. They had different, more lenient, halachas than the Orthodox.

Once Nathan retired, Marsha was more eager to see the clothes than the photo album. She and Hannah emptied each drawer and scrutinized its contents. They tsked over the moth-damaged woolens, though Marsha thought some could be repaired. The clothes in the closet, however, they tried on, a good use of the full-length oval mirror in the corner.

"I think some of the older everyday outfits could be worn now if they were shortened to a fashionable length," Marsha said.

"By the way, thanks for writing to me with advice on what to wear this weekend."

"What are you wearing to the wedding?"

Hannah pulled out her sleeveless V-necked yellow formal gown, and seeing Marsha's uncertain expression, said, "There's a matching jacket for the ceremony."

They returned to the closet, and Marsha shot Hannah a grin. "Let's try on the flapper dresses, just for fun."

Twenty minutes later Nathan was awakened by their giggling, and curious to see what was so amusing, he knocked on the door. When it opened to reveal the two smiling women in full Roaring Twenties regalia, his foul mood dissipated.

Shaking his head and chuckling, he addressed Hannah. "You should bring one of these back for Purim."

"Now that you're awake, we can go upstairs and see what's up there," she replied.

To Hannah's relief, the third floor was not a dusty cluttered attic, but a series of small well-kept rooms that had presumably been servants' quarters. Their contents, however, were an idiosyncratic mixture of living room, bedroom, and office furnishings.

"Look at this." Nathan called them over to an enormous rolltop desk where he busily opened and closed the many drawers and compartments. The admiration in his voice was clear.

"It belonged to Zayde's father," Marsha said. "His office was in the house in those days, but nobody's used it for years. I bet Auntie Dora will let you have it."

"Look at these beauties." Hannah's voice rang out from the adjacent room. "Are they real Tiffany lamps?"

When Nathan and Marsha joined her, Hannah had already removed the sheets covering nine of them, two pairs and five individual lamps. "I'd love to see them lit up."

"They are pretty, but they don't give much light," Marsha said. "There used to be more, but most got broken or stopped working."

"Do you think Auntie Dora would let us have a couple?" Hannah asked. "We could fix them if they don't work."

"Let's take them all downstairs and see what happens when we turn them on," Marsha suggested.

"And unroll the rugs too," Nathan added. "We could definitely use some of those."

Marsha chuckled. "Don't be surprised if a cloud of moths fly out."

Hannah pointed to a small upholstered chair in the corner. "Isn't that the same as in Minnie's room?" When Marsha thought it was, Hannah directed Nathan to sit in it. "I thought Minnie's was comfortable, and if you agree, maybe we could use them in our bedroom—recovered with new fabric."

"It feels fine to me." Nathan blinked back tears. "I would like to have a chair my mother sat in."

"Wait," Marsha interjected. "There should be a couple of matching footstools."

It took several minutes to find them, and during the hunt Nathan got his chance to ask Marsha what his mother was like.

"I remember she was always nice to me, not ignoring me like my other aunts did. And she was so pretty." Marsha sighed. "I wish I could tell you more, but she moved away before I was born, so I only saw her a few times a year. I do know that the family, especially Zayde, complained about her becoming Orthodox."

When Hannah stepped out of her room Sunday afternoon dressed for the wedding, Nathan was waiting in the hall. Neither had ever seen the other in formal clothes, and they gazed at each other in delighted awe. She had to admit there was something about wearing a tuxedo that made a man look especially attractive. She took his arm to keep from tripping in her long gown as they came down the stairs.

Auntie Dora was waiting below, garbed like a queen in a beaded rose-colored dress. "Don't you two make a handsome couple," she gushed. "Minnie would be so proud."

Nathan grasped the opportunity. "Auntie Dora, what was my mother like? You probably knew her best."

"I was her older sister, so I may have a jaundiced view," she began. "Minnie was a surprise baby, born several years after the rest of our siblings. She became Papa's favorite, and I thought he spoiled her terribly, always buying her new clothes when mine were hardly worn and our brothers got hand-me-downs."

Hannah smiled inwardly at how Rae always looked forward to getting Hannah's outgrown clothes and how disappointed Rae was at eventually wearing a different size.

"She was smart and headstrong, always getting her way, which is why Papa gave in and let her go away to college," Dora continued. "It served him right when she came home and told him she was going to marry your father. I liked Sol, and it was obvious Minnie adored him, so I helped Mama talk Papa into a big synagogue wedding here rather than having some Orthodox rabbi marry them quietly in New York."

"Everyone has been so nice to me," Nathan interrupted. "What did my grandfather have against Orthodox Judaism?"

"Actually, it was *my* grandfather who rebelled against Orthodoxy, as soon as he got off the boat," she replied. "He married a girl from a Reform family, though some of us ended up Conservative and Minnie went all the way back to Orthodox. That infuriated Papa, and they had some terrible quarrels. He saw her and your father as being critical of their non-Orthodox observance—which your parents probably were." Her reminiscences were interrupted when Uncle Barney arrived to drive them to the synagogue.

Nathan wanted to say something to defend his parents in the car, but then remembered that he himself had judged Cousin Marsha harshly for carrying his tallis on Shabbos. So he was silent until they entered the spacious foyer.

"Wow," Nathan whispered to Hannah as they surveyed the elegant crowd. "It's like we walked into a Fred Astaire movie."

They took their seats, and Nathan pondered how strange it was that he now felt perfectly comfortable next to Hannah in the same pew where he'd experienced such discomfort sitting near her the previous morning.

As the radiant eighteen-year-old bride came down the aisle, Hannah vacillated between eager anticipation of her own upcoming nuptials and an awareness of how old she must appear in comparison. The Conservative wedding service was much the same as Orthodox ones she'd attended and ended with the identical glass stomping and "mazel tov" shouts. But the beautifully decorated ketubah, prominently displayed in the reception hall, was not. Hannah read it carefully and confirmed that it contained the clause Isaac Goren had told her about.

The ten-piece orchestra, clad in white dinner jackets, looked and sounded like it belonged in a Fred Astaire movie too. When the dancing began, Nathan kept his moves restrained out of concern that he'd be judged a show-off. But as the evening progressed, his liquor consumption increased and his inhibitions lessened, so Hannah encouraged him to let go a little. After the newlyweds cut the cake and made their exit, followed by many of the elderly guests, the band broke into more modern tunes, including some by Elvis Presley. Unable to resist the lively new rock and roll rhythms, Nathan led Hannah, who had now removed her jacket and bared her shoulders, through a few of their showier moves. Their expertise was soon noticed, and some of those preparing to leave sat down again to watch. The musicians also took note of their skill and widened their repertoire to showcase the talented couple.

It was long after midnight when the wonderful evening ended. Nathan and Hannah stayed up even later packing and then had to get up early to catch their train. When they thanked Auntie Dora for her hospitality, she held out a worn dog-eared book.

"I'm not sure you'll want this old Conservative siddur, but it was your mother's." Dora showed them the bookplate inscribed *Property of Minnie Trachtenberg*. "Minnie left it here when she moved out, and it occurred to me that Mama might have saved it."

Hannah didn't wait for Nathan's reply. "Of course we want it." After davening at the Trachtenbergs' synagogue, Hannah had intended to obtain a copy of a Conservative prayer book for herself.

Dora must have heard Hannah's enthusiasm. "I have some of the new edition if you want any."

Hannah intended to ask Nathan on the train about adding the Lieberman clause to their ketubah. But before she got up her nerve, his head was nodding toward her shoulder. So she began perusing the new prayer book, only to fall asleep somewhere in New Jersey.

The next thing she knew, Nathan was telling her to wake up. They were at Penn Station.

The following week, Nathan spent nearly every day at the new residence with Hannah, putting away wedding presents and choosing the art they wanted from Sarah Goren's studio. Auntie Dora had enthusiastically approved their furnishing choices and insisted they take some of her old artwork as well. Plus, Hannah wanted him to finally attend services at the Eisins' shul.

So he didn't see Benny again for two weeks.

"Jesus, where have you been hiding?" Benny exclaimed when he walked in Friday afternoon and saw Nathan making dinner. "I am going crazy with no one to talk to."

This was the closest Benny came to swearing, so Nathan took a deep breath before apologizing. "I'm sorry, but I've been busy preparing for my wedding and getting the new place ready for us to move in. You could call me at Spektor—you know my schedule. Or at the Eisins'. Here's the number."

"Between patients and teaching, I have no time on weekdays."

"Are things going okay with Sharon?" Surely nothing terrible had happened or Hannah would have told him.

"This is not about Sharon." Benny paused for emphasis. "Keep this to yourself, but one of my new patients is Rav Brenner, the tutor who abused the Fishkoff boys."

Nathan stopped basting the chicken and gave Benny his full attention. "The child molester? I can't believe it."

"His rebbe made him see me, but he just spouted a bunch of *mishegoss* about being misunderstood, it not being his fault because the boys enticed him, and besides there were no witnesses so who are you going to believe—a rabbi or a bunch of crazy kids?" Benny shivered in disgust. "On his second visit, he denied everything and accused Mrs. Feinstein of orchestrating a vendetta against him. Then he refused to say another word, no matter how I tried to reach him."

"Are you going to see him again?"

"Maybe a few more times so he cannot lay the failure on me." Benny clenched his fists in frustration. "I hate to give up if there is any chance of helping him, but I cannot waste my time on him when there are children who would benefit from my help."

Nathan hadn't seen Benny so discouraged since his friend discovered that Spektor's psychology department was more focused on experiments than on Freud. "Annie tells me things are improving between you and Sharon, that she answers your letters and has started suggesting compromises she wants you to make."

"I guess so, although she is still not ready to see me."

They set the table, said the blessings to welcome the Sabbath, and sang a few songs. After Nathan served the food, he judged Benny to be in a more receptive mood. "Listen, Annie says Sharon does want to reconcile but is scared. So, assuming you've negotiated the major compromises, I came up with a great idea on how to get you two at least talking to each other, and maybe even back together, at our wedding."

Benny looked skeptical, but Nathan continued. "Annie intends to ask Sharon to go with her to that new fancy mikveh on the Upper West Side, to show her the ropes." Nathan smiled conspiratorially. "I checked the place out, and it meets even your ridiculously demanding standards."

Benny must have gotten the idea because a hint of a smile played around his lips. "Actually, one of the compromises I am willing to make for Sharon is relaxing my mikveh standards from ridiculously demanding to minimally demanding."

"Now comes our part," Nathan continued. "I'm glad you didn't get your hair cut on Lag b'Omer, because you're coming to my barber with me before the wedding. But first I'll teach you how to dance with a woman. You'll be all dressed up and looking so handsome, Sharon won't be able to resist you once she's in your arms."

"And how do I get her in my arms?"

"That's the easy part. I'll start dancing with her first, and then you cut in. She's not going to make a scene and stalk off, not in front of everyone at our reception."

"So when do my dance lessons start?"

"Tonight, after dinner. Then we'll practice tomorrow and see how you progress." Nathan faltered. He knew what he needed to say, but it was a delicate subject now that Benny and Sharon had separated.

Benny reacted to his hesitation. "What? Spit it out."

"You needn't teach me about marital relations. I'll find someone else or learn it myself."

"I appreciate your desire to spare my feelings, but a promise is a promise, and besides, I doubt anyone else could teach you better," he said. "Still, I am glad you brought up the subject. I have some homework for you."

Nathan gulped. "Homework?"

"I want you to review the *sugyiot* from Niddah 31, Eruvin 100, Shabbos 140, and Nedarim 20, in that order. Also, you should read the Kinsey Report on female sexual behavior."

"But that's eight hundred pages long."

Benny raised an eyebrow. "So, you are familiar with it."

Nathan knew he was blushing and tried to speak calmly. "I saw a copy once but didn't get past the title page."

"I'll loan you mine. Don't worry. It's not like Talmud. You can skim it."

NINETEEN

NATHAN WASN'T SURPRISED at how quickly Benny learned the basic dance steps. But he was surprised, and apprehensive, when Benny called Sunday saying he needed Nathan to meet him at his parents' house on Monday morning. Benny was downstairs when Nathan arrived, and after thanking him for coming at such short notice, handed him a heavy paper bag containing his homework textbook. Together they made the climb to Reb Stockser's third-floor study.

When Nathan saw Reb Stockser and his son Hershel seated behind the massive black wood table, stony expressions on their faces, his trepidation heightened. He realized that Benny had assembled a beis din, a rabbinic court of three authorities in Jewish Law. The last time he'd seen them was six years ago, at Benny's June wedding. The last time he'd been in this room was the year before that, when Benny told his father he intended to be a psychologist, not the next rebbe. Nathan had a bad feeling that this encounter might be even more harrowing.

The room looked almost the same. The red carpet was several shades darker, and there was a discernible path worn between the doorway and the desk. The heavy glass that previously topped the table was gone. The musty old-book odor was even stronger, and now there was that distinctive old-man smell mixed in.

The two Stockser men had changed greatly. Hershel, now age twenty, was a brunette mirror image of Benny before he'd shaved off his beard and *payess* to attend Columbia. Nathan had only known Hershel as a thin, pale, sickly child, but judging by Hershel's current girth, his new treatment must have allowed him a normal diet. Reb Stockser's hair had already gone from gray to white when Benny married, and in the intervening years it had thinned considerably. With his deep wrinkles and bony hands, he made Nathan think of an old, shriveled apple.

The chair to his left was vacant, and Nathan took it. He'd never officiated as part of a beis din and was curious how the theory worked in practice.

First Benny presented his case. In a dispassionate voice, he shared the explicit and painful stories of the Fishkoff brothers and other patients who'd been sexually abused by Rav Brenner. He explained how the bar mitzvah tutor stopped shortly before his victims turned thirteen and could legally testify against him. "And if they do go to their parents or other teachers, they are told: 'You are forbidden to say *lashon hara*, derogatory things. There's no proof! There are no witnesses. You cannot make this public.'" Benny did a good imitation of frightened authorities.

"You believe these boys?" Hershel asked.

"Absolutely. And several are no longer boys," Benny replied. "I also believe their mothers, to whom some of them complained. It takes courage for these women to speak up when they know our community will react with denial to avoid the painful reality."

Reb Stockser sighed. "What about the man himself?"

"First I went to Brenner's rebbe, who initially took the tutor's part that the boys either misinterpreted his actions or made up stories about him. Typical blame-the-victim response."

Hershel squirmed with discomfort. "His rebbe maintained that Brenner was innocent?"

"I think the rebbe believed me because he forced Brenner to come see me," Benny said. "At first Brenner wrapped himself in the cloak of righteous innocence. But when it became clear that I knew what he'd done, he was completely unrepentant, even declaring that the boys seduced him and enjoyed the sex acts. Then he resisted therapy altogether."

"What do you want from us?" Reb Stockser asked.

Benny's expression hardened as he returned his father's gaze. "I have two adult patients Brenner abused as children, including the brother of the Fishkoff suicide. Both will go to the police with me since the rabbonim won't intervene. They understand the risks and legal consequences."

Nathan understood why Benny needed a beis din. "So we must decide if the mesirah prohibition against informers applies."

"Of course it applies," Hershel said. "Maimonides forbade handing a Jew over to heathen authorities, even if he is wicked and a sinner, even if he causes distress and pain to fellow Jews."

"But *dina demalchuta dina*" (the law of the country is the law)—Benny locked eyes with his brother—"has been halacha since Talmudic times. If New York statutes say child sexual abuse is illegal, then it is also against

Jewish Law." Before Hershel could object, Benny continued. "The *Sifsei Kohen* maintains that one is permitted to report any repeat or chronic abuser to non-Jewish authorities in order to prevent further abuse."

"Even for those who might support mesirah, the prohibition does not apply when there is a public menace." Nathan was determined to support Benny's efforts to stop Brenner from abusing more boys. "In his gloss to the *Shulchan Aruch*, Isserles states, 'A person who attacks others should be punished. If the Jewish authorities do not have the power to punish him, he must be punished by the civil authorities.'"

"What about the shame this brings on the community?" Hershel asked. "The difficulty for the abused boys' families to find *shidduchim* for their children?"

"The Mishnah in Sanhedrin 73a is clear: A *rodef*, one who pursues his fellow to kill him, or pursues after *a male* or a betrothed maiden to rape them, must be killed." Nathan emphasized the word "male" before continuing, "So Brenner, who sexually abuses boys, should certainly be considered a rodef."

"But permission to kill the rodef does not apply when lesser means would prevent the forbidden acts," Hershel objected.

"Exactly." Nathan didn't smile, but he was pleased at how easily he'd maneuvered Hershel into supporting his position. "In the case of a rodef intent upon inflicting physical harm, one must do something to stop him."

Nathan and Hershel argued for thirty minutes until Reb Stockser lifted his hand. "In my opinion, even though this man's sin is great, and he shows no repentance, we may not turn the matter over to the secular authorities. For it is certain that they will punish him with incarceration, which is inconsistent with halacha, and it is forbidden to inform on a person for a matter where the punishment is unfounded in Jewish Law."

Struggling to hide his outrage, Nathan stared at Reb Stockser in disbelief. "Which means that, since according to Jewish Law, rape is resolved with a fine and secular law punishes through imprisonment, it is forbidden to report a Jewish rapist to the police?" He didn't expect an answer and he didn't get one.

"Wait while I telephone the man's rebbe," Reb Stockser said. "In the meantime, my wife wants to say something to Nathan."

Nathan found Benny's mother in the kitchen. Compared to her husband, Mrs. Stockser seemed not to have aged at all. Of course, her real hair was hidden under her *sheytle*, but she stood up straight and had hardly any wrinkles, even when she smiled.

Which she did when she saw him. "Mazel tov on your upcoming

marriage, Nathan. I'm glad you and my Benyomen are still friends." Then
her smile disappeared as her chin quivered. "And he needs one badly now."
She looked like she wanted to say more, but Hershel called for them to
return.

"Here's what the rebbe suggested," Reb Stockser began. "If Benyomen
doesn't go to the police, Rav Brenner will continue in therapy indefinitely
at the rebbe's expense. There will also be more money to pay for Benyomen's
other patients' therapy." He stopped to let this sink in. "Hershel and I can
do nothing."

Before Nathan could react to the attempted bribe, Benny slammed his
fist down on the thankfully no longer glass-topped table. Then he locked
eyes with his father. "You didn't make my childhood miserable with your
silence, training me to be a tzaddik, so I could allow Jewish children to be
abused. We're done here." He stood up straight so he towered over Reb
Stockser. "You wanted me to be a tzaddik to the world. Well, you got yourself one!"

Nathan was so desperate to talk to Hannah about his experience on
Benny's beis din that, even though Shavuos began that evening, he walked
to the Eisins' after his last class ended. He ate sparingly and ignored the
usual dinnertime banter. By the time everyone else had finished their meals,
the atmosphere was so strained that the family rapidly found excuses to
leave him and Hannah alone.

She let him speak uninterrupted, and when he was done, all she could
do at first was sigh. Benny might be outraged, and Nathan along with him,
but she wasn't the least bit surprised that the rabbonim didn't want him to
go to the police. Not after the way her article for the *Freiheit* got quashed.

But she had to say something. "It's good you came over here to get your
anger out. You would have been stewing over it all night, and who knows
how worked up you'd have been in the morning."

"You bet I'm angry, and not just at the rebbe's blatant bribe, which
does nothing to stop more children from being abused. I'm angry at how
everyone uses me."

"Uses you?" This was not what Hannah expected to hear.

"People have used me for years, and I'm sick of it. Reb Stockser used
me to keep Benny from becoming a goy, and later to talk to Benny despite
his silent treatment." Nathan hadn't intended to say more, but it all poured
out. "My father used me to check his manuscripts at the Seminary even
though it led to all sorts of rumors about me at Spektor, and to avoid confronting his guilt over my mother's death by not telling me anything about

her. Then Benny used me to break through to Joey even though it risked my friendship with the boy; Rav Klein, to attack my father behind my back when his book came out; and Sharon, to unload her unhappy feelings about Benny while making me keep them secret." He stopped, aghast at all the resentments he'd built up.

"And me, interviewing you as an excuse to get you to teach me Talmud?" she asked tentatively, aware that she too was guilty. While her first interview had begun innocently enough, she'd concluded with the blatant proposal that he teach her Talmud.

He shook his head vehemently. "Not you. I wanted to teach you Talmud, and I knew exactly what I was risking when I agreed to do so." He thought for a minute before saying quietly, "That's not quite true. I didn't know I'd risk falling in love with you."

She smiled and took his hand. "Or that you'd risk making me fall in love with you."

"Benny said it was the excitement of secretly engaging in such risky and forbidden behavior that made us fall in love."

"That wasn't the only reason, but it probably helped."

He chuckled. "Like when Marilyn Monroe says that a man being rich is like a girl being pretty. It's not why you marry someone, but it certainly helps."

They sat holding hands for some time as Hannah pleasantly recalled their early Talmud studies. "Nathan, I know it won't match the modern furniture we bought, but I'd like to put your father's table and chairs in our dining room." She squeezed his hand gently. "To remind us of how we fell in love studying together." It would also make her remember the mansion where her father had grown up eating at an identical set.

His heart swelled at her being so sentimental. "I'd like that too."

She thought back to how well he'd responded when she told her about Steven. "I'm glad we can be so open with each other."

"Speaking of being open . . ." He told her about his idea to get Benny and Sharon dancing together at the wedding reception. "Please don't tell Sharon about it."

"I'm sure your intentions are good, but—"

"I know, the road to Hell is paved with good intentions," he interrupted. "But since their negotiations are going well, I thought this could be what gets them over the hump."

When Hannah had lunch with Sharon that week she shared Nathan's report about what happened in Reb Stockser's study. Sharon wavered between pride at Benny's courage in confronting his father and sadness at his being so alone.

"Can't you bring yourself to talk to him?" Hannah asked. "He loves you."

"I know, but I'm afraid that if we talk, if I hear his voice, I'll give in too easily and make another bad bargain."

"Tell me the truth. If Benny agreed to all your conditions without harboring any resentment, would you go back?"

Sharon didn't hesitate. "In a heartbeat."

"Then you must be strong and stick to your guns."

All Hannah could do was hope their negotiations worked out by the time Sharon saw Benny at the wedding. Then Nathan's crazy idea might actually work. Next week she'd have lunch with Sharon on Monday; later that afternoon she'd take a train to Boston to spend three days with Aunt Elizabeth's lawyers and the foundation staff. Then she'd drive both of them back to Brooklyn so her aunt could attend the wedding.

Nathan arrived at his Williamsburg apartment Friday afternoon to find Benny pacing the living room. Benny didn't wait for Nathan to put down his briefcase before bursting out, "He's gone. The mamzer is gone."

Nathan had a sick feeling he knew who Benny meant. "What do you mean he's gone? Where did he go?"

"He got on a plane to Israel last night, the first one he could get after Shavuos ended."

"What happened?"

"We went to the police Monday, and a detective took our statements. Apparently there were already reports about Brenner, but nobody had been willing to file charges." Benny slammed a fist into his other palm. "The detective called me this morning. They halted the investigation because Brenner left the country."

Nathan tried to control his growing anger. "So now he's free to abuse Israeli boys."

Benny's eyes narrowed, and he spoke in such a cold, harsh voice that Nathan drew back in alarm. "And who tipped him off? My father—my own father. That phone call warned his rebbe."

Nathan could no longer control his fury. He swore at length, cursing Reb Stockser with every English and Yiddish profanity he knew, for all the times he'd hated Benny's father over the dozen years he'd known him. Nathan had lived in New York City his whole life, so he knew all kinds of foul words. He'd just never used most of them before.

When he finally fell silent, Benny looked at him in awe. "Thank you. I couldn't have said it any better myself."

Refusing even to attend Hasidic services, Benny spent all of Shabbos with Nathan. Trying not to spoil the holy day by discussing Brenner's absconding, they davened together at home. Nathan kept losing his place in the siddur, yet despite the abysmal atmosphere, Benny seemed as transfixed by his prayers as any Hasid, perhaps more so.

At lunch, Nathan was determined to find out how Benny did it. And to get an answer to Hannah's question. "How can you pray for restoration of the Temple sacrifices?" he asked. "I find the whole thing appalling."

Benny blinked his eyes in confusion for a moment. "For Hasidim, prayer isn't about the actual words but the connection to God. The Baal Shem Tov taught that one who reads the words of prayer with great devotion may come to see the lights within the letters, though he does not understand the meaning of the words he speaks." He looked at Nathan earnestly. "Such prayer has great power."

Nathan nodded slowly. "Go on."

"Every day we must pray with a different *kavanah*," Benny continued. "This cannot happen when you pray by rote, saying the same words yesterday as the day before, forming the words out of habit but without heart. We must send out our prayers to God from the heart: praising and thanking Him, confessing our sins to Him with repentance, pleading with Him for blessings for our spiritual and bodily needs. This is true prayer."

Then he hesitated. "Yet sometimes, because of carelessness and lack of attention, our tongue says the prayer while our spirit wanders away somewhere. Then prayer is merely words, not true prayer at all. And God knows the difference."

Nathan sighed. "I didn't have any kavanah today. I don't know why I bothered to pray."

"If we never prayed except when we knew we'd have kavanah, we would never pray," Benny pointed out. "Not all prayers are meaningful to someone all the time. Focus on those that bring you closer to God."

And ignore the others, Nathan thought. "How can you pray with fervor when such terrible things are happening?"

"This is exactly when I most need to pray."

Which reminded Nathan, "Have you written Sharon about the beis din?"

"No, and I don't intend to. I want my letters to focus on my desire to

stay with her and my offers of how I can change to make that happen."
Benny wavered and then added, "And how much I love her."

"You know Annie and Sharon see each other often, and they talk on
the phone as well. So by now Annie has probably told her anyway." *It's a
relief not to be in the middle anymore.*

They were trying to decide whether they should practice dancing, go
for a walk and discuss Nathan's Talmud homework, or take a Shabbos
schluff when they heard a light tapping on the door. Nathan opened it and
stepped back in astonishment as Benny's mother entered and hesitantly
peered around.

Before he could say anything, Benny jumped up and called out, "Mama,
vus tisti du?" (What are you doing here?)

Nathan invited her in, also speaking in Yiddish to demonstrate she
needn't try to use English for his sake.

Mrs. Stockser looked up as if addressing Heaven and continued in
Yiddish. "If my son doesn't visit me on Shabbos, then I will come visit him."
When Benny was too stunned to reply, she sighed heavily. "My Benyomen,
my treasured firstborn, I love him more than life itself. How I suffered
when his father stopped speaking to him. Nothing is more painful for a
mother than to see her child suffer, but his father would not let me comfort
him."

Nathan could tell this was going to be a long visit. He offered her a
chair at the table and asked if she'd like some water or perhaps some iced
tea.

"Iced tea, please." She sat down across from Benny. "Now when my son
suffers, I cannot stand idly by. I will not stand idly by." She looked at him
until he met her gaze. "I know you are angry about Rav Brenner and how
the rabbonim protected him. I am angry as well."

"How do you—" Benny began, but she interrupted him.

"I am the rebbetzin. Women come to me with their tsuris, not Pinchas.
They want I should keep their secrets. So I know all about Rav Brenner, *er
zol hobn paroys tsen makes bashotn mit oybes krets*" (he should have Pharaoh's
ten plagues in addition to Job's scabies). "Yetta Feinstein came to me months
ago."

"There is nothing we can do about him now," Benny said. "He is in
Israel."

"True, but on another matter that causes you pain, I hope I am not so
helpless." She drank some tea and turned to Benny. "So, *nu?* Tell me why
your wife left you so perhaps I can persuade her to return."

Nathan gulped, but to his surprise, Benny detailed Sharon's many complaints. It took several glasses of tea.

When Benny finished and Nathan had little to add, she shook her head and sighed. "Poor Sharon, and poor little Zisse too. Think how difficult it was for Zisse, uprooted from her home in Jerusalem and coming to live thousands of miles from her family to marry Hershel. Such a shy little thing, hardly speaking to anyone. I see how Sharon took her silence personally, but it didn't help that Sharon never spoke to Zisse. Or that Sharon sat most of Shabbos in her room."

"So that was merely a misunderstanding?" Benny asked.

She nodded thoughtfully. "That I can fix. But I apologize for not stopping the women who talk too fast," she added. "If you convince Sharon to stop pretending she doesn't understand Yiddish, thus putting a stumbling block before the blind, I will have them speak slower."

Nathan had no doubt the rebbetzin could do this. He wasn't so sure about Sharon.

She again addressed the ceiling. "*Ach*, I knew Sharon would not dress properly unless I taught her. And when she rejected my help, I should have found another way to reach her." She sighed and turned to the men. "Now, a question for you, Nathan. Your betrothed, she has beautiful hair?"

"Yes, she does," he replied, puzzled why she'd changed the subject so abruptly and what Hannah's hair had to do with Benny and Sharon's estrangement. "Her name is Hannah Eisin."

She looked at Benny. "Your Sharon also has beautiful hair, which she refuses to cut off."

"I like her hair long," Benny said.

"For married Haredi women, it is forbidden any man sees their hair except their husbands. So they cover it with a sheytle, which often looks better than their own hair. But it is too much work to keep hair nice when it's hidden under a sheytle most of the time, especially after having children. So they cut it off." She looked at the men expectantly.

"Why should Haredi women cover their own hair with someone else's nice-looking hair?" Nathan asked. "Doesn't that defeat the entire premise of the halacha, modesty?"

"Even worse," Benny said. "At home their husbands see them with unattractive cut hair."

"When I married Reb Stockser, he wanted I should wear a sheytle like back in Russia. Of course I have several, and all look better than my real hair; only the finest sheytle for the rebbetzin." She grimaced instead of displaying pride, and Nathan understood that she would rather not wear the wig.

"Mama, what would happen if you wore a *tichel* to hide your hair?" Benny asked. "Wouldn't other women start wearing them?"

"You've seen your father's temper. What do you think would happen?"

Nathan shuddered at the memory of Reb Stockser's fury when he'd innocently mentioned the nascent State of Israel. For Reb Stockser there could only be a religious Eretz Yisroel, established by the Messiah, and he'd viciously attacked anyone who supported the Zionist cause. Including Nathan's father.

"I don't want to fight with Tateh. That's why I can't see him anymore." Benny leaned closer to his mother. "But you and I will find ways to see each other."

Mrs. Stockser dabbed her eyes with a handkerchief. "Not like with your sister, although with her I can still write."

Benny's jaw dropped open, and it was a full minute before he spoke. "I thought Malke died in Israel. We sat shiva for her."

"Pinchas made us do that when she left the kahal and became a Zionist."

"But . . . how . . . ?" Benny trailed off.

"Malke wanted to escape your father and his temper, and she convinced her husband to make aliyah to Israel. Pinchas never forgave them for joining the Lubavitch. And I never forgave him for making our family act like she was dead, and worse, forbidding me to even mention her name. *Danken him!* I discovered her address."

Benny sat there silently blinking his eyes, and Nathan suddenly wondered if Benny might also have cousins in America, like he did. "Mrs. Stockser, you were born in the city. Is your family still there?"

She shook her head. "My community was decimated by the Spanish Flu forty years ago. I was the only survivor of our rebbe's family." She winced. "So when I was sixteen, I married the widowed Pinchas Stockser, and what remained of my people joined his Hasidim."

When Nathan made no effort to hide his disgust at the thought of Benny's teenage mother forced to marry middle-aged Reb Stockser, she concluded with, "It wasn't the match I wanted, but I did my duty."

Sunday, Hannah furiously began writing an article about the Rav Brenner debacle. The *Freiheit* would never publish it, but maybe this way she'd purge her outrage. Though it needed editing, she brought it along when visiting

Sharon the next day. As she anticipated, Sharon was eager to read the story, so eager that when the phone rang, she asked Hannah to get it.

"Goren residence," Hannah answered.

"This is Rivke Stockser," a woman said in Yiddish. "I'm calling for Sharon Stockser."

Hannah was so startled she nearly dropped the receiver. "I'll see if she's available." She walked back to Sharon and whispered, "Someone named Rivke Stockser wants to talk to you."

Sharon's eyes opened wide. "Oh God, it's Benny's mother. I hope he's all right."

Hannah made a fast decision. "This is Hannah Eisin, Nathan Mandel's fiancée," she said in Yiddish. "Sharon can't talk now. May I take a message?"

"I assume you know I was several hours at Nathan's on Shabbos listening to my son's version of the rift between him and my daughter-in-law," Rivke began.

"Yes, Nathan told me about it." She tried to keep all emotion out of her voice.

"So you understand why I must speak with Sharon in person."

"Hold on. I'll ask her, but I doubt she'll want to see you when she won't see Benny." Hannah hoped Rivke could be a useful ally, but she didn't want to get the woman's hopes up.

"She shouldn't worry she'll fall into my arms as soon as she sees me and then agree to new compromises without realizing the cost. Not like she might do with my son if she sees him."

Impressed with Rivke's insight, Hannah gave Sharon the message and added, "I think she understands you and might help."

Sharon took a deep breath. "All right, but only if you're here too. You can translate her Yiddish for me and my English for her. I don't want any more misunderstandings."

Hannah went back to the phone and explained Sharon's conditions. At the last minute, she let Rivke know that Nathan had told her about Malke.

"I'll be there in thirty minutes," Rivke replied. "And I'll inform Sharon about Malke myself."

She was there in twenty, which was just enough time for Sharon to change into something decent and fix her hair while Hannah made tea and set out a plate of rugelach.

At first glance, Hannah would not have guessed Rivke was Haredi. Her navy dress, while modestly covering her elbows and collarbone, was similar to clothes other well-to-do matrons wore. It would have taken an expert to recognize that her perfectly coiffed brunette sheytle was a wig and not her own hair.

When Hannah reminded her why she was remaining, Rivke nodded in approval. "Yetta Feinstein speaks well of you and says your Yiddish is excellent."

"*A dank*. I have spent many years working to perfect it."

Rivke thanked Sharon for seeing her, but neither made a move to show affection or to take any of the refreshments on the coffee table. She began by turning to Sharon and shaking her head. "I am very upset about this miserable business my Benyomen has uncovered and even more upset at the pain it is causing him."

Rivke winced when Hannah translated "miserable business" into English as "child molesting" but didn't correct her. "Just because a son is grown doesn't mean his mother cares for him less than when he was a boy. I still regret I was not permitted to comfort Benyomen when my husband was raising him in silence, and I still hate my husband for the pain he made Benyomen and me suffer. So I will not sit idly by while Benyomen, and you, suffer now."

Hannah was amazed to hear this. Not that she didn't sympathize with Rivke.

"I see you are shocked I hate him, but my arranged marriage was not a romantic fairy tale," Rivke said. "I was forced to marry a widower more than twice my age, one who saw me as nothing more than a vessel to perpetuate his lineage and relieve his physical needs. I bore his children, but other than that I tried to have as little to do with him as possible. Once Hershel became ill, I devoted myself entirely to his care."

Sharon's chin quivered, but she said nothing.

Rivke turned to Sharon and continued. "You and I are the two people who love Benyomen the most, but I cannot comfort him as you can. I understand how you hoped Benyomen's people would be your people and his God your God. But that cannot be."

That roused Sharon from her silence. "Why not?"

"Hasidic men and women have separate spheres. The women have their own closed community and don't easily open it to others. Their children are primary, not Torah study and not praying in synagogue. Those are for men, like Benyomen's God is." She looked helplessly at Hannah. "*Ach*, I cannot explain it."

Hannah knew this distinction was crucial and hoped she could clarify it for Sharon. "Rivke doesn't mean that Hasidic men and women don't have the same God, only that they have different relationships with God. Which is why their prayers are also different."

Rivke nodded. "I don't see how Sharon can join our women's world. It is difficult enough for outsiders who want full entry, yet she is only with us on Shabbos and chagim."

"But Benny is only there then," Sharon protested. "And he no longer looks like a Hasid."

"Benyomen is not a newcomer. Plus he is the rebbe's son and a *talmid chacham*," his mother countered. "He may look a little different, but when he's with us, he dresses like a Hasid and, more importantly, acts like one."

Hannah realized that she'd better step in. "For Hasidim, the outside world is populated by evil goyim, especially Jewish goyim, and one cannot deny that Sharon brings with her a weekly reminder of that outside world and the freedom it offers."

"Sharon, I am so sorry I wasn't more welcoming after you and Benyomen married," Rivke said. "I admit I wasn't pleased with the match, but I should have paved the way for you. I wish I could have shown you how important it is in our community to wear proper clothes for Shabbos, like I did with Zisse—who, by the way, admires you greatly and wishes you two could be better friends."

Hannah hoped that Sharon would accept Rivke's apology, but Sharon shot back, "It infuriates me that he, and all of you, call our daughter Yutke when her name is Judy."

"But that's what Yutke means in Yiddish," Rivke protested. "Little Yehudis, little Judith."

Sharon looked down in embarrassment, but she said nothing.

Rivke tried again. "I should have insisted the women speak slower so you could learn Yiddish more quickly. I should also have realized you'd miss spending Shabbos and Pesach with your own family. Not that I could change my husband's demand that you and Benyomen always come to us. Believe me, I had no say in the compromises he required of you."

To Hannah's relief, Sharon didn't argue. "I could have been less rebellious and met you halfway when you offered assistance, but I mistakenly assumed Benny would provide all the advice I needed. By the time I understood how important the right clothes were, or how insulting it looked when I kept to my room and shut myself off from the other women, it was too late."

Hannah felt like sighing in gratitude at the apparent progress Rivke's intervention was facilitating, but she didn't dare make a sound that might interrupt the growing rapprochement. Thankfully, there was no need for

Sharon to admit what they all knew, that she'd deliberately pretended to know less Yiddish than she did.

Rivke smiled at Sharon's confession. "My Benyomen is a rebel too. Otherwise he would be the next rebbe and not a psychologist, and he would not have married you."

"If Sharon weren't a rebel, she wouldn't have married him," Hannah added.

"Sharon, look at me." Rivke sounded sad and serious. "I am deeply ashamed of my part in this. In particular, I must ask forgiveness for not being supportive enough when your son died." She dabbed her eyes with a handkerchief. "It is the rebbetzin's responsibility and burden to put the community's needs above her own family's. Everyone's children were sick and dying, plus so many still grieved and suffered over the horrors of what happened in Europe. But that is no excuse."

Sharon began to cry, and moments later the two women were weeping on each other's shoulders. Under such circumstances, Hannah's eyes could not remain dry either. Once they were all cried out, Rivke explained what happened to Malke.

"I doubt I'll ever meet my Israeli *ayniklakh*," she said between sniffs. "But I want to know those in America, and to watch them grow up." She looked at Sharon hopefully. "What do you want I should do to make things better?"

"Will you help me choose some proper clothes?" Sharon asked.

"Gladly," Rivke said. "It would be a pleasure to go shopping together."

Hannah thought of something. "Please don't let your husband know about their negotiations. He mustn't put pressure on Benny."

Rivke's eyes flashed. "Pinchas will hear nothing from me, though I'm confident Benyomen would resist his interference."

Their conversation was halted by Judy's cries from the bedroom. Rivke asked to remain a little longer with her granddaughter and suggested helping Sharon go through her closet to find outfits the Vinitzer community would find acceptable.

Hannah would have liked to see that, but she had a train to catch. Then, all the way to Boston, she tried to focus on other ways Sharon and Rivke could repair their relationship rather than on what it must be like to be married to a man you loathed.

TWENTY

IT WAS STILL LIGHT when Hannah's taxi let her off outside Aunt Elizabeth's building in Beacon Hill. Carrying her overnight case, she climbed the stairs to the first floor. Aunt Elizabeth took a long time to come to the door, and Hannah tried to hide her dismay at how pallid and haggard she looked.

Elizabeth must have noticed her reaction because, after embracing her niece, she said, "Don't worry, Annie. I'm having a blood transfusion in two days, so I'll be all perky and pink-cheeked for your wedding."

Hannah was grateful when her aunt went to bed early. Nathan wouldn't tell her what homework Benny had assigned, though he did admit some of it was from the Talmud. So she'd brought the Kinsey Report along to review its relevant sections. She'd bought the book when it first came out in 1953, curious to see what was normal for single women like her. Thus she learned about masturbation, including the various techniques women used. To her surprise, and relief, close to 40 percent of devout Jewish women had masturbated to orgasm by age twenty, considering it less sinful than premarital relations.

She was pleased to read that masturbation contributed to a high rate of sexual satisfaction in marriage. Her main focus tonight, however, was on marital relations and methods married couples used as foreplay. As she'd expected, nearly all married women her age experienced simple and deep kissing and both manual and oral stimulation of their breasts. They also received manual genital stimulation from their husbands and gave it to them. But she was taken aback that two-thirds of them received oral genital stimulation and only slightly fewer performed it.

Who initiated it? How did they learn how to do it? Would Nathan want to do that, and what would he think if she asked him to? What if he asked her to do it? What if, despite all her best efforts, he couldn't get hard enough to consummate their marriage?

Kinsey didn't have any answers to these questions.

Hannah and Aunt Elizabeth had a leisurely breakfast the following morning, and promptly at ten o'clock the doorbell rang. Hannah opened it to admit two men holding large briefcases. Aunt Elizabeth introduced Hannah to her lawyers, James Dewey and his son James Jr., who sat down at the dining table and began pulling out documents.

During the next two hours, they informed Hannah of the extent of Elizabeth Covey's estate, how it would be distributed among her beneficiaries, and what Hannah's duties as executor would entail. Of course their office would do much of the actual work, and the Deweys would be there to assist her at every step.

It was all very professional and very condescending.

When they finally left, briefcases emptied, Aunt Elizabeth sighed and rolled her eyes. "I know they sound pompous, but they are excellent lawyers whose firm has served my family for years. I do wish they would talk less and let their work speak for itself, but I suppose they think they need to explain everything in excruciating detail."

"Especially to women," Hannah said. Thankfully, she could replace them with a New York firm later. "Now that they're gone, I'd like us to go over these papers together to be sure I understand everything."

"Good idea. And when we're done, you can drive us over to the RMV and reregister my car in your name."

"Oh, Aunt Elizabeth, thank you." *My own car. I will have my own car.*

"My driving days are over, so you might as well have it now. You'll need it for your honeymoon anyway."

Hannah gazed around the living room in awed surprise. After spending so many summers in Aunt Elizabeth's austere farmhouse, she wouldn't have expected such an extensive collection of tchotchkes that they occupied several cabinets and bookcases. "What will happen to all your knickknacks?"

Aunt Elizabeth must have heard the incredulity in Hannah's voice because she chuckled. "There are a lot of them, but I couldn't refuse gifts from people I helped on my nursing missions. I have things from all over the world now, but their value lies in the memories they evoke, not their monetary worth."

"Would it be all right if I took some of the Israeli ones?" Hannah asked shyly, reluctant to appear presumptuous. "To remind me of our time together there."

"I would be honored if you did."

That night, when Hannah studied the Marital Coitus chapter, she couldn't help thinking about her and Nathan experimenting with various techniques. Thus she was too aroused to sleep when she finished reading. Usually when she brought herself to orgasm, she did it quickly, furtively. This time, with the intent of soon instructing Nathan and imagining it was his hands caressing her, she noted which actions gave her the greatest pleasure. It was an edifying experiment, and she fell asleep both intellectually and sexually satisfied.

In the morning Hannah drove Aunt Elizabeth to the Covey Foundation office, where her experience was the polar opposite of that with the attorneys. Here people were deferential and eager to hear her views. Employees had their own portfolios reflecting their areas of expertise, and she was regaled with enthusiastic descriptions of their projects. They were proud of their work and delighted when she asked questions. It was much better than reading the staid yearly reports.

At a luncheon for the staff, Hannah sat with the team who administered the archaeological grants and impressed them with her fluent Hebrew. They agreed with her suggestion that having an employee who read and spoke Hebrew would enable them to process more grants for projects in Israel. Afterward, Aunt Elizabeth insisted Hannah stay longer to meet with the administration while she took a taxi to the hospital for her transfusion.

When Hannah finally returned from her whirlwind day, excited rather than exhausted, she was delighted to see her aunt looking perfectly healthy. *Maybe with treatment Aunt Elizabeth will have many more years to live.* With that hope in mind, she slept well, and after breakfast they closed up the apartment and packed the blue roadster for the drive back to Brooklyn.

With Hannah away, Nathan spent his evenings on Benny's homework. On Monday and Wednesday, thankful that Abba was living miles away and thus unable to question his subject matter, Nathan pored over the Kinsey Report on female sexuality. The first thing he learned, to his surprise—and relief—was that masturbation was nearly universal among men and apparently did no harm whatsoever. *Too bad I didn't know that ten years ago.*

Back then he didn't know that what he did covertly and ignominiously even had a name, let alone that anyone else did it. He'd discovered it by accident. Waking prone in the morning with his penis swollen and irritated, he'd had to rub only briefly against the mattress to receive a pleasurable relief. That evening he was horrified, and ashamed, to see the stained sheet and vowed to never do it again. But his pledge was impossible to keep.

He took some solace in using a T-shirt from the hamper to protect the sheets and his secret vice, as he called it, from discovery. For he knew, from whispered asides from other students, that this was a disgraceful activity, unbefitting a yeshiva bocher. It was a small consolation that he wasn't the only one, and he eventually learned that a cold shower was effective at diminishing his need.

Annoyed at being thus distracted, Nathan pushed these memories away and returned to Kinsey. He was soon astonished to find that women also masturbated and that those who did achieved more orgasms once married. So while it would be helpful to know what Hannah did, just the idea of asking her mortified him.

The thought of discussing any of this with Benny was embarrassing enough.

With Annie's sexual satisfaction as his goal, Nathan studied the chapters on Pre-Marital Petting and Marital Coitus with the concentration he usually reserved for Talmud. She certainly enjoyed necking in her father's car, but would going below her waist revive her college trauma? The Kinsey Report said nothing about how women responded sexually following rape.

Since Tuesdays and Thursdays were his regular Talmud study nights, he spent those on the sugyiot Benny assigned—none of which were taught in yeshiva. He began with Niddah 31, as recommended. There he learned that, according to the rabbis, if the man emits seed first, the resulting child will be a girl, but if the woman does, she will bear a male. Should they emit seed simultaneously, it could be either gender.

Rashi explained that just as a man emits seed during his sexual climax, so too a woman experiences a climax during which she emits seed. Thus a man who wants sons should endeavor to make his wife climax first. Nothing in the Talmud surprised Nathan anymore, but he was still impressed that the Rabbis detailed sexual techniques a man could use to ensure this.

The first seemed obvious; the man, like the mighty men of Ulam in Chronicles who sired many sons and grandsons, should restrain himself and delay his climax until after hers. Ramban explained that the man should stimulate his wife for some time before penetration so she would emit seed quickly when he entered, and thanks to Kinsey, Nathan had a good idea of what to do. Rava recommended another method, that the man who wants to make all his children males should perform the mitzvah deed twice in a row. Rashi commented that the woman would be so aroused by the first act that she'd surely emit her seed first the second time.

Puzzled, Nathan consulted Kinsey, which said nothing about women emitting seed when they climaxed. Rather, women ovulated monthly, apparently whether they had sexual relations or not. He understood why Benny wanted him to study this sugya. Never mind the Rabbis' faulty premises; the important thing was how to make Annie climax before he did.

Next he opened Tractate Eruvin to page 100, where Rami bar Chama said that a man is forbidden to force his wife into marital relations, that he must first obtain her consent. Rami quoted a Baraita that a man who cohabits and then repeats the act is a sinner, Rashi commenting that this is bothersome to the woman. Rava then reiterated his adage that one who wants male children should perform the mitzvah deed and repeat it. To Nathan's relief, the Gemara easily resolved the contradiction. The Baraita referred to a situation where the husband repeats the act without his wife's consent, while in Rava's case the woman does consent. Nathan understood that Benny hadn't recommended this sugya merely to reinforce Niddah 31. It taught an important new rule: the wife must consent to each marital act.

The brief sugya in Shabbos 140 seemed incomprehensible, with Rav Hisda teaching his daughters that in sexual foreplay the man holds a pearl in one hand and a kiln in the other. The woman should allow him the pearl at first but not the kiln. Only after they both are suffering does she offer it to him.

Thank Heaven for Rashi, who explained that pearl is a euphemism for breast and kiln for womb. If Nathan understood him properly, the man is supposed to hold his wife's breast with one hand while he caresses the place between her thighs with the other. But she should not allow him to enter that place too soon, not until their passion has grown and they are tormented by desire. This seemed to reinforce another part of Niddah 31 by detailing how the mighty men of Ulam stimulated their wives before they entered. It also matched what Kinsey reported as the ways husbands usually aroused their wives prior to penetration.

Imagining himself following Rashi's explicit instructions on Annie almost sent Nathan to take a cold shower, but he was too curious about what was in Nedarim 20 that Benny wanted to save for last. This sugya began oddly with the Ministering Angels describing sexual practices that produce defective children: overturning the table makes for lame children, kissing *that place* makes them mute, and looking at *that place* makes them blind.

"Overturning the table" apparently referred to a sexual position the angels didn't like. But while the commentators couldn't agree which it was, the ones they argued about were the same that Kinsey said were most common: woman on the bottom, woman on top, and from behind. The "place" the angels didn't want men to kiss or even look at was evidently the same as what Rav Hisda called her kiln, and until he read in Kinsey that more than half of married men performed oral sex on their wives, Nathan had never even imagined doing such a thing.

But all these were permitted by the Sages, who taught that a husband and wife may engage in whatever sexual practices they like—with consent. Like kosher meat from the butcher, which can be served roasted, salted, cooked, or stewed. Rabbenu Tam made the halacha clear by stating that even occasional nonprocreative sex is permitted provided the couple does it as a supplement to procreation. And that explicitly included oral sex.

Now Nathan needed that cold shower.

Hannah drove at a more sedate pace than Aunt Elizabeth would have, so they arrived at the Eisins' brownstone barely in time for dinner. After the meal she hurried to call Nathan. To spare Aunt Elizabeth having to climb so many stairs, Deborah made up the foldout couch in the living room, and the two women were still talking together there when Hannah went to bed.

She didn't fall asleep easily, for Nathan told her that the moving van from Philadelphia had arrived, and she was anxious to see how everything looked. She was also mulling over what Benny wanted Nathan to read before their sex lesson. Nathan wouldn't divulge the pages of the Talmud he was supposed to study, but he promised to teach them to her during their honeymoon.

He did reveal that Benny wanted him to read the Kinsey Report, at which point Hannah acknowledged that she had a copy and was reviewing it as well. Then he surprised her by confessing that he'd seen it in her bedroom the day he hid there from Naomi. They laughed in embarrassment, and he joked that at least they'd be on the same page once they were married.

After they hung up, Hannah sobered. *What if we aren't?* She still hadn't found the courage to ask him to add the Lieberman clause to their ketubah.

When Hannah, Deborah, and Aunt Elizabeth arrived at the new apartment the next day, Nathan and his father were waiting for them. Solomon greeted Elizabeth gently but said nothing about her illness, and Hannah was glad he hadn't seen her before the blood transfusion.

She was astonished at the apartment's transformation.

"I tried to arrange everything like we decided earlier," Nathan told her. "But some of it didn't seem to fit, and I still had to leave room for the dining room set. So I asked Sarah Goren for help, and we moved things around and rehung some of her art. I hope you like it."

"It looks wonderful," Deborah gushed. "The rugs are lovely."

Hannah surveyed the living room in awe. "I wasn't sure Auntie Dora's Oriental rugs would go with our furniture, but somehow they tie together Abba's armchairs and the modern stuff."

Nathan sighed with relief. "You can thank Sarah. She suggested reupholstering the dining chairs to match the living room drapes."

"Now I want to see the second floor."

Unlike downstairs, the master bedroom looked exactly as Hannah imagined it. The bedroom chairs from Auntie Dora, with slipcovers in the same fabric as the drapes, could have been sitting on either side of the fireplace fifty years ago. The oval mirror from Minnie's bedroom stood in the corner near the window, with the two matching rugs on either side of the bed adding the finishing touch.

Hannah knew Nathan couldn't stay for Shabbos dinner. Only his father would be joining them. Nathan would be spending Friday night and Saturday with Benny. But Saturday night they'd go out dancing, just the two of them, and she'd be driving her new car. That would be the last time they'd be alone together until the wedding.

She couldn't believe how the four months had flown since their sudden and unexpected engagement.

Benny was already there when Nathan got to his apartment Friday afternoon, and his friend's smiling welcome was a pleasant change from the previous week.

"I think your plan for getting me and Sharon back together at the wedding might work," Benny said over dinner. "With my mother now involved, negotiations are going faster."

"What have you agreed on?"

"None of our children will be raised in silence," Benny began. "They will attend schools like the one you and Hannah did, not Haredi schools."

"What else?" Those seemed obvious to Nathan.

"Sharon has agreed to let my mother help her choose clothes that don't mark her as an outsider. Then Mama will arrange for Sharon and Zisse to spend some time together, and she'll speak to the other women so they'll be nicer to her." Sounding proud of his mother, Benny added, "I couldn't have done that by myself."

"What about Shabbos?" Nathan asked. This was the all-important compromise.

"We will try to spend Shabbos with Sharon's family as often as with mine and avoid staying with my family when she needs to visit the mikveh." Benny sounded less confident. "And somehow we'll arrange the chagim so we're not always in Williamsburg."

"You know, it would be easier if you moved back to Brooklyn and found a place within walking distance of both families."

"But commuting to Columbia wouldn't be."

Nathan wasn't sympathetic. "Sharon made the sacrifices before. Now it's your turn."

"She wants me to wear a wedding ring. Are you going to?"

"Of course. That's what married men do these days."

"But the halacha is that the man acquires his wife by giving her a ring," Benny objected. "She doesn't acquire him."

"This is the twentieth century. People don't acquire each other," Nathan said. "Annie's dad and her stepbrother, Dovid, both wear wedding rings, and most of my married friends do too."

"Okay, I'll wear a ring. But all this is moot if your dancing scheme doesn't work."

"So let's practice."

Thankfully, Benny had improved to where Nathan rarely had to do any back-leading, but what would happen if Benny lost concentration? After half an hour Nathan decided to find out.

"I've been thinking how dancing is like sex," he began. "Keep things simple at first—you both need to know the steps, a good physical connection is important, as is recognizing if your partner is enjoying the activity or struggling."

Sure enough, Benny stumbled.

"And you must keep control of your body," Nathan added. "A couple should be able to dance and talk at the same time."

"Couples don't usually talk while making love, and it's impossible to control your body during orgasm," Benny retorted. "But I have to be able to speak with Sharon, so let's keep talking and dancing until I can do both without difficulty."

It took a while, but eventually Benny succeeded. "Enough about me and Sharon. Let's talk about you and Annie." His demeanor switched to what Nathan thought of as his professorial mode. "Start with Kinsey now, and we can study the Talmud sections Shabbos afternoon."

Nathan found the book, and they began going over the chapters he'd read. Benny didn't care whether Nathan masturbated or not, but it could be useful for Nathan to know if Annie did.

"I'm supposed to just ask her outright?"

"Of course not. You should approach the subject gradually."

"Is that what you did?"

"Actually, no," Benny admitted. "Sharon knew a lot about sex, from her reading and from what her mother taught her, so she showed me what to do."

Nathan was caught between wanting to know what Benny had learned and not wanting to invade their privacy. When he hesitated, Benny quoted from Tractate Berachot, where one of the Talmudic rabbis discovers a student hiding under the bed while the rabbi and rebbetzin have marital relations. The student defended his spying by stating, "This is Torah and I must study it."

"You're inviting me to hide under your bed?"

"Metaphorically," Benny replied.

"So what did you learn from Sharon?" Nathan asked.

Benny explained exactly how she liked him to caress her breasts and between her legs. "You need to be gentle down there so she doesn't get overly sensitive."

"And to think I didn't know what a clitoris was until last week."

"You're lucky. Kinsey hadn't published his report on female sexual behavior when I got married."

"I'd really like to make her climax first, at least in the beginning." Nathan didn't try to hide his anxiety. "So I don't leave her frustrated."

"I understand. It's difficult when you have to separate after the first night."

"Annie and I won't have that problem. She was wounded by wood," Nathan said.

"So you are already discussing the subject. Good." Benny nodded. "That's enough for tonight."

Benny headed to Abba's bedroom and Nathan to his own. He knew it shouldn't matter what Benny thought about masturbation, but he was still relieved that Benny didn't care whether Nathan did it or not. Because after that lesson, and imagining doing all those things with Annie, Nathan needed to.

They tackled the Talmud texts after lunch on Shabbos. Nathan had only one question about Niddah 31. "The way Rava says a man should do it twice in a row makes it sound easy. But when it's just me, I'm done after one orgasm."

"It's not easy except perhaps for teenagers," Benny agreed. "But if you climaxed quickly at first, you should be able to harden again in a few minutes, although you may need some stimulation from your wife. Fortunately, it will take you longer the second time, which is why she will likely climax before you."

"She's supposed to stimulate me?"

"According to Kinsey, a woman rarely has to do anything to arouse her husband the first time. He can be ready to enter just by thinking about it," Benny explained. "But women are not like that. They need actual genital stimulation, just as most men do the second time."

Nathan didn't have questions about Eruvin 100. Of course a man shouldn't force his wife. However, he needed Benny to clarify Shabbos 140, since not all commentators agreed with Rashi's interpretation.

Benny did. "A pearl clearly symbolizes the breast, so I think forge or kiln refers to the vaginal passage's heat."

Nathan could feel his own heat rising below and forced his mind onto the final sugya. "It's interesting that Nedarim 20 begins by criticizing the very behavior it ends up permitting."

"You do not need to study psychology to recognize that forbidding something only makes it more attractive."

Nathan smiled. "Which helped me and Annie fall in love to begin with."

"Were you surprised to read about kissing that place?"

"I was," Nathan admitted. "Also when Kinsey reported that most married men do exactly that."

"I knew this sugya, but I needed Sharon's encouragement to do it properly."

"You, who didn't touch her until the wedding, do oral sex?"

"Of course, although not at first. It took me a while to develop the best technique." Benny continued by providing a detailed, and explicit, explanation of the various methods he used to arouse his wife. "You should be able to tell if you're doing it right by her breathing getting faster and by the sounds she makes. It seems strange, but the more she moans, the better she likes it. And when she is about to climax, you will think she's in pain, but do not stop."

"I read something about that in Kinsey," Nathan said.

"One last thing. For a man, the ecstasy of sexual relations strengthens the love he feels, while for a woman, her love intensifies the physical pleasure she feels." For a few moments Benny's psychologist's persona cracked and allowed Nathan to perceive the fullness of Benny's love for Sharon and his pain at their separation.

Nathan was too overwhelmed by sadness to speak for a minute. "I think you'll get Sharon back, but whatever happens with your marriage, you can count on me to be there for you."

Benny looked embarrassed at having his emotions so easily read. "Any other questions, or can I go take a *schluff* now?"

"What time are you coming over next Friday?" Nathan was glad the uncomfortable discussion was finally finished. He needed to think about what he'd learned.

"Around four so I can see your new place in the daylight."

"Good. Now I need a Shabbos *schluff* myself." Nathan yawned. "Annie and I are going dancing tonight, and I expect we'll be out pretty late."

Benny was still there when Hannah arrived in the blue roadster. "Your new haircut looks very nice," she told him. "I'm sure Sharon will like it."

"Will she be wearing a dress like yours?" Benny asked, staring at her spaghetti straps. He didn't look pleased with the prospect.

"We're getting married in a synagogue." She tried not to sound annoyed. "Everyone in the wedding party will have their arms and chest covered."

He still heard her irritation. "I'm sorry. I'm nervous about your wedding, about seeing her again."

Nathan chuckled. "You're nervous about our wedding. How do you think I feel?" He took Hannah's arm. "*Shavua tov*, Benny. See you next Friday."

Once in the car, Hannah said, "I'm feeling optimistic about Sharon and Benny. According to her, he writes some persuasive love letters and has agreed to nearly all the changes she wants, as well as some additional ones his mother suggested." *Now I need to put aside my fear of your anger and ask you to change our ketubah.*

"I'm glad to hear it," he replied. *Especially after seeing how Benny truly feels.*

"She's still worried that Benny will be angry with her for leaving so abruptly without sharing her unhappiness earlier."

"Then it should be one of her compromises that in the future she'll tell him if something is wrong and not let problems build up," he said. "I'll encourage him to write her about that."

"Good idea. I'll urge her to do the same."

Finding a parking place wasn't easy late on a Saturday night. "Next time we'll take a taxi," Hannah promised. "But I wanted to show you my new car."

They were walking through the smoke-filled vestibule when Nathan froze.

"Why are we stopping? What's wrong?" she asked.

"My old dance partner is here."

Hannah recalled what he'd said about her. "The one who violated halacha by traveling early on Saturday night and then tried to hide it? The one who abandoned you in a restaurant when you refused to marry her?"

"I didn't refuse to marry her," he protested. "She asked if our relationship was heading for marriage and I answered no."

"Don't even think about leaving, not after how long it took us to park." Curious about the rival she'd bested, Hannah took his arm and urged him forward. "Besides, we've wanted to hear this band for a long time."

Nathan had thought about leaving, but she was right. Even so, he pretended he didn't see Barbara as they walked past the smokers into the dance hall.

But Barbara saw him. "Nate, what a nice surprise." She gestured toward the pudgy young man standing at her side. "May I introduce Stanley Leiber"—she paused for emphasis—"my husband."

Nathan shook Stanley's damp hand and made his own introduction. "Barbara and Stanley, this is my fiancée, Hannah Eisin. We're getting married next Sunday."

Hannah smiled and greeted them with the usual pleasantries. If Barbara had wanted to show off her marital status while Nathan was still single, he'd thwarted her by bringing his own bride.

Barbara persisted. "Nate, come dance with me, and we'll show them how it's done. Stanley could use a breather." When Nathan hesitated and looked questioningly at Hannah, Barbara continued. "Please, for old times' sake."

"I don't mind watching," Hannah said truthfully. "I don't get to see you dance when I'm your partner."

Barbara's cologne was cloying compared to Hannah's, but he overcame his reluctance when the music started. If Barbara wanted to put on a show, well, then, he'd give them one. He noted with satisfaction that she was a little rusty but was too kind to comment about it. Indeed, he didn't say anything as he led her through the most complicated routine he could think of. But there was no spark between them, and compared to his eagerness to dance with Annie, Nathan realized there never had been.

Hannah kvelled over how well Nathan led Barbara through her paces, but Stanley looked so displeased she took pity on him. "How did you two meet, Stanley?"

He was happy to enlighten her. "We met two years ago when both our families summered in the Catskills, and we had what I thought was a summer fling. But after spending last summer together, I realized it was the real deal." He stopped to watch his wife dancing with another man, then turned back to Hannah. "We got married just before Passover."

"Mazel tov." Clearly Stanley was Barbara's fallback option when she'd asked Nathan about his marriage plans. Stanley didn't ask about her and Nathan, but Hannah told him anyway. "Nathan and I went to grade school together and lost contact for a few years, but we found each other again last year." Let Barbara assume he'd reconnected with Hannah after she'd rejected him.

After the music stopped, Nathan walked Barbara back to Stanley and took Hannah's hand. When the next tune turned out to be a slow one, she shared what Stanley had told her.

"I guess she really wanted to get married and wasn't too particular about to whom." Nathan felt more relief than rancor. "You're sure you didn't mind me dancing with her?"

"Not at all. I loved seeing you dance. You were great."

"I generally don't like being a show-off. It's boorish."

"When we dance together at our wedding, you can show off all you want."

As they pulled up to Nathan's apartment, both were reluctant to leave the car's close quarters. Savoring Annie's perfume, he leaned over to kiss her good night, and she responded with enthusiasm. His studies with Benny fresh in his mind, Nathan pulled her onto his lap. Usually she kept their petting within limits; he could kiss her lips and her neck as much as he wanted, and she cooperated fully in French kissing. Recently she'd encouraged him to caress her breasts outside her clothes, but unhooking her bra was too complicated an obstacle to going further.

Tonight there were no limits. Feeling relieved at having abandoned what would surely have been a contentious discussion, Hannah wanted to find out how aroused she would get if there were no restraints. Her dress had a built-in bra, so he could simply unzip the back and then reach around for her bare breasts. He seemed hesitant at first when she encouraged him to do so, but as soon as his fingers found her nipples and she gasped with pleasure, it was full speed ahead. She was soon so focused on the amazing sensations that erupted between her legs when he squeezed her nipples, now swollen and erect, that when his other hand reached under her skirt and began making its way up her thigh, she spread her legs to make it easier for him.

His fingers were fumbling to get inside her panties when suddenly a bright light from outside blinded them. All activity ceased as they gazed up into a policeman's stern visage. Hannah promptly slid off Nathan's lap and back into the driver's seat.

"Let me see your driver's license and registration."

Desperate to draw the man's attention away from Annie, who was frantically attempting to rearrange her clothes as she groped for her purse, Nathan said he didn't have one.

Frightened and mortified, Hannah handed over her papers.

The policeman scrutinized them and shook his head. "Aren't you two a little old for this kind of hanky-panky?"

"We're getting married next Sunday, Officer." Nathan hoped that would excuse their misbehavior, or at least lessen any punishment.

"Well, don't let me catch you out here again." He returned Hannah's documents. "Now say good night and go home."

Nathan let out his breath as he and Hannah watched the patrol car's receding taillights until it disappeared around the corner. She giggled with embarrassment, and in a minute they were laughing so hard the tears ran down their cheeks.

When they regained their composure, Nathan gave her a chaste kiss and headed for his front door. He was no longer the least bit aroused. Being interrupted by the police was even more efficacious than a cold shower.

By the time Hannah got home, her body had calmed. But she couldn't rid herself of an overwhelming feeling of shame at being caught by the police in such a compromising situation.

Yet thinking about it still made her chuckle.

TWENTY-ONE

HANNAH HAD ALREADY turned in all the Israel interviews the *Freiheit* would publish in the next four months, but since she was going into the office anyway Monday for a bridal shower lunch, she decided to give Moe her article about Rav Brenner and the students he'd molested.

She'd been home only an hour when he called. "This is a dynamite story, Annie, but I can't publish it."

"I know, but maybe you can put it in the hands of some Haredi *machers* so they'll realize it's too late to try to cover up the scandal."

"How much of this is true?"

"It's all true, even the yeshiva student who tried to slit his wrists in Spektor's bathroom. But to protect the victims' families, I didn't use their real names. I said that at the end."

"I think you should say it at the beginning."

"Okay. You can make that change." *Wait, why does Moe want changes if he isn't going to publish it?*

"What about Benjamin Stockser? Does he know you identify him?"

"He approved the article before I gave it to you," she said. "He was disappointed when I told him it probably wouldn't be published. He wants people to realize that these things happen in his community. Then victims won't be ashamed to come forth, and perpetrators will stop getting away with it."

"Maybe I'll make it look like I do plan to print it, let it get circulated privately, and see what happens." He broke off, and she could imagine him nodding. "At least more victims, and their parents, will learn that Dr. Stockser is available to help them."

"Thank you so much. We'll see you at the wedding."

"I wouldn't miss it."

Hannah hung up and gave herself a big hug. Moe had called her story "dynamite." He was going to make sure it got read.

After Aunt Elizabeth went to bed, Deborah told Hannah she wanted to speak with her, that she'd come upstairs after Rae and Jake were asleep. Hannah had been expecting her mother to discuss marital relations with her before the wedding, so she was surprised when Deborah brought up Aunt Elizabeth's poor health instead.

"Elizabeth's doctors say her leukemia is getting worse."

"Oh no." Hannah looked at her mother in dismay. "I thought the blood transfusions would help her more."

Deborah blinked back tears. "I tried to convince her to spend her final days with us, that I want to take care of her like she took care of us all those times we were so ill."

"She didn't just take care of us. She saved our lives." Hannah thought back to how Aunt Elizabeth had dropped everything to nurse Mama back to health from childbed fever, then helped Papa recover from being wounded in Spain. After he died she had put aside her own grief to diligently care for Hannah at the farmhouse.

Deborah wrung her hands. "But now, when we have the opportunity to help her, she demurs, saying she'd rather return to her friends, church, and hospital in Boston."

"Then we'll have to go to Boston too, when the time comes."

Two nights later, Hannah and her mother did have "the talk" she'd expected. Deborah began by sitting on the twin bed next to Hannah's. "Unlike most mothers, I have quite a bit of sexual knowledge."

"You don't need to go into details," Hannah interrupted. "I've got a copy of the Kinsey Report on females."

"Kinsey doesn't discuss quality, that some experiences can be utterly sublime and others I wouldn't wish on my worst enemy."

Hannah confirmed that she knew about the latter. "You were raped by Cossacks when you were barely in your teens, and your grandfather died trying to protect you." She wanted to spare her mother the trauma of talking about it and herself the trauma of hearing details that would chafe her own wound.

Deborah gasped. "I spoke of it only once, when you were little, yet you remember."

Hannah, convinced Mama didn't want to discuss it further, changed the subject. "You met Adam Blum in Vienna . . ." She trailed off, hoping her mother would continue the sentence.

Deborah did. "Adam loved me, and I started sleeping with him. I was no longer a virgin, so there didn't seem to be any reason to stay chaste," she explained. "I wanted a lover to erase all memories of what the Cossacks did."

"Did he?" Hannah hoped Nathan would do that for her.

"Nobody could, not even Michael. But I'm getting ahead of myself." She hesitated for a few moments. "Adam Blum was gentle and sweet, but so anxious it took several tries before he was capable. He never did learn how to satisfy a woman."

What if Nathan has the same problem? But Hannah asked instead, "You weren't worried about pregnancy?"

"I thought the soldiers' brutality had made it impossible. I was astounded—and overwhelmed with joy—when I realized Michael had gotten me pregnant." She paused again and smiled. "He was the one who showed me how pleasurable making love could be."

Hannah had an alarming thought. Papa wasn't religious; he didn't have any church telling him what to do or not do. Maybe Nathan wouldn't think it was right to do all those things that Kinsey wrote about.

"What about Dad? Does he do what Papa did?"

"He does now, after I taught him," Deborah replied. "Dancing works best when a man leads, but the woman should lead when it comes to lovemaking."

Their conversation had gotten sufficiently intimate that Hannah felt brave enough to ask her mother the question she'd asked so many strangers. "Do you go to the mikveh?"

"I don't need to. I haven't gotten my period in years."

"I mean when you were younger, after you married Dad." Before her mother could answer, Hannah continued. "I interviewed a lot of Orthodox women and was astonished that most of them did not follow Jewish Law when it came to niddah."

"They didn't?" Deborah sounded surprised but not judgmental.

Hannah shared what she had discovered. "None would say how many days they separated from their husbands, but they weren't reticent about admitting that they usually used their own bathtubs instead of an official mikveh." She caught herself before revealing that Nathan's mother had immersed in a Russian bath.

Deborah sighed. "I never liked going to the mikveh. One evening it was freezing outside and I didn't want to travel home with wet hair, so I used our bathtub instead," she said. "Sam either didn't notice or didn't want to bring up the subject, so I stopped going in the winter. It was so much more convenient that eventually I switched to using our bathtub all the time."

"Dad never said anything to you about it?"

"No. All he needed to know was that I was niddah when I separated our beds and that I wasn't when he saw them back together twelve days later. He probably assumed I wanted to bathe after immersing in a mikveh that who knows how many people had used before me."

"Did you abstain for the seven extra clean days?"

"He expected us to, so we did," she replied. "But not being hot-blooded youths, it wasn't much of a sacrifice."

Hannah was left in a quandary. Of course Nathan would expect her to follow halacha; he was an Orthodox rabbi. And attempting to deceive him was out of the question, not after what happened with Barbara. She'd just have to find a sanitary mikveh and bring a hair dryer. At that moment Hannah chickened out and decided that the week before the wedding was too late to discuss changing their ketubah.

The movers arrived early on Thursday, forcing Nathan to scramble out of his pajamas into jeans and a T-shirt to let them in. Once the van was loaded, he did a final search around the apartment, then left the keys on the kitchen counter and climbed into the truck's cabin. It was only as they turned the corner that nostalgia hit Nathan. This was real. He had left behind the apartment he'd grown up in, the only home he'd known. But when the moving van turned onto Eastern Parkway, his spirits rose. The trees were lush and green, flowers bloomed in front gardens and window boxes, and the buildings' wooden trims were neatly painted.

Nathan was almost giddy with excitement when the van pulled up in front of his new residence. He directed the men to put the containers with his clothes in the master bedroom, then set to work unpacking them while they unloaded the rest of the truck's contents. Then he took the photo of Hannah that had been on his bedside table and carried it into his office, where cartons of books were stacked.

He had just opened a box when he heard Joey Goren shouting below, "Hello! Anyone home?"

Nathan came down to greet his friend. "Joey, glad to see you. When did you get in?"

"My flight landed late last night." Joey gazed around in admiration. "Nice place. My father told me you were moving in today, so I thought I'd come help."

"Perfect timing. I've got a ton of books to put away."

"Would you like me to stay here tonight?" Joey asked. "They say a bridegroom isn't supposed to sleep alone the week before his wedding."

"That would be great. Abba snores so loud, I'd rather he continued to sleep downstairs."

They worked steadily through the morning. Nathan knew that wherever they shelved the books now would likely be where they'd stay, and he was determined to be methodical in their placement. It was an ideal time to catch Joey up on the last six months.

So he was surprised to hear Leah Goren calling from downstairs, "Take a break, you guys. It's way past lunchtime."

She had every kitchen cabinet door open, surveying the contents. "You have plenty of dairy dishes." Then she glanced into the dining room, where the china cabinet from Nathan's apartment was still empty. "It doesn't look like you have enough for meat meals though."

"Annie's aunt gave us the dairy stuff, but most of the recent gifts have been other kinds of meat items, like pots, pans, and silverware," Nathan explained. "I don't understand why." *Maybe I shouldn't have given our old dishes away to that Jewish charity.*

Church bells were chiming three o'clock when Nathan walked into his classroom and saw he'd be partying instead of teaching. An enormous cake sat on his desk next to presents from the department store where he and Hannah were registered. There were tables of food set up against the walls, plus schnapps for toasts. Nearly all the faculty were present, including Rav Rabinovich and Rav Klein, but not the dean.

When the taxi dropped Nathan off late that evening, he was exhausted. Abba and Joey helped carry in the heavy gift boxes, and the three men made short work of opening them.

Joey started laughing when he saw their contents. "I guess you don't have to worry about not having enough meat dishes now." Then a look of alarm wiped the smile off his face. "Oy, it will take us hours to wash them."

"No, it won't. We have an automatic dishwasher." Nathan pointed out the appliance. "I'll go next door in the morning and ask Naomi how it works. They have the same one."

Hannah waited for Sharon to get settled in the car. "I know this should be an enjoyable experience, but I'm still nervous. I've heard so many complaints about local mikvehs." They had planned for a special prewedding outing: first the mikveh, then a beauty salon, and finally lunch at a popular kosher restaurant.

"This mikveh is the nicest in New York," Sharon assured her. "When I made our appointments and told them you were a bride, they promised you wouldn't be disappointed."

There was a parking lot nearby, which was a good start.

Hannah felt relieved that there was no sign, or other identifying marks, to indicate the building's purpose. The lobby had a feminine feel, with pastel walls and furnishings. Their entrance must have alerted someone because a matronly woman opened the inner door, welcomed them, and confirmed their appointments.

"I'm Mrs. Schneider." She handed them each a brochure, then waited while they read it. "Do you have any questions?"

Sharon replied, "I don't think so. My husband is an Orthodox rabbi, and she's marrying one."

The woman smiled. "Then you probably know more than me." She led them to a pink-tiled dressing room with a shower and a large bathtub.

Hannah was relieved that everything was neat and hygienic. A mirrored wall had a long counter with an array of grooming products, including a handheld hair dryer. One tall open cabinet held fluffy white towels and terry-cloth robes. Another had empty shelves and hangers for their clothes and purses.

"Do you want to prepare separately or share the same room?" Mrs. Schneider asked. "Brides who bring a friend often want company."

Hannah and Sharon had discussed this earlier. "We'll share a room and immerse one after another," Sharon said. "That way we can each make sure it's done correctly."

The woman didn't seem to mind being superfluous. "Take as much time as you need."

Hannah carefully followed the instructions for cleaning herself so nothing would interpose between the mikveh's water and her body. Realizing she was looking forward to the spiritual experience, she paid particular attention to areas that tend to collect schmutz: between her toes, under her fingernails, inside her ears, and *pupik*. She washed, rinsed, and combed her hair until there were no knots.

Under Sharon's watchful eye, Hannah waded down the steps into the water, which was pleasantly warm and smelled faintly of chlorine. Thankfully, it wasn't at all cloudy. She made the blessing and dunked, surfacing three times as Sharon said, "Kosher," to indicate she'd completely submerged.

Hannah didn't know what to expect, but shouldn't something feel different from being underwater in a swimming pool? Shouldn't there be a sense of holiness or transformation? Yet it felt much the same as slipping beneath the surface in the bathtub when she was a child. She hid her disappointment and resolved to be grateful that at least the experience wasn't as awful as some of the women she'd interviewed reported.

When Sharon asked how it went, Hannah said, "Now I understand why our great-grandmothers cut their hair when they married. Can you imagine walking back from the mikveh with wet hair in the middle of a Russian winter?"

Sharon scoffed at that. "Just because it was necessary for Jewish women in the eighteenth century doesn't dictate continuing the custom in the twentieth."

At their next stop, the hairdresser, Hannah knew exactly what to expect. After all, this was her third beauty salon visit in as many months. Hannah had originally planned to get married with her hair up, concealed under her veil. Most Jewish women were brunettes, and those who weren't were redheads like Sharon and Naomi. Jewish blonds were such rare creatures that Hannah was regularly assumed to be a shikse, which was no compliment. With her hair up, its color would be less obvious. Yet tradition held that a Jewish bride wore her hair down because this would be the last time she showed her hair in public. Though Hannah had no intention of covering her hair after marriage, she wavered between hairstyles.

Until six weeks ago, when Grace Kelly's wedding photos were splashed on every newsstand.

Nathan wasn't the only one who thought Hannah resembled the blond actress, and there was no denying that their two bridal gowns looked similar. Grace Kelly had gotten married with her hair up, so rather than invite further comparisons, Hannah decided to wear hers down.

Sharon, however, hadn't had her hair done professionally since her own wedding. She selected a fancy upswept style, quite different from the casual way she usually wore her lengthy tresses.

"Now that I've been to the mikveh, Benny and I will be able to touch again," she declared. "I hope he'll be encouraged rather than deterred by how elegant I look."

"What are you expecting to happen?" Hannah wasn't prepared to tell Sharon about Nathan's plan.

"I don't know, Annie, but I hope something good. It's time for more than love letters."

Hannah had no sooner gotten home and settled in to write more thank-you notes than the phone rang. Hoping it was Nathan, she raced down to pick up the extension in Samuel's office.

It was.

"How did everything go this morning?"

"Fine." She was ambivalent about sharing her disappointing mikveh experience, so instead, she asked him, "How about you?"

"I learned how to operate the dishwasher." He sounded proud of himself. "Folks at Spektor threw me a party last night and gave us at least service for twelve of our meat dishes, plus lots of serving pieces."

Hannah didn't think you were supposed to run such fancy dishes through a dishwasher, but before she could decide how to tell Nathan that after he'd done so much work, he continued. "It even has a 'fine china' setting, though I didn't use any soap. I mean, it's not like the dishes were actually dirty."

"They will be after your family Shabbos dinner tonight."

"Listen, the reason I called is that Cousin Marsha wants to show you the wedding present they brought up."

"Another present? In addition to all the furnishings from Auntie Dora's house? Nathan, it's too much."

"This is a small one. I wanted you to see it before we get back from our honeymoon."

"Cousin Marsha can come over anytime. I'm not going out again."

He lowered his voice so she could barely hear him. "Are you still planning to come to the aufruf tomorrow?"

"I am, but I'll sit way in the back with Sharon so I don't flaunt that I'm seeing you so soon before our wedding," she replied. "Speaking of Sharon, she's ready to see Benny again, but she's still nervous about talking to him."

"He's nervous about seeing and talking to her too." He took a deep breath. "Frankly, I'm also nervous about it."

"Are you having second thoughts about your little plan?"

"Third and fourth thoughts too. But it's a little late now."

"I think it will be okay. Sharon understands that her using the mikveh means they'll be able to touch. She told me she's looking forward to it."

He sighed with relief. "I'm nervous about our wedding too, not that I'm having second thoughts about it." Actually, he was more nervous about the wedding night.

"I can't wait for us to be married already."

"We should say goodbye. Cousin Marsha will be there any minute."

Hannah wanted to keep talking. "Only two more days."

"Only two more days," he replied. "Have a good Shabbos. I love you."

Hannah no sooner replied, "I love you too," than the doorbell rang. "She's here. I've got to go."

Nathan's cousin broke into a wide smile when Hannah let her in. "It's so good to see you again. You look gorgeous."

"I had my hair done this morning. I'm glad to see you too."

Marsha held out a flat rectangular box. "Nathan already opened it, but I wanted to see your reaction."

Hannah unfolded the tissue paper and sighed with pleasure. "This is beautiful. Thanks so much."

It was a framed photo of her and Nathan dancing at the Trachtenberg wedding. The two of them looked handsome and sophisticated in their for-malwear; plus the photographer had captured them smiling at each other so their affection was unmistakable.

"Everyone at the reception was so impressed by your dancing. They could hardly believe Nathan is an Orthodox rabbi." Marsha lowered her voice. "Uncle Barney and Uncle Max wouldn't say it to Nathan's face, but they weren't shy about their astonishment that he could be the son of such sanctimonious prigs . . . though I expect it was partly the alcohol talking."

"So you think the difference in observance was at the bottom of the breach between Minnie and her family?"

Marsha nodded. "I asked some pointed questions later and learned there was a giant fight when Aunt Minnie refused to attend the family's Seders anymore, complaining that their house wasn't sufficiently *kosher l'Pesach.*"

"Oy gevalt!" was all Hannah could say. *How ironic that someone in Minnie's family had given her and Abba all those beautiful Pesach dishes and silver.*

"I think my grandparents in particular felt threatened, that the Judaism they practiced wasn't good enough for her. Of course, everyone thought it was all Solomon's fault." Marsha shook her head. "No wonder Zayde blamed him when Aunt Minnie died while he was away at shul on Shabbos."

"I hope they can be civil to him this weekend," Hannah said.

"Me too. But if they aren't, you'll know why."

Everyone else left for shul early Saturday morning, but Hannah wanted to arrive later and slip in unnoticed. So she waited until Aunt Elizabeth's taxi arrived to start walking. Elizabeth wasn't Jewish, so she needn't observe their Sabbath. Hannah had never given any thought to how old or infirm Jews attended services if they couldn't walk, but now it seemed to her that

Conservatives had the right idea when they permitted driving to synagogue on Shabbos.

Congregation Israel of Brooklyn was on Eastern Parkway, so Hannah walked past the Gorens' apartment building. Sharon, who wanted to get to shul well after Benny, was waiting for her. She was wearing a fashionable forest-green suit that covered all the areas Haredi women are supposed to keep hidden.

"I love your hat," Hannah said. The wide-brimmed cartwheel style covered all of Sharon's hair.

"Thanks. It's pretty and it protects my face from the sun." She shook her head gently in wonder. "Can you believe that Rivke got it for me, along with this outfit? She took me and Zisse out shopping at some exclusive store for wealthy Haredi women, and it was actually fun."

"She has excellent taste in clothes. You look like the mysterious beautiful woman in a detective movie."

Sharon blushed. "Your dress and hat look nice too. You'd never catch me wearing fuchsia, but the color becomes you."

As Hannah planned, they blended with the crush of people who arrived at services shortly before the Torah reading. The men's section was more crowded than usual, and by the youthful appearance of many of the occupants, Hannah guessed they were either Nathan's students or his father's. She recognized a contingent of the Trachtenberg family and sighed to see them sitting as far as possible from Nathan's father.

In a normal aufruf, one without a rabbi bridegroom, the cantor chanted from the Torah scroll while the groom and his male friends and family recited the blessings. But Nathan knew the Torah as well as any cantor, and after hearing him merely recite an aliyah in Philadelphia, Hannah was eager to hear him sing the lengthy section of Torah assigned for that Shabbos.

She was not disappointed. When Nathan began chanting, her heart swelled with happiness and pride as she watched him, the man she was about to marry, continue reading. She hadn't really expected to become Mrs. Nathan Mandel when she scribbled those words in her grade-school notebooks, but by some miracle, tomorrow that would become her name. She didn't share the Talmudic belief that God spent a lot of time matchmaking, yet it seemed more than a coincidence that she and Nathan should have encountered each other, let alone fallen in love.

Sharon gasped as Benny came up for his aliyah. Hannah, who'd seen his new haircut, had to admit that, despite having lost some weight, he looked very handsome. His eyes searched the women's section until they found Sharon. When she returned his gaze and gave him a shy smile, he, and Hannah, sighed with relief.

Sharon's anxiety returned when the Torah service was done. "We should go soon," she told Hannah. "You don't want to be seen here when people start leaving."

"All right," Hannah replied. "We'll lunch at my place." She understood that it was Sharon who was eager to leave early.

Nathan had never been a fan of so-called Kiddush Clubs, where men left Shabbos services before the haftarah in order to socialize over schnapps and whiskey, only to return, inebriated, for the final prayers. He objected to the custom even more when a small group, including his uncles, joined in at his aufruf.

He was still standing at the sanctuary entrance, receiving congratulations with Samuel Eisin, when Benny, wearing a grim expression, appeared and gestured that he needed to speak with Nathan.

"Your father and another man—I think one of your uncles," Benny whispered, "are arguing in the men's room. Do you want me to break it up?"

This was exactly what Nathan had feared, that the bad blood between Abba and the Trachtenbergs would erupt, alcohol-fueled, during his wedding weekend. But not in the men's room. Nathan couldn't recall how or when he knew, but it was inviolable that men never spoke in the restroom, not even in a whisper. Yet his father and uncle were shouting at each other. Excusing himself from his guests, he turned to Benny. "I'll go with you."

Samuel headed in the opposite direction. "I'll get the rabbi."

Nathan could hear the loud angry voices from the hall. Abba accusing Barney of abandoning Nathan for over twenty years, only to turn up now to celebrate. "Where were you all when we were starving during the Depression?"

Barney rehashed his family's complaints. "You were the one who refused to eat at our home. We weren't *frum* enough for you."

Nathan was steeling himself to go inside and enter the fray when Louis Katz ran past him. Suddenly all was quiet, and a moment later, Louis exited, each hand with a firm grip on one of Abba's and Barney's arms. Max followed meekly behind.

"Come," Louis said to Nathan. "We're going to my office."

Once everyone was seated, Louis asked Nathan to explain the problem. Which Nathan, with a great deal of discomfiture and reluctance, did. When he got to the part where his parents refused to go to the Trachtenbergs for Pesach, Abba broke in.

"That wasn't my doing," he declared. "I went to your family Seders for years before Minnie and I married. I thought we should be lenient rather than insult your parents, or if it was that important to Minnie, she should come down early and help remove the hametz. But she insisted that her father had to finally realize that she was an adult and accept her autonomy."

Louis shook his head. "It's a shame how much strife different kashrus standards cause in Jewish families these days."

Nathan knew he couldn't avoid addressing his mother's death, but Abba brought the subject up first. "You can hate me all you want for being responsible for Minnie's death, but it wouldn't come close to how much I hate myself." He swallowed hard. "I should have stayed home with her, no matter how much she pushed me to go to shul."

Barney and Max exchanged surprised looks. "You didn't know what would happen," Max said sympathetically.

"It was cruel not to let me know about Shai's death," Abba continued. "He was my best friend, my only friend."

"I know Mama sent you a letter," Max explained. "Although if you didn't get it, there was no way you'd be expecting it."

"We thought you were so angry you wouldn't even attend Shai's funeral," Barney said.

The men sat quietly in the rabbi's office. The hostility was gone, replaced with melancholy over opportunities missed.

"Gentlemen, I hope we will not see a repetition of this kind of incident tomorrow." Louis sounded like a teacher admonishing some wayward students.

The three men shook their heads, then stood and left.

Nathan gazed at Louis with awe. "That was masterful, the way you defused the situation. Getting smicha at Spektor didn't teach me to do anything like that. Where'd you learn how?"

Louis shrugged. "On-the-job training, I guess."

Now that tensions between the Trachtenbergs and Abba had eased, Nathan was looking forward to a relaxing evening before what he expected would be his frenetic wedding day. The company—Abba, Benny, Joey Goren, and his parents—had known Nathan and each other for years, and Nathan expected a congenial exchange of stories of their various interactions with him and Hannah.

But Joey remained sullenly silent until Benny said, "What's bothering you, Joey? Do you want to tell me privately or share it with us now? Nathan deserves to have cheerful attendants tomorrow."

Joey locked eyes with Benny. "You think I shouldn't be upset that you—." He gazed around the room. "All of you kept Benny and Sharon's separation secret from me for months. How did you expect me to feel when I found out about it only after I came home?"

"We didn't want you distracted from your schoolwork," Leah Goren explained.

"We hoped it would be temporary," Isaac added. "That they'd be back together by now."

Benny shook his head and sighed. "I understand your anger, and I apologize for my part in causing it. From the very beginning I feared my relationship with Sharon would interfere with your therapy, so I tried to keep the two separate. Which has not always been successful."

Nathan, dismayed at the direction the conversation was taking, broke in. "But if all goes according to plan, they'll be back in each other's arms tomorrow." He proceeded to detail the scenario they'd worked out.

Abba, looking pleased and surprised, turned to Benny. "You and Sharon have agreed on your compromises?"

"For the most part," Benny replied. "Among other things, I will eat more often at my in-laws', having some Shabbos dinners there, and I will maybe sometimes go to their shul. It was easier than I expected at the aufruf."

Isaac Goren looked skeptical. "How are you going to manage that living in Manhattan?"

"We will find an apartment within walking distance to both my parents and hers, probably in Bedford-Stuyvesant. It will be a schlep to Columbia, but it's a sacrifice I am prepared to make."

"You're moving to a Negro neighborhood?" Leah's expression was full of dismay.

"You can't find someplace safer?" Abba asked.

"Bed-Stuy is no more dangerous than other parts of Brooklyn," Benny replied. "And much cheaper than Manhattan."

Nathan had helped Benny research the neighborhood. "Just because some white folks let Realtors scare them into selling cheap doesn't mean there aren't still Jews around," he said.

Benny looked Isaac Goren in the eye. "I would rather have us living among Negroes than where Polish and Italian hoodlums harass us, or worse, for killing Jesus."

No one could dispute that.

Only Nathan knew that Sharon and Benny hadn't decided where to spend the holidays, since Benny was still too angry to see his father. But all were aware that Sunday's activities would begin early, so the evening soon drew to a close. Isaac and Leah said their goodbyes, and Abba disappeared downstairs.

Joey made a request as the three young men got ready for bed. "Maybe it would work better if I were dancing with Sharon when Benny cut in?"

With Joey's parents gone, Nathan could tease him. "Wouldn't you rather be dancing with Rae?"

Benny's eyes widened. "You did not tell me you were interested in anyone."

Joey blushed and grinned. "You're not the only one keeping secrets. We've been writing to each other since Pesach."

TWENTY-TWO

HANNAH AWAKENED early Sunday morning, too early. It was still dark, and the clock's luminescent hour hand pointed to four. She rolled over and went back to sleep, only to wake again at sunrise. Hoping for several more hours of shut-eye, she pulled the covers over her head. But a bride was never supposed to sleep alone just before her wedding, a custom Hannah considered absurd, so Rae was in the other twin bed. Thus Hannah woke again when her sister did, even though she wouldn't be eating breakfast. The bride and groom fasting until the ceremony was another Jewish wedding custom, one she judged as nonsensical as not sleeping alone. She'd never forgotten a humid summer afternoon wedding where the groom fainted during the Sheva Brachot. But going against tradition seemed to be judged as harshly, or more so, than violating Jewish Law. Like New Yorkers jaywalked with impunity but wouldn't dare wear shorts to synagogue or a funeral. It was a mystery.

She came downstairs in her traveling clothes, suitcase in hand. Nathan's bag was waiting in the foyer, and she put their luggage in the roadster's trunk. She could see her wedding gown and veil hanging in the family sedan—they would have been crushed in her small car. Concrete evidence that she was actually getting married. Everyone else in her family was already wearing their wedding attire, but Hannah would get dressed in the synagogue's special bride's room.

The photographers were there when she arrived. They took pictures of her alone, her with her family, her with her female attendants. The process was overwhelming, but thankfully, it kept her too occupied to be nervous.

The only person not in the photos was Nathan.

Nathan was down the hall at the groom's *tish*, Yiddish for "table." Hannah could hear the men laughing and shouting as Nathan attempted to *drash* while his friends and family heckled and interrupted him. Considering how many of them were Jewish scholars, Hannah doubted he would get many words in edgewise. While the men were thus raucously occupied, Hannah and the women—there were far too many to fit in the bride's room—gathered in the social hall, where the band had begun to play.

Hannah, flanked by her mother, Aunt Elizabeth, and Auntie Dora, grew increasingly anxious as she received the women's good wishes. She nearly panicked when the music abruptly stopped. That meant the men were waiting to begin her *bedeken*, when she and Nathan would finally see each other as he set her veil in place. Some said the ceremony was based on the Bible story where Jacob married Leah instead of Rachel, the sister he loved and expected to wed, because Leah was already veiled so he couldn't see her face.

But Hannah liked the explanation that came from Rebecca veiling herself when she saw Isaac in the field, thus setting herself apart for his eyes alone. Jacob ended up with both Leah and Rachel, plus their handmaids Bilhah and Zilpah, but Isaac had only one wife—Rebecca.

At first Hannah thought this was merely another odd ritual. But to look into each other's eyes as Nathan slowly lowered her veil was an unexpectedly intimate, and romantic, act. They might have gazed at each other longer, but the band broke into a new klezmer tune to inaugurate the procession to the huppah, the wedding canopy, under which they would be married. She and Nathan had refused to use either Wagner or Mendelssohn's music, and it was fun choosing from the many Jewish selections their band had in its repertoire.

Hannah's heart swelled with love as Nathan, dressed in crisp light gray linen, his bow tie and matching handkerchief the same turquoise blue as the bridesmaids' gowns, took his place beside Abba for their walk down the aisle. Next came her friends Naomi and Sharon, resplendent in the blue gowns that beautifully highlighted their red hair, followed by her maid of honor, Rae. Her pulse racing, Hannah stood in the hall as Naomi's daughter and Jake, flower girl and ring bearer, fidgeted at the sanctuary's door. Slowly the music came to a halt. This was the signal to go in.

A Yiddish processional melody, "*Tsu der Khupe Marsh*," began and the congregation stood as Hannah, flanked by Deborah and Samuel, began her long walk to Nathan's side. She was glad to be veiled. Her expression would be obscured, while she could see everyone looking at her. But Hannah only had eyes for Nathan, who gazed at her with such love and tenderness that her heart melted.

The rest of the wedding was a blur. Thankfully, Benny produced the ring promptly, and Nathan had no trouble placing it on her finger. She tried not to giggle when she caught his eye as Deborah cried behind them while the Sheva Brachot were chanted. Finally, she let out her breath with relief when Nathan crushed the glass with one loud stomp, sending them racing down the aisle to the privacy of the bride's room.

At last they were alone.

A table was set up for them to break their fast. But first they threw their arms around each other and kissed, and kissed, and kissed some more. Eventually they sat down to eat, and Hannah gave Nathan his ring.

"I can't believe how beautiful you look," he said with awe. "And how lucky I am."

There was nothing for her to say to this but "I love you too."

They gobbled down their meal, pausing now and then to exchange smiling glances.

"What's in that big manila envelope at the end of the counter?" he asked.

"Our honeymoon itinerary."

"What itinerary? I thought we were going to your aunt's farmhouse in Canada."

"We are, but Durrell Point is more than eight hundred miles from here. It takes three days to get there, so Mama and Aunt Elizabeth arranged for us to stay in two lovely places on the way." She laid the envelope's contents on the table.

He picked up the brochure for a lakeside bed-and-breakfast near Shrewsbury, Massachusetts. "This one looks very nice."

"That's where we'll stay tonight." She gave him what she hoped was a sensuous smile. "We want to arrive at today's destination before dark."

He grinned in return. "Not after a long tiring drive."

"Leave it to Aunt Elizabeth to find us an inn at Bar Harbor tomorrow night. That's near my grandparents' historic home." She told him about last summer's visit. "Too bad we won't have time to see it on this trip."

They silently took a few final bites as Nathan grew impatient to get to the reception and start dancing. "How long are we supposed to wait in here?"

"Long enough for folks to have their hors d'oeuvres." As if reading his mind, she added, "We can't just go out on our own. The bandleader is supposed to introduce us."

Before Nathan could protest, they were interrupted by a gentle knock on the door. It was the photographer, who kept them occupied for another half hour, until Samuel arrived and declared it time to join the party. Next came their grand entrance, followed by a long and lively Hora dance, after which everyone else returned to their seats for lunch.

Hannah was glad she and Nathan had eaten earlier, because the photographers had them moving from table to table, greeting their guests. Nathan was increasingly restless, until the bandleader finally intervened.

"Pictures can wait," he insisted. "Nobody will get up and dance until the bride and groom do."

Grateful beyond belief, Nathan and Hannah headed to the dance floor, where they strutted their stuff to enthusiastic applause. Next Nathan danced with Deborah, who easily followed his lead, while Hannah danced with Dad. Then other relatives were called up. It seemed that they waited forever to be back in each other's arms.

It was only when they danced past the Gorens' table and saw Sharon's expectant expression that Nathan realized he'd better get his scheme started. Hannah asked the band to play the slow, romantic "You'll Never Walk Alone," which was the signal for Nathan to ask Sharon to dance. Hannah watched anxiously as time slowed until Benny stood up, leisurely approached the dancing couple, and tapped Nathan's shoulder. Another eternity passed until Sharon nodded in acquiescence, Nathan stepped aside, and Benny took his place. Hannah, who'd been holding her breath, let it out in a long sigh of relief.

Nathan hurried to get Hannah back on the floor, but there were too many dancers in the way to keep an eye on Benny and Sharon. People wanted to congratulate them, and then the photographers needed more pictures.

By the time they were free, Benny and Sharon were gone.

Then Hannah saw Joey and Rae dancing together. "Let's go see if Joey knows anything," she said to Nathan.

"I think your plan worked," Joey told them. "I saw the two of them talking together for a while until Sharon stopped by our table and asked her parents to watch Judy overnight." He shot them a grin. "Then she and Benny left together."

Hannah and Nathan hugged each other with joyful relief. "We should cut the cake," she said. "We have a long drive ahead of us."

The sun had just begun to set when Hannah parked at the Inn at Lake Quinsigamond. She and Nathan laced arms and admired the multicolored sky reflected in the water until the bellman came out to greet them.

"Welcome, Mr. and Mrs. Mandel. Our best suite is waiting for you." He led them up the wide staircase. "The kitchen is closed; however, we kept a pot of vegetable soup hot. There is also bread and a selection of fruits and cheeses."

He opened the door and promised to be right back with their soup. Hannah headed for the bathroom while Nathan put their suitcases in the bedroom. He'd expected a large bed, but the fireplace was a pleasant surprise. There were two closed doors; one opened to a good-sized mirrored closet where Nathan was glad to find two terry-cloth robes inside. He worried that being in street clothes when he started what he hoped would be a slow, gentle seduction could trigger Hannah's rape memories. These robes could avoid that potential problem.

But first it was time for dinner.

Hannah was back in the living room and Nathan was in the bathroom when the bellman returned with their soup and a bottle of champagne nestled in a bucket of ice. The living area was furnished with a dining table set for two and a nearby buffet. Through the French doors she could see a balcony overlooking the lake that promised to be a pleasant spot for breakfast. *Breakfast—everything would be different at breakfast.*

"I'm on duty until midnight," the man said as he opened the champagne and filled two fluted glasses. "So don't hesitate to call if you need anything." Without the slightest hint of a smirk, he concluded with "Have a good evening."

Thinking, *He'd better not be popping in until midnight,* Hannah bolted the door after the waiter left. The soup smelled wonderful, and she realized how hungry she was. Suddenly shy, she was relieved when Nathan joined her, having removed only his coat and tie. How embarrassing if he'd undressed already while she hadn't.

"*L'chaim.*" Nathan lifted his champagne glass toward her.

"*L'chaim,*" she responded, and took a sip. She'd avoided alcohol ever since college, but surely that was unnecessary tonight, and it might help her relax. Besides, the champagne tasted good, and she was thirsty. So she drained the glass.

Nathan, who was prepared not to drink if Hannah didn't, emptied his as well. "To our lives together," he said as he refilled their glasses. He hoped she'd give him a sign when she felt ready for bed. Just thinking about what they'd soon be doing was getting him more aroused every minute.

"To our long lives together," Hannah toasted him back. After that they ate in uncomfortable silence. By the time they polished off the fruit and cheese, the bottle was empty.

Hannah, a bundle of nerves waiting for something to happen, recalled her mother's advice about the woman leading and was tipsy enough to feel uninhibited. "So, shall I get undressed in the bathroom and you in the closet or vice versa?"

Nathan, who'd been pondering how to bring up the awkward subject, quickly agreed to use the closet. When he stepped into the bedroom, clad only in a robe, Hannah was still in the bathroom. He turned off one lamp after another until only flickering flames lit the room. He didn't want to make love for the first time in total darkness, but having a light on seemed too brazen. This was ideal, and hopefully as different from a frat-house room as possible.

He was trying to decide whether to get in bed first when the bathroom door opened. Hannah was wearing a lace peignoir set, and her body was silhouetted by the light behind her. Then, when she closed the door, he could see glimpses of bare skin through the lace. His respiration quickened, and his mind went blank except for his pent-up desire. He remained frozen to the spot, unable to take his eyes off her.

Hannah saw Nathan's eyes widen in a combination of astonishment, appreciation, and lust. She couldn't look away, and a burning between her legs ignited in response. Shyness and anxiety left behind, she raced into his embrace. Minutes later, without knowing exactly how it happened, his glasses were on the bedside table and they were naked together between the sheets.

Nathan, afraid to rush her, limited his kissing to her face, neck, and shoulders and let his hands caress her back.

Hannah could feel his erection when her hips, through no volition of her own, began pushing up against his. Eager for more than kissing, she moved his hand around to cup her breast. Like in the car before their wedding, his fingers fondling her nipples produced a surge of heat below, but now there was no policeman to interrupt them. Her breathing accelerated as her need forced her to propel his hand down toward the source of what was now a fiery longing.

Nathan remembered his studies and replaced his fingers on her breast with his lips. Hannah let out a soft moan, and he was glad he'd been warned that this was a sign of desire, not pain. He tongued her nipples and was rewarded with louder moans as his hands moved steadily up her thighs until they ultimately reached what the Talmud called "that place." His fingers, slippery with her wetness, explored every fold and crevice until he found the tiny nub he hadn't known existed until ten days ago. Hannah writhed under his ministrations, and it took a tremendous amount of willpower not to enter right then and bury himself in her.

Abruptly, her lower lips grew more swollen and that small nub felt larger and engorged. Judging her about to climax, he climbed on top, but he'd been fully aroused for too long. Just the feel of her warm skin pressing against him was overwhelming. So overwhelming that he was helpless when merely attempting to enter was all it took to send him over the edge.

His momentary ecstasy was followed immediately by devastating guilt.

No, no, no! Nathan's mind screamed at him. He'd studied so diligently how to make Hannah climax first, but losing control before he'd even entered and leaving her on the brink of orgasm was beyond dreadful. It was a complete and utter disaster.

He wanted the earth to open up and swallow him.

She was murmuring something consoling like "It's all right; things will be better next time," but Nathan couldn't abandon her to her frustration. Not their very first time. He hadn't planned on trying this so soon, but as the old saying advised, "Desperate times call for desperate measures." He reversed position and gently spread her legs so he could stimulate her orally.

Hannah had worried so much about Nathan not getting sufficiently aroused that she hadn't considered that he might climax so soon. Now she was planning how she'd clandestinely get to the bathroom and bring herself to orgasm when she felt his tongue probing around her inflamed and throbbing flesh. She squirmed and whimpered, but he seemed determined to continue.

In less time than Hannah thought possible, she was on the brink again, but this time there was no stopping. Her rapture reached new heights until it seemed she would swell up and burst. Suddenly her cries reached a crescendo as wave after wave of contractions seized her.

Afraid to stop too soon, Nathan forced his mouth to remain in place until she wrenched her body away. He was wallowing in his failure when he felt her hand moving down his belly.

Hannah wasn't about to leave her marriage unconsummated on their wedding night. She reached down and chortled softly to find him not as limp as she'd anticipated. Indeed just touching his skin, smooth and supple under her fingers, was a great restorative. Only a few gentle strokes and squeezes made him ready again. She rolled over and pulled him on top of her.

Nathan groaned as her tight passage enveloped the most sensitive part of his body. After just climaxing, the intensity of his pleasure was almost painful. With Hannah's legs wrapped around him, he let her control the depth and timing of his thrusts as he gave himself over to the marvelous feeling of her damp heat surrounding him. When she began to convulse around him and his release came, it was as if his semen was burning its way out.

Hearts pounding, they lay limp and sweaty in each other's arms. Hannah somehow managed to lift her head to kiss him good night. "Thank you," she whispered. "It wasn't what I expected—it was better."

"My pleasure," he murmured, too exhausted to say more. He then turned on his side so they were snuggled together like two spoons. His last thought before sleep overtook him was the Yiddish saying, *Der mentsh trakht un Got lakht.* (Man plans and God laughs.)

When Nathan woke, waves of joy inundated him as he turned to see Hannah lying next to him. She was still asleep, her blond tresses spread over the pillow as her bare arms and shoulders overhung the blanket. If someone had told him last week that he didn't love her enough, he would have called that person a liar. But Benny was right. Nathan couldn't explain it, but his love *was* stronger now that they'd coupled. He fingered his wedding ring and recited the broche for seeing an especially beautiful person: *Baruch atah Adonai, Eloheinu Melech ha'olam, shekacha lo beolamo.* (Blessed are you our God, Ruler of the Universe, who has such [beautiful things] in His universe.)

He was yanked out of his admiration by a soft knocking on the door to their suite. It was room service, who quickly set up the morning meal. Then they were gone, leaving the scent of coffee behind. Hungry as he was, Nathan had no intention of eating breakfast alone. But there was plenty of coffee. He poured himself a cup and considered what had happened, and what had almost not happened, the night before.

He was still trying to mentally balance his humiliating failure against his ultimate triumph when the door opened and there was Hannah. Her hair was mussed and she was wearing the lacy nightgown and matching robe, only this time the dimly lit bedroom behind her made them opaque.

She covered a yawn with her hand. "Hmm, I thought I smelled coffee."

"Good morning, Mrs. Mandel." He fixed her coffee with cream and a little sugar, the way she liked it. "Breakfast is served."

She didn't sit down. "I know you needed to let room service in, but I was frightened to wake up in an empty bed."

"I'm sorry that I wasn't there as well. I was looking forward to our waking up together."

"Oh, Nathan. I love you so much."

A moment later she was in his arms, and a minute after that they were back in bed. Ignoring any concern about appearing brazen, Hannah was determined to lead. "That thing you did with your mouth down there to make me climax," she whispered, "could you do it again?"

This time Nathan was resolute not to let the ecstasy take him unaware. "I'd be delighted."

So he did, and she did.

Once inside her, he managed to last a sufficient amount of time that they both reached orgasm, if not simultaneously, at least close enough not to matter.

Hunger woke Hannah an hour later. Reluctant to worry Nathan, she stayed in bed and leaned on her arm to gaze at him, now her husband. Without his glasses he looked different, and admiring his dark wavy hair, she suddenly imagined Superman and Clark Kent with a beard. The comparison was so incongruous it made her giggle. She rolled over and tried to quiet her laughter, but that only made her quake with repressed mirth.

Of course Nathan couldn't sleep with her shaking next to him. Her back was toward him, so he feared she was crying. "Are you all right? Is anything the matter?" Chas v'chalila he'd made her remember being raped.

He saw his mistake as soon as she turned over, but with embarrassment added to the mix, she was giggling so hard she couldn't speak. "What's so funny?" he asked.

It took a little while for her to calm sufficiently to enlighten him. He looked at her skeptically, until she gave him a quick kiss and explained, "When you're not wearing your glasses, you do have superpowers."

Now it was his turn to look abashed.

"I'm serious," she continued. "What you did was marvelous. Where did you learn it? And don't tell me it's from the Talmud."

"It is from the Talmud," he asserted.

"That was the homework Benny gave you?"

"Part of it." He told her how Benny explained sexual relations being different for a man than for a woman. "Until last night, I wouldn't have thought it possible for me to love you more."

This time she kissed him longer. "Maybe that's why they call it *making love*." She smiled seductively.

He returned her smile. "I brought all four tractates with me so we can study my homework together when we get to the farmhouse. They're in my briefcase."

Her growling stomach interrupted their pillow talk. As soon as Nathan went into the bathroom, Hannah donned her peignoir and headed for the balcony. The eggs and toast had cooled to ambient temperature, and the fruit was no longer cold. But the view of the lake was excellent and the coffee was still hot in its carafe. It was definitely a good morning.

After bathing and dressing in comfortable clothes, they drove to their next destination, Bar Harbor, arriving in time for dinner. Again Hannah knew what she wanted Nathan to do in bed, and he was happy to do it.

Twice.

The next morning Hannah woke first. Still drowsy, she pondered what Benny had told Nathan. Certainly there could be no comparison between what she and Nathan did versus her only other sexual experience. But men weren't the only ones affected as he had been; she also felt that her love for him was stronger. She didn't want him to be alone in the bedroom when he awakened, but she didn't want to lie there doing nothing. *If only I had something to read.*

She remembered his volumes of Talmud. She tiptoed into the living area, opened his briefcase, and examined its contents. She was debating which tractate to start with when she noticed a periodical tucked away. It was clearly not a scholarly journal, but she'd never seen any popular magazines in his apartment.

She gulped when she saw the title. *Playboy: Entertainment for Men*, dated May 1956. An attractive redhead's face graced the cover; her eyes were closed and a blanket decorated with cartoon rabbits came up to her chin. Hannah's first instinct was to shove his copy back where she found it and grab one of the Talmuds. But curiosity got the better of her.

She knew about *Playboy*; it was displayed at many newsstands. Now was her chance to see what all the fuss was about. She took it with her, settled back into bed, and opened to the table of contents. Her opinion of the publication rose when she saw a short story by Erskine Caldwell, author of *Tobacco Road* and *God's Little Acre*, both novels she'd read in college. Farther down was an article "Training Your First Wife" by Shepherd Mead, labeled satire.

Was that why Nathan had this particular copy? She tried to turn to Mead's entry, but the center page unfolded to reveal a three-page color photo of a nearly naked buxom blond titled "Miss May—Playboy's Playmate of the Month." The woman did bear a superficial resemblance to Hannah, but would Nathan have acquired the magazine for that? She checked the outside cover and realized he hadn't bought this copy at all; there was a subscription label addressed to an unfamiliar man in Brooklyn.

She read Caldwell's story, which was clever and funny. Mead's article, however, was so irritating she had to keep reminding herself it was satire. Then the blanket shifted, and she lowered the magazine to see Nathan staring at her with an expression that combined shock and mortification.

"This isn't what you think, Annie," he said in a panic. "They have copies at the barbershop, and the owner gave me one because he knew I was getting married."

"I'm not upset. I wanted something to read and thought of Talmud, but this was too intriguing." If anything, he should be upset because she'd rifled through his briefcase. "The writing is surprisingly good, though I suspect most men probably don't read it for that."

Relief coursed through him. "I read the 'Training Your First Wife' article, and while I knew it wasn't serious, I still didn't find it amusing."

She couldn't resist teasing him. "How did you like Miss May? I thought she was very nice looking." As she anticipated, his face flamed.

But his reply was both unexpected and inspired. "She doesn't hold a candle to you."

Now it was her turn to blush. "So, what do you want to do this morning? We could get an early start"—she looked into his eyes—"or we could stay in bed a little longer."

Nathan couldn't believe his ears, yet she had to be propositioning him. Of course he wanted to. "Well, since we're still here and haven't dressed yet . . ."

It was good that they managed a somewhat early start, since the drive took more than eight hours and they forgot that Prince Edward Island was in a later time zone. But the sun didn't set there until nine, so they still got to Aunt Elizabeth's farmhouse before dark.

They walked outside to stretch their legs. The waning crescent moon was barely visible, and the stars were coming out. Hannah took Nathan's hand and led him down the path to the beach, where he marveled at the starlit canopy overhead. In Sea Gate there was too much light from the city to see so many stars, and in Peekskill the forest had concealed much of the night sky. They stood together, breathing in the salty sea air, taking in the awesome scene. Finally Hannah yawned, and Nathan felt an answering wave of sleepiness. The farmhouse, lit from the inside, was a beacon in the dark night as they climbed back.

They slept late and then snuggled together in the brass double bed. Nathan got up first and, investigating the kitchen, was pleased to find that someone had left coffee, eggs, a quart of milk, and a bowl of blueberries in the refrigerator. Inside a paper bag on the counter were four cinnamon rolls that looked home baked and smelled delicious. He started the coffee and returned to the bedroom to admire Hannah while listening to a concert of birdsong.

When she opened her eyes, she smiled to see him there, and he kissed her good morning. Then he went to the kitchen to make breakfast and give her privacy to get dressed. They had agreed not to dally in bed their first day so they could go out shopping for provisions before the best items were gone. They had many long days ahead of them to dally as much as they liked.

Buying groceries in Little Pond was an adventure. Their first stop was the bakery, which, Hannah informed Nathan, began making bread at dawn and closed at noon or whenever everything was sold. Despite having eaten a hearty breakfast, her mouth watered as soon as she smelled the fresh bread. They bought enough baked goods to last until Friday. Next they drove into the countryside to find Aunt Elizabeth's favorite produce stands. Blueberries were obviously in season, but Hannah was thrilled to find strawberries and rhubarb too.

Nathan, who'd previously bought all his produce from the same Haredi greengrocer, was impressed with the quality of fresh vegetables, all picked that morning. Like the bakery, these stands closed when their supplies ran out. When they returned to the farmhouse, he had bags of spinach, sweet peas, asparagus, early potatoes, and several kinds of lettuce to carry in.

Late that afternoon, they went out again to meet the returning fishing boats and purchase what looked best, which Hannah judged to be halibut. That evening, Nathan ate the best dinner ever, including two vegetables he'd never tasted before—rhubarb and asparagus. Afterward, they took a walk under the starlit sky and went to bed early.

It was as if he'd been cast ashore on an island of unimagined delights.

The following two weeks fell into an idyllic pattern. Most mornings they made love, after which Nathan prepared breakfast. Then they packed lunch for picnics on the deserted beach or in the forest. If it was warm, they went swimming. Eventually it was off to the harbor, where they bought the fish Hannah would cook for dinner. They experienced only one rainstorm, during which Nathan assisted in making strawberry-rhubarb jam to bring home. After the storm cleared, Hannah was able to procure a variety of fresh mushrooms, another new food for Nathan.

After dinner they studied Nathan's Talmud homework, which inevitably led to what it called "using the bed."

Hannah was amused, and impressed, that the Rabbis believed women released seed at climax. "Do you realize that other cultures back then didn't think women made seed at all?" she asked Nathan. "Greeks and Romans believed the man's semen contained a homunculus, a tiny fully formed baby."

Nathan responded with a perfect quote from Tractate Niddah. "There are three partners in a child: the father, the mother, and the Holy One, blessed be He. The father provides the white seed that forms the child's bones, sinews, brain, and white of the eye. The mother provides the red seed that forms the flesh, hair, blood, and black of the eye. The Holy One gives the soul, intelligence, hearing, eyesight, and ability to speak. When a person dies, the Holy One takes away His share and leaves the father's and mother's." Nathan wasn't sure he remembered the text exactly, but that was the general idea.

"Oh, Nathan, that's beautiful," Hannah said. The Rabbis were more enlightened than she'd thought.

They would have stayed at the farmhouse longer, since Hannah's menses was late, but Nathan wanted to get home before Abba left for Israel. So Hannah drove like a demon was chasing them, and they got back with an hour to spare before Abba's taxi arrived to take him to the airport. In her haste to get to the bathroom, she rejected Nathan's offer to carry her over the threshold, which was just as well since, as she'd feared, her period had begun.

Sighing with disappointment, she waited until Abba was gone to tell Nathan they needed to move their beds apart.

It took him a moment to recognize the implication. "At least nobody can accuse us of jumping the gun, Annie." He hadn't expected a pregnancy so soon, but he could see she was feeling let down and wanted to cheer her up.

It didn't work. "I really thought I might be. I mean, I was a few days late, and we'd been doing it every day . . ." She trailed off with a sad sigh.

He suddenly thought of what might really cheer her up, or at least take her mind off their failure. "Do you think it's too late to call Benny?"

"I don't know. What do you think? You know him better."

They debated for a few minutes until Nathan made the decision. "I don't care how late it is. I'm going to call anyway."

They rushed to the phone, and Hannah held her breath while he dialed. Somebody eventually answered, and Nathan's face lit up. "Sharon," he said loudly so Hannah would hear. "It's good to hear your voice. Yes, we just got back. Can you speak up so Annie can listen too?"

He held the receiver between them, a difficult task since Hannah was literally jumping with joy. "I moved back in the day after your wedding," Sharon began. "Now we're looking for a new apartment in Bed-Stuy."

"I have an idea," Hannah broke in. "Nathan and I are going to Sea Gate on July first, and we won't return until after Labor Day. You could stay here while we're away."

Nathan was taken aback by her audacity but admitted it was a good idea. "It would be easier for you to search for a new place if you're living in Brooklyn. Benny's already stayed here, so he knows where everything is."

Sharon paused and they heard her calling to Benny, "It's Nathan and Annie on the phone. They just got back and want us to stay there this summer while they're in Sea Gate."

They smiled at the excitement in Sharon's voice, and then things quieted as she and Benny had a whispered conversation.

Benny got on the line. "We accept your very generous offer. Thank you, for everything."

Nathan had no sooner hung up than Hannah grabbed him in a joyous bear hug. "Sharon sounded so happy. I can't believe we got them back together."

TWENTY-THREE

"GEVALT." NATHAN ABRUPTLY let her go and took a step away. "We shouldn't be touching. You're niddah."

"Sorry, I forgot." Hannah gave him a skeptical look. "Are we really going to not touch each other at all?"

"We're not allowed to even hand things to each other."

She rolled her eyes. "I don't know how oversexed these Rabbis were, but we're responsible adults. We're not going to run off to bed if I hand you a cup of coffee."

"I agree it's highly unlikely, but that's halacha."

"You mean it's another fence around the Torah," she protested. "Because the Rabbis didn't trust people to follow the Torah, they added all these extra restrictions. Like not allowing an organ in shul because musical instruments were prohibited on Shabbos to prevent someone from carrying one, which is forbidden work."

"I know," he interrupted her with a sigh. "Nobody can carry an organ. But we can't just abandon these fences; so much of Jewish Law stems from the building and rebuilding of them."

"I don't understand why Orthodoxy makes Judaism so complicated and difficult. The prophet Micah told us what God wants: only to do justice, to love mercy, and to walk humbly with your God." She challenged him. "Besides, you're a rabbi. You don't need fences to keep you from accidentally sinning. You know the law."

"Being a rabbi, I have to set an example."

"If you don't want us to hand things to each other even during my white days, I won't. But I think it's a completely unnecessary inconvenience," she said. "And rather hypocritical considering how it didn't matter if I was niddah when we went dancing before we were married, nor if any of your other dance partners were. Not to mention that I was still niddah when that policeman caught us fooling around in my car."

Nathan realized further arguments were useless. When he let her have the last word, Hannah was glad she'd made the lenient decision about underwear she'd use during the seven clean days. With that in mind, she'd bought some black panties at Martin's; it was the darkest color they had.

Hannah drove them to the Sea Gate cottage on July 1 with enough time to unpack and go shopping before lunch. One bedroom had a double bed, another had twin beds, plus there was a pair of hammocks on the screened-in porch. While Hannah put things away in the kitchen, Nathan made up the beds. For now they would sleep in the twin beds, then switch to the double after Hannah immersed.

Nathan davened at the nearest Orthodox synagogue before dinner. Normally he would have prayed at home, but they needed to learn where the local mikveh was, and it would be too embarrassing for Hannah to ask a roomful of strange men such an intimate question. Thankfully, someone gave him the address of a mikveh a few blocks away.

Five days later Hannah scrupulously prepared and drove to the address Nathan provided. At first she thought she must have gotten it wrong because the place was a small ramshackle house, but she gathered her courage and knocked on the door. An elderly woman opened it, and while appearing surprised to see Hannah, led her to a door at the end of the hall.

The woman reached in and switched on a light. "I hope you know what to do, honey," she said. "Part of the reason the rent's so cheap here is that I have to let people use that pool downstairs."

"I'll be fine by myself." Hannah let out a relieved breath. She would just as soon not be supervised.

She walked down a short flight of stairs and stared at the small, dimly lit room in dismay. There were no towels, no place to sit, and only one clothes hook. She couldn't help gulping in disgust at the murky water, a strange shade of green. She remained paralyzed for a few minutes, waiting for her nerves to settle so she could step in, but that gave her time to detect the subtle yet undeniably fetid odor.

Without even sticking her toe in, she went upstairs. "I forgot to bring a towel," she told the woman as an excuse. "I'll have to come back later."

Hannah drove off in a panic. How could she possibly find another mikveh tonight? She'd read that the ocean was a kosher mikveh, but it wouldn't be safe to go in the water alone after dark. Then she remembered the fancy hotel they'd passed on the way. Maybe she could get a room there with a large bathtub.

The clerk looked at her suspiciously when she walked in without luggage, but after she presented her driver's license and paid cash for a suite, he gave her a key. The tub was indeed spacious, and when she finally returned, her hair still damp, Nathan got her into bed so fast there wasn't time to acknowledge how she'd deceived him.

The guilt hit her in the morning, but she couldn't bring herself to confess what she'd done when he was so loving and affectionate. He'd certainly be disappointed in her, and angry too; which he'd have every right to be. But there never seemed to be a good time to tell him, and as each day passed, it was easier to continue as if nothing untoward had happened. Next month she wouldn't wait until the last minute to find a mikveh. And if there wasn't a nice one nearby, she'd ask Nathan to help her immerse in the ocean.

A week later Hannah had put the experience out of her mind. Until, as they walked hand in hand on the beach, Nathan casually asked, "So how was that mikveh I found for you?"

She froze, desperately trying to think of the least terrible answer. Lying and saying it was fine would be easiest, but that would be compounding her sins. Yet there was no way to tell the truth without, at the least, upsetting him, and at the worst—she didn't want to imagine the worst.

When Hannah didn't reply immediately, Nathan had a sinking feeling in the pit of his stomach. The longer she faltered, the greater his dread.

Finally, she realized the truth was her only option. "It was awful, so repulsive I couldn't even put my toe in." In a shaking voice, she explained what she'd done and apologized for not telling him. "I know I should have come back right away, but I was so panicked I couldn't think straight."

Nathan dropped her hand immediately and stepped away. "Oh my God. You're still niddah." He gulped. "And we . . ." He couldn't bring himself to say it.

The revulsion on his face hurt more than if he'd hit her. "Don't look at me like I have the plague," she retorted. "My body is no different than it was last month."

His rage erupted. "How could you violate halacha like that?"

"Like what?" She narrowed her eyes in defiance. "The vast majority of Jewish women don't immerse at all, and even most Orthodox women don't use a mikveh. I did the best I could at the moment, and I regret not inspecting the place in advance."

He ignored her contrition and the insinuation that he should have inspected the mikveh before recommending it. "How can you possibly know what most Orthodox women do?"

"First, because I know there aren't enough mikvehs in New York for all the Orthodox women who live here." Her voice rose as she defended herself. "Second, because I interviewed dozens and dozens of them."

"I don't care what most so-called Orthodox women do. You're my wife, and I expect you to follow Jewish Law."

"Right, like your mother did," she spat out.

That silenced Nathan for a moment. "What do you mean—like my mother did?" he finally sputtered.

"I interviewed her best friend, who told me that not only did your mother not immerse in a mikveh, but she didn't wait the seven clean days either."

"That's impossible. Abba would never allow it."

"He didn't know." She gave Nathan a hard stare. "And he never asked." Then she began to explain how he was conceived.

"That's enough. I don't want to hear it." He began striding back to their beach house. Then he turned and blurted out, "You can sleep in whichever bed you want. I'll be on the porch."

He was almost out of sight when Hannah burst into tears.

For the rest of the week they maintained a frosty relationship where they spoke to each other only when necessary and never got close enough to touch. Claiming she needed a larger table where she could spread out, Hannah spent much of the day at her parents' cottage, trying vainly to focus on translating stories in the Israeli newspapers her dad brought her.

She'd confessed her sin and apologized, but he'd rejected her contrition. *Now the ball is in his court.*

At the same time Nathan tried to keep busy preparing a new curriculum for his Intro to Textual Criticism class; after all, he'd been teaching the same material for seven years. But not being able to share it with Annie made him miss her presence more. *How could she deceive me like this? It's a million times worse than Barbara hiding how she violated the Sabbath.*

Neither slept well, as each tossed and turned while their emotions fluctuated between resentment, disappointment, and complete wretchedness. And for Nathan, intense sexual frustration. He didn't know how much longer he could keep from reaching out for her, especially now that he knew what he was missing. His only option was to avoid her as much as possible.

Exacerbating Hannah's misery, she eventually got her period again. Nathan felt relieved, and ashamed of that relief, that he had not fathered a *ben niddah*, a child conceived while the mother was niddah. Yet he couldn't avoid thinking that, if Hannah was correct about his mother, he himself was a *ben niddah*. Which only made him feel worse.

Six days later, she had just toweled off and pulled on her first pair of black panties, when Nathan, assuming, she was sleeping late like usual, walked into the bathroom. She grabbed the nearest towel to cover her breasts, but it was too small, thus presenting him with an image that was a near replica of the blond playmate in his *Playboy* magazine. But she wasn't smiling.

His body responded with a flood of desire and his mind with outrage. "Are you deliberately trying to torment me?" he demanded. "Or just trying to provoke me?"

Horrified by his open expression of fury and lust, she screamed back, "How dare you come in without knocking? Get out."

Further incensed by her defiance and aroused by her lascivious appearance, he took a step toward her without realizing how small the bathroom was. She tried to move away, but she was already up against the bathtub. She was trapped.

The terror in her eyes brought Nathan to his senses. What the hell was he doing? He knew Annie had been raped, and here he had her cornered in the bathroom, where she was completely vulnerable. *Look at her; she's trembling.*

He backed out the door. "I'm sorry I interrupted you," he said softly. He gently closed the door behind him, the image of her wearing only those skimpy black panties seared into his brain.

Hannah collapsed onto the toilet seat and tried to calm herself. They couldn't go on this way, but she could neither keep waiting for Nathan to apologize nor go back to that Sea Gate mikveh. She had seven days to find a new approach.

Horrified at the extent of the disgust that had made him view Annie like a leper, Nathan decided to see for himself the mikveh she'd rejected. Introducing himself as a rabbi there to inspect the mikveh, he immediately got an earful from the woman who let him in.

"I wondered when somebody would finally do something about that filthy pool down there." She led him down the hall and shivered with revulsion. "It's not my job to clean it, only to let water in from the roof when it rains and let the old water drain out."

As soon as the door opened, Nathan was assaulted by the stench. He forced himself to peer inside, where a glance at the film floating on the water was enough to send him reeling.

Unable to restrain his curiosity, he asked, "Do many women come here?"

"Hardly any, and those who do come after a storm has freshened the water a bit." She stopped to think. "The only one who's been here this summer was a blond who left right away—not that I blame her."

Nathan thanked her for her time and made a beeline for the front door. He couldn't get away fast enough. Annie had been right not to immerse there, but she should have come back and had them figure out what to do together. Even so, he was ashamed to admit that she had good reason to fear his reaction if she told him what she'd done.

That afternoon, Hannah was alone at her parents' cottage attempting to work when the doorbell rang. Having no desire to see anyone, she ignored it, but a few minutes later the back door opened.

"Anybody home?" Naomi's voice called out.

"I'm in the dining room." Hannah mentally kicked herself for forgetting that Naomi would be spending August in Sea Gate. It gave Dad such pleasure to have all his children and grandchildren together for a month in the summer that for years he'd been renting a beach cottage nearby for Dovid's family to join them.

Naomi's eyes narrowed as she surveyed Hannah. "Are you all right? You don't look well."

Cognizant of the dark circles under her eyes, Hannah admitted, "I've been having trouble sleeping . . ." She tried to keep her voice steady, but her chin quivered and she couldn't continue.

Naomi sat down next to Hannah and put her arm around Hannah's now shaking shoulders. "What's the matter? What happened?"

It took a while, but Hannah told her.

"Oh, Annie, I'm so sorry. Who would have guessed that Nathan has such a temper? How awful for you."

Hannah didn't want to discuss how awful it was any longer. "What mikveh do you go to when you're here?"

"Luckily, I've either been pregnant or nursing, so I haven't needed a mikveh. But I hear there's a decent place in Bensonhurst."

"I was thinking about immersing in the ocean, but I can't do that by myself. I'd need someone to hold my robe and"—she smiled weakly—"make sure I don't drown."

Naomi thought for a moment. "I could go with you and hold your robe, but I doubt I could keep you from drowning. I can't swim and don't think I could run for help fast enough."

"Holding my robe should be enough. I'm a good swimmer."

"Okay. But if you change your mind and want to check out the Bensonhurst mikveh, I'd like to go with you. It shouldn't be that big a schlep if you're driving."

Back at their cottage, Nathan knew he had to do something to heal their breach before it was time for her to immerse again. In desperation, he called his colleague Louis Katz.

"Nathan, what a pleasant surprise," the young rabbi said. "I thought we wouldn't start our premarital work until after the holidays. I hope you had a nice honeymoon."

"We had a most excellent honeymoon." Nathan tried not to sound bitter.

Louis must have heard something in Nathan's voice. "And after the honeymoon?"

"Not so good," he confessed. "Listen, let's not talk about it on the phone. We're summering in Sea Gate. How'd you like to take a walk on the beach and breathe some fresh ocean air?"

"Considering it's ninety degrees and 95 percent humidity in the city, how about tomorrow afternoon?"

Louis, sporting a wide Panama hat, was true to his word and arrived just after lunch. As the two rabbis walked along the water's edge, Nathan described his predicament. "I don't know what to do," he lamented. "I love her, and it drives me crazy that I backed away like she had the plague when the reality was that she'd merely used the wrong bath."

"Hannah is right that most Orthodox women don't use the mikveh, and I doubt most Orthodox men care." Louis sighed in resignation. "When we were planning the new building, we asked the Sisterhood to raise some money for a mikveh—they're very expensive these days, with all the complicated plumbing needed to meet building and health codes. But the women weren't interested; they preferred to fund the school."

"That's a shanda."

"Teaching at Spektor has kept you cloistered. You only see men, and the most observant ones at that," Louis pointed out. "As a pulpit rabbi, I have to do the best I can with the Jews I serve. Still, I don't know who was more shocked, the bridegrooms upon hearing that they're only allowed to sleep with their wives half the month or me at learning how few of them knew this."

"I can't force Annie to go back to that filthy mikveh." He punched his fist into his other hand. "But I can't just accept our violating halacha."

Louis smiled. "You taught her Talmud though."

"That's different; there are various opinions." *But is it really so different?*

"Maybe one of these days Orthodox rabbis will confront the fact that the vast majority of their congregants regularly violate niddah laws." Louis shook his head. "But I suspect that they will just continue to be willfully blind."

Nathan recalled assuring Benny's father that Sharon and her family observed *all* the Commandments. It had never even entered his mind to doubt that the Goren women used a mikveh.

They jumped back as a large wave rushed toward them, and Louis began to laugh. "How it is, my learned friend, that you failed to notice that the oldest, largest mikveh is literally at your feet?" He made his point by splashing Nathan.

"Immerse in the ocean?" Nathan didn't know whether to laugh or cry. "Of course. I can't believe I didn't think of that."

"Now you have to apologize to your wife."

"But she was the one who misled me." Yet he was the one who made it obvious he'd found her repulsive.

"You forced her to. You broke one of the most important rules of marriage: never ask your wife a question if you're not prepared for her answer."

A wave lapped at their feet as Nathan considered Louis's advice. "Maybe it's just as well I never took a pulpit."

"I don't know about that," Louis replied. "Rashi said: Any idiot can forbid out of ignorance, but it takes a true scholar to find the leniency to permit."

"You sound like a Conservative rabbi."

"Don't tell anyone, but if it weren't for my father wanting me at his shul, I probably would be."

Nathan waited until he judged the moment right, a few days later when they were washing the dinner dishes. "Annie, I'm really sorry. I'm an idiot."

She put the wet plate on the counter behind her instead of where he could reach it to start drying it. "Do you mean you're sorry that you're an idiot or you're sorry and you are an idiot?"

"Both actually, I guess."

He looked so miserable she didn't wait for him to explain. "I've been thinking, and maybe on the evening I'm supposed to immerse, we could take a walk along the shore." She gave him a shy smile. "Then, when it's dark, you could hold my robe while I immerse in the water."

He smiled back at her, overjoyed that she'd already had the same idea he'd planned to propose. "That sounds lovely, although I might have a better idea."

"Go on."

"What if we immersed in the ocean together?" He looked at her imploringly. "Please, it'll be fun." And he'd feel less sinful for having had sexual relations with a niddah.

"What if other people see us?"

"They'll just think we're out for an evening swim. We'll go in our bathing suits, then take them off when the water's deep enough. I'll hold yours while you immerse, and then you can hold mine." His eyes met hers, silently begging her compassion. "And when summer's over we can figure out something else."

Hannah let herself replace the memory of the disgust he'd shown previously with his current penitence. "Let's just take it month by month for now." *Please, God, let me be pregnant by then.*

"If you don't mind, could we sleep in the same room again? In the twin beds?"

She was flooded with relief. "Yes, I'd like that too."

"I know you're busy with work for the *Freiheit*, but I'd appreciate your help with preparing my new fall curriculum. I want to start with a simple amended text, one so obvious even my most disapproving students can't challenge it . . ." He trailed off, unable to decide how to explain what he needed without insulting her.

But she recognized what he was reluctant to say. "And you want to test it on a novice like me. Because if you can get me to understand it, then your Spektor students surely will too."

"Exactly." Nathan sighed. *How well she knows me.*

They gazed at each other with solace and joy. Even so, Hannah wished that she could at least hand him the wet dishes instead of putting them down near him.

When Hannah woke during the night, she was reassured to hear Nathan's soft breathing mixed with waves breaking on the shore. Somehow they had stumbled through their first marital crisis and were going to study Talmud together again, but she would still need to formally atone for her actions and ask Nathan's forgiveness before Yom Kippur.

She knew he'd forgive her for deceiving him, but would he ever fully trust her again? And how could she forgive herself for divulging his mother's secret?

She'd never get to sleep if she wallowed in guilt, so she turned her mind to questions she wanted to ask Nathan. Why are the rules strict for a niddah but lenient for the *ba'al keri*, who had a seminal emission? Why does *minhag yisrael din hu* only apply to make things stricter for women, not more lenient? Why do we allow medieval rabbis who believed in demons and thought a niddah shouldn't even enter a synagogue make halacha for us today? Why are men so squeamish about menstruation anyway? If the majority of people violate one law regularly with no consequences, won't they come to disrespect other laws?

To Hannah's disappointment, when she asked him over breakfast, Nathan had no good answers for her. It was some consolation that he had the same questions, but she put away her qualms when he cleared the dishes and laid the Talmud volume on the table.

"We're going to look at something odd in the third Mishnah in Tractate Kiddushin." Since they were sharing one book and Hannah was still niddah, Nathan was careful not to touch her as he pointed to where she should read. He tried to be just as careful that it wasn't obvious he was doing this.

"When a man says to his friend: 'If your wife gives birth to a female, behold the girl is betrothed to me,' she does not become betrothed." Hannah waited to see if Nathan wanted her to continue to the next sentence, which had an unusual set of parentheses around it.

Instead, he explained the first sentence. "Kiddushin is not valid if the man tries to betroth someone in the future whom he could not currently betroth," he said. "For example, he cannot betroth a woman if she is not Jewish and has not yet converted, or if she is a slave and not yet freed. Here the man couldn't betroth the friend's daughter now because she doesn't exist yet. So the Mishnah rules his Kiddushin invalid."

Intrigued, Hannah continued reading. "But when the woman is obviously pregnant, such a betrothal is valid. And if a girl is born she is betrothed to that man." She looked at Nathan in confusion. "I don't see a problem, except that the text is in parentheses, so there must be something strange about it."

"The problem is that the last sentence contradicts the beginning of the Mishnah by giving us a case where a betrothal that could not occur at that time is still contracted." He smiled as if about to impart a secret. "Don't read the commentary about the parenthetical clause yet. Just keep in mind that it's there when we go to the Gemara."

Fascinated, Hannah found the discussion in the text about the man who tries to betroth an unborn child. "I see a difficulty. The Mishnah that the Rabbis quote in the Gemara is different," she exclaimed. "It has only the first clause, where the man wants to betroth his friend's unborn child. Then it ends with 'He has said nothing.' It doesn't have the part about the wife being pregnant."

"Exactly. That last sentence was added later, replacing 'He has said nothing.'" His expression was triumphant. "Now look at that commentary on the Mishnah."

"Maharsha declares that the final clause does not belong in the Mishnah, that its inclusion is a mistake." Her voice rose with enthusiasm. "So the correct version of the Mishnah is the one quoted within the Gemara, not the one that begins the chapter."

"Indeed. We have old Mishnaic manuscripts, including one from fifteenth-century Cambridge, that omit the extra clause and also conclude with 'he has said nothing.'" Nathan was proud of this part of his new curriculum. "Most modern editions of the Mishnah note the discrepancy."

"Where do you think the error came from?" *This is incredible.*

"In the Gemara, right after the Mishnah quote, Rav Chanina says it applies only in the case where the friend's wife is not pregnant." He pointed at the text. "See, he continues that if the wife is pregnant, the betrother's words stand."

"That is a direct challenge to the Mishnah, which concludes that he has said nothing." She suddenly recognized what he was getting at. "You think someone added Rav Chanina's words to the Mishnah later."

He beamed at how she'd arrived at the correct deduction. "So you had no trouble understanding what I wanted to demonstrate?"

"I understood it, but then I've been studying with you for over a year and know how you teach," Hannah replied. "It was hard to restrain myself from reading Maharsha's comment."

"I'm not sure I can stop my students; they'd read it automatically."

"Maybe you could start with the Gemara," she suggested.

They spent the rest of the morning discussing how Nathan could best present this lesson to his students without giving away Maharsha's conclusion too soon. They were still working on it when Naomi came over and announced that lunch was ready.

Then, after a pleasant meal with the entire Eisin clan, Hannah found a moment to take Naomi aside and happily explain that she didn't need her friend's help. Nathan would make sure she didn't drown.

The next afternoon at sunset, they carried a picnic basket, blanket, and two towels to the water's edge. Nathan spread out the blanket, and they ate dinner as the sky darkened. The half-moon wouldn't rise for hours, so it was soon completely dark except for Coney Island's lights in the distance.

To mask her nervousness, Hannah tried to be lighthearted. "I'm not sure we should do this." She giggled as the waves wet their feet. "My mother always said to wait thirty minutes after eating before going swimming."

"So it's a good thing we're not going swimming," he said.

Soon they were up to their waists, and Hannah slowly went in deeper until her breasts were submerged. Just watching her slip the straps of her bathing suit off her shoulders was sufficient to arouse Nathan. Still, he was conscientious to observe that she fully immersed three times before she put her suit back on. Then it was his turn to go underwater, which he did as quickly as possible.

As soon as Nathan had his suit on again, Hannah pulled him into an embrace. But it took only a few kisses before he reached for her hand and hurried them toward the cottage.

Lying spent between the soft cotton sheets, Nathan resisted the pull of sleep. He wanted to luxuriate in this delicious moment. With Annie's head on his chest, he was overwhelmed with gratitude for the gift this amazing woman had bestowed on him, pleasure and passion beyond his wildest imaginings. He'd stayed inside her as long as he could, until a final contraction forced him out. Now he kept her close, savoring the feel of her smooth skin against his. Waves of tenderness washed over him as he smelled the sea on her hair, felt her chest rise and fall as she breathed. He could hear love songs playing on a distant radio, but none could describe the intensity of his feelings. He suddenly thought of the Torah, specifically Genesis 2:24. "Hence a man leaves his father and mother and clings to his wife, so they become one flesh." Soon he would fall asleep and his hold on Annie would loosen, but until then he wanted to cling to her like ivy on a wall, never to be separated. And when they woke in the morning, they would become one flesh again.

Hannah lay still, not quite asleep, the sounds of waves breaking on the beach in her ears. She was utterly satiated by the climaxes he had given her. Rapture that was indescribable, unimaginable before. Cradled in his arms, she snuggled closer, listening to his strong and steady heartbeat. Something seemed to expand inside her chest, filling her with an emotion so powerful she couldn't describe it. You loved a song, a movie, a book, a particular food, or your family. But that affection paled compared to this ardor that warmed and heated her. No wonder poets described "kindling the flame of love." She let out a long sigh. Just contemplating the feeling gave her immense joy. Snippets of love songs ran through her head; she always found them insipid, made up by lazy lyricists who copied each other. "Love is a many-splendored thing"—what on earth did that mean, she'd asked herself last year when the movie came out. Now she understood how the dictionary defined "splendored": full of marvels, magnificence. It was what she felt.

Thinking Nathan had dozed off, she softly whispered the quote from Song of Songs, "*Dodi li va'ani lo.*" (My beloved is mine and I am his.)

But he must have heard because he leaned down and gently kissed her forehead.

A few days later Joey Goren arrived to spend the week with them. As Hannah expected, he spent much of his time with Rae. The four of them went dancing every night, and then Joey tactfully slept on the porch so Hannah and Nathan had the cottage to themselves. Sharon and Judy came up to visit, but Benny stayed back to tend to his patients. Sharon confided that he didn't like the beach—or rather, he didn't like being confronted with all those unclothed bodies.

Hannah was disappointed when she became niddah again in early August. But when Deborah walked over in the morning with a telegram that Aunt Elizabeth was declining rapidly, Hannah had only one thing on her mind—getting herself and her mother to Boston as soon as possible.

They had been gone two days when Rae came over as Nathan and Joey were having breakfast. "Nathan, there's a call for you."

Only the Eisins' cottage had a telephone, so Hannah phoned him there daily. But those calls came at night.

Nathan's heart immediately started to pound. "Is it Annie?"

"No, it's Benny Stockser."

Only slightly relieved, he raced over to find Benny still on the line. "Sorry to bother you so early, but since Annie is away, could Sharon and Judy stay with you and Joey awhile?" When Nathan stopped to think, Benny continued, his voice rising with anxiety. "Sharon is doing poorly with the heat, and it would be a mitzvah to bring her some relief."

"Is she ill?"

Benny hesitated. "Her impairment is only temporary, and I am sure she will be better when the weather cools."

There was something cagey in Benny's tone, so Nathan pressed him. "What's the matter with her? Has she seen a doctor?"

"She does not need to see a doctor, but since you are so nosy, I can say we likely will not be going anywhere next Pesach."

Nathan didn't need college mathematics to realize that Sharon had gotten pregnant soon after the wedding. He couldn't resist teasing Benny. "Apparently dressing you up and teaching you to dance made you irresistible."

"Sharon was pretty irresistible in her fancy gown too."

"I'm glad you had such a satisfactory outcome," Nathan said. "Of course Sharon and Judy are welcome." He couldn't wait to tell Annie the good news.

"They will be there in a few hours, then. And while I have you on the line, how are things in Boston?"

"Annie's aunt wants to spend her last days at home, so Annie and Deborah are up there with her. It won't be long now."

Hannah had to hide her shock at the change in Aunt Elizabeth and her apartment. The cabinets and bookcases that held her treasured mementos were empty, a sign that part of her was already gone. Elizabeth had always been a lanky woman, but now she was just skin and bones. She reclined in a rented hospital bed, too weak to get up or even speak more than a few sentences.

The day Hannah and Deborah arrived, the pastor at Elizabeth's church came by to meet them and give Hannah a sealed envelope. He praised Elizabeth's good works and called her one of the most pious and generous women he'd ever met. Hannah and Deborah agreed with him completely.

After her mother went to bed, Hannah sat across from Elizabeth and opened the envelope. There were business cards from the pastor, doctor, mortician, banker, movers, attorneys, plus a dress shop and a literary agent, along with a lengthy letter.

My dearest Annie, it read. *Hopefully I will still be alive when you get this, because I need you to take my power of attorney, which is in the top right drawer of my secretary desk, to the bank and empty my safe-deposit box. In it you should find ten $1,000 bonds. Clip the coupons for July and buy a black dress and hat for my funeral, which is already arranged. To accommodate your Jewish customs, I ask to be buried quickly.*

As the heir to all my movable property, you are entitled to anything you want from my apartment. My attorneys will arrange for the other items to be donated. I would especially like you to take my secretary desk, as it gives me pleasure to imagine you using it for your writing. On the subject of writing, you will find my journals in its bottom drawers. I urge you to use their contents to write my life story.

Ah, Hannah thought, that explains the movers and the literary agent.

Very few women, or men, for that matter, have seen as much war and suffering as I have and still managed to die in bed. So I think readers would find my biography interesting.

Hannah had no doubt they would.

Here Aunt Elizabeth shed her New England reserve. *When I chose to become a missionary nurse, I accepted that I must forgo husband and children. Then, after Michael's death, I became attached to you. The summers we've spent together have brought me unexpected joy. It has been a blessing to watch you grow to become the lovely and talented young woman you are, and I am thankful that the Lord has allowed me to live long enough to see you married to such a fine young man.*

It was signed, *Your loving aunt, Elizabeth.*

For several minutes, Hannah held the letter to her chest as tears streamed down her cheeks. Then she remembered her aunt's journals. There were at least a dozen of them, each labeled with opening and closing dates. What a bittersweet legacy she'd been entrusted with.

TWENTY-FOUR

HANNAH'S FIRST WEEK in Boston brought many visitors: Covey Foundation employees, nurses Aunt Elizabeth worked with, and women from her church. The doctor arrived early each morning before hospital rounds, and the pastor came every other afternoon. Thus Hannah and her mother had some respite during the day. The next week, however, Elizabeth constantly needed someone familiar nearby. Though she slept a great deal, she could open her eyes at any moment and panic if Hannah or Deborah wasn't there. So they divided their time into two shifts.

By nature a late riser, Hannah took the nighttime. In those wee hours, she pored through Elizabeth's journals. She wasn't afraid of being alone with someone so close to death; during her summers in Israel, especially the first one, she'd seen so many dying people, it no longer unnerved her.

Thankfully, Aunt Elizabeth did not appear to be in pain.

The unsettling thing now was Elizabeth speaking to people who were dead. The first time it happened, Hannah thought her aunt was talking to her. But when she heard her addressing someone named Michael, she listened carefully and realized Elizabeth was conversing with her brother, Hannah's father. When this happened, which was more often as days passed, Hannah became an unobtrusive eavesdropper. Elizabeth sometimes spoke to her mother and her older brother, but mostly she talked to Michael. The family was apparently eager to see her, because she would say how she was looking forward to seeing them again too. Hannah found these strange monologues both fascinating and disturbing.

One conversation in particular made Hannah weep. Elizabeth was talking to Michael when, to Hannah's astonishment, Elizabeth mentioned her name. She went on to congratulate Michael on what a fine daughter he'd produced, then teased him about the irony that despite his great antipathy toward religion, Annie had become an observant Jew.

That was Elizabeth's last communication with the other side. Saturday she refused to eat or drink, clenching her teeth tight against even a spoonful of her favorites. That night her breathing was especially noisy, and when Hannah took her hand to calm her, she was startled by how cool and dry Elizabeth's skin felt, like a fragile piece of old parchment.

Eventually Hannah dozed off, only to wake when the room lightened at dawn. Aunt Elizabeth's hand, which Hannah had been holding earlier, had slipped off the bed and was now dark purple. When Hannah lifted it back onto Elizabeth's belly, she felt no pulse. There was no breathing either. Her eyes filled with tears as she sighed with resignation, but also with relief.

"*Baruch Dayan haEmet*," Hannah whispered and went to wake her mother. The doctor would be there soon, and he would set everything in motion. Until then Hannah and Deborah would guard the body together.

Sunday was Hannah's eighth clean day. The mortician came midmorning and, confirming Elizabeth's wishes, scheduled the burial for Monday afternoon. Once he'd removed her aunt's body and the clothes she'd be buried in, Hannah took a few hours to visit the very nice mikveh the receptionist at the local shul had recommended. Though the Rabbis taught that no immersion could remove the impurity of death, she came out of the water feeling spiritually and emotionally cleansed.

Hannah was thankful that the hospital bed had been removed by the time she returned. Having skimmed through Elizabeth's journals, she knew that her aunt would always be alive for her in their myriad pages. She wanted to remember her that way, not like in her final days.

Nathan and Samuel arrived in the late afternoon, and she was even more grateful when her mother and her dad checked into a hotel after dinner. While Nathan would have preferred a hotel room as well, his job was to console his mourning wife, and if she wanted to remain in the Covey apartment, then so would he. *And try not to think about the fact that someone died here less than twenty-four hours earlier.* Hannah had given him a hug when he arrived, so he assumed she wasn't niddah. He'd learned his lesson not to ask about her mikveh attendance.

Yet when she led him to the double bed in what was clearly the main bedroom, he had to ask, "This isn't where your aunt, uh, slept?"

Hannah understood what bothered him. "No. We brought in a hospital bed for her. Mama and I slept in this one . . ." She trailed off as she choked up.

"I'm so sorry." He took her in his arms so she could cry on his shoulder.

But despite her heavy heart, the sobs she needed to let loose didn't come. "As deaths go, it was a good one." She proceeded to tell him about Elizabeth communicating with the dead.

His eyes widened with awe. "I've heard stories of things like that, but never firsthand."

"I missed you so much," she whispered.

"I missed you too."

She gazed at him lovingly, and he began kissing her wet cheeks. Instead of stopping him, she lifted her head to kiss his lips. He was nuzzling her neck when she pulled back.

"Are we permitted to do this?" she asked. Not that she wanted to stop. "Don't worry. I went to a kosher mikveh this morning. But aren't mourners not supposed to use the bed?"

Nathan was prepared for this question. "There is no Jewish Law that mandates mourning for an aunt, never mind whether she's Jewish or not," he replied. "Still, I expect you'd want to observe at least some bereavement practice."

"So what should I do?" Hannah spoke slowly, but she kept her arms around him. She wanted to honor her aunt's memory and mourn her in a respectful way, but she yearned for his comforting touch.

"The one thing you shouldn't do is refrain from prayers and mitzvos," he said. "Since mourning is not mandatory for you, it doesn't override other halachic obligations."

"Like the mitzvah to be fruitful and multiply?" She let him hear the hope in her voice.

When he smiled and nodded, she kissed him again, more passionately than before, and he responded in kind. Without saying a word, she pulled him onto the bed.

When they snuggled together afterward, Nathan thought of another thing he should say. "Benny told me it's not uncommon for couples to make love after a funeral. Something about a psychological need to affirm life."

Deborah and Samuel attended the private burial on Monday and drove back to Sea Gate after the memorial service at Elizabeth's church the next day. As principal mourner, Hannah remained in Boston until she'd greeted everyone who wanted to pay their respects. Even so, she and Nathan were back in their seaside cottage for Labor Day.

Judy was napping when they returned, and Sharon hurried to embrace Hannah. "I'm sorry for your loss," she whispered. Then she turned to

Nathan, a smile on her face. "Benny and I found the perfect apartment. We start moving in this weekend."

"I'm glad things are going well for you." Hannah gave Sharon a quick wink.

It was a superstitious Jewish custom, based on fear of the evil eye, not to mention a pregnancy until it was physically obvious. Some said nothing until the child was safely born, leaving the family rushing around like crazy buying baby things and setting up the nursery.

Sharon sat down and began describing the new place. "It's a great location in Bed-Stuy, the entire third floor above a corner drugstore. The building's owners are an older Jewish couple whose children have moved away, but they refuse to leave their second-floor apartment."

"So you'll each have one floor?" Nathan asked.

"Even better," she replied. "They're letting Benny use two rooms near the second-floor entrance for his office." She sighed with pleasure. "A six-room apartment, within walking distance of both our parents. With windows on three sides. My mom and Aunt Leah have been packing our things all week, and the movers are coming on Sunday."

"But next Wednesday is Erev Rosh Hashana," Hannah interjected. "Can you get settled in time?"

"We vacate this place next Monday, so you can count on us for Tuesday," Nathan offered. "And Wednesday morning if need be."

That Tuesday, Hannah and Nathan drove to Benny and Sharon's new address, a brick building that had clearly seen better days. First Benny showed off his two-room suite consisting of a waiting room, bare except for two wooden chairs, and an office with a desk set, two bookcases crammed with psychology texts, and an overstuffed club chair.

"What? No couch?" Nathan teased him.

Benny smiled wanly. "Maybe after next month's paycheck."

They climbed the second flight of stairs, a few steps creaking under their tread, and entered a whirlwind of activity. Empty boxes were piled in one corner of the living room and unopened ones, labeled with the room they belonged in, took up an entire wall. Books waiting to be shelved sat next to partly empty bookcases.

Hannah, seeing more "kitchen" boxes than anything else, took one and headed for where she could hear women's voices. She passed through the dining room, where an ornate chandelier dwarfed the dinette set below, and noted that it needed cleaning. A swinging door led to the kitchen, where Sharon, Leah, and Sarah were putting things away. The kitchen brought back memories of similar rooms in Hannah's childhood apartments. The cupboard that used to be an icebox, the white porcelain stove on legs and the freestanding cabinets all looked original. Only the refrigerator, awkwardly squeezed in next to the door, was of postwar vintage. She felt self-conscious that her and Nathan's brownstone was so much nicer. She didn't want Sharon to envy them but couldn't think of anything to prevent it.

"This kitchen is huge compared to our old one," Sharon said. "Look, there's room for our Pesach dishes on the top shelf."

"You'll have more room when you get a china cabinet for the dining room," Leah Goren said. "It looks naked without one."

"If you have any dust rags," Hannah said. "I'd like to tackle that chandelier."

Soon she was stepping from one dining chair to another to wipe away the schmutz. She could see Benny and Nathan in the living room, companionably sorting through books and putting them away. Everyone seemed determined to complete all the unpacking that day, so she worked as late into the night as the others.

At bedtime, Nathan gazed fondly at Hannah as she picked up her hairbrush. One of his small marital pleasures was watching her nightly ritual of giving her blond tresses a hundred strokes. Seeing her in a negligee was an enjoyable bonus.

Hannah knew Nathan relished her grooming routine and waited to start until he was present. "It's strange, but Benny and Sharon's apartment brought back memories of all the seedy places Mama and I lived in before she married Dad."

He didn't want to complain about the Bed-Stuy apartment, but he had to agree. "I wasn't expecting it to be so dingy."

"I'm not surprised. Probably nobody's lived up there for years."

"I didn't realize Benny is so broke he can't afford a couch."

Hannah turned away from the mirror as an idea came to her. "I inherited everything in Aunt Elizabeth's apartment, but until now I was only planning to take her secretary desk."

His eyes lit with comprehension. "You're hiring movers anyway, so Benny and Sharon might want some of her furniture."

"Even better, I'll move all her things down here. They can take what they want and the rest can go to Brooklyn charities."

"That should save Benny and Sharon some money."

A sudden feeling of dread enveloped Hannah. "Nathan." Her voice lowered with anxiety. "This is Benny's sixth year as assistant professor. What if Columbia doesn't give him tenure?"

"Well." He stopped to think. "They would likely give him an additional year in his current position to look for another job. Unfortunately, though, people who don't get tenure usually have to move somewhere else."

They looked at each other in dismay. Hannah couldn't speak; the prospect was too awful to contemplate. She finished with her hair and went into the bathroom to brush her teeth.

"Of course someone as brilliant as Benny will get tenure," Nathan called to her, trying to sound confident. "He's a genius."

Over the next ten days, with texts spread out on their familiar dining table, now in their own home, Hannah and Nathan studied the section in Tractate Rosh Hashana about the importance of intent in fulfilling a mitzvah. The discussion was ostensibly about hearing the shofar, a topic some rabbinic authorities would say was irrelevant for women since they were exempt from that time-bound mitzvah. Moreover, it included a debate between Talmudic rabbis Rava and Abaye, whose complex legal disputes all authorities would forbid women to study.

As far as Nathan was concerned, any Talmud study that omitted the two preeminent sages was incomplete at best and bowdlerized at worst. But now that Annie was his wife, he could teach her whatever he wanted.

Hannah, too, was eager to resume their studies, especially since Rava and Abaye's dialectics were no longer off-limits. Now she would learn the same Gemara men did.

As usual, she started with the Mishnah. "If someone passed a synagogue and heard the shofar, if he directed his mind to it, he has fulfilled the mitzvah. If not, he has not fulfilled the mitzvah." She was slightly disappointed that the Gemara was so straightforward. "Abaye said this meant that the listener must have intent to hear the shofar blown on Rosh Hashana, but Rava said the Mishnah meant only that the listener realized he'd heard a shofar blast rather than thinking it was a donkey braying."

Hannah burst out laughing. "Their local shofar blower must have been terrible for anyone to mistake a donkey braying for his shofar blast." It was so good to study Talmud again, and now in their own home.

"I once heard a donkey braying at the zoo." Nathan chuckled. "And I know some guys whose shofars sound worse."

"But what about the man who hears a donkey on Rosh Hashana and thinks it's a shofar?" she asked.

"He hasn't fulfilled the mitzvah, but he believes he has."

The debate went on to consider the man who happened to read the words of the Shema at the time he was commanded to say the prayer, thus fulfilling a mitzvah without intent, and one who slept outside in a sukkah longer than the week the mitzvah required because it was cooler, thus violating, without intent, the prohibition against adding extra days to a festival.

Hannah had no trouble following the Gemara, but she had so much to add to the discussion that it took an entire week to get to Rava's conclusion that "Though transgressing a prohibition does require intent, fulfilling a mitzvah does not."

To Nathan's gratification, she quickly saw the advantage in following Rava's view, which made it easier to gain merit for fulfilling mitzvos since they could be done inadvertently.

"So according to Rava, only those who deliberately violate a prohibition have transgressed." She gave Nathan a sly look. "What about the women who think a Russian bath is a kosher mikveh and immerse in it? Or in their own bathtubs?"

"Rava would say such women haven't sinned," Nathan admitted. "But those using their own bathtubs haven't fulfilled the mitzvah either."

"Those booklets they hand out to newlyweds are merely lots of admonitions and no explanations," she challenged him.

"Which is why rabbis have a responsibility to follow halacha. So people will know what to do from their model." As soon as he said it, he realized that with a private ritual like mikveh, it was unlikely anyone would know where, when, or even if a rabbi's wife immersed.

"Speaking of the mikveh . . ." She took a deep breath. "It's only a few days until Yom Kippur, and I need to ask you to forgive me for using that hotel bathtub." After Mama married Dad, their children would ask each other for forgiveness during the High Holy Days, but mostly for juvenile transgressions like taking someone else's things or calling each other names. How she and Nathan performed the ritual now could prove crucial for their marriage.

Thankful that she'd raised the subject first so it wouldn't look like he was chastising her, he looked deeply into her eyes. "Not only do I forgive you, but I take complete responsibility for not inspecting that local mikveh first. It was putting a stumbling block before the blind." Then he added, "Can you forgive me?"

She let out a sigh of relief at his accepting some of the blame. "I forgive you, but even so, I should have told you about the problem instead of hiding it."

He looked at her plaintively. "I feel awful about how I looked at you with revulsion afterward, but I don't know how to atone for it because I don't understand why I behaved that way or how to ensure it won't happen again."

She was too hurt to make it easier for him. "You mean why abruptly, after we're married, I become loathsome when I have my period when it never bothered you before?"

"I never knew about it before, but that's not why." He struggled to find a good analogy. "Pigs are just as clean as cattle, probably more so, but it would upset me terribly to find out I'd eaten pork." When she rolled her eyes at this, he said, "I know; it doesn't make sense."

"Sounds like brainwashing."

"I need to think about that. But first I really need you to forgive me for frightening you in the bathroom at Sea Gate, especially after knowing your history. I promise I'll always knock first." He gave her a small smile. "And I'll try to control my temper."

"Of course I forgive you. I knew you had a temper after that weekend in Philadelphia, and I still married you." That was easy; now she had to ask him to do the hard forgiving. "I promised your mother's friend that I wouldn't tell anyone how she'd violated halacha to get pregnant with you, and then I not only broke that promise, but I told *you* about it . . . the person who'd be most hurt to hear it." She looked up at him and sighed. "You're not the only one with a temper."

He leaned over and put his arm around her. "I forgive you, and I'm grateful for everything I've learned about my mother, whether I like it or not."

It was the day before Kol Nidre, and Hannah was pacing with impatience until a truck horn blared outside. She showed the movers where to put Aunt Elizabeth's secretary and her boxes of Israeli souvenirs, then drove behind them to Benny and Sharon's. Reb Stockser had asked Benny to come talk to him today, and to Nathan's consternation, wanted Nathan to join them. But if Reb Stockser wanted to ask for forgiveness, they both had to go.

"Benny's not home yet," Sharon said when she saw Hannah. "I guess I'll have to figure out where everything goes without him."

It took some time for Sharon to decide which items she wanted and for the movers to unload them. Hannah was glad they'd brought all of her aunt's furniture, because Sharon kept additional things, like rugs and lamps, that Hannah hadn't considered.

"What an improvement." Hannah beamed. It wasn't just the new furnishings, although Sharon's meat dishes did look lovely in Aunt Elizabeth's china cabinet. New curtains hung at clean windows, and Sarah Goren's art adorned the walls.

"I can't thank you enough." Sharon embraced Hannah when the movers left. "Would you like some tea and honey cake while we wait for our husbands?"

They sat at the new dining table. "Speaking of honey cake, how did Rosh Hashana go?" Hannah asked, honey cake being traditional to invoke a sweet New Year.

"It was wonderful. We stayed at my parents' so I wouldn't have to walk so far to their shul, then had Shabbos dinner here to celebrate our first week in our new home."

Before Sharon could ask Hannah about her New Year, they heard heavy footsteps coming up the stairs. The door slammed open, and the two scowling male faces told Hannah that things had not gone well.

Sharon hurried to calm her husband. "Look how nice everything looks, Benny." Then she turned to Nathan. "We're just having some tea and honey cake; come join us."

Benny's visage softened as he gazed around the room. A moment later Judy raced down the hall and grabbed his hand. "Tateh, Tateh. Come see my new big-girl bed."

When he was out of sight, Nathan said, "It's been a long day, and I can see you've been working hard. Let's save the tea and cake for another time."

They drove home in silence, Hannah increasingly worried that something awful had happened. Her fears were confirmed when, as soon as Nathan closed the front door behind them, he sank onto the nearest chair and held his head in his hands.

"I thought the way Benny and Reb Stockser fought over Talmud was horrendous, but this was so bad I was afraid they'd come to blows." He shuddered at the memory. "Each thought the other should be the one seeking forgiveness, and when that became obvious, the battle escalated so painfully that I lost my temper and told Reb Stockser exactly what I thought of him."

"Oy. Gottenyu." Her voice was almost a moan.

"I've never been so ashamed in my life, especially since I just repented to you for my bad temper."

"Did you apologize?"

"I didn't have a chance. He screamed at both of us to get out and not come back." Nathan cringed at the memory. "At least on the walk back

Benny and I forgave each other—me for making things worse for him and him for getting me involved in the first place."

Nathan wouldn't say more and begged off to take a shower. Hannah remembered she still needed to put away Aunt Elizabeth's mementos. She hadn't wept at the burial or funeral service, but as she took out each item and recalled how, when, and where in Israel Aunt Elizabeth had received it, her tears began to fall. By the time the last box was empty, she was all cried out.

The phone rang insistently early the next morning. Half-asleep, Nathan stumbled down the stairs, but what he heard jolted him fully awake.

"Who was it?" Hannah mumbled. She sat up when she saw him getting dressed.

"That was Sharon. I have to meet Benny at the hospital." His face was pale, and he took a deep breath to calm himself. "Reb Stockser had a stroke, and it's my fault."

Hannah thought it was Reb Stockser's own fault for refusing to forgive Benny. Parents should take the initiative to forgive their children first, teaching by example. "Nathan, you had every right to vent your outrage at Reb Stockser. You were there when Zelig tried to cut his wrists. And it was Reb Stockser who set the molester's flight in motion."

Somehow they made it through Yom Kippur. The next night, Benny called Nathan to keep them informed. So Hannah learned that Reb Stockser's right side was paralyzed and it was impossible to understand anything he said, but he wasn't dying. Benny was thankful none of his congregants knew about the fight except Rivke and Hershel, who'd overheard it. Even so, for their sake and the sake of the community, Hershel had begged Benny to spend Yom Kippur with them, which Benny did, explaining to Nathan that he had much to atone for and needed to do it in his own shul, where he wouldn't be distracted by an unfamiliar *nusach*.

Benny also told Nathan that Hershel, to his astonishment, had asked them both for their forgiveness for not supporting them against his father in the matter of Rav Brenner. At first Hershel couldn't believe such an accusation about the rabbi, whose public life was exemplary in righteousness and *chesed*. And then, when forced to acknowledge the truth, he was ashamed he'd been too much of a coward, afraid of his father's wrath, to do so openly.

When Hannah asked about Sharon, they learned that she'd attended the morning service with Rivke and Zisse. Though the dark green outfit she'd worn to the aufruf was a tight fit, Sharon squeezed into it, thus announcing her pregnancy to any woman with discerning eyes.

When Hannah's period still hadn't started a week later, she told herself the delay was probably due to the extra stress. Yet her hope grew until Simchas Torah, when she broached the subject with Nathan over dinner. "In case you haven't noticed, it's been three weeks since I went to the mikveh in Boston."

He looked up from his plate with a startled expression. "I have noticed, Annie, but I didn't know how regular you were." His face reddened as he fumbled through the conversation. "I mean, it seemed long enough, and I hoped you might be, but I didn't want to say anything in case you weren't, and I figured you'd say something eventually . . ."

She chuckled at his discomfort. "I'm saying something now."

"So you think you are?" He didn't dare say the word itself. He'd been so worried about how to deal with her needing to use the mikveh again that he'd been afraid to hope the problem would be temporarily solved.

"I suspect I am. I hope I am."

"But you're not throwing up or anything."

She shrugged. "Not all women do."

"So when will you know for sure?"

Hannah was fairly sure already since she'd never been this late. "In about eight months," she joked. When he rolled his eyes, she laughed and continued. "I took a urine sample to Mama's doctor this morning. They have tests to confirm it."

Abba returned from Israel on the first day of the World Series, played again between the Dodgers and the Yankees. He was tanned and overflowing with energy. He couldn't stop talking about Israel: the land, the archaeology, the food, the amazing mix of Jews from all over the world.

"Nathan, you and Hannah should go next summer," he urged them again, having gotten no reply the first three times.

They exchanged smiles, and Hannah nodded at Nathan, who said, "Abba, we'd love to go to Israel, but next summer wouldn't be the best time."

"We'll be occupied here at home," Hannah replied, hoping he would understand their delicacy.

"What could possibly occupy you so much you can't take some time away from . . . ?" His eyes opened wide as he realized what they implied. "You mean?" He too couldn't say it aloud.

"Yes. They injected my urine into some frog, and it—I mean she— began to lay eggs," Hannah said with a grin.

Speechless, Abba gazed from one to the other until a smile lit his whole face. Nathan enfolded his father in an embrace and whispered, "Abba, we only just heard from the doctor's office, so please don't say anything yet. We weren't planning to tell the Eisins until after Hannah's first appointment."

But it became increasingly difficult for Hannah and Nathan to hide their happiness, so Hannah decided to atone for not telling Naomi about their romance by confiding her pregnancy. Then she took pity on her family, especially her dad and brother, after the Dodgers lost the World Series to rival Yankees in the seventh game by the humiliating score of nine to nothing.

Cocooned in their own little world, Hannah outlining how she'd write Aunt Elizabeth's memoir and Nathan collaborating with Louis on a new premarital counseling protocol, they had little contact with Benny and Sharon. They spent minutes staring at each other and smiling, and in their spare time, poring over Dr. Spock's *Common Sense Book of Baby and Child Care*. But they weren't so entranced that they neglected her responsibility for Aunt Elizabeth's estate. Referred by Samuel, Hannah switched to a New York law firm. Then she and Nathan spent several days in Boston showing the Covey Foundation's staff that the charity was in competent hands.

Hannah was fascinated by what was happening to her body; she hadn't realized she'd need new, larger bras sooner than new panties. Or that her breasts would become so tender she couldn't bear Nathan touching them. She smiled at how he, concerned that pregnancy could decrease her desire for lovemaking, had suggested a way for her to signal her interest.

Blushing and stumbling over his words, he eventually confessed how watching her remove her gloves used to excite him. "But now that we're married and in our own home . . ."

"I usually take them off when you're not around," she said, finishing his sentence.

"So . . . uh. I thought, uh . . ." He hesitated before quickly adding, "You could take off your gloves in front of me when you want us to use the bed that night."

As it turned out, watching his face as she slowly slipped off her gloves after their evening walk left her as eager as he was.

Their bubble burst at month's end when Hannah received a phone call from Moe Novick, urgently needing to see her. Over coffee that afternoon in her new home, she informed him that the Israel articles she'd already written would be her last. To her surprise, he wasn't at all upset. "You can't imagine how obsessed everyone has become with Israel," Moe began. "Publishers are desperate for books about the country."

Hannah nodded. "Now, while interest is high."

Back in early July, just home from their honeymoon and struggling with her refusal to use the Sea Gate mikveh, she and Nathan had been too distracted to care that Egypt had seized and nationalized the Suez Canal. But they couldn't ignore the latest news that Israel, Britain, and France had invaded the Canal Zone and attacked Egypt. With Israel at war again, they and the American Jewish community turned their collective attentions to the Middle East.

"Indeed. But books with plenty of human interest, not boring historical treatises." Moe put down his cup and looked her in the eye. "We've been printing your interviews for years, and they're very popular. And you have more we haven't published yet."

"But not enough for a book."

"Our publisher wants you to put your best interviews together in chronological order, and then we'll turn them into a book." His voice rose with enthusiasm. "It would be like a history, but told through individual stories. We'd include photographs too."

"But people have already read them."

"Annie, people don't remember what they read last week. They certainly won't remember what they read five years ago. And so what if some of them sound familiar?"

He had a point. Her excitement growing, Hannah knew it wouldn't take long to put such a book together; she could even use some of her new stories about Aunt Elizabeth. "How soon do you need it?"

Seeing he'd intrigued her, Moe sighed with relief. "They want the book out for Hanukah."

Hannah swallowed hard. There was no time to procrastinate. "I'll do it, but I won't be able to do anything else for the *Freiheit*."

He opened his briefcase and laid a large envelope on the table. "I've put together a preliminary version from what we have, but you can rearrange the stories however you like. You should also decide where to incorporate the new material."

She was astounded that they were giving her so much control. "I assume the publisher will be sending me a draft contract. I'd like to go over it with my dad."

"Good." He finished his coffee and stood up. "The publisher knows you're a woman—we had to use your legal name—but they are leaving it up to you what kind of author bio to include."

Hannah couldn't delay telling him the news any longer. "Moe, I won't be coming back to the *Freiheit* next year. We're expecting a baby in the spring." Plus, there would be the Covey Foundation to administer. Aunt Elizabeth may have had a hands-off management style, but she'd been doing it for decades. Hannah would need time to learn the ropes.

"Mazel tov. I figured a little Mandel would come along soon," he said. "We'll miss you."

"I hope we'll still see you at Pesach."

"You're sure I'll still be invited once I'm not your boss?"

She saw the twinkle in his eye. "Nathan's father wouldn't have it any other way. Who else can he argue Israeli politics with?"

Moe's expression sobered. "Keep this under your hat, but I'm planning to officially free the *Freiheit* from Communist Party control. I'll maintain the paper's commitment to the Jewish left, of course, but it will espouse an independent brand of democratic socialism."

Hannah was astonished. "I know my parents will be pleased, but why now?"

"With Khrushchev denouncing Stalin's crimes, countless new revelations are coming out." His voice hardened. "You know about the Doctors' Plot, of course, but I recently learned that at the same time Stalin was also executing a great many of the Soviet Union's leading Yiddish cultural figures. Some of whom were personal friends of mine."

Her first thought was what would you expect from the leader who signed a nonaggression pact with Hitler, but she prudently kept that to herself and, instead, just commiserated with him on the great loss to Yiddishkeit.

Two hours after Moe left, Hannah was still recovering from the shock of suddenly becoming a published author. She intended that credit would go to "H. M. Covey," but how she'd compose her bio could wait until she'd actually finished the book.

TWENTY-FIVE

WITH HANNAH ENGROSSED in her urgent new project, Nathan knew it was time to bite the bullet and reach out to Benny. Guilt over responsibility for Reb Stockser's stroke ate at him constantly, making it difficult to kvell over Hannah's pregnancy and book contract. He tried to reassure himself that in the past he and Benny had gone months without contact and that Benny would have called if anything important changed. But the longer he delayed, the guiltier he felt.

Yet something important had happened, because when Nathan ultimately did call, Benny wanted to walk and talk.

They met at Prospect Park on Sunday. Benny was there first and greeted Nathan with a hearty "Mazel tov. Sharon tells me Annie is feeling well."

"Yes, *keinehora*," Nathan replied. "How is your father?"

"He seems to have stabilized." Benny sighed. "He is still partly paralyzed, but they have him up in a chair, and at least Mama can usually figure out what he is saying."

"So what happens to your Hasidim now?"

"Honestly, I do not know. That is why I need to talk to you."

Nathan's stomach tightened. "I'm listening."

"First, though Yom Kippur is behind us this year, I need to ask your forgiveness for being such a terrible friend."

Nathan started to protest, but Benny waved away his objections. "You have been my best friend—my only friend—for almost a dozen years. You helped me through all kinds of tsuris and ordeals, but what have I done for you? Now I owe you so much for getting Sharon back together with me that I can never repay you. All I can do is confess my failings and try to appease you."

Before Nathan married, he would have agreed with Benny. "Don't sell your friendship short," he said. "If it weren't for your lessons, Heaven only knows how long it would have taken me to figure out how to satisfy Annie in bed. Thanks to your advice, our marriage got off to an excellent start." He thought for a moment before adding, "And if my friendship enables you to help more abused children, that's repayment enough."

"I am not so sure about that. My father is unlikely to recover, at least not sufficiently to resume his position as rebbe." Benny started walking faster. "Hershel is terrified to take over. He has no confidence that he can help people and thinks he does not know enough Talmud. He believes *Shamayim* arranged our argument before Yom Kippur to precipitate our father's stroke, so I would be forced to become rebbe."

"You're not forced to do that. Your father released you to be a psychologist."

Benny stopped but didn't meet Nathan's eye. "My guilt at causing his stroke is forcing me. But a good part of me shares Hershel's belief that it was *Shamayim*'s design."

Nathan was astonished, and relieved, that Benny also thought the argument caused Reb Stockser's stroke. He didn't think Heaven was involved, however. "I've been feeling guilty too, but all it's done is make me afraid of talking to you. Now I'm sorry I didn't talk to you sooner."

"Forgive me for not realizing that you would feel responsible too."

"I do. Now forgive me for losing my temper right before Yom Kippur, especially after I've been trying diligently to control it." Suddenly Nathan had an idea that he thought Benny should hear. "If Heaven had anything to do with your father's stroke, maybe it was punishment for his enabling that pedophile to get away."

To his surprise, Benny nodded slowly. "I have wondered that myself."

"So what are you going to do?"

Benny took a deep breath. "I do not know. Hershel wants me to come back."

Nathan's jaw dropped. "After all the effort you've made to become a psychologist, you're going to give it up?"

"That was my initial reaction too."

"What does Sharon think about this?"

"She is conflicted and wants to know what you think."

The fall foliage brought back memories of Sharon confiding her marital troubles to him last year without Benny's knowledge. But this time both of them wanted his advice. "You said your *initial* reaction, which implies you've reconsidered."

"I am not sure I have a future as a child psychologist. One of my funding sources wants me to study what is wrong with these children that they make up such accusations." Benny's pained expression gave way to resignation. "But if I were rebbe, I could fight the problem from the inside."

"You and Sharon would be profoundly unhappy," Nathan objected. "And what about all the children you're treating?"

"Sharon and I will be unhappy if we do not have enough money to live on either, but you are right. I cannot imagine abandoning my patients, and if I cannot do my research, how will anyone know what kind of therapy is useful?"

"Isn't there some way to help your brother? Until his confidence grows?"

"Even if there were, that does not get me tenure."

"I can't help you at Columbia, so tell me what's happening in the community while your father is incapacitated?"

"Nobody knows how badly he is doing. Mama talks to him, tells us what he wants, and Hershel does it while everyone prays for his recovery."

"Is that a problem?"

Benny's chin quivered. "Not while my father lives."

Nathan thought for a long time before giving up. "I wish I could help you, but I don't see any good options."

That night he told Hannah how sad and frustrated he felt after leaving Benny at the park. But sadly, she couldn't think of anything to help either.

Hannah's book, *Israel Stories*, came out in the middle of Hanukah and received several good reviews in the local papers. It contained a short author biography that read simply, "H. M. Covey, a native of New York City and journalist for the *Freiheit*, received an MA in journalism from Columbia University before spending 1950–1953 in Israel volunteering with refugee groups."

Hannah no longer tried to hide her author alias from people she knew, but Nathan was more circumspect at Spektor. He didn't openly brag about his wife's dual identity, but if *Israel Stories* came up in conversation, he wasn't shy about revealing that his wife had written it. Samuel and Deborah, however, couldn't resist telling friends and colleagues about their talented daughter. And with Naomi given free rein to her love of spreading good news, Hannah's pseudonym was no longer much of a secret in Brooklyn.

Hannah didn't mind. Her new book was doing well enough that the publishers asked if she had anything else for them. When she described Aunt Elizabeth's life story, they lost no time in offering her a contract for it, which she accepted gladly. And later, there were all those boxes of her special writings.

Giving in to exhaustion, she slept late, took naps, and went to bed by nine o'clock. Her pregnancy was obvious; she was almost as big as Sharon.

Naomi was happy to pass on her maternity clothes, whispering to Hannah that three children were all they could afford on Dovid's yeshiva teacher salary. When Naomi admitted that she didn't know how they'd manage if not for the free rent, Hannah was glad that only she, Nathan, and Dad knew that the brownstone duplex had been included in her share of Aunt Elizabeth's estate.

Reb Stockser's condition remained unchanged. Benny helped Hershel behind the scenes but confided to Nathan that their mother was really in charge. And doing an excellent job of it.

The last night of Hanukah, Hannah couldn't get back to sleep after she got up to urinate, she was so worried about all the molested patients Benny wouldn't be able to help and all the research he wouldn't be able to do. Oddly, her thoughts turned to Leon Shertov, the KGB officer who defected to the United States and whom she'd shepherded around Columbia the day he lectured to the Russian department.

During their hours together, they shared details of their early lives, the kind of confidences only complete strangers who will never see each other again reveal. He had a fascinating history, and she encouraged him to write about it. Months later, he sent her four stories. She'd put them away, determined to edit them and get them published.

But once she began studying Talmud with Nathan, Shertov's stories lost their urgency. Indeed, until that moment, she hadn't given them any thought. Yet she clearly recalled looking for the chairman of Columbia's Russian department and passing an office door labeled with a name, followed by his designation as the Bakhmeteff Professor of Russian studies.

That was the solution to Benny's problem!

The Covey Foundation would establish an endowed chair in child psychology at Columbia University for him.

That morning she got up before Nathan or his father and made the coffee. They were surprised, and Nathan relieved, to find her in the kitchen so early. They were even more surprised when she shared her plan.

"You know about these things, Abba," she said. "How do I make it happen this year?"

"One thing I can tell you is that your lawyer should make the initial inquiries."

"But Benny is researching child sexual abuse," Nathan reminded them. "What if Columbia turns her down?"

Abba shook his head and chuckled. "No university turns down that kind of money, even to study a subject so disturbing and offensive that few will name it. Besides, Columbia has already sullied itself by accepting funds from the Communists to establish that chair in Russian studies."

"I'd like to call it the Elizabeth Covey Memorial Chair," Hannah declared. "And leave my name—our names—out of it.

"Even though it sounds like a sure thing, I don't think we should tell Benny or Sharon," Nathan cautioned. "Let him learn about it through official channels."

"Unless you want everyone to know you control a good deal of wealth, I think we shouldn't mention it to anyone." Abba took his coffee and went back downstairs.

When he was gone, Hannah turned to Nathan. "I'd also like for the Covey Foundation to fund something to memorialize my father and your mother. I'm considering scholarships for children whose parents were working people as a tribute to Papa. What do you think would honor Minnie? College scholarships for women?"

"That's very thoughtful of you, Annie." He took her hand and squeezed it gently. "Every day you make me more thankful I married you."

She yawned and then leaned over to kiss him. "I'm very thankful I married you too, but I didn't sleep well worrying about Benny, and now I can't keep my eyes open."

He helped her stand up. "Let's get you back upstairs then."

When Nathan arrived at Spektor the next day, he was alarmed to find Rav Klein pacing the hall outside his office, ubiquitous cigarette in hand. "Mandel, I need your help."

Nathan put down his briefcase, hung up his coat, and followed Klein downstairs. Once in his office, Rav Klein handed Nathan an aerogram from Israel, written in Yiddish.

"What should I do about this?"

When Nathan was a student, his Talmud professor had regularly asked him to explain articles in the secular newspapers. America, with its free press and relative lack of anti-Semitism, was nothing like Jewish life in Eastern Europe. After he and Annie became engaged, Nathan acknowledged that he owed Rav Klein more than gratitude. So he continued to answer his old teacher's questions.

Nathan scanned the missive and then reread it. "This rabbi in Israel isn't happy about Spektor establishing a women's college. He asks how you can permit such a travesty."

When Samuel announced that the women's school's first classes would start the following fall and that he would be one of its trustees, Nathan had wondered the same thing. After all, Rav Klein was the one who canceled Spektor's annual senior show because women attended it.

Klein took a drag on his cigarette and scowled. "America is not Lithuania; New York City is not Vilna." He began what Nathan anticipated would be a lengthy tirade. "Here there are female doctors, lawyers, and professors. Here young women from prominent Jewish families are expected to attend college, and if possible, one of the prestigious goyish women's universities."

"That's true." Nathan marveled that Klein knew so much about what went on in American Orthodox homes.

"You're surprised I don't fight it." It was part statement, part question. "Then what should an educated God-fearing Jewish father do? Chas v'chalila he should send his daughter to a secular or goyish college, especially one where men and women sit together in class. Yet it is unthinkable her education should end with high school."

"So you approve of Spektor's college for women?" Nathan asked in amazement.

"They didn't need my approval, only that I don't object. Demand was there, money was there, so fighting *vet helfn vi a toytn bankes*." (Would help as much as cupping a corpse.) He lit a new cigarette. "But the Israel rabbonim don't understand that."

"Universities in Israel admit women and the rabbonim don't prevent it," Nathan said.

"The rabbonim have no control over Israeli colleges. Here I will have some influence on the curriculum."

Suddenly realizing that he wouldn't have to deal with Klein's interference if he taught at the Seminary, it took a few "ahems" before Nathan noticed Klein clearing his throat.

"Mandel, I've heard that Reb Stockser is unlikely to continue as Vinitzer rebbe."

"What about it?" Although it no longer surprised Nathan, it never ceased to amaze him how quickly Klein obtained all sorts of confidential information.

"Tell your friend Rav Stockser that he has my backing against any potential usurpers. There is no question that, despite his youth, he is the most learned talmid chacham among the Hasidim."

"Thank you. I'm sure he'll appreciate it."

Nathan was halfway back to his own office when he realized that the business about the women's college had been an excuse for Klein to send a confidential message of support to Benny.

At the same time, Hannah was on the phone with her new lawyers, who insisted she leave everything to them. They'd let her know when it was time to sign the checks. Thus reassured, she went back to bed and didn't get up until noon. She took a leisurely walk, then polished the menorah and put it away with their other ritual objects.

By the middle of January, Hannah understood why the second trimester of pregnancy was called the honeymoon period. The continuous afternoon nausea that never got bad enough to make her vomit was gone, she had plenty of energy to devote to Aunt Elizabeth's memoirs, and her sex drive . . . well, every day she did what she privately called her glove striptease. She and Nathan spent a wonderful week in Boston during winter break learning firsthand about the Covey Foundation. Sometimes she thought she'd felt the baby move, but she wasn't sure. Both Naomi and Sharon said they felt life later in their first pregnancies than in subsequent ones.

Bundled in her warmest coat, a new one now that her regular clothes didn't fit anymore, Hannah waved for the taxi that would take her to this month's prenatal appointment. The weather had been below freezing for several days, but at least it wasn't snowing. Dr. Isaacson had promised she'd get to hear the baby's heartbeat this time; otherwise, she'd be tempted to put off this visit until the following week. Judging by the empty waiting room when she arrived, Hannah saw that other expectant mothers had done just that.

Once on the exam table, she waited impatiently for the doctor to place his stethoscope on her belly. But instead of giving her the ear tips, he continued to slide the diaphragm back and forth. Then he stopped and asked the nurse to listen.

My God, he can't find the heartbeat. But everything's fine; it has to be. Sometimes it takes a while to find the right spot. Why is it taking him so long? Please, God, don't let anything be wrong. Please let my baby be all right.

Hannah's dread heightened when he told the nurse to get Dr. Rubinstein. The next few terrifying minutes seemed like hours until a balding man in a white coat with a stethoscope around his neck entered after a cursory knock. He introduced himself and, without ado, leaned over to listen to her belly.

He stood up almost immediately, a satisfied expression on his face. "Mazel tov, Mrs. Mandel. You're having twins."

Hannah gulped. "You mean there are two of them in there?" No wonder she was as big as Sharon.

Dr. Isaacson chuckled. "That is what having twins means." Then he grew serious. "I'm sorry if the delay alarmed you, but when I heard two heartbeats, I wanted to be certain there were only two babies. Dr. Rubinstein specializes in high-risk pregnancies, and he will be seeing you from now on."

Hannah's anxiety heightened. "High-risk?"

Dr. Rubinstein explained. "All multiple births are considered high-risk." He turned to look at her chart. "And since you are pregnant for the first time at age twenty-six, you are considered an elderly primipara, which puts you at higher risk than an eighteen-year-old."

Hannah grinned as a mask to hide her apprehension. "I didn't expect to be called elderly for several more decades."

The doctor didn't crack a smile. "I want to see you every two or three weeks instead of monthly, and that will increase to weekly as you get closer to term." He perused her chart and nodded. "There is no protein in your urine, and your blood pressure hasn't started rising. Have your husband come to your next appointment, and the nurse will show him how to monitor it."

With that, he instructed Hannah to see the receptionist to arrange her follow-up visit and to be sure to pick up the booklet on having twins.

Sitting in the taxi's back seat, Hannah gazed at her expansive waistline with a mix of excitement and trepidation. *Two babies. Dear God, I'm going to have two babies.* Only one thing was certain—if one of them was male, his name was going to be Michael.

Her family's reaction to the news ranged from Naomi's ecstatic delight to her parents' eager excitement to Nathan's openmouthed shock to Abba's abject fright. Hannah's feelings fluctuated depending on her companion. With Naomi, her enthusiasm was tempered by thoughts of all the extra work twins would entail. With her parents, she kvelled at Mama's pride at finally becoming a bubbe. With Abba, while she understood the source of his fear, she conveyed confidence in modern medicine and her doctor's expertise.

With Nathan, however, she was honest about her ever-changing emotions. Once he got over the surprise, however, he was determined to focus on practical matters and relieve her of as much anxiety as possible. Despite their pledge not to keep secrets, his fears would stay hidden.

"Whether we use my income or your inheritance," he said, "I want to hire all the nurses, housekeepers, nannies, or other help we need to care for our babies. This is no time for economy."

She smiled up at him. "Don't forget a diaper service." She loved how he called them "our" babies, not "the" babies like everyone else. "I doubt I'll actually need a nurse before the birth, but I think Abba wouldn't agonize so much if we had one."

"I agree," Nathan replied. *I won't agonize so much either.*

The following Shabbos, Louis Katz sat down next to Nathan at the Kiddush lunch. "Mazel tov! My wife heard that you and Annie are expecting twins."

Nathan tried to hide his surprise at how quickly the news had gotten out. "Yes, the doctor confirmed it on Monday."

Louis lowered his voice. "So immersing in the ocean worked out well for you?"

"Obviously. But it will be too cold, and inconvenient, to immerse there again after the birth."

"I have another possibility if you're interested, one available all year."

"I'm interested," Nathan replied.

"Good. Can you meet me at the Turkish baths on Fulton later this week?"

They agreed on Tuesday morning, and at ten thirty Nathan stepped out of a taxi in front of Yusuf's Turkish Baths. Signs announced that men's hours were morning and late afternoon until sunset. Women's hours were midafternoon and evenings until closing.

After paying the entrance fee, which included the use of a locker and a towel, Nathan followed Louis into the changing room, where signs warned that all patrons must shower thoroughly before entering the baths. Thankfully, the damp air smelled more herbal than rank. Then it was out of his clothes and, his lower body wrapped in the towel, through a swinging door into the bathhouse.

Here the air was more humid, and Nathan watched as steam rose from some of the pools. They entered a warm pool, and after becoming acclimated to that temperature, transferred to a hotter one. Louis stretched out until only his bald head was visible above the water.

"Ah." Louis closed his eyes and sighed. "This is the life."

"Definitely." Nathan had gone to the *schvitz* with Abba, but sitting in a steam room with a bunch of *alte kakers* smoking cigars was not his idea of tranquility. Relaxing in this large hot bath on a frigid winter day was more like it.

They soaked until Louis broke the silence. "My wife enjoys it so much she comes here even when it's not time to immerse."

Nathan recognized why Louis had brought him here. He gazed around the room, scrutinizing the pools. "I'm not sure about the hottest ones, but these others contain at least one hundred gallons of water."

"Plus, they're drained and disinfected regularly."

"They look kosher. Have you checked the plumbing?"

"The pipes are inside the walls." Louis locked eyes with Nathan and spoke slowly. "Even if I could, why would I want to?"

Nathan swallowed hard. The Sages, when they knew they couldn't change the people's behavior, advised that it was better for Jews to sin in ignorance than in defiance. He wondered if in a case where the plumbing was inaccessible, wouldn't it be better that women use the Turkish baths that possibly were kosher mikvehs rather than home bathtubs that undoubtedly were not?

"I understand why you wouldn't," he told Louis. "Another reason I'd have difficulty as a pulpit rabbi."

After they showered and got into their clothes, they took separate taxis—Nathan to Spektor and Louis back to the synagogue. Nathan was relieved to be alone in the cab; he had much to think about. Annie would need to immerse after their babies were born, perhaps as soon as eight days after if one of them was a boy. The doctor warned that multiples usually came before their due date, and thus theirs could be born as early as May. Even if the ocean were warm enough then, which was unlikely, eventually Annie's menses would return and she would need to immerse in the winter.

Should I be strict and insist she schlep into the city or be lenient and permit the Turkish bath? After all, the Sages declared that a judge should rule leniently in case of doubt. So maybe just let her know about the Turkish bath and accept her decision?

When Nathan and Hannah returned from her next doctor's appointment, they found a note from Abba to call Benny immediately. Hannah's first thought, not surprisingly, was that Sharon's baby was coming early, while Nathan, knowing Abba wouldn't have written "immediately" unless it was bad news, prepared himself for a major deterioration in Reb Stockser's condition.

Sharon answered the phone, and Nathan learned that he was right. Reb Stockser had suffered another stroke, more severe than the first, and Benny was at the hospital. They quickly settled on a plan of action. Hannah would drive to Sharon's to keep her company and sit with Judy if necessary. Nathan would call when he finished teaching, and they could decide what to do then.

Barely able to squeeze behind the roadster's steering wheel, Hannah drove to Bed-Stuy and was surprised to find a young Hasidic woman there with Sharon.

"Hannah, I'd like you to meet my sister-in-law, Zisse," Sharon said in Yiddish.

Hannah, recalling that Benny's brother, Hershel, had recently married, replied politely, also in Yiddish, "Pleased to meet you."

"Mama Rivke wanted to speak with her sons privately." Zisse looked around cautiously and whispered, "I'm expecting, too, and she thought I shouldn't be at the hospital around so many sick people."

Nobody felt like talking. Sharon got up to look out the window a few times, while Zisse sat smoothing the nonexistent wrinkles in her skirt. Hannah, waiting until Nathan called, resolved to be patient.

Zisse broke the awkward silence. "Sharon has been so kind to me since Reb Stockser's illness. Things like showing me how to go shopping or take the bus, but most important, teaching me how to be friendly but not too friendly, with the Vinitzer women. As their future *rebbetzin*, I can't have favorites."

"I could have used a mentor after I married Benny," Sharon concurred.

"Until Sharon took me under her wing," Zisse continued, "I was so afraid of inadvertently getting off to a bad start that I hardly spoke to anyone."

"Hannah is the H. M. Covey who writes all those articles in the *Freiheit*, and she has a new book out." Sharon handed Zisse a copy from the nearest bookshelf.

Zisse sighed and gave the book back. "I don't read English that well."

"My newspaper articles are in Yiddish," Hannah said. "I'll see that they send you a set of them. You could use them to help you learn English by translating the book."

Sharon returned the book to the bookcase and looked out the window. "Gottenyu. They're back. Benny, Hershel, and Rivke, heading for the stairs."

The trio soon came through the front door. Hershel's eyes were red-rimmed, but Rivke's and Benny's faces were like statues.

Benny stopped when he saw Hannah. "Tell Nathan my father passed away earlier this afternoon, and I would appreciate him attending the funeral with me tomorrow."

"*Baruch Dayan ha'Emet*" (Blessed is the True Judge), Hannah intoned.

Rivke took her arm. "Please also phone your editor and tell him to run Pinchas's obituary. Afterward, I'd like you to stay with us a little while."

"Of course." Hannah went to the kitchen to make the call, then waited a bit longer for Sharon and Zisse to receive the bad news.

Reb Stockser's death was more relief than sorrow for Hannah; everything she'd heard about the man had made her despise him. After what she considered a decent interval, she joined the family around the dining table. At first Hannah thought the seating, Hershel and Zisse on one side, Benny and Sharon opposite them, and Rivke at the head with Judy on her lap, was to keep each couple together. But it wasn't long after Hannah took the empty chair that she realized Rivke was now head of the family.

"I'm glad you're here, Hannah," Rivke began, speaking Yiddish. "There will be no shortage of rumors, claims, and allegations about the Vinitzer succession. I want you should report what we said and agreed here." Then she turned to Benny. "You have the best memory. I want you should recall for us what was decided at the hospital."

"When my father told his Hasidim that he had given me permission to study psychology, his transfer of the *tzaddikate* to Hershel was merely tacit," Benny explained. "True, he took Hershel under his wing and treated him as an heir, but he never put it in writing."

"There was no will?" Zisse's eyes were wide with astonishment.

Hershel shook his head. "After Tateh's first stroke, writing one became impossible."

"As I have told Mama and Hershel many times," Benny continued, "I have no interest in, desire to, or intention of becoming the Vinitzer rebbe. I have consented to function as their *av beis din* only because they pressed me, and because I am a greater talmid chacham than any challenger." He said this as a statement of fact, without a hint of pride.

"Benny's expertise will help his family avoid a disputed succession," Sharon said.

Hannah nodded. Obviously, Benny and Sharon had already agreed on his becoming chief rabbi for the Vinitzer courts, a position for which he was uniquely qualified. Rivke had surely been part of that decision too; her easy manner with Judy showed how relations between mother and daughter-in-law had warmed. Rav Klein had probably used his influence as well.

"The three of us agree that as Vinitzer rebbe, Hershel will receive the people's *kvittlach* and *pidyonous*" (petitions and donations), Benny continued. "He will meet with them privately to hear their appeals and offer the traditional blessings for *bonei, chayei* and *m'zonei*" (children, health and sustenance) "that only a tzaddik can personally bring down from Heaven."

"I expect Mama to do that for the women," Hershel said.

Hannah tried to be nonjudgmental, but she found it offensive that Hasidim had a practice of bringing monetary contributions to the rebbe along with requests for his assistance. It was bad enough they believed he had a unique connection to God.

Now Rivke took the reins. "We are in agreement over Hershel's and Benny's separate responsibilities and that while Hershel will deliver the majority of sermons, Benny may give some on occasion," she declared. "Rest assured that I will not allow any dispute over Pinchas's succession."

"I didn't know Hasidic kahals could have both a rebbe and a chief rabbi," Hannah said.

"Few rebbes are like Pinchas, both a tzaddik and a Talmudic scholar," Rivke explained. "Many kahals have their own rebbe, but legal disputes go before a beis din headed by a true talmid chacham."

Hannah would have liked to hear more, especially about how Rivke was going to prevent challenges to young Hershel becoming rebbe, but the phone rang. Sharon went to answer it and was back a minute later to tell Hannah that Nathan was on the line. He already knew about Reb Stockser's death and funeral; the *chevra kadisha* had spread the word at Spektor. She should wait for him at Benny's; he'd take a cab.

In less than fifteen minutes there was a knock on the door. Hannah was impressed he'd gotten there so fast, but it wasn't Nathan. It was a delegation of Hasidic women bringing what would be the first of eight days' worth of meals for the mourners. Without a word, they deposited the many dishes and covered plates in the kitchen. Then, as they were leaving, Rivke stood and, appearing to Hannah like a queen acknowledging her subjects, silently took each woman's hand and held it briefly.

On the ride home, Hannah told Nathan everything she heard that afternoon.

"I wouldn't put it past Reb Stockser to deliberately avoid writing a will in order to pressure Benny to become the rebbe after he passed away," he replied sourly.

Hannah had also considered that, but she didn't want to speak ill of the dead. "I hope appointing Benny as av beis din won't interfere with his professional duties," she said. "Especially since we're arranging that psychology chair for him."

TWENTY-SIX

THE NEXT MORNING a taxi picked up Nathan, then Benny, to deliver them to Reb Stockser's home prior to the funeral. The final mile took the longest, and Nathan's impatience grew as the cabdriver threaded his way through the crush of men. Eventually he let them out a block away, where Benny's presence parted the crowd like Moses at the Red Sea. Nathan had heard about the massive funerals Hasidim held for their rebbes, but it was claustrophobic to be in the midst of one. Their men normally dressed in black, but today there were no caftans, and despite the cold, no fur *shtreimels*. Benny and Hershel dressed in the plainest possible black coats and hats. Nathan wore the only black suit he owned, an old one that added physical discomfort to his already considerable emotional turmoil.

At the cemetery, the ocean of men and boys separated for the coffin to pass, followed by Hershel, Benny, and other prominent males. After the men, Rivke and Zisse led in the women; Sharon's advanced pregnancy kept her at home. Once everyone was seated, a seemingly endless number of rebbes delivered eulogies, while Nathan fumed and clenched his fists as he speculated which ones had known about the child molester.

Finally Benny spoke. He began by praising his father's scholarship and devotion to his people. Then, carefully and adroitly, he shifted the subject to mesirah and its application in America, particularly to Jews who, negligently or purposefully, injured other people. He quoted familiar and obscure pieces of Talmud, Midrash, medieval and modern commentaries. It was an extraordinary display of erudition, and of chutzpah. Nathan could see most men's eyes light with awe, but some flashed with anger. He himself wanted to stand up and cheer.

Toward the end, Benny beckoned Hershel to come forward.

"Though I am the eldest, I pray you should stand by Hershel, for it was our father's will, and his heart's desire, that my brother should take his place." He put his arm around Hershel's shoulder. "I am honored he has chosen me as av beis din."

Hershel, his pale skin luminous in contrast to his dark beard and *payess*, prayed that the congregation's merit and piety would unite to his benefit and allow him to lead them. He would be a symbol for them, a modest one, confident that Messiah would come soon and thus he would not have to be their rebbe long.

The people nodded in approval at his display of humility. Whether Hershel truly felt this way, Nathan admired his effort to distinguish himself from Benny. But what came next was as unexpected as it was remarkable. The men had begun leaving the grave, thus tacitly permitting women to come up, when Rivke reached the site and broke out in anguished sobs, drawing everyone's attention.

Women were expected to remain silent at funerals. Yet when the men saw whose anguish was breaking the customary solemnity, they didn't dare protest. Everyone could see and hear as she turned to the coffin and, between sobs, begged her late husband for forgiveness and prayed that he would be an advocate on high for all the Jewish people. While not speaking officially at the funeral, the widowed rebbetzin had still shown she would not be marginalized.

Her triumph was complete, Benny told Nathan, when later that night the young men chanted in the street below Hershel's window, "*Yechi adoneinu, moreinu, v'rabeinu*" (Long live our master, our teacher, our rebbe), formally accepting him as their new rebbe.

Nathan got to the shiva minyan early the next day so he'd have a chance to talk with Benny alone. "Your eulogy was brilliant, absolutely brilliant."

"Thanks. Your praise means a lot to me."

Nathan shook his head in wonder. "When else would you get the opportunity to exhibit your scholarship while admonishing every rebbe between Boston and Philadelphia? And in a place where they had to sit and listen to you?"

"Those who received my veiled message will understand that my courts will not tolerate child abuse," he declared. "And that victims will find protection and justice there."

"Did you write it down? I'd like Annie to read it."

"Usually I do not know exactly how I am going to drash in advance," Benny replied. "But this was too important to risk leaving anything out, so I wrote an outline. Then I made a copy for Sharon so she would know what I would be doing. You and Annie are welcome to keep mine."

"You don't have to talk about it, but it must have been quite a bombshell that your sister is still alive and in touch with your mother."

"I've gotten over the shock and moved on to feeling relieved," Benny replied. "But Hershel is pretty upset. Mama didn't tell him until yesterday."

Hannah filled with admiration and pride as she heard about Benny's eulogy and Rivke's noisy breach of custom. All week, as Hannah sat shiva with Rivke, Zisse, and Sharon, the women discussed the event with her. At first she was surprised they would confide in an outsider, but then she remembered that no one was supposed to address the mourners until they were spoken to. However, Hannah wasn't an official mourner. Plus she spoke Yiddish. So the women talked to her, particularly when shiva resumed after a hiatus for Shabbos. By then it was clear that, despite her non-Hasidic appearance, she was a good friend of the new rebbe's mother, wife, and sister-in-law.

Hannah's obvious pregnancy was their opening to offer advice, at length, on the subjects about which every Hasidic woman is an authority— childbirth and babies. That she was carrying twins only increased their interest, and each considered herself an expert on baby items. What and where to buy, how much to pay, and most importantly, how long would it last? Hannah, feeling privileged at their acceptance, and a little amused, took in every word.

Baby carriage versus stroller, twin stroller versus two regular strollers, bassinet versus crib: each was thoroughly debated with the assumption that the twins would be the first of more—many more—children. Several women recommended Radio Nurse, which allows the mother to listen in on the nursery, for peace of mind. For going out, Paddi disposable diapers were the best. One woman, aware that Hannah drove a car, had a cousin whose brother-in-law used something called a Car-Baby auto-crib that hung behind the front seat. Hannah tried to remember everything.

She was pleased at how many women spoke fondly of Sharon and expressed hopes that it would be another boy for her and Rav Benyomen. All shared their pleasure that he would be back in the community serving as av beis din. Most seemed to know about his friendship with Nathan and enthused that Hannah must be proud to be married to such a talmid chacham.

Spending a week with them, Hannah could see the attraction of Hasidism. In such a close-knit society, women could feel mutually cared for, supported, and comforted. But when one woman's eyes filled with tears as she praised Rav Benyomen for all he does for the *kinder*, Hannah suspected she had just met the mother of one of his patients.

Yes, this was a warm, secure community for families—as long as they hid their shameful secrets and pretended, willfully blind to any suffering beneath the surface, that all was perfect. But if you were shut out, it would be a cold and lonely existence. Look what happened to Benny's sister.

Hannah saw some of these women again a month later, at the bris of Benny and Sharon's new son. Either because circumcision was a male mitzvah or because Bed-Stuy was too distant from Williamsburg, there were far fewer women here than at Reb Stockser's shiva. Confined to the bedrooms, they cooed over the dowager rebbetzin's new grandson and inquired gently about Hannah's health, but they ignored Sharon's mother and aunt.

Hannah had to admit that a bris was one of the rare times she was glad to be separated from the men.

She hadn't given it much thought when Rivke wore a black tichel at her husband's funeral instead of her sheytle. Sharon had also worn a tichel during shiva, for change was coming for the Vinitzer women. For her son's bris, Sharon wore the most beautiful tichel Hannah had ever seen. The material matched her coffee-colored dress perfectly, and it sparkled with tiny gold accents. Rivke's tichel, which matched her dark dress as well, could best be described as elegant.

Zisse wore a sheytle, and the rest of the women appeared equally divided between the two head coverings, except Leah and Sarah Goren, who wore hats. Hannah herself had put her hair up under a cloche that covered most of it and kept her head warm in the cold weather. She wondered what other changes Rivke would pioneer. In particular, would Rivke make a trip to Israel to see her daughter and grandchildren there?

Hershel's appearance halted her speculations. It was time to bring the baby out.

In the living room, Nathan fidgeted in one of the large chairs. For the umpteenth time, he regretted having agreed to act as *sandek*, the man who holds the baby while the circumcision is performed. But David Goren had adamantly refused this role traditionally given to the boy's grandfather, professing that he was too squeamish.

Nathan couldn't see over the men milling around, but he heard them hush and then recite, "Blessed be he who enters." That meant Hershel and Zisse, the *kvatterim*, were bringing the infant to Benny. Another tradition was that this honor went to a childless couple, as a *segulah* that they would soon be carrying their own healthy newborn. Hannah had told Nathan that Zisse was pregnant, but many of the Hasidim might not know, so there was a question of whether Hershel and Zisse should do this. Benny said it was minhag, not halacha, and deferred to Rivke, who said of course they should do it. It would be a *segulah* for a healthy pregnancy and birth, while refusing the honor would be tantamount to announcing the pregnancy.

Nathan gulped nervously as Benny pronounced the father's customary invocation, that he was ready to fulfill the mitzvah of *bris milah*. Of course, Benny wouldn't be doing the actual circumcision; that was the mohel's job. Nathan's job was to hold the boy as still as possible. Unable to keep his hands from trembling when Benny handed him the baby, Nathan wished he could be anywhere except where he was. When he felt Benny squeeze his shoulder reassuringly, he shut his eyes and took a deep breath.

Thankfully, it happened quickly. The mohel made his broche, "*Baruch atah Adonai* . . . Who commands us concerning circumcision," and the newborn began to yowl. Nathan let out his breath and, along with probably every man in the room, relaxed his clenched thighs.

Now it was time for the blessing everyone was waiting for, the one announcing the boy's name. The mohel cleared his throat and waited for quiet before intoning, "May this child, named in the House of Israel, Mordecai ben Benyomen, become great. As he has entered into the covenant, so may he enter into Torah, *huppah*, and *ma'asim tovim*" (Torah, marriage, and doing good deeds).

There was a long silence before the first "mazel tov." Everyone had undoubtedly expected them to name the boy Pinchas, after Benny's recently deceased father. Nathan understood that Benny and Sharon had no intention of giving their son a name with such unpleasant associations, but fortunately it was customary to name a boy Mordecai who'd been born on Purim. Benny would also be admired as generous in allowing his brother Hershel, the new rebbe, to name a son after their father, the old one.

Thankfully, Nathan and Hannah didn't need to discuss names. A son would be named after her late father and a daughter after his mother. If they had two girls, the second one would be Elizabeth, and a second boy Leib after Deborah's heroic grandfather.

Two weeks later, Hannah and Nathan waited anxiously for Dr. Rubinstein to check her blood pressure as she stood, sat, and lay down. Her feet and ankles had been swelling since the bris, but the swelling mostly went away during the night. The last couple of days, however, not only were they still swollen in the morning, but now her hands were puffing up too.

"It's a good thing you called," the doctor said. "Mrs. Mandel is developing hypertension, and she has protein in her urine. Both symptoms are not uncommon with multiples, but we need to monitor her urine for protein and try to lower her blood pressure."

Hannah's stomach clenched. "What should I do?"

Dr. Rubinstein opened a small box labeled ALBUSTIX and pulled out two slender strips of paper with a small green square at the end. He dipped one in a cup of water and the other in Hannah's urine specimen. The square on the water strip looked unchanged, but the one from Hannah's urine had gone from green to blue.

He handed her the box. "You should test a first-morning urine sample daily, record the result and bring that log to your visits. Call if the protein level increases significantly."

"What about my blood pressure?" Anxiety would only make it higher, so Hannah tried to remain calm.

"The most important thing is to rest, drink lots of water—not coffee, tea, or soda—and keep your feet elevated. Here's a pamphlet about preventing preeclampsia." He handed the booklet to Nathan. "Go over it together now so I can answer your questions before you leave."

When they finished reading it, Hannah was even more worried. "It says that I should stay off my feet but also that walking is recommended."

"Short walks are good to keep the fluid from pooling in your legs, but avoid standing," Dr. Rubinstein explained.

"It advises immersing in water up to her shoulders." Reading this, Nathan immediately thought of the Turkish bath. "What temperature water and for how long?"

"Tepid water, not too hot, for as long as she likes." The doctor waited, and when he saw they had no more questions, added, "You should check your wife's blood pressure twice a day now, and call if it rises abruptly."

"We were thinking about hiring some help if Hannah has to be off her feet for long periods," Nathan said. Outwardly calm, inside he was a bundle of nerves.

"The receptionist can give you business cards for the visiting nurses we recommend."

Their appointment was over. Neither dared question the booklet's advice to curtail sexual relations, not when it could cause premature labor.

Nathan had Hannah drive by the Turkish bath on their way home. He hadn't decided if it would be an acceptable mikveh, but he needed to inform Hannah about the place. Once she saw the pools, his very intelligent wife would surely come to the same conclusion as Louis Katz. Yet when she returned from the baths that evening, with the result that her edema had decreased and her blood pressure was somewhat lower, she said nothing about immersing there for other than medicinal purposes. Since the last thing Nathan wanted was to raise his wife's blood pressure in a stormy debate about mikveh use, he merely expressed thanks that she was doing better and, with some relief, put away the visiting nurse cards.

There was more good news the next night when Benny phoned and, without first asking about Hannah, launched excitedly into his announcement. "Nathan, you will not believe what happened today."

"What? Did little Motel" (Yiddish for Mordecai) "say his first words?" Nathan joked. He had a good idea what Benny was calling about.

"This is serious. Professor Altman came into my office today, closed the door, and looked at me with such a solemn expression that I thought for sure my tenure application had been denied."

"But . . . ?" He beckoned Hannah to get on the extension.

"Not only were they giving me tenure, but I was getting it because some charitable foundation in Boston wants to endow a chair in child psychology." Benny stopped to catch his breath. "It is a miracle, an Adar miracle."

"As they say, 'when Adar enters, joy increases.' Things are doing fairly well over here too." Nathan told him how soaking in the Turkish bath had reduced Annie's edema and hypertension.

"I will start saying *Mi Sheberach* for her. Hannah bas Devorah, right?" There was a long silence, and then Benny said slowly, "But she writes as H. M. Covey?"

Nathan had assumed Benny would figure it out eventually, but this was fast. "Yes, her birth father was Michael Covey, *zichrono livracha*. Samuel Eisin adopted her."

"And Elizabeth Covey?"

"His sister, my aunt," Hannah broke in.

"We greatly appreciate your giving us her furniture . . ." Benny was clearly waiting for one of them to enlighten him further.

"My Covey grandparents were wealthy, but they disinherited my father for being a Communist and marrying a Jew." Hannah explained how the foundation was founded and what kind of charities it funded. "When my aunt took over, she gave priority to supporting children and higher education, which your endowed chair combines perfectly."

"I cannot thank you enough for suggesting this to her."

"You were doing research nobody else was likely to underwrite, research vital for learning how to help these children. Plus, she doesn't have any donors or board members to propitiate." Reluctant for even such close friends to know about her wealth, Hannah was careful to let Benny assume that Aunt Elizabeth had established the chair prior to her death.

"Elizabeth Covey was a maverick," Nathan said in admiration. "She excelled at doing things other women couldn't or wouldn't. I wish I could have known her longer."

Hannah changed the subject before the truth came out. "What are you and Sharon doing for Pesach?"

"We are undecided. But considering that we have always spent Pesach with my family, we will probably go to the Gorens' this year," Benny replied. "What about you?"

"We'll see how Annie is feeling, but the plan is to go to her parents for the first Seder and her dad's cousins, the Helfmans, for the second night, like we did last year."

As soon as they hung up, Nathan hugged Hannah as closely as he could despite her extended belly. "Thanks to you and Benny, psychologists will finally have to take this scourge seriously," he said.

"I doubt it will stop many child molesters, but I can take some satisfaction that as Benny publishes his research, more victims will get treatment," she replied. "They say *mit a leffl ken men dem yam nit oys'shepn*" (you can't empty the ocean with a spoon). "But Benny's work should at least lessen the damage a little." Still, she felt guilty, knowing it was somewhat unethical to fund a friend's employment.

"You should have great satisfaction," Nathan declared. Then he quoted from Tractate Sanhedrin. "Whoever saves one life, it is considered as if he saved an entire world."

"It just occurred to me," she said slowly, "that I can ask the foundation staff to find other scholars interested in researching this subject. There's no reason there shouldn't be additional Elizabeth Covey Memorial Chairs in Child Psychology at other universities." And she wouldn't so much be specifically supporting Benny as supporting his field of research.

"Now that you mention the foundation staff, I think you should consider having them come to New York for meetings."

Hannah didn't have to consider it long. The train ride to Boston took almost an entire day, door to door. "Good idea. I could meet with senior staff here quarterly, and we could take the twins with us to Boston twice a year during school vacations."

A few days before Pesach, however, Hannah was disappointed, and frightened, to learn that going to the Helfmans for the second-night Seder was out of the question. Her blood pressure and urine protein level had risen significantly, so much so that Dr. Rubinstein prescribed complete bed rest, with the exception of using the toilet and moving from bed to couch.

She was ending her eighth month, and every day she didn't give birth was another day the twins had to grow and mature.

She didn't argue when Nathan said it was time to hire a nurse.

So, Mrs. Porter, a maternity nurse with over twenty years' experience, moved into the empty second-floor bedroom. Which, Hannah expected, would very soon, *keinehora*, be the nursery. Mrs. Porter did the cooking, shopping, and laundry, but mostly she kept an eye on Hannah. She also took over measuring Hannah's blood pressure, a responsibility Nathan was relieved to relinquish.

Hannah, feeling increasingly ungainly, looked forward to spending many pleasant hours in bed doing nothing but working on Aunt Elizabeth's life story. But as soon as word spread about her condition, it seemed that every woman she knew felt obligated to visit. Naomi, Deborah, and Rae dropped in daily while Tante Essie, Sharon, and Leah Goren were there several times a week. Even Rivke and Zisse came to call. Sometimes Hannah felt oppressed by her confinement, but mostly she was grateful for the company.

Plus there were women from Congregation Israel, including Louis Katz's wife, who, upon hearing that Hannah had visited the Turkish bath for medicinal purposes, confessed to using it as a mikveh—with her husband's knowledge.

Hannah nodded thoughtfully. Those warm Turkish baths, with their well-appointed dressing rooms that even supplied hair dryers, would be a blessing in winter.

But Nathan expected her to immerse in a kosher mikveh, and she was unlikely to change his mind. Suddenly she had an epiphany. *What if we install a mikveh at home? I own the building now. I can remodel it however I want.*

In less than five minutes she was on the phone with Naomi, with instructions to get Rabbi David Miller's book on niddah from the synagogue library. An hour later they were perusing chapter nineteen.

"It doesn't look too complicated," Hannah pronounced. "I bet Dad's contractor could make one in no time."

Naomi's eyes lit with enthusiasm. "They could do it while you're in the hospital so it would be ready when you come home with the babies."

"It could go under the stairs, like in this illustration, and get its water from the kitchen. It would hardly need any new plumbing." Hannah's voice rose with enthusiasm. "And you could use it too."

"That would be amazing," Naomi gushed. Then her face clouded. "But what if Nathan doesn't think it's kosher enough? This book is over twenty-five years old."

"I'll wait and show it to him after Pesach," Hannah replied. "If he doesn't approve this design, maybe we can find a way to make it kosher." *Best say nothing now and avert the inevitable confrontation. It will be months before I'll need to immerse anyway.*

Hannah refused to miss either Seder, so Deborah stipulated that she would host the first one like usual, but in the Mandels' dining room. Tante Essie would host the second one next door at Naomi's. Samuel and Nathan gently carried Hannah downstairs, enabling her to truly fulfill the mitzvah of reclining during both Seders. Chol HaMoed passed uneventfully, with Nathan and his father, both on school break for the week, bumbling fretfully around the house and getting in Mrs. Porter's way.

At night, with Nathan's arms around her, Hannah snuggled closer and tried not to think about the dangers of her high-risk pregnancy. She could tell he was worried; he tossed and turned in bed, and even the smallest noise made him jump. So she said nothing of her own fears. Until the babies came, telling him how frightened she was would only make him more anxious.

She didn't mention building a home mikveh either.

On the last day of Pesach, a Yom Tov with as many halachic constraints as the first two days, Hannah woke up feeling poorly. Nathan and Abba were downstairs, dressed and ready to walk to services, when Mrs. Porter stopped them.

"Mrs. Mandel is experiencing several symptoms that concern me," she informed them. "I would like to call her doctor."

Nathan's throat tightened, but he was determined to appear calm. "His office is closed for the chagim." He barely eked out the words.

"Then we need to page him."

"What's the matter with her?" Abba asked. "Phone calls aren't permitted today unless it's a matter of *pikuach nefesh.*"

"She feels nauseous and her head hurts."

Nathan didn't think that sounded like pikuach nefesh, but his father's expression clouded with fright. "Gottenyu, just like Minnie," Abba whispered.

"Her blood pressure is up, as is her proteinuria," the nurse added. "We cannot wait until sunset."

Nathan raced to the kitchen and frantically dialed the doctors' number. "The paging company can't reach Dr. Rubinstein or Dr. Isaacson," he called out from the kitchen. "But they'll keep trying."

When he returned to the living room, his father, face ashen and struggling to breathe, was lying on the couch while Mrs. Porter loosened his tie. "Call for an ambulance," she ordered Nathan. "No, call for two ambulances."

Paralyzed with fear, his mind unable to function, Nathan just gaped at his father.

"I'll do it, then. You get his tie off." She gave another command. "Then go upstairs, find your wife's hospital bag, and sit with her until the ambulance comes."

Hannah didn't open her eyes when Nathan came in. "We couldn't reach your doctors, so just to be safe, Mrs. Porter is calling an ambulance to take you to the hospital." It took every ounce of self-control to say nothing about Abba's collapse.

"The light makes my headache worse, but I'm really thirsty," she said. "Could you get me some water?"

"Of course." He filled a cup from the bathroom, and she drank greedily. Then he sat next to her and held her hand. Chas v'chalila she should realize anything was amiss downstairs and cause her blood pressure to rise even higher.

Within minutes they could hear sirens. Terror consumed Nathan as he watched out the window until the ambulances arrived, thankfully with their sirens quieted. Soon Mrs. Porter came up the stairs.

"I'll stay with Hannah now," she said. Then she mouthed, *You go with your father.*

Nathan leaned over and kissed Hannah gently. "I'll see you later. I love you." *Please God, don't let these be my last words to her. Don't let this be like with my mother.*

When the second set of attendants brought Hannah downstairs and lifted her into the ambulance, Naomi was waiting on the stoop. "I'll walk over to your folks' house and tell your mom what's going on," Naomi said. By agreement with Nathan she let Hannah assume the men had gone to synagogue.

Mrs. Porter got in back with Hannah and they drove off. Thankfully, the ride wasn't long because Hannah was feeling increasingly nauseated. As gently as the ambulance attendants were in moving her onto a hospital gurney, she vomited on the sidewalk.

"Don't worry," Mrs. Porter said as Hannah tried to apologize. "At least you weren't in the ambulance."

The bright lights hurt Hannah's eyes, so she continued to keep them closed, but she could hear everything. Mrs. Porter was apparently known at the hospital because the admitting staff and obstetric nurses took Hannah's information from her without question. They even let Mrs. Porter accompany Hannah into the exam room, where the light was thankfully dimmer.

"Could somebody change the linen on this gurney?" Hannah asked. "I think I just peed on it." It was mortifying first throwing up at the hospital entrance and then urinating in bed.

Mrs. Porter felt the wet sheet and pushed the call button. "Mrs. Mandel's water has broken."

Now Hannah was frightened. If her babies didn't come soon enough, they would want to induce labor or, chas v'chalila, perform a caesarian section.

It wasn't long before a doctor came in. He put his stethoscope on Hannah's belly, listened intently, and heaved a sigh of relief. "Are you feeling any pain or contractions?"

"My lower back is sore," she acknowledged. "But it's getting worse."

"And it will continue to worsen," he said. "You are officially in labor."

"So my babies are coming today?" Excitement temporarily overcame her fear.

"Most definitely." He gently ran his hands over Hannah's belly. "Both twins are head down, which is good." He then left one hand in place while he looked at his watch. "Did you feel that? That was a contraction."

A few minutes later, Hannah moaned. "I felt that one."

"I'll be back in twenty minutes or so." He turned to Mrs. Porter. "Please time her contractions and let me know if they speed up suddenly."

When the doctor returned, he informed them that Dr. Rubinstein would be there shortly, which added a modicum of relief to Hannah's other emotions.

In the cardiac wing of Brooklyn Memorial, Nathan paced the hall reciting Tehillim (Psalms) while the doctors examined his father. Somewhere in this large edifice, Hannah was also being treated. Since ancient times, Jews prayed Tehillim in times of trouble and distress, and Nathan tried to say them carefully, with kavanah, to keep his mind off what might be happening to his two loved ones, especially Annie.

But he kept thinking about the Mishnah quote in the Orthodox siddur about women dying in childbirth because they neglect niddah. His own mother died that way and apparently had not followed niddah laws. Annie had also not observed niddah properly and was now in mortal danger from complications of her pregnancy.

However, he kept reminding himself, the vast majority of modern Jewish women neglect niddah, and almost none die in childbirth.

That Mishnah was obviously incorrect, not to mention causing unnecessary fear, yet it remained in the siddur. But the Orthodox Ashkenazi siddur text wasn't canon; Sephardic communities recited different prayers. The Conservative movement revised their prayer books periodically and had at some point deleted that offensive passage.

Maybe Benny didn't care about the actual words he prayed, but Nathan did. And he didn't want to pray that fearsome lie or even see it in his siddur.

TWENTY-SEVEN

TO NATHAN IT SEEMED FOREVER, but he had been waiting less than two hours when Dr. Grossman came out and informed him that this time his father did not appear to be having a coronary. Even so, they would keep him overnight for observation. Nathan could see him, but only briefly so his father could rest.

"Abba, you really scared me." Nathan gave his father a long hug. "But you look a lot better." It was true. Solomon Mandel's color was good, and he was breathing easily.

"I'm sorry I frightened you, but all those horrible memories coming back . . ." He took a deep breath to calm himself. "How is Annie doing?"

"I'm not sure." Nathan had been too scared to even approach the maternity wing. Whatever was happening there was out of his control, and as long as he didn't know anything definitive, he could continue praying for Annie and their babies. "She's over in maternity, and I can't see her."

"Go over there and ask what's happening," Abba commanded. "I won't be able to relax until you have a report."

Nathan hugged Abba again and went to check the directory. Maternity was on another floor, so, reciting more Tehillim, he hurried that way. The receptionist acknowledged that a Hannah Mandel had been admitted, and when Nathan identified himself as her husband, she said Mrs. Mandel was in labor and directed him to the appropriate waiting room.

It was the same waiting room where, two years ago, he'd sat with Benny while Sharon labored with Judy.

He struggled to come to grips with Annie being in labor, which at least meant she was alive. Before he got up the nerve to knock on the inner door to ask how she was doing, a nurse came out and called his name. Nathan jumped up and learned that his wife's labor was progressing well, and she was expected to give birth later that day. No, he couldn't see her, but yes, they would tell her he was here.

364

Tears of joy streaming down his cheeks, he returned to Abba's room. "Those maternity nurses won't tell me anything," Nathan complained. "All they say is that Annie's labor is progressing and our babies will be born when they're ready." In truth he was elated by the news, but it seemed prudent to kvetch.

Abba looked upward and closed his eyes. "*Gott tzu danken.*"

Nathan prayed quietly until his father fell asleep. When he returned to the maternity waiting room, he was surprised to find Deborah there. Obviously, she had violated halacha to get here, but he wasn't about to chastise her when he was so glad for her company.

Hannah didn't care how her husband and mother had gotten to the hospital on this Jewish holy day. She'd been there five hours, and her painful contractions, now coming every minute and barely subsiding before the next one started, kept her fully occupied. If it weren't for Mrs. Porter encouraging her while massaging her back, Hannah couldn't have endured it without screaming. She'd expected to get what Naomi and Sharon called "twilight sleep," but Dr. Rubinstein said those drugs slowed labor, and it was imperative that the babies be born as quickly as possible. Her positive response to the magnesium infusion had encouraged him to let her labor naturally in hopes of avoiding a caesarian, which had its own risks.

One advantage of twins, he told her, was that their small size made for an easier delivery.

If this was an easy delivery, Hannah thought, Heaven save her from a hard one. Just when the pains reached such a crescendo that she begged Mrs. Porter to find a doctor to give her something to stop them, she felt an urge to push. For a moment she was embarrassed that she might move her bowels right there in the labor room, but then she recognized the difference.

When Mrs. Porter returned with Dr. Rubinstein, he declared it too late for drugs; the babies were coming. Attendants wheeled Hannah into the delivery room, where she couldn't have stopped pushing even if she'd tried. Her muscles were out of her control, and they wanted, needed, to push those foreign bodies out of her.

Thank God it didn't take long.

"It's a girl," Dr. Rubinstein declared triumphantly when the first baby emerged. "At least a five-pounder," he added as he passed the wailing newborn to the nurse standing by.

One big push and the next baby followed its sister. "Mazel tov, Mrs. Mandel," he called out. "You also have a son."

The boy's cries weren't as lusty as the girl's, and he wasn't as big. As Dr. Rubinstein predicted, she was a little over five pounds, but her brother weighed only four and a half.

Hannah lay back on the table, physically exhausted yet mentally exultant. *Hallelujah! It's over.* The pain was gone, and her babies, though small, appeared healthy.

In the waiting room, Nathan and Deborah watched in quiet gratification as the sun set. Mrs. Porter had relayed the good news, and they were eager to visit Hannah. They'd already viewed the newborns through the nursery window, where two nurses had brought the twins right up to the glass. Deborah started crying, but Nathan was disappointed in his unemotional response. To him, his dark-haired babies looked indistinguishable from many others in their little bassinets, although his boy was significantly smaller. They definitely didn't resemble him, his father, Annie, or her mother.

Nathan raced back and forth between the maternity waiting room and the cardiac ward with each update, until finally, he and Deborah were allowed into Annie's room, which she shared with five other women. Her bed was at one end, and Nathan was thankful for the modicum of privacy this afforded. She looked beautiful, a little tired, but beautiful nonetheless.

According to halacha, she was niddah now, which meant he couldn't touch her or even hand something to her.

So he stood there helpless and miserable with envy as Deborah and Annie embraced. It wasn't fair, this extra fence around the Torah. Did the ancient rabbis really believe that without their fences a man would jump into bed with his wife immediately after she'd given birth? Didn't Rashi disapprove of making many fences, saying Judaism shouldn't be difficult for the people?

This is why there are so many Reform and Conservative Jews. Also, he had to admit, why some so-called Orthodox Jews ignored such fences. Like women who immersed in their bathtubs and husbands who refused to wait seven clean days.

Deborah must have decided that the new parents should have some time alone together before Yom Tov was over and visitors began arriving. "I'll wait downstairs for Sam," she said.

Once Deborah was gone, two attendants came in wheeling the babies' bassinets. "Oh, I'm sorry," one said. "We didn't realize the father was still here. But you insisted on nursing and they're hungry." This last statement came with heavy disapproval.

"Surely my husband can stay and watch," Hannah replied, undaunted. "He may as well start getting used to the sight now."

Intimidated by Hannah's authoritative demeanor, the attendant said, "Yes, ma'am," and pulled the privacy curtain around the bed. She placed the boy, wrapped in a blue blanket and wearing a blue cap, in the crook of Hannah's right arm and the girl, in pink, in the left. Then she left in a huff.

Hannah followed Sharon's detailed instructions and leaned over so her nipple was next to her daughter's mouth. The remaining attendant helped by stroking the baby's cheek, and to Hannah's surprised delight, the newborn latched on and began to suck. The baby boy had a bit of trouble at first, but the attendant encouraged Hannah to keep trying, and once he started nursing, he wouldn't let go. A sharp cramp in her belly startled her, but the pain didn't diminish her happiness.

Watching his euphoric wife nursing their twins, Nathan couldn't restrain his tears. The attendant passed him a box of tissues and then, presence no longer required, slipped outside.

Sharon had warned Hannah about such a reaction, but Nathan's sobs went beyond weeping for joy. "Nathan." Hannah kept her voice soft so as not to startle their babies. "Are you okay?"

He pulled his chair closer to unburden himself. First about his father's health scare and then about hers. "I've never been so terrified in my life. I was sure you were both going to die."

"But everything's fine now," she said soothingly. She didn't want to think about all the disastrous outcomes that had been averted—not now with the newborns in her arms.

"No, it's not." He proceeded to share his anger and frustration at not being able to touch her when he most needed comforting. Then his eyes filled with new tears. "I never questioned halacha until we started studying together."

"But you've studied Talmud for years. You know it's written by men, not God," she said. It unnerved her to see Nathan so distressed. "Why shouldn't you question laws created hundreds of years ago, when people's lives were very different? Why else did God give us svara?"

"Svara" was a Talmudic concept that referred to a person's moral intuition and common sense, ideally informed by Jewish learning. According to the Rabbis, when one's svara conflicts with halacha, svara has the power to override even Torah law.

He used a tissue to blow his nose, and then his eyes twinkled. "I'm probably the only man in the world whose wife brings up svara in an argument."

"Are you kvetching or kvelling?"

He gave her a small smile. "Some of each."

"Speaking of svara, I used it to overrule Dr. Rubinstein when he tried to discourage me from nursing." Hannah felt very proud of herself. "He said that I wouldn't have enough milk for twins, so I countered that why else was a woman created with two breasts. When he said formula was modern and scientific, I pointed out that women have been nursing babies for millennia and I didn't see how scientists could improve on a mother's own milk. After all, my mother nursed me and I turned out fine."

He couldn't suppress a grin. "Sounds more like *af tsu lokhes* than svara."

She chuckled in return. "You know me well."

"I know you like to question authority."

Suddenly her expression turned serious. "On that subject, do you think you could help dry my face? My hands are occupied." *Will his svara be strong enough to override this fence around the Torah?*

Nathan knew she'd chosen a good test for him. It wasn't a matter of pikuach nefesh; he could ask a nurse to do it. But not drying her cheeks while she was in the hospital nursing his babies was one fence too many. He stood up and slowly removed a tissue from the box. Then he approached the bed, hesitated, and took a deep breath before gently wiping the wetness away.

"Thank you." She locked eyes with him before adding, "I really appreciate it." She wanted it clear that she appreciated a great deal more than the Kleenex itself.

Surprised that breaking that fence left him feeling liberated rather than guilty, Nathan stayed until she finished nursing. Then, finding Deborah, Samuel, and Rae in the waiting room with Leah Goren, he took some time to fill them in on the day's events.

When he got to his father's room, Isaac Goren was there visiting, and Nathan recounted what he'd told the others. He said nothing to any of them about tearing down halachic fences, however.

Abba beckoned Nathan to sit next to the bed. "While Dr. Grossman doesn't think I had a major coronary, he can't rule out a small one. You know how he lectures me about working too hard . . ." He sighed with resignation. "He reminded me that I'm almost sixty-five, and I should be thinking seriously about retirement if I want to live long enough to enjoy my grandchildren."

"But they need you at the Seminary, Abba. You're irreplaceable."

"No, I'm not." Abba's eyes bored into Nathan's. "We've been studying Talmud together for fifteen years, and I've taught you everything I know about text criticism. You've been teaching the subject and coauthoring papers with me for seven years."

"The Seminary has long planned to offer you your father's position when he retired," Isaac Goren said. "With full tenure, a larger salary, and extra funding to attend conferences."

It immediately entered Nathan's mind that nobody at the Conservative Seminary would scrutinize what he did outside of class, and he realized how much it still rankled that somebody, or somebodies, had spied on him with Annie and then reported back to Spektor's dean.

"For years you've complained about the hostile atmosphere in your classroom, how the Haredi students resent what you teach and attack your methods," Abba said.

"I guarantee Nathan won't have antagonistic students at the Seminary." Isaac Goren turned to Abba. "Your classes are so popular, there's a waiting list for seats."

Before Nathan could respond, Abba added, "Teaching at the Seminary hasn't turned me into a Conservative Jew."

"I know," Nathan replied. *Not that it would be so terrible if that happened.* "But I have to think about it and discuss it with Annie."

Abba and Isaac Goren exchanged triumphant smiles before Abba addressed his son. "Good. At least you're considering it."

With Hannah in the hospital, this was Nathan's first night not sharing a bed with her in eight months. He hadn't realized how much he'd miss snuggling together or how cold the bed would be without her warm body nestled next to his. He was still wound up from the roller coaster of emotions he'd experienced that morning, and hearing the doctor describe Annie's narrow escape only added to his turmoil. He resolved that whatever Mrs. Porter charged, they'd pay her double.

He was also cognizant that he'd deliberately transgressed niddah prohibitions that afternoon by drying Hannah's face. Somehow he doubted it would be a one-time sin that Yom Kippur atoned for. In earlier times rabbis had modified, or at least adjusted, halacha to respond to changes in society, even creating legal fictions. But once medieval codes were written and disseminated via printing press, halacha became fixed. After Reform Judaism arose in protest, halacha ossified further, to the point where laws of mesirah now protected Jewish child molesters from punishment.

With a shock he realized his opponents were right. Seeing how Talmud contained variant texts could undermine the immutability of Orthodox halacha. Had it done so for him? Or maybe it was studying Talmud with a woman? Or both?

Perhaps the Conservatives had the answer. Louis was right that being cloistered at Spektor had left Nathan ignorant of conflicts between Orthodox halacha and the modern world. In the meantime, while he wrestled with his evolving beliefs, he knew that so long as he was teaching at Spektor, he would have to give the appearance of Orthodox observance. But what about his behavior at the hospital? Did he want to become a hypocrite, behaving one way in public and another in private? Worrying about new spies reporting to the dean?

Samuel and Benny, along with everyone at Spektor, would feel disappointed, maybe even betrayed, if he left to teach at the Seminary. But what would Annie want?

Hannah slept poorly for obvious reasons: besides the excitement of giving birth to twins and having to feed them every hour or two, the maternity ward was a near-constant source of commotion. Plus, Dr. Rubinstein had explained to her and Nathan how close a call she'd had, that without Mrs. Porter things might have ended badly. But in the back of her mind lurked guilt for seducing Nathan, an Orthodox rabbi, into violating niddah halacha, as well as apprehension over their need to discuss its implications. She had thought they had an advantage over Sharon and Benny because she and Nathan didn't need to compromise their level of observance.

But she was wrong.

There was no denying that she and Nathan were at odds over how to observe niddah and mikveh. Her pregnancy had only delayed confronting the issue. Now, they'd have to face it.

The next morning Nathan was in line to sign the visitor log when he heard a familiar voice. "I hoped I'd see you here to wish you mazel tov." Louis Katz clasped him around the shoulder. "You don't have to wait in this long line. There's a separate sign in for clergy."

"But—" Nathan started to protest.

"Rabbis get few enough privileges in the world, enjoy this one while you can," Louis said. "Too bad I didn't see you earlier. You could have joined our minyan."

"Where do you meet?" Nathan asked. It would be convenient to daven here before coming upstairs to see Annie and the twins.

"The hospital has a very nice chapel. Come, I'll show you once you have your visitor name tag."

Nathan's was labeled RABBI MANDEL in large letters, and he felt self-conscious as he and Louis walked to the chapel. The room was softly lit, and several people sat quietly in the pews, some reading and some with eyes closed.

"You're welcome to stay." Louis turned to leave. "I've got a lot of congregants to visit."

Nathan opened a Conservative siddur and savored the peaceful silence as he davened. When he turned to leave, he stopped short as he saw the inscription above the door. It said, "Chapel dedicated to the memory of Margaret Taylor Covey." There couldn't be another Covey family giving money to hospitals, and with Aunt Elizabeth being religious, it made sense they would fund a chapel.

Upstairs in Hannah's corner of the maternity ward, Hannah confirmed to Nathan that Margaret Covey was her grandmother, and her own middle name was in memory of this Margaret. "I've only seen the foundation's recent reports. It might be interesting to see what projects it supported years ago." She looked pensive. "I wonder if the hospital has records of donations going that far back."

When Nathan returned after his last class, his father had been discharged, the twins were asleep in the nursery, and Annie was in a private room. "What's this?" he asked her, half seriously. "I register as a rabbi at the visitor check-in and my wife gets her own room?"

Disappointed that he made no move to hug or kiss her, Hannah shook her head. "I should have known somebody here would get excited if they learned I was Margaret Covey's granddaughter." She felt more annoyance than gratitude. "I suppose we'll be hearing from the hospital's fundraisers pretty soon."

"Would that be such a bad thing?"

"I suppose not, but I don't like so many people, especially strangers, knowing I have money. I'll need to be more circumspect in the future," she said. "By the way, I asked Mrs. Porter if she could stay on with us to help with the twins once we were all discharged. I said she could go on vacation while we're still in the hospital."

"Excellent idea. I'm glad you thought of it."

"Also, the pediatrician examined our babies and recommended the boy not be circumcised at eight days, but to delay until he's bigger."

Nathan gulped back his fear. "But he's all right otherwise?"

"He's fine," she quickly reassured him. "The doctor only wanted us to wait two weeks."

Nathan did a quick mental calculation. "Since we can pick any day we want, how about the second Sunday in May?"

"Mother's Day, very appropriate. Then we can name both of them on the same day."

But there was still another matter to discuss. They sat silently for a few moments before they both said, almost simultaneously, "We need to talk about yesterday."

"I apologize for taking advantage of your emotional state, but I'm not sorry I made you touch me." Hannah launched her first salvo. "I think having too many fences insults our ability to think for ourselves and control our own behavior."

To her surprise Nathan not only concurred but told her about Abba retiring from the Seminary. "But unless, or until, I leave Spektor, I have to follow Orthodox halacha, even the laws I disagree with." He looked at her with sad eyes. "Which means you do too."

Hannah could see that Nathan was torn about changing jobs. "I'd be thrilled for you to teach at the Seminary, but you shouldn't do it just for me." *Hopefully, that will make my position clear without being pushy.*

"Even if I taught there, I'd still want us to observe the same halacha." *But not necessarily the same as I do now.*

"What if you want to observe Shabbos totally and I want to write some letters, or if you want to keep strictly kosher and I want to eat fish in a regular restaurant?" she asked, testing him.

"Never mind Shabbos and kashrus. Let's talk *tachlis*. We can't each observe niddah in a different way." Nathan looked her in the eye. "Thankfully, how we keep niddah is a private matter, not obvious to others. Using svara, I hope we can agree on our own level of observance, which fences we'll keep and which we won't."

Amazed and awestruck that he was willing to negotiate halacha, Hannah realized he'd given this much thought. "It's important to me that we be able to touch and hand things to each other," she said.

"First we need to define niddah," he interrupted. "Are we talking d'oraita, for seven days total, or derabanan, for seven extra clean days?"

She looked at him in astonishment. "If you're giving me a choice, I'd certainly prefer d'oraita." Observing niddah would be easier if it only lasted seven days from the start of her period.

"Not really. I just want us to agree on the basic halacha before we get to the fences." He wasn't surprised that she chose the less onerous option. "Derabanan, then?"

"All right." She didn't hide her regret. "Now back to touching. I think we should touch platonically while I'm niddah; otherwise any touching at all becomes something sexual. So I'm willing to act like brother and sister while I'm niddah."

"Very well," he replied. *She has a point.* "In public or just in private?"

"Now we need to define public and private." Hannah was relieved they were able to discuss this reasonably, without Nathan getting angry. "I want us to be able to touch in our house and at my parents' even if other people are there, but I'll let you decide about what to do at the Gorens' or Benny and Sharon's."

This was more complicated than Nathan had considered. At least if he wanted to move toward Conservative Judaism, he was confident that Annie would support his decision. "None of those people are likely to know when you're niddah, so I'm willing to touch at our friends' homes. It would also be okay if you took my arm at the movies or theater, but maybe not at shul." He suddenly realized that once he left Spektor, nobody there would be watching them and then complaining about him being lax about niddah.

"I suppose we couldn't hold hands, because siblings don't do that." Hannah had one more activity to clarify. "Can we go dancing?"

"I'd rather we not dance while you're niddah."

She sighed and acquiesced. "I supposed once I'm niddah again, our twins will keep us so busy we'll be lucky to have any time at all to go out."

"What about mikveh?" This would be the difficult choice, so Nathan needed to hear what she wanted first.

"Summer is no problem. We'll immerse together in the sea."

"I look forward to it." He waited for her to continue.

"Dr. Rubinstein recommended a very hygienic mikveh in the city for my first immersion, so I'll go there before the bris." Then she hesitated. If she was going to bring up building a home mikveh, this was the time to do it.

But Nathan beat her to it. "Don't worry." He smiled and explained, "Naomi showed me Rabbi Miller's book. You know she can't keep a secret." He basked in her expression of delighted surprise.

"Oh, Nathan. Do you think it's kosher enough?"

"Rabbi David Miller is an authority in this matter." The rabbi's home mikvah would certainly be better than the doubtfully kosher Turkish bath.

"And you agree with locating it under the first-floor stairs?" She couldn't believe it had been so easy.

"The carpenters are already at work. Since our stairs are across the wall from theirs, Naomi suggested making it bigger and having an entrance on their side too. It should be finished when you and our babies come home."

For a moment Hannah was speechless, but tears of joy welled in her eyes. Finally she held out her arms. "So can I have a hug?"

He gave her the same kind of hug he'd given Auntie Dora, and he felt fine, without even a twinge of guilt. Nor, to his relief, was there any revulsion.

When they finally let go, Hannah decided to be bold. "I know I should have asked you before we got married, but there's something I'd like you to consider doing for me." *If he's going to teach at the Seminary, he might be open to changing our ketubah.*

He could tell she didn't think he'd do it. "What?"

"I'd like you to write me a new ketubah, one with the Lieberman clause." When she saw his frown, she quickly added, "Or one with something similar. Nobody else needs to know." He was quiet for so long she was sure he was trying to control his temper, but then he surprised her.

"I know all newlyweds think they'll never get divorced, and I certainly hope we don't," he said slowly and deliberately. "But I think it's better to put the clause in and not need it than to leave it out and cause more trouble later." He knew he'd made the right decision by the look of gratitude and adoration she gave him.

When he got home, he decided that not upsetting Sam or Benny was insufficient reason to remain at Spektor compared to the advantages of switching to the Seminary. Once teaching there, Nathan realized, he'd daven the weekday services in their chapel with the students and other faculty—using the Conservative siddur. He wouldn't be confronted with the Orthodox prayers about women dying in childbirth and for rebuilding the Temple.

And if he and Annie wanted to explore Conservative Judaism, it was no one else's business. He just needed to find two witnesses for the new ketubah, Jews who wouldn't object to its contents. Which left out most of his friends and colleagues.

Hannah and Nathan anticipated a large attendance for the combination bris and baby naming, so they held the ceremonies at Congregation Israel. More people would likely attend on a Sunday, when the morning minyan met at the reasonable hour of eight thirty. Just because Nathan would be teaching at the Conservative Seminary in the fall didn't mean they'd be joining a Conservative synagogue. Abba had taught there for years and davened at an even stricter Orthodox shul than theirs.

Their new ketubah, witnessed by Isaac Goren and Louis Katz, was safely stored in their bedroom at home, no one else the wiser. And their new mikveh, its construction overseen by Nathan, was discreetly hidden beneath the first-floor stairway. Naomi had immersed in it twice and was effusive in appreciation.

Under Mrs. Porter's watchful eye, the synagogue's bride room became a temporary nursery. But much of the time the babies were out in the sanctuary, usually in Hannah's and Deborah's arms. Benny and Sharon brought both Judy and baby Mordecai, and Hannah couldn't get over how much larger their son was compared to hers.

The ceremonies began when Hannah *benched gomel*, the prayer of thanksgiving said after recovering from a serious medical problem or completing a dangerous journey. "*Baruch ata Adonai, Eloheinu melech ha-olam, ha-gomel l'chayavim tovot she-g'malani kol tov.*" (Blessed are You, Lord our God, ruler of the world, who bestows goodness on the undeserving and who has bestowed every goodness upon me.)

As she returned to her seat, it hit her how close she had come to not surviving childbirth. By the time she sat down, she was trembling. Nathan squeezed her hand, then came up to give the drash they had written together.

He started by reminding everyone, in the unlikely event that any Jews needed reminding, that it was Mother's Day. When the laughter died down, he soberly explained that both he and Hannah had lost parents at a young age, his mother in childbirth and her father at Guernica, both in this month of Iyar. He spoke of his mother's efforts in the creation and acceptance of the OU kashrus hechsher and of Hannah's father's exemplary work as a journalist and war correspondent. He had to halt several times to control his emotions before declaring that he and Hannah would honor their late parents by naming their son and daughter after them.

He continued by quoting Exodus, Deuteronomy, and Leviticus, where the Israelites are commanded to "honor your father and mother" in the first two texts and "revere your mother and father" in the latter. According to Rashi, Nathan pointed out, the Torah mentions mother before father in Leviticus because it is evident to God that a child reveres—or fears—a father more than a mother. But regarding honor, in Exodus and Deuteronomy the father is mentioned first because it is evident to God that a child honors a mother more than a father.

Then he launched into a Talmud discussion from Tractate Kiddushin, which starts, "Our Rabbis taught: What is 'revere' and what is 'honor'? 'Revere' means a child doesn't stand in the parent's place nor contradict their words. 'Honor' means children must care for their elderly parents' physical needs." He quoted more Rashi and Tosafos, moved on to Maimonides, and finally some twentieth-century scholars.

Hannah's heart swelled with pride as the congregation hung on his every word, words she had a significant part in writing. He concluded with a nod to Hannah to bring their daughter up to the bimah. He put his hands on the baby's head, and using the feminine Hebrew of the blessing said at a bris, they recited together, "May this girl, named in the House of Israel Mina bas Natan, become great. So may she enter into Torah, huppah, and *ma'asim tovim*."

The more traditional attendees might be offended, but it was important to Hannah that her daughter enter into Torah alongside her son. For the circumcision, she retreated to the bride's room with little Mina. As Sharon had warned, hearing her son's cries made Hannah's breasts leak milk, but she'd prepared by starting to nurse Mina. Thus she was ready for baby Michael when he was brought to her.

Both children were asleep when Hannah and Mrs. Porter wheeled out the baby carriages and parked them next to the table where Hannah and Nathan would have lunch. Of course everyone gushed over how little and sweet the twins were, while Nathan and Hannah's feelings were a mix of relief and gratitude that the ceremony was over, set against a background of protectiveness and devotion.

They managed to eat as a seemingly endless line of relatives, friends, and acquaintances offered congratulations and blessings. Few Jews attended a wedding without being invited, but a bris was open to all who wanted to celebrate the mitzvah, especially one held at a synagogue. Observant men considered it an obligation to do so, thus bringing Solomon Mandel, Rav Klein, Isaac Goren, and much of the Seminary and Spektor faculties and student bodies together under one roof with Moe Novick and the *Freiheit*'s secular male employees.

Nathan's maternal relatives waited until the end to have more time to chat. Cousin Marsha cooed over the babies, who were starting to wake up. "They are absolutely adorable, and I think it's so cute for twins to be named Mickey and Minnie."

Hannah and Nathan stared at each other in disbelief and dismay at the realization that they had named their children after Disney cartoon characters.

But then Nathan's eyes began to twinkle.

Hannah finally shook her head and smiled back at him until eventually neither could restrain their laughter.

AUTHOR'S NOTE

FIRST I'M GOING TO address the two questions all my beta readers asked.

1. Since *The Choice* is inspired by the work of Chaim Potok, how did you get permission from the Potok estate? Short answer: I didn't. This book is *not* authorized by the Potok family. Long answer: *The Choice* is what intellectual property lawyers call a "transformative" work, one that uses some elements of another copyrighted work for purposes of criticism and/or commentary under the Fair Use Doctrine. Just as *The Wind Done Gone* was ruled to be a fair use of *Gone with the Wind* for retelling Margaret Mitchell's tale using the slaves' point of view to criticize the 1860s South, in my case *The Choice* exposes the unequal and inferior position of women in traditional Jewish Law, a subject that was omitted from the work of Chaim Potok. Unlike *The Wind Done Gone*, however, I have only alluded to the world that Potok evoked in his work rather than retelling his stories.

2. How can you have your Orthodox rabbi character frequenting dance halls? Isn't mixed dancing forbidden? Short answer: Violating some prohibitions is less egregious than violating others, especially the ones most people are violating. Long answer: From the early 1900s and continuing into the 1940s and 1950s—the big-band era and the dawn of rock'n'roll—Orthodox Jews, like other New Yorkers, patronized dance halls. According to Orthodox synagogues' monthly bulletins from that time, which I found in the Central Library's Center for Brooklyn History, many held regular dances in their social halls. Photo collections show that, except for the Haredi, Jewish men and women danced together at weddings. We also know this was common because the great midcentury *posek* Rabbi Moshe Feinstein ruled first that a man shouldn't remove his yarmulke upon entering a theater, cinema or dance hall even though frequenting these venues was prohibited. Then again, two years later, Feinstein ruled that otherwise

observant Jews who participate in mixed dancing should still wear their yarmulkes so as not to add another violation to their already sinful behavior.

Now on to how I wrote *The Choice*.

When I began research for the Rashi's Daughters series in the early 1990s, there was little in the genre of Jewish historical fiction—only *As a Driven Leaf* by Milton Steinberg, *The Fixer* by Bernard Malamud, and *The Source* by James Michener—none written by women. Anita Diamant's *The Red Tent* wasn't published until 1997. My characters were actual historical figures, so my investigation was like doing genealogy. For the Rav Hisda's Daughter series, my characters were from the Talmud, which made them a mix of historical and legendary. So I studied what the Talmud said about them, plus what life was like where and when they lived.

I was inspired to write *The Choice* by what was left out of Chaim Potok's first two novels, *The Chosen* and *The Promise*, as well as his later *Davita's Harp*, but I gave my characters different names and invented new ones. I used Jewish names popular in those times, chosen from my own family as much as possible—for example, grandsons Nathan and Benjamin, niece Hannah, and daughter Sharon. It was months, maybe years, before I recognized that I'd given my protagonists, Nathan and Annie, the same names as my own parents. What would Benny's friend Dr. Freud say about that?

I did use a real name for one of my fictional characters. Afraid to inadvertently shame an actual man by giving his name to the pedophile, I called him Rav Brenner after convicted child molester Rabbi Lewis Brenner, whose original charges included fourteen counts of sodomy, sexual abuse, and endangering the welfare of a child. He was permitted to plead guilty to a single count of sodomy.

It was while reading the chapter on American Orthodox women in Jenna Weissman Joselit's *New York's Jewish Jews: The Orthodox Community in the Interwar Years* that I chose niddah for the central conflict between Hannah and Nathan. Hannah, like most twentieth-century American women, would be disinclined to use an old, typically unsanitary mikveh, while Nathan, an Orthodox rabbi who had no idea how few Jewish women actually immersed in them, would insist that his wife follow halacha. As readers can imagine, it wasn't easy doing research on this subject, but I now have a collection of mikveh manuals, including one from 1965 that listed only three "ritulariums" in New York City.

Though I was writing fiction, I wanted to be accurate about my characters' milieu in mid-1950s Brooklyn—what books, movies, and other entertainment they'd have enjoyed, what was in the news, what kind of clothes and music were popular. I made it a point to include serendipitous events like the discovery of a successful polio vaccine, the Brooklyn Dodgers' 1955 World Series win, the secret selling of the Dead Sea Scrolls to Israel, Grace Kelly's wedding, Stern College for Women's founding at Yeshiva University in 1954, the Suez Crisis, and events in the USSR associated with Stalin's death. I tried to make it clear that many of my characters are speaking Yiddish.

After the first Rashi's Daughters volume was published, I was surprised and dismayed by all the criticism I received for purportedly getting the halacha wrong. Yet I was confident that my research was correct; it was those critical readers who'd incorrectly assumed that Jewish Law was the same back in eleventh-century France as the Orthodox today practice it. I suspected I would have the same problem with *The Choice*, for though my book is set merely seventy years ago, the practices of all three branches of Judaism have changed.

Until the Reform movement arose in Europe in the early nineteenth century, there were no separate Jewish denominations. Not that all Jews observed the same laws in the same way. For example, men were limited to one wife at a time in Ashkenaz and women there were not permitted to initiate divorce, while in Sepharad men could have multiple wives and women were able to divorce their husbands. But European Reformers wanted a more assimilated Judaism than that mandated in medieval codes. So they permitted work on the Sabbath, prayed in the vernacular, and no longer required prayer shawls (tallit) or head coverings in shul. They declared dietary laws (kashrut) and the ancient purity/impurity system (including niddah) obsolete.

Orthodox Judaism originated in the mid–nineteenth century in response to the Reformers' innovations. Orthodox Judaism, which claims that both Torah and Talmud are authoritative and fixed regarding Jewish doctrine and observance, thus requires modern Jews to uphold ancient Jewish Law. It rejects positions held by both Conservative and Reform Judaism, which are flexible in interpreting Jewish Law in modern times. Until the early 1950s there was little difference between Conservative and Orthodox practice in America. That changed after Eastern European Holocaust survivors arrived determined to revive and maintain a strict Orthodox lifestyle.

The founders of Conservative Judaism, largely immigrants interested in more traditional Judaism in an American context, had no intention of starting a new denomination. In the early twentieth century they launched a rabbinical school in New York that they hoped would become the unifying institution of all opponents of Reform. But American Orthodoxy, gaining self-definition, promoted its own seminary, later to become Yeshiva

University. Conservative leadership accepted its differentiation from Orthodoxy, establishing its own synagogues and publishing its own prayer books.

Today, Reform has grown more traditional, bringing back Hebrew liturgy, head coverings, and tallit to the synagogue, although the latter two items are worn by both genders. Indeed, it can be hard to tell the difference between Reform and Conservative services on Friday evenings, particularly since both denominations ordain women. Their two main disagreements are about (1) who is a Jew—Reformers consider someone a Jew if either parent is Jewish and the person was raised Jewish, while Conservatives consider people Jewish only if they have a Jewish mother, though both movements accept each other's converts; and (2) the importance of halacha—Reformers affirm that halacha is nonbinding or optional, while Conservative Judaism remains halachic, embracing the binding nature of Jewish law, though with modern principles considered.

Regarding Conservatives' niddah restrictions, their Committee on Jewish Law and Standards stated the following in 2006: "The menstruant should refrain from sexual relations for seven days beginning with the first day of her flow" (not seven days after its conclusion), "some physical contact can continue between partners during the woman's menstruation as long as it is limited to that which is generally accepted in society between siblings," and "an outdoor, in ground swimming pool [may] be used when a *mikveh* or other source of living water is not available."

Meanwhile, Orthodoxy has split into its own groups. Most obvious, there are Modern Orthodox Jews, who engage in many aspects of modern, secular culture, and ultra-Orthodox Jews (sometimes called Haredi, Yeshivish, or "black hats"), who tend to insulate themselves from modern mores. Among the ultra-Orthodox, the strictest are the Hasidim, a sect (some say a cult) of isolated communities, each following a specific rebbe. A major difference between Hasidic and Yeshivish communities in America is that the former speak Yiddish and the latter English. Modern Orthodoxy has divided into Neo-Orthodoxy, Religious Zionism, and Open Orthodoxy, the latter of which began ordaining women in 2009. Modern Orthodox rabbis no longer forbid women to study Talmud, and it may surprise readers to learn that back in 1979 Rabbi David Silber founded the Drisha Institute for Jewish Education in New York to provide women with the opportunity to study Talmud and other Jewish texts.

Last, but not least, particularly for a novel with "Talmud" in the title, here's where readers can find the sugyiot my characters studied—chapter 1: Pesachim 108a; chapter 4: Kiddushin 29b, Sotah 21b, and Rosh Hashana

20a; chapter 6: Megillah 23a; chapter 7: Yoma 85b; chapter 9: Shabbos 21a; chapter 11: Kiddushin 34a; chapter 12: Berachos 57b; chapter 16: Niddah 66a; chapter 18: Shabbos 31b; chapter 20: Niddah 31a, Eruvin 100b, Shabbos 140b, and Nedarim 20a; chapter 22: Niddah 31b; chapter 23: Kiddushin 62a; chapter 24: Rosh Hashana 33a; and chapter 27: Kiddushin 31b. I invite readers to learn the details of what they say at https://www.sefaria.org/texts/Talmud.

I encourage readers to visit my website, https://www.thechoicenovel.com. There they will find my bibliography, author Q&A, speaking schedule, reading group questions, reviews, and other fascinating information— including a video of highlights from the seventh game of the 1955 World Series.

GLOSSARY

Please note that all Yiddish words are in italics.

Abaye: Head of the Babylonian Talmud academy in Pumbedita in the fourth century CE. Hundreds of debates between Abaye and Rava (head of Mechoza academy) are cited in the Gemara.

abba: Hebrew for Father.

a dank, a sheynem dank: Thanks, thanks very much.

af tsu lokhes: In spite of authority.

aliyah/aliyos: Being called up to read from the Torah in synagogue.

alte kaker: Elderly man, old fart.

Ashkenazi: Descendants of Jews who lived in France and the Rhineland valley before migrating eastward to Slavic lands (e.g., Poland, Lithuania, Russia) after the Crusades.

aufruf: Ceremony on the Shabbos before a wedding, when the groom has a special blessing.

av bes din: Head judge of a Jewish court.

ayniklakh: Grandchildren.

ayver: Penis.

ba'al keri: Man who had a seminal emission.

Baraita: Tradition in the Jewish Oral Law, contemporary with but not part of the Mishnah.

Baruch Dayan haEmet: "Blessed is the true Judge," said upon learning of a recent death.

bashert: Meant to be, predestined mate.

borech Hashem: "Bless God's name," thanking God for something good that should happen.

bris [milah]: Circumcision.

broche: Blessing.

bubbe: Grandmother.

chacham: Wise man, Torah scholar.

chagim: Jewish holidays.

challah: Jewish bread served on Shabbat.

chas v'chalila: Heaven forbid.

cherem: Excommunication.

chesed: Kindness.

chevra kadisha: Burial society.

Chol HaMoed: Semiholiday middle days of a weeklong Jewish festival.

chutzpah: Brazen nerve, audacity.

dank: Thank.

danken himl: Thank Heaven.

daven: To pray.

derabanan: Law from the Talmudic rabbis.

d'oraita: Law from the Torah.

drash: Sermon or brief teaching on a passage from the Torah (aka d'var Torah).

esrog: Citron, citrus fruit used during Sukkos.

frum: Religious, observant, pious.

Gemara: Rabbinical analysis of and commentary on the Mishnah, forming the second, and largest, part of the Talmud.

get: Religious divorce decree.

gevalt: Exclamation of shock or fear.

Gottenyu: Oh my God.

goyim: Non-Jews.

Hadassah: Jewish women's organization supporting Israel.

haftarah: Reading from the Prophets in synagogue.

halacha: Jewish religious law.

Halvah: Fudgelike Jewish candy.

hametz: Leavened food, forbidden during Pesach.

hamish: Friendly, warm.

Haredi: Ultra-Orthodox Jews.

Hasidism: A charismatic Jewish movement founded in the eighteenth century emphasizing piety and joy.

Havdalah: Ceremony marking the end of Shabbos.

hechsher: Symbol on food package indicating the contents are kosher.

HIAS: Hebrew Immigrant Aid Society.

huppah: Wedding canopy.

IDF: Israel Defense Forces.

JDC: Joint Distribution Committee.

Kaddish: Prayer said for deceased family member.

kahal: Hasidic community.

kashrut/kashrus: Jewish dietary laws.

kavanah: Intention, state of focus, and devotion during prayer.

keinehora: "No evil eye," said when announcing good news.

ketubah: Jewish wedding contract.

Kiddush: Prayer said over wine to sanctify Jewish holiday; also the meal served after morning services at synagogue.

kinder: Children.

klezmer: Jewish folk music.

klutz: Clumsy person, bungler.

Kol Nidre: Prayer chanted on the eve of Yom Kippur.

kvatterim: Couple who bring the baby into where bris takes place.

kvell: Take pride/delight in.

Lag b'Omer: Jewish holiday a month after Passover.

latkes: Potato pancakes eaten at Hanukah.

l'chaim: To life, said as a toast.

leyne: Chant Torah reading.

ma'asim tovim: Good deeds.

macher: Important person, big shot.

Maimonides: *See* Rambam.

mamzer: Bastard.

matzah brei: Fried egg and matzah.

maven: Expert.

mazel tov: Congratulations.

mechitza: Partition in Orthodox synagogues to separate men and women.

Megillah: Biblical Book of Esther, read at Purim.

mesirah: Informing on a fellow Jew to the secular authorities.

mikveh: Bath used for ritual immersion.

minhag: Custom.

minyan: Quorum of ten adult Jews required for certain public prayers; in Orthodox synagogues the ten must be men.

Mi Sheberach: Prayer for the sick.

mishegoss: Craziness, insanity.

Mishnah: A terse collection of early rabbinic legal traditions written in Hebrew that was passed down from teacher to students through memorization and recitation by generations of scholars. This assemblage of Jewish laws and practices, known as the Oral Torah, forms the first part of Talmud.

mitzvah/mitzvos: Commandment from God.

mohel: Ritual circumciser.

musar: Jewish ethical movement prescribing moral discipline.

niddah: Menstruating or menstruant.

nu: So?; Well?

nudzh: To pester or nag.

nusach: Style or melody of a Jewish prayer service.

payess: Long side curls/earlocks worn by Hasidic males.

Pesach: Passover.

pikuach nefesh: To save a life.

pogrom: Organized massacre of Jews in Russia and Eastern Europe.

pupik: Belly button.

Purim: Jewish spring holiday celebrating events in the Book of Esther.

rabbonim: Orthodox rabbis.

Rambam: Rabbi Moses Bar Maimon, aka Maimonides. Twelfth-century Sephardic Jewish philosopher and one of the most influential Torah scholars of the Middle Ages.

Ramban: Rabbi Moses Bar Nachman, aka Nachmanides. Thirteenth-century Spanish Jewish scholar.

rasha: Bad man.

Rashi: Acronym for Rabbi Shlomo ben Isaac, medieval commentator par excellence who wrote commentaries on both the Talmud and the Hebrew Bible.

rav: Ordained rabbi.

Rava: Head of the Babylonian academy in Mechoza in the fourth century CE. Hundreds of debates between Rava and Abaye (head of Pumbedita academy) are cited in the Gemara.

rebbe: Rabbi leader of a Hasidic sect.

rebbetzin: Rabbi's wife.

Rosh Hashana: Jewish New Year.

sandak/*sandek*: Man who holds the baby during the bris.

schlimazel: Someone with bad luck.

schluff: Nap, sleep.

schlumpy: Slovenly, rumpled, dowdy.

schmutz: Dirt.

schvitz: Communal steam bath; also to sweat.

Seder: Home service at the Pesach table the first and second nights of Passover.

segulah: A protective/benevolent ritual.

Sephardi: Descendant of the Jews who lived in Spain and Portugal.

Shabbat/*Shabbos*: The Sabbath, Judaism's day of rest and seventh day of the week.

shalom aleichem: Jewish greeting (literally, peace to you).

Shamayim: Heaven.

shammes: Synagogue official, not clergy, who manages day-to-day duties.

shanda: A shame, scandal.

shanda fur dei goyim: (Jewish) embarrassment at a fellow Jew doing something disgraceful where non-Jews can observe it.

shavua tov: A good week.

Shavuos: Jewish late spring festival celebrating the giving of the Torah, Pentecost in Christianity.

Shema: Major Jewish prayer, said upon waking and going to bed.

Sheva Brachot: Seven blessings recited at a Jewish wedding.

sheytle: Wig worn by ultra-Orthodox women to hide their own hair.

shidduch: Arranged marriage.

shikse: Non-Jewish woman.

shiva: Weeklong mourning period for close relatives.

shofar: Ram's horn, sounded on Rosh Hashana.

shomer Shabbos: Rigorously observes Sabbath restrictions.

shpilkes: On pins and needles (state of agitated suspense).

shrayen: Scream, yell.

shtetl/shtetlach: A Jewish village in Eastern Europe.

shtiebel: Small neighborhood synagogue.

shtreimel: Fur hat worn by Hasidic men.

shul: Synagogue.

Shulchan Aruch: Code of Jewish Law, authoritative in Orthodoxy, compiled in sixteenth century by Josef Karo.

siddur: Prayer book.

Simchas Torah: Jewish fall holiday.

smicha: Rabbinic ordination.

sugya/sugyiot: Talmud passage discussing a specific issue.

svara: Talmudic term meaning moral intuition, reasoning that appreciates social relationships and real-world situations.

tachlis: Heart/substance of a matter.

tallis: A ritual prayer shawl.

talmid chacham: Jewish learned scholar, Talmud expert.

Talmud: The collection of Jewish Law and tradition consisting of the Mishnah and the Gemara, compiled and edited between the third and sixth centuries. It is the central text of Rabbinic Judaism and the primary source of Jewish religious law (halacha) and Jewish theology.

tchotchke: Trinket.

tichel: Head scarf worn by Orthodox married women.

tiflut: Lechery/immorality [Rashi], triviality [Rambam].

tish: Literally, table; groom's prewedding reception.

Tosafos: Medieval commentaries on the Talmud, written in the eleventh to thirteenth centuries by Rashi's disciples.

treif: Nonkosher.

tsuris: Trouble, problem.

tush/tuchus: Derriere, buttocks, rear end.

tzaddik: A most righteous, holy man.

tzimmes: Big deal or fuss (literally a stew made with chopped fruit, vegetables, and/or meat).

vatrushka: Russian pastry.

yahrzeit: Anniversary of a relative's death.

yarmulke: Skullcap worn by Jewish men.

yeshiva: Secondary Hebrew/Talmud school/academy.

yeshiva bocher: Adolescent Yeshiva student.

yichus: Family status/prestige.

Yom Kippur: Day of Atonement, ten days after Rosh Hashana.

Yom Tov: A Jewish festival. As on Shabbos, Jews do not work and instead celebrate and pray.

Yoreh Deah: Second chapter of *Shulchan Aruch*; deals with kashrut, conversion, mourning, and niddah.

zayde: Grandfather.

zemiros: Hymns sung around the table during Shabbos and Jewish holidays.

zichrono livracha: May his/her [a deceased person's] memory be a blessing.

THE CHOICE BOOK GROUP
DISCUSSION QUESTIONS

1. What made you want to read *The Choice*? Did it live up to your expectations?

2. The author takes characters inspired by Chaim Potok and ages them into young adults in Brooklyn in the 1950s. If you read Potok's *The Chosen*, *The Promise*, or *Davita's Harp*, did reading *The Choice* change your opinion of those novels? In what way? If you have not yet read Potok's books, are you now going to?

3. Discuss how the author depicts Hannah and Nathan, Sharon and Benny, and the world in which each lived. How did your perception of religious Jews change after reading the novel?

4. Although *The Choice* is set in 1950s Brooklyn, what similar issues do modern women face today?

5. The topic of family purity or *niddah* is rarely discussed publicly among Jewish women. Did you know about the laws of niddah? Do you think most Orthodox Jewish women fulfill the mitzvot of niddah? Why or why not?

6. Why do you think many Jewish women do not fulfill the mitzvot of niddah, neither visiting a mikveh nor abstaining from sexual relations during the extra seven clean days? Do you or did you ever observe these? Why or why not?

7. Many Talmudic texts are brought into the story. Which did you find most interesting? Why? Have you studied Talmud before?

8. Were you offended or disturbed by the subplot involving child sexual abuse by Orthodox Jewish men, especially clergy? Explain your answer.

9. What surprised you most about the book? Were you surprised that Nathan, ordained as an Orthodox rabbi, went out dancing or kissed women he was dating?

10. What other books by this author have you read? How did they compare to this book?

11. If you could ask the author one question, what would it be?

ACKNOWLEDGMENTS

MANY THANKS TO Rabbi Beth Lieberman for editorial guidance that never let me forget that my Talmud scenes should be about more than just Talmud, thus forcing me to take this book to a higher level, and for her steadfast friendship over the course of this ten-year project.

Kudos to my sister Nancy, who read my manuscript and Potok's early novels before pelting me with opinions as to which subjects I should address in my book and which are better left out. And to my daughter Emily, a voracious reader and fan fiction writer, who spent hours critiquing my early drafts and never hesitated to lambast any scenes that didn't measure up to her exacting standards. She introduced me to the podcast *Writing Excuses*, which offers advice on how even seasoned authors can improve their writing.

Penina Lopez, my uniquely qualified copyeditor who had attended Bais Yaakov schools and is fluent in Yiddish, applied invaluable expertise to the challenging task of creating consistent spelling for words in a language that has no agreed-upon transliteration.

Thank you to master storyteller and super-agent Al Zuckerman for scalpel-sharp line edits and his faith in me.

My publicists Rachel Gul of Over the River Public Relations and Steve O'Keefe of Orobora collaborated to create great press kits—Rachel got the word out to the trades and Jewish media, while Steve focused on online book marketing. I could never have imagined a team as superb as they have been.

To all those who encouraged me over the years to write another novel via Goodreads, Facebook, and personal emails—I am happy to deliver this. I hope you like it.

Finally, I offer my love and gratitude to Dave, my husband of over fifty years. When I can't think of a certain word for a specific situation in a scene, he stops what he's doing to provide exactly the one I need. He doesn't complain about my late nights working on book business, is always ready with a silly pun or dad joke when I need cheering up, and even manages to mostly tolerate my addiction to Pokémon Go.

ABOUT THE AUTHOR

MAGGIE ANTON is an award-winning author of historical fiction as well as a Talmud scholar with expertise in Jewish women's history. She was born Margaret Antonofsky in Los Angeles, California, where she still resides. In 1992 she joined a women's Talmud class taught by Rachel Adler. There, to her surprise, she fell in love with Talmud, a passion that has continued unabated for thirty years. Intrigued that the great Jewish scholar Rashi had no sons, only daughters, she started researching the family and their community.

Thus the award-winning trilogy Rashi's Daughters was born, to be followed by National Jewish Book Award finalist *Rav Hisda's Daughter: Apprentice* and its sequel, *Enchantress*. Then she switched to nonfiction, winning the Gold Ben Franklin Award in the religion category for *Fifty Shades of Talmud: What the First Rabbis Had to Say about You-Know What*, a lighthearted in-depth tour of sexuality within the Talmud. Her latest work, *The Choice: A Novel of Love, Faith, and the Talmud*, is a wholly transformative novel that takes characters inspired by Chaim Potok and ages them into young adults in 1950s Brooklyn.

Since 2005, Anton has lectured about the research behind her books at hundreds of venues throughout North America, Europe, and Israel. She still studies women and Talmud, albeit mostly online. Her favorite Talmud learning sites are *Daf Shevui* and *Mishna Yomit*, provided daily via email by the Conservative Yeshiva in Jerusalem at https://www.conservativeyeshiva .org/learn/.

You can follow her blog and contact Anton at her website, www.maggie anton.com. You can also find her on Facebook and Goodreads. And if you liked this book, please give it a nice review at all the usual websites.